In the Midnight Rain

In the Midnight Rain

Ruth Wind

HarperTorch
An Imprint of HarperCollins*Publishers*

HARPERTORCH
An Imprint of HarperCollins*Publishers*
10 East 53rd Street
New York, NY 10022-5299

ISBN 0-7394-1090-3

Printed in the United States of America

For my husband Ramm,
who has a heart made of music.

ACKNOWLEDGMENTS

Some books are written in a white-hot heat, in secret, or alone. This is not one of them. Thanks to Rosalyn Alsobrook, who took time from a brutal schedule to answer a zillion questions, and Eve Gaddy, who also answered questions, acted as guide through her town, and generously read the manuscript to help catch errors. Thanks to Susan Wiggs for an early and detailed critique of an embryo manuscript that was obviously not going to fit into my usual formats; Krissie Ohlrogge for nudging me toward a plot point that was right under my nose; and Teresa Hill, who valiantly and cheerfully read (and read and read), suffered through months of writer terrors, and always had the right words ready.

Love and thanks go to my mother-in-law, Lurelean Samuel, for her generous, entertaining stories of growing up in Mississippi in a world that is now gone; my grandmother, Madoline Putman, whose stories of sin and redemption, told so alluringly in her soft, genteel drawl, provided the voice in my head as I wrote; and Lynette Cole, whose long conversation over a four-hour perm gave me the idea for this book in the first place.

And finally, deepest and most sincere thanks to Meg Ruley, warrior woman, and Laura Cifelli, wise woman.

Against the day of sorrow
Lay by some trifling thing
A smile, a kiss, a flower,
For sweet remembering

GEORGIA DOUGLAS JOHNSON

PROLOGUE

Sometimes, when the wind was just right, she could hear the blues.

Once the rainy winter passed into spring, she liked to sit on her porch late at night, held in a kind of wonder beneath the moon and tall pines. She rocked in a cane-bottomed chair, smelling the green and copper moisture coming off the water, and she listened, nodding in time as cicadas and crickets whistled their song to the night. From the dark trees sometimes came the whirring, nearly silent beat of wings, followed by a swallowed screech of death, a sound not everyone could hear, but she did. She heard everything.

What she liked best was hearing the blues. The music sailed down the channel made by the river, ghostly guitar and haunted harmonica, even the hint of a man's ragged voice. It came from Hopkins' juke joint, upriver a mile or two on the Louisiana side of the Sabine River, and spilled with yellow light and blue cigarette smoke into a forest as dark as sin, as warm as a lover's mouth. It floated toward her over the stillness hanging above the water. Sometimes she imagined they were playing it just for her.

She'd close her eyes and let that music creep under her skin, seep into her bones. She let a part of herself get up and dance while she rocked steady in her chair. Every so often, she let that ghost of herself sing along while she silently nodded her head to the beat. The slow, sexlike rhythm filled her with memories of a man's low, dark laughter and a baby's sweet cry; with the song of Sunday-morning church and the blaze of morning over the east Texas pines.

She rocked and danced, nodded and sang, and thought as long as she could die with the blues in her ears, everything would be all right.

1

The sky was overcast and threatening rain by the time Ellie Connor made it to Pine Bend at seven o'clock of a Thursday evening.

She was tired. Tired of driving. Tired of spinning the radio dial every forty miles—why did the preaching stations always seem to have the longest signal?—tired of the sight of white lines swooping under her tires.

She'd started out this morning at seven planning to arrive in Pine Bend by midafternoon in her unfashionable but generally reliable Buick. She'd had a cute little Toyota for a while, but her work often took her to small towns across America, and if there were problems on the road, she had discovered it was far better to drive American. Since she'd lost a gasket in the wilds of deepest Arkansas, this was the trip that proved the rule.

The gasket had delayed her arrival by three hours, but at last she took a right off the highway and drove through a small East Texas town that was closing itself down for the evening. She had to stop at a gas station to get directions to the house, but finally she turned onto a narrow road made almost claustrophobic by the thick trees that crept right up to its edge. It hadn't been paved in a lot of years, and Ellie counted her blessings—at least she didn't have to look at dotted lines anymore.

Something interfered with the radio, and she turned it off with a snap. "Almost there, darlin'," she said to her dog April, who sat in the seat next to her.

April lifted her nose to the opening in the window, blinking against the wind, or maybe in anticipation of finally escaping the car. Half husky and half border collie, the dog was good-natured, eternally patient, and very smart. Ellie reached over to rub her ears and came away with a handful of molting dog fur.

As the car rounded a bend in the road, the land opened up to show sky and fields. A break in the fast-moving clouds overhead suddenly freed a single flame of sunlight, bright gold against the purpling canvas of sky. Treetops showed black against the gold, intricately lacy and detailed, and for a minute, Ellie forgot her weariness. She leaned over the steering wheel, feeling a stretch along her shoulders, and admired the sight. "Beautiful," she said aloud.

Ellie's grandmother would have said it was a finger of God. Of course, Geraldine Connor saw the finger of God in just about everything, but Ellie hoped it was a good omen.

April whined, pushing her nose hard against the crack in the window, and Ellie took pity and pushed the button to lower the passenger-side glass. April stuck her head out gleefully, letting her tongue loll in the wind, scenting only heaven-knew-what dog pleasures on that soft air. Handicapped by human olfactory senses, Ellie smelled only the first weeds of summer and the coppery hints of the Sabine River that ran somewhere beyond the dense trees.

The road bent, leaning into a wide, long curve that ended abruptly in an expanse of cleared land. And there, perched atop a rise, was the house, an imposing and boxy structure painted white. Around it spread wide, verdant grass, and beyond the lawn, a collection of long, serious-looking greenhouses. Trees met the property in a protective circle, giving it the feeling of a walled estate. Roses in a gypsy profusion of color lined the porch and drive.

Ellie smiled. It was a house with a name, naturally: Fox River, which she supposed was a play on the name of the owner, Laurence Reynard.

Dr. Reynard, in fact, though she didn't know what the doctorate was in. She knew little of him at all, apart from the E-mail letters she'd received and the notes he'd posted in a blues newsgroup. In those writings, he was by turns eccentric and brilliant. She suspected he drank.

She'd been corresponding with him for months about Pine Bend and Mabel Beauvais, a blues singer native to the town, a mysterious and romantic figure who was the subject of Ellie's latest biography. Ellie had had some reservations about accepting Reynard's offer to stay in his guest house while she completed her research, but the truth was, she did not travel without her dog, and it was sometimes more than a little difficult to find a rental that didn't charge an arm and a leg extra for her.

As she pulled into the half-circle drive, however, Ellie's reservations seeped back in. E-mail removed every gauge of character a body relied upon: you couldn't see the shifty eyes or the poor handwriting or restless gestures that warned of instability. And arriving in the soft gray twilight put her at a disadvantage. She'd deliberately planned to get here in daylight in case the situation didn't feel right, but that blown gasket had set her back too many hours. At the moment, she was too tired to care where she slept as long as her dog was in her room.

Pulling the emergency brake, she peered through the windshield at the wide veranda. Two men sat there, one white, one black. It hadn't occurred to her that Reynard might be black, though thinking of it now, she realized it was perfectly possible. She gave the horn a soft toot—something she hadn't done in years but that suddenly seemed right—and the white guy dipped his chin in greeting.

Ellie stepped out of the car and simply stood there a minute, relieved to change postures. The air smelled heavily of sweet magnolia and rose, thick and dizzying, a scent so blatantly sensual that she felt it in her lungs, on her skin. She breathed it in with pleasure as she approached the porch, brushing her hands down the front of her khaki shorts, trying to smooth the wrinkles out. "How you doing?" she said in greeting.

They both gave her a nod, but nobody jumped up to welcome her. Ellie hesitated, wondering suddenly if she had the address wrong or something.

A raggedy-looking mutt was not nearly as reserved as the men. It jumped up and barked an urgent alert. Anxious to make a pit stop, April started to follow Ellie out of the car, but Ellie said, "Stay," and with a little whine, she did.

A low voice said, "Sasha, hush." The dog swallowed the last bark and perched on the edge of the steps and waited for Ellie to come a little closer. Its tail wagged its whole rear end.

Ellie resisted the urge to fiddle with her hair. It was mussed and wild with humidity, but nothing short of a shower was going to fix it. She settled for shoving her sunglasses on top of her head, which drew the worst of it out of her face so she could at least see as she walked to the bottom of the steps and looked at the men in the low gray light, trying to decide if she had the right place.

The black man was the older of the pair, maybe in his mid-forties or a little more. Judging by the length of his legs, propped on the porch railing, he was tall, and his skin was the color of polished pecan. A neatly trimmed goatee with a few betraying curls of white framed a serious mouth. His eyes were large and still.

Ellie could imagine this face behind the notes Reynard had written.

But it was the other man who snared her attention. Darkness lay in the hollows below slashes of cheekbone, and along the fine line of his jaw; peered out from large eyes of a color impossible to determine in the low light. Her mind catalogued other details, his bare feet and worn jeans, the shadow of unshaved beard. His hair was thick and long, of indeterminate color. A skinny white cat sat serenely at his ankle.

Ellie looked from one to the other. "I give up," she said. "Which of you is Dr. Reynard?"

The white man rose with a half smile. Ellie had the faint sense that she'd been tested, but also that she'd passed. "That would be me," he said. "You must be Miz Connor." It was a bourbon voice, smoky and gold and dangerous, and Ellie heard the unmistakable sound of money in the blurred Southern vowels. "We've been waiting for you."

Ellie took a breath against the sudden wish to stand straighter, toss her head, somehow be prettier. "You somehow don't look the way I pictured you, Dr. Reynard," she said mildly.

"Call me Blue. Nobody calls me anything but Blue around here." He inclined his head, and a wash of that thick, wavy hair touched his shoulder. "You're not what I was expecting, either, to tell you the truth."

"I'll tell if you will."

He paused, then gave her a slow grin, one that hid all the darkness and brought out the charm. "A woman named Ellie who writes biographies says middle-aged librarian to me." The grin said he knew she'd forgive him.

"Ditto," Ellie said. "A man who spends all his free time talking trash in blues newsgroups with a whisky at his elbow—I was thinking a Keith Richards look-alike. Middle-aged and worn out."

A surprised chuckle rolled out of him. "Dissipated, maybe," he said, lifting a finger. "Worn and ragged by hard living, definitely. But I don't spend all my time on the computer. Just nighttime."

The black man laughed softly. Ellie had forgotten he was there. Reynard gestured. "Miz Connor, this is Marcus Williams."

Ellie nodded politely. "How do you do?"

He answered, "Just fine, thank you," a Southernism she'd forgotten.

"Well," Reynard said, straightening, "can I get you something? I have some sweet tea, maybe some lemonade, and"— he held up his tumbler with a sideways grin—"good Kentucky bourbon."

"Much as I'd love to, I'm going to have to say no tonight. I'd just like to get settled." From the car came a deep, pointed bark. Ellie glanced over her shoulder. "And my dog urgently wants to get out."

"No need to make him suffer." He gestured. "Go on and let him out."

"She," Ellie corrected automatically, and hesitated. "You sure?"

"She won't cause any damage my own haven't at some time or another." April, as if overhearing the conversation, let loose another sharp alert. The mutt on the porch, unable to resist any longer, rushed down the steps and licked Ellie's fingers. Reynard grinned. "Let your dog out, sugar, before she busts."

"Thank you." Ellie hurried back to the car, the mutt at her heels, and opened the door. "Come on, sweetie." April leaped out and rushed to the grass to squat with an almost blissful look of relief on her face. To keep the mutt busy, Ellie rubbed her soft gold ears. "You're kind of cute."

From the porch, the black man snorted. "Rat-dog."

Ellie smiled over her shoulder. "She must belong to you, then, Dr. Reynard."

"Marcus is a dog snob, that's all. Don't mind him." He whistled softly, and the mutt ran full tilt up the stairs, halting barely in time to avoid smashing into his knees. He bent down to give her that hearty pat men seemed to always bestow on dogs. As if to claim his attention, the skinny white cat circled around his ankles and Reynard stroked her back absently.

Watching, Ellie felt a little of the vague tension in her ease. He didn't appear to be unbalanced or particularly strange—it was probably safe enough. As if he noticed, Reynard straightened and eyed her, taking a swallow of the whisky in his hand. In the dusky stillness, ice clinked. "Now that your dog's all right, are you sure you don't want something to drink?"

His voice mesmerized her, that slow rolling depth, and it took a moment before she realized he'd asked her a question.

Which was answer enough in her mind. "No, thank you. Really."

"I'll get the key, then. If you want to drive on back down the road, I'll meet you over there." He pointed through the deepening gloom toward a path that seemed to lead to the greenhouses, which glowed a soft green against the twilight.

Ellie finally spied the small house set beneath a stand of live oak and loblolly pines. She clicked her tongue for her dog. "Nice to meet you," she said to Marcus.

"Good luck with your biography."

"He told you?"

"Mabel's our only claim to fame, so we're kind of proprietary."

Ellie smiled. "I promise to do my best."

"Can't ask no more than that, I reckon."

She whistled for April and got back in the car, only realizing as she drove that she was humming under her breath. "There's a red house over yonder . . ." and her mind was playing it, the Jimi Hendrix version, threaded with that smoky sex sound that had made him such a god among women.

She rolled her eyes at her subconscious, which had an annoying habit of coughing up the most embarrassing, corny soundtrack for her life—like flying into LAX and finding herself humming "LA International Airport"—and made herself stop before he heard her.

Blue. She glanced in the rearview mirror. She wished his name were Laurence.

As he cut through the open meadow between the house and the old slave quarters, converted in the twenties to a guest house, Blue told himself it was liquor making his skin feel hot. He'd worked hard in the sun all day, the warmest they'd had so far. Probably had a little sunburn. And the bourbon on an empty stomach had gone to his head.

But as Ellie stepped out of the car at the guest house, he found his attention snared again. She was not his usual type. He liked soft, shapely blondes. Women who wore gauzy sundresses you could see through just a little bit. Women with easy laughter and soft edges and no causes to champion. The less serious the better.

Bimbos, Marcus called them. Blue preferred to think of them as easy to get along with.

Either way, Ellie Connor did not fit the profile. Small and too thin, with angles instead of softness, khaki shorts instead of floaty skirts, and curly black hair that fell in her face instead of that swing of blonde he found so appealing. From her posts, he'd known she was strong and smart and knew her mind, an impression reinforced now by the set of her chin and the sharp, no-nonsense way she met their eyes back there. It wouldn't surprise him at all if she had a revolver in the glove box—she struck him as a woman who wouldn't leave much up to fate.

But even she had to struggle, trying to lift a big suitcase out of the trunk.

Blue stepped forward. "Let me get that for you."

"Thank you."

He grabbed it while she picked up some other things and followed him to the porch, waiting behind him silently as he unlocked the door. Inside, he flipped on the lamp by the desk. "This is it. Small, but comfortable."

She put a soft-sided case on the table. "It's beautiful," she said, and it sounded sincere.

"Thought you'd like it," Blue said, shoving hair

out of his eyes. "I took the liberty of dragging out some of the material we talked about"—he pointed to a neat stack of books and files on the desk—"and had Lanie—she's my aunt, who lives with me—order some groceries to be delivered. She got most of the staples, coffee and milk and things, but if there's something you don't see, just holler. Nearest store is about five miles down the road, back the way you came."

For a moment, she just looked around her. In a lazy way, he zeroed in on that mouth again. She might not be his type in a lot of ways, but that was one hell of a mouth. Bee-stung, his mama would have said.

The light was better in here, and he could see the exotic cast to her features, a faint tilt to her eyes, high cheekbones; together with all that glossy black hair it made him think maybe Russian or East European.

"Ah!" she said suddenly, and moved across the room to the counter, putting her hands on a CD player. "Excellent. I carry a portable with me, but this is much better." She turned, and looked straight at him. "It's really very nice of you to offer your hospitality this way," she said, and a knowing glitter lit her eyes. "Although I suspect you were drinking when you extended the invitation."

Blue winced. "Guilty." Not unusual of a late evening, which was when he generally signed on to the Internet, looking for a good argument. "How'd you know?"

"Your notes have a different tone. And you transpose letters."

He crossed his arms, smiling to cover his discomfort. "Here I thought I was being so sly, and all the time, I might as well have been hootin' in some club."

"Not exactly. It was really just a guess."

"Well, bourbon or not, I was sincere. The place is yours as long as you need it. I'm glad you're doing the biography. It's long overdue."

"And whatever the circumstances, I'm grateful. I really hate looking for a place to keep April, and I won't leave her in a kennel."

At the sound of her name, the dog swept her tail over the hardwood floor. "That speaks well of you, Miz Connor."

She looked at him, all calm sober eyes, and Blue looked back, and all the months of notes back and forth rose up between them. He'd liked her sharpness, a certain diffidence edged with wry humor. They'd stuck mainly to discussing the blues, but every so often, they'd go off on a sidetrack and he'd catch an intriguing glimpse of something more: a hint of anger, or maybe just passion, mixed in with the steadiness.

"It's really a shock to see how different you are from how I imagined you," he said impulsively.

Something flickered in her eyes, there and gone so fast he couldn't really place it, before she tucked her hands in her back pockets and turned her face away. A sliver of gold light from the lamp edged her jaw, and Blue found himself thinking he liked that clean line. She had very fine skin. It made him think of the petals of an orchid in one of the greenhouses. "Ditto," she said, and again raised her head and looked at him with that directness.

He wasn't used to women who looked so straight at him.

As if she thought better of it, she moved to the table and unzipped the soft-sided case, revealing dozens of CDs in their plastic cases, and scooped up a handful. It was a restless gesture, the kind of thing a person did to fill up an awkward moment, and Blue realized he ought to take the hint and leave her to settle in.

But a person's taste in music said more about them than they ever realized, and he couldn't resist peeking into the case. "What do you have here?" He pointed. "Mind if I look?"

"No. Of course not."

The CDs were piled in a jumble. "They have cases now that'll stack 'em up for you."

She made a rueful noise. "Yes, but they don't carry enough." She smiled at him, a quick bright flash. "I need my dog and my CDs to feel secure."

He lowered his head, oddly unsettled. He looked at the titles, wondering if he really wanted to know that much more about her, but he didn't stop sorting through them. Blues, of course. He *tsked* and took out a Lightnin' Hopkins recording, shaking his head.

She plucked it out of his hands. "You've made your feelings plain about the Delta style, Dr. Reynard. Unhand my classics."

He grinned. They'd had quite an argument about various styles. Blue didn't like the tinny sound of Delta, and she didn't care for jazz, which he considered just short of sacrilege. "Gonna have to turn you on to some good jazz, darlin'," he murmured, and bent back to the case.

Besides the blues, there was a huge variety. A little alternative rock and roll, some country he thought of as "story" songs, some classical. "Baroque, huh?" he said, pulling out a couple of cases from that period and flipping them over to look at the lists.

A flicker of surprise crossed her face. "You like it?"

"You sound surprised, sugar." He tossed the CDs back, the unsettled feeling growing along the back of his neck. "A man might say the same about you. Never saw you in the other music newsgroups."

"Do you visit others?"

"Some." That made him think about her comments on his drinking when he posted. Embarrassing. "Well," he said, straightening. "I guess I'll leave you alone. In the morning, I'll be glad to take you around town—show you where the library is, and introduce you to some of the folks who might have some stories to tell."

"You don't have to put yourself out, Dr. Reynard."

"Blue."

"Blue," she repeated. "I'm sure I can find my way around."

"I'm sure you can. But things'll go better if you let me take you." He lifted a shoulder. "It's a small town."

Still, she hesitated. Then, "All right. I'll see you in the morning."

"Don't let the bedbugs bite," he said. On the way out, he paused to scratch April's ear.

Out in the night, with lightning bugs winking all through the grass, Blue stopped, feeling a little off-balance. He put a hand to his ribs and took in some air, then blew it out and shook his shoulders a little. In his mind's eye, he saw the bulging, soft-sided case and the big, well-trained dog. Security, she'd said. Music and a dog. Security for Miss Ellie Connor with the tough set of her shoulders and her head-on way of looking at him.

He shook his head. Probably just a case of the girls looking prettier at closing time. He needed some food, some sleep. But when he stepped back up on the porch, he said, "She's not just into the blues. She's got classical in there. And REM. Even some Reba McEntire."

Marcus nodded and wordlessly handed him a fresh glass of bourbon, an offering of solace.

Blue drank it down, taking refuge in the burn, then poured another and put the bottle down on the wooden floor of the porch. After a long space of time, filled only with the lowering depths of the night and the faint squeak of the porch swing, he rubbed his ribs again.

"Not one of your bimbos there, that's for sure," Marcus said.

"No, I don't think so."

"Hell of a mouth."

"Yep." Blue drank.

A dark, rolling laugh boomed into the quiet. "Oh, how the mighty do fall!"

"Not my type."

"Mmmm. I saw that." Marcus stood and put his glass on a wicker table. He pulled his keys out of his pocket. "I think I'll go curl up with my woman."

"Hell with you, Marcus."

Laughter was the only reply.

2

In the little cottage, Ellie irritably brushed hair off her face, feeling the long drive in her weary shoulders and the fine film of grit on her skin. April carefully sniffed the floor, following some invisible trail through the living area, into the kitchen, over to the corner. Then, obviously satisfied, she slumped down in front of the sink with a *whuff*.

"First things first," Ellie said. She opened the plastic grocery bags that contained the heavy ceramic dog dishes, filled one with water from the sink and put it in the corner where it wouldn't get kicked. April wagged her white-tipped tail as Ellie opened the ten-pound bag of dry food and filled the other dish. She put it on the floor. "Been a while since breakfast, I guess."

The dog attended to, Ellie dug through the cabinets, finding the staples Blue had promised—nothing terribly appetizing, though, until she opened the fridge. "Beer," she breathed. "Thank you, God." She screwed off the top of a long-necked Pearl, and without bothering with a glass, took a long swallow. It was cold and crisp. Her dry throat sucked it deep, and she drank a third of the bottle without stopping.

Next to the beer was a promising container covered with foil, a sure clue that whatever was under it was home-cooked, likely by the unknown Lanie, who had probably also been responsible for the extravagant vase of blue asters and ivory roses on the counter. Ellie lifted an edge of the foil covering the bowl and saw piles of golden fried chicken, the batter dotted with specks of black pepper. Her stomach growled. Although she'd been intending to wait until she showered to eat, she grabbed a breast from the pile and dug in.

It was even better than it looked, and Ellie let go of a genuine moan of pleasure. Southern fried chicken, the real McCoy—so savory she suspected it might even have been fried in bacon grease. She leaned on the counter, beer in one hand, and devoured the breast with the other, barely stopping to breathe.

And as she stood there, barefooted and tired and aware on some low level of the sound of cicadas starting up their nightly song, a wave of almost violent gratitude overtook her. The past few years, she'd been in Minnesota and Montana and Washington and California, all over the country doing research for various biographical projects. She'd been lucky to discover a chatty, hip style that gave her a popularity not ordinarily found in her field, and though she wasn't rich, she made enough to get by. For six years, she'd been on the road, researching and writing and generally enjoying the process.

But Mabel had brought her back South. Standing in the sweet little cottage, with real fried chicken in one hand and a cold beer in the other, and the smell of river faint on the air, she felt both relieved and uneasy. She wasn't far from home.

Carefully, she wrapped the bone in a piece of plastic bag and threw it away under the sink where April wouldn't be tempted to dig it out again, then wandered over to the desk pushed up under the windows that faced the big house on the hill. On the desk were the piles of background material on Mabel, and she flipped open the file curiously.

The biography was due in seven months. No, she amended, looking at the Wilson's Garage calendar stuck to the wall with a blue thumbtack. Six months and twenty-four days. Most of the career documentation and music background was done—the easy stuff. What remained was much more difficult—and rewarding—part of Ellie's work: discovering the personal influences, the story of the life that had given the music its heart.

In this case, there was also a mystery to solve, because Mabel Beauvais had disappeared off the face of the earth in 1953. Most everyone assumed she was dead, and nearly all the indications pointed that way, but Ellie wanted to find out for sure, put the mystery to rest. The best place to find those clues was right here in Pine Bend, where Mabel had been born and raised.

Six months and twenty-four days. She let go of a sigh, and a curl over her forehead sailed up and landed back in her eyes. She wondered if she'd have to ask for an extension—and if she did, how she'd possibly stretch the advance money another couple of months. When she'd started the biography in a fit of enthusiasm nine months ago, she'd never dreamed Mabel's hometown would lie so close to her own—or that such a small fact would cause her to drag her feet like this.

Oh, get real, Connor.

Okay. Honesty. In some dark, secret place in her mind, Ellie had known Mabel Beauvais was from Pine Bend and that she'd be a great subject. Ellie had just been biding her time until she was ready to dig into her own life. Consciously, she'd chosen Mabel as her next subject because of a single photograph she'd glimpsed in the Ann Arbor library while finishing up her last project. Unconsciously, the choice had been prompted by Ellie's growing need to find out about her own father.

That was the thing about the brain, she thought, and drank some more of her beer, leafing through the material in the folder. You went along thinking you knew what you were doing, and all the time, you were doing something else entirely.

Two years ago, Ellie's grandmother—her only living relative—had had a heart attack. She appeared to be fully recovered. She walked four miles every morning, watched her fats, took care of herself just as she should. But Ellie had been forced to face the fact that the woman was past eighty. She wouldn't live forever. Once she was gone, Ellie would have no people left—unless she could find her father.

It embarrassed her a little, this sudden quest. It

seemed needy and whiny, so much that she had barely admitted to herself that she was here to find him. It seemed so pitiful, somehow, to even want to track him down. Her mother had not been, after all, a woman of sterling character. She'd never let on to Ellie's grandmother who the father of her baby was. Maybe she hadn't known. Maybe she had good reasons for hiding the truth. Added to that, Ellie was uncomfortable with the idea of tracking down a man who'd probably made a home and a family by now and might not even remember a wild hippie child who landed in Pine Bend in 1968.

But, sometimes lately, when Ellie was hip-deep in the life of another person, she'd find herself wondering about the details of her father's life. Wondering who he was. What he dreamed about. How he laughed. Biographies started with parents. Who had hers been? Had they loved one another? Had they just been two lost souls meeting in the dark?

Mabel and her mama. Lost women. She looked out the door, in the direction of the town she couldn't see. Somewhere out there were the answers to both her quests. Mabel's story had been written here. Someone would know something.

And somewhere, someone would also know who Ellie's father was. Unlike her other research projects, this one was a little trickier. She had no name, not even a photograph, only the postcards her mother had sent to her grandmother in the summer of 1968, all postmarked Pine Bend.

Not much to go on. As she made her way to the

shower, she thought that might not be so bad. What would she do with a father, after all these years, anyway?

Blue showered and made some roast beef sandwiches, but he was still restless as night tightened around the house. His body was tired from the long day, but his mind circled and paced, without any sense of real direction. From the apartment his aunt Lanie lived in, he heard the hollow laugh track of a comedy on television.

He washed up his dishes and put them in the drainer and looked out the window at the small house nestled beneath tall, fragile pines. A light was on, and he wondered what the woman was doing. What music she was listening to.

Music. He rubbed a hand across the flat of his ribs, thinking of that CD collection. His experience with women and music had been that they fell into a couple of categories. There were bubble gum lovers, who never really got past the style they loved in high school, the ones who ended up keeping the radio tuned to the country station, or the oldies, or Pure Rockin' Soul on 92.

Then there were the serious ones. Serious women and serious music, the fans of classical, the ones who allowed movie themes and maybe some Celtic stuff into the mix, a little New Age, but didn't tend to dip into anything as plebeian as country or Southern rock.

Ellie's collection had looked like his own. All over the place. He wasn't sure why it bugged him, but as he'd been looking through that case, he'd felt a warning.

He turned away from the window and, determined

to avoid the temptation of bourbon and the Internet, wandered outside, Sasha trailing him hopefully to the door. "Stay," he said, closing the door behind him, and ambled in the cool night down a well-worn path through the meadow to the greenhouses.

There were three of them. The smallest and oldest was a work space, mainly, where new starts for baby plants of various kinds could be tended carefully. The second, quite a bit larger, was the most experimental, and the one that had generated a lot of attention in botanical circles. A man from Stanford was coming out tomorrow to see it, and both Blue and Marcus had been working their asses off this week to make a good showing.

But his favorite was the big one. Even as he approached, a lot of tension he'd been holding in his shoulders slid away. Against the dark canopy of sky, the roof arched palely. From within the glass walls glowed pockets of pinkish grow lights, tucked away in various corners where the ecosystem would not be bothered.

He stepped inside and closed the door behind him, then paused for a moment, closing his eyes to stand, hands loose at his sides, his senses opening to the feel and smell and sound of it. A rich fragrance bloomed here. Moist earth provided the grounding note, primal and fecund, evoking pictures of an abundant harvest. Below that was another elemental—water, softly metallic. Blue could see it in his mind's eye—condensation on the panes of the greenhouse and the leaves, and collecting in silver droplets that dripped from the roof and coalesced into pools.

And over those base notes floated the airy elegance of the flowers themselves, their varied trademarks unique and not always harmonious. Tonight, a newly bloomed cymbidium overpowered the rest, like the tuba in a band. Unmistakable, overt, beautiful.

He listened and felt—the thick, humid overlay he found so comforting, and the scrabbling, tiny sounds of lizards, the fluttering of birds awakened to an intruder, the squeaking little cries of tiny mammals. He even imagined he could hear the bugs who thrived in such a fertile world—the spiders and the predators, the beetles and the dragonflies. An entire host of insects.

Only then did he let himself open his eyes. By day, it was a splendor almost too great for the eye, and sight blotted out the less vigorous but no less enchanting sensory pleasures of smell and hearing and touch. By night, the flowers and leaves formed a haunting backdrop, mysterious and colorless and a little dangerous.

Better than bourbon, though sometimes he forgot that lately. Sometimes a way of living just got to be a habit. As he moved in his bare feet through the world he'd created, headed for a the potting bench, he decided maybe he'd been a little too dependent on the bourbon at night.

Or not. He scowled and stuck his hands into the cool, sweet-smelling black earth in a barrel, pulling up fistfuls of it to admire the glitter in the low light. The whole damned country was drinking-impaired in his opinion—scared to death to let themselves go. Gotta run, gotta compete, gotta be at peak form ninety-seven hours a day.

Not for him. A few bourbons at night did not a drunk make, and he'd be damned if he'd let some skinny little thing with her blurred country voice make him feel ashamed of a perfectly civilized habit.

In the morning, Ellie called her grandmother. Geraldine Connor answered a cellular phone she kept in her apron pocket—a phone Ellie paid for and insisted that Geraldine keep on her person at all times—from the garden. Ellie could hear birdsong in the background. "Hey, Grandma," Ellie said. "What are you doing?"

"Hi, darlin'! I'm pulling weeds. How was the trip?"

"Fine. Lost a gasket in some little town in Arkansas, but they fixed it and I got here safe and sound."

"And your host? He all right?"

Ellie hesitated for a split second. "He's fine. Very nice. The cottage is pretty, and there's a lot of room for April to run." To forestall any comment, she added quickly, "Do you have something to write with? I have the numbers for you."

But Geraldine smelled a rat. "Hold on, child," she said with an edge of irritation. "I have to go inside and get me a pencil. So, is he a young man, this Dr. Reynard?"

"Not that young. Mid-thirties, I guess." Ellie moved to the desk, looked out the window toward the house, realized what she was doing and paced back to the sink. "He has greenhouses."

"For what?"

"I have no idea."

"I still say it's crazy, taking a man you don't know up on an offer like that. Only heaven knows what kind of person he is." The screen door to the kitchen slammed, and in her mind's eye, Ellie saw the red vinyl and chrome chairs that matched the red Formica table. Right now, her grandmother would be opening the drawer to the left of the sink, her junk drawer that really was very junky, and digging through it to find a pencil. "I'm ready for the number," she said. "Go ahead."

Ellie read it off the phone. "It should only take me a few weeks to get this research done, and then I'll come home and finish the book there."

"Child, I keep telling you I'm doing just fine. You don't have to change your life around to take care of me."

"I'm not coming to take care of you. I just want to spend some time with you. Unless," she added with a grin, "you don't want me there."

"Don't be silly."

"All right then. I'll keep you posted, but I'm guessing I'll be done by the end of the month." She looked at the calendar on the wall and quelled the faint sense of panic the date gave her.

"Well, you do what's right for you, child. I still think you're chasing a pipe dream."

Ellie knew that Geraldine did not mean Mabel Beauvais. "Aren't you even curious?"

"Heck, no! Why would I care all these years later who your mama was sleeping around with?"

Ellie rolled her eyes. Though in truth it probably

had happened just that way, it was faintly painful to hear it said aloud. "Anyway, that's a side trip. I have to get this biography done."

"Mmmm. So, is he good-looking?"

"Who?"

"You know very well."

She did, but lying made her feel bad. With a sigh, she admitted, "Handsome is really too mild a word."

A *tsk*. "Don't lose your head this time."

"No, I've learned my lesson. Pretty is as pretty does."

Satisfied that she'd warded off immediate danger, Geraldine said, "I'll be praying for you like always. I love you."

"I love you, too, Grandma. I'll call you in a day or two."

Keeping the warning in mind, Ellie did nothing to particularly improve her appearance before Blue came to fetch her. She wore serviceable cotton shorts, crisp and neat but a long way from sexy, with an equally clean, pressed blouse. She wet her hair and combed it away from her face, fastening it with a thick scrunchie, and was going to skip the makeup, but in the end compromised with just a little blush to counter her sallowness, telling herself it was simply self-respect.

A white lie that was revealed the instant she opened the door to his knock. "Morning," he drawled.

Ellie sucked in a breath. Along with the rose scent of the air came the smell of clean man. She'd been trying to tell herself she'd exaggerated his appeal overnight. She hadn't.

"Morning," she said. She closed the door behind her, and let him open the truck door for her. He climbed in the other side.

"How about some breakfast?" he asked.

"That would be great."

"Good." He started the truck and reached for the radio. "You mind?"

She shook her head. He clicked the knob and Ellie expected to hear rock and roll or maybe soul or blues. Instead, a cheerful swirl of swing filled the cab. She grinned, forgetting her self-consciousness, and raised her eyebrows at him.

He was backing out of the spot in front of the cabin, and caught her gaze only as he turned back to shift. "What? You don't like it?"

Damn, she thought. Not just blue eyes. Course not. Everything about him was more, and his eyes made her think of that moment between night and daylight, light and dark, hope and despair, all caught in that single moment. "No, actually, I do like it." She inclined her head in a gesture of dismissal. "I just wouldn't have expected you to. It's awfully New York."

He winked. "Stick around, kid. I'm full of surprises."

Ellie chuckled, and the tension in her eased. So he was gorgeous. She could get around that. "Tell me about the town," she said.

He entertained her with wry tales of fortunes won and lost as they drove the short distance into town. "And here," he said with a wry tone, "we have the main event. Pine Bend, all three thousand people."

They drove down a sleepy main street, lined with buildings mostly erected a century before, interspersed with the odd McDonald's and up-to-the-minute gas station. One side street was blocked off, and Ellie saw earth movers and other heavy construction equipment. "What's going in there? Wal-Mart?"

"We're not big enough for Wal-Mart yet," he said with a grin. "That's a Vietnam war memorial going in." He slowed behind a truck hauling a horse trailer and glanced in the mirror. "Marcus—the one you met last night?—is in charge. It was supposed to be dedicated Memorial Day, but they're aiming now for Fourth of July. We'll see."

Ellie looked at him. "Really?"

His face shifted the slightest bit, and she suddenly saw again the darkness that had lain below his cheekbones last night. "Yeah. Believe it or not, this little bitty town lost forty-two people to that war."

"Why so many?"

A shrug. "Patriotic, I guess."

He turned the corner by the courthouse, a huge, elaborate affair built of red stone, and waited for a car to pull out in front of an obviously popular café. The driver waved, giving Ellie an openly curious look, as he pulled out. Blue waved back and took the open spot. "Here we are."

It looked like home, Ellie thought as she stepped out. The courthouse with its wide lawns and thick stands of pecan trees, the trucks and farm vehicles in the streets, the mix of white and black on foot on the sidewalks, busy on errands before it got too hot.

"What do you think?" Blue asked.

She smiled. "Homey."

The café had the same feeling. It had obviously been standing in the same location for decades, but the walls had been redone in a green-and-white ivy print, and the green vinyl covering on the booths and chairs looked new. The waitresses wore slacks and polo shirts, green and white, with tennis shoes. One was on her way to deliver an order when she caught sight of Blue. She immediately changed direction. "Hey, handsome," she said.

"How you doing, Julie?" Blue drew Ellie forward by her elbow. "This is my houseguest, Ellie Connor."

"Hi," she said without enthusiasm. Ellie quelled a smile. "Right this way. Table for two by the window." She let them move by her and settle in, then added, "I know how you like to watch the girls go by."

"Thanks." Blue shot Ellie a glance wickedly dancing with amusement.

"Old girlfriend?" Ellie guessed when the woman walked away.

"Yeah—seventeen years ago." He didn't laugh aloud, but she saw the twitch of his lips. "Somebody's got to be irresistible, right?"

"Noble of you to take it on."

A studied shrug, charming and self-deprecating at once. He leaned forward and lowered his voice. "Her husband left her a few months ago. She's just feeling lonely."

"I'll try not to be too threatening," Ellie whispered

back, then looked at the waitress. Auburn-haired, trim, and tall, she had the kind of well-tended prettiness Ellie always associated with Texas women. She chuckled. "I'm sure she's just terrified."

Ellie didn't look away fast enough, so that outrageous blue of his eyes slammed into her hard, again, and once caught, it was hard to make herself look away. "Any woman who knows anything would kill to have your mouth," he said.

Which made it nearly impossible to keep from doing something like pursing her lips or wiggling them or biting them or something. "I wasn't fishing for compliments," she said, and opened the menu.

"Oh, sorry. I thought you were."

Ellie glanced up, and caught him grinning. "Touché."

He lifted his chin toward the menu. "The biscuits and gravy are terrific. You should try them."

As they came out of the restaurant into the glorious sunlight, Ellie lifted her face and breathed deeply the moss and magnolia smell of the air. She patted her belly. "That was so good. Thank you."

"My pleasure, ma'am. Good to see a woman who eats like that." He gestured down the block. "Let's go see Rosemary. She ought to be there by now."

"Terrific." Ellie had been corresponding with Rosemary Grace, a niece to Mabel Beauvais, and although Rosemary didn't remember her, she had promised Ellie access to family letters and photographs.

"It's just down the block," he said, lifting an open

hand to someone passing down the street. "We can walk."

Ellie fell in beside him, taking pleasure in the morning and the easy camaraderie she felt with Blue. It had been there from the beginning in their E-mails, but last night she'd been made uncomfortable by his good looks. This morning, the other feeling was back, and she could relax.

It was also pleasant to realize she was really in a small town for a change. She loved them, loved the easy flow of relations, things like the simple wave he'd returned, the nods he gave to people they passed. The air was moist on her skin, the late spring sunlight not yet the weight it would be later in the day.

Across the street stood the rosy-colored courthouse with a proper dome and pillars across the front. Thick bluegrass and pecan trees spread away from it to the sidewalks, providing an oasis of shade and comfort and a sense of stability. A white frame church with a steeple stood on the corner. On this side of the street was an assortment of shops—a bakery sending a scent of fried dough into the morning; a shoe shop, with a sign that boasted the prices of heel repair; a beauty parlor; and at the end, Rosemary's Book Stop.

Yes, she knew this world. It surprised her how much she'd missed it.

A plump, neat black woman in her mid-forties struggled with a key in the front door of the bookstore. Obviously the Rosemary of the shop's name. She kicked the door impatiently as they approached.

Blue chuckled. "Morning. You need some help?"

"Oh, fiddlesticks," the woman said, and stepped back. "It jams all the time lately. I don't know what's wrong with it."

Blue had it open in a moment, and gave her the keys with a flourish. "Needs some WD–40, that's all. I have some in my truck. I'll be right back." He headed down the block, then turned back, grinning at them. "Where are my manners? Rosemary Grace, this is Ellie Connor."

Rosemary raised her brows. "We'd have managed, Blue."

"Now I'll get the WD–40."

"You do that. Come on in, Ellie," Rosemary said. "I'm fifteen minutes behind, and it makes me mad to be late. They have these streets so torn up over that damned memorial you can't get through."

Ellie followed her into the store, watching as she flipped on the fluorescent lights and dropped her purse on the counter. It was a wide room, and every inch of it was packed with books that perfumed the air with notes of faint dust and paper and glue. Old books, she saw as the light spluttered on; old paperbacks and hardcovers of every imaginable genre, neatly alphabetized. Boldly lettered signs high on the wall guided the browser to particular sections: science fiction and fantasy, history and biography, mystery.

"I have to do just a couple of things," Rosemary said, heading for the back. "If you can hang on just one minute, I'll be right with you."

"Take your time," Ellie said. "I'm in no hurry at all."

The room was split in half, with new books on the other side of the cash register. With writerly approval, Ellie noticed the books were displayed face-out as much as possible, and there were tags quoting reviews or recommendations from obviously local readers beneath them: "Delbert Reese says this is a good military history." She smiled. Everything was clean and organized, shelved with a logic that often seemed to defeat small booksellers. Rosemary knew her business and took it seriously.

Bless her heart.

Toward the back, an open archway had a computer-generated banner over it: *Romance for everyone!* Ellie peeked in and saw a large, charming room, pleasingly bright thanks to a big window to the back showing a parklike view of trees and a small stream. Easy chairs, worn but inviting, nestled in corners, with small lamps nearby for easy exploration. Ellie went down the two steps into the room and wandered through.

The new books were displayed with the same care and attention as the books in the other room, the covers displayed face out, with small, typed tags beneath some of them.

"There you are!" Rosemary said. "You read romances?"

"I read everything," she said with a wry smile. "Or I used to. My job now requires so much reading, I don't ever seem to pick up books for pleasure." She gestured. "This room makes me want to start."

Rosemary gestured to one of the chairs. "Have a seat."

"Oh, I don't want to keep you from your business. I was just hoping we might be able to set up an appointment."

"Don't be silly. If someone comes in, they'll look around." As if to illustrate she had all the time in the world, she settled in one of the chairs next to the window and smoothed the burgundy challis skirt over her knees. "Please, join me."

"Thank you."

An electronic *ding* sounded. Both Rosemary and Ellie looked toward the front of the store. Blue called out, "It's me!"

Rosemary answered him, and turned back to Ellie. Her eyes were large and very dark, almost black, and there were golden freckles over her nose, giving the middle-aged face an air of eternal youthfulness. "Now, why don't you tell me how you decided to write a biography of my aunt." She gave the word aunt the elongated *ahh*. "She was quite a character, but I can't imagine how you came across her. There hasn't been much written."

"No," Ellie agreed. "That's one reason it makes such a great story. I stumbled over her by accident. I was finishing up some research on another blues musician, and found a picture of her." Ellie remembered the afternoon clearly—sitting in the stacks at the University of Michigan's Ann Arbor library, a group of Chinese students murmuring behind her, and the oddly compelling picture of a beautiful woman laughing, as if to defy the world. "She was with Smokin' Joe Reese, and there was this look on his face"—Ellie paused and shook her head with a smile—"like he would eat her up if he could. But she was laughing, like she didn't even notice. I loved how free and beautiful she looked, but the tag line on the photo said she disappeared three days later." Ellie spread her hands. "It just pierced me. I wanted to find out who she was."

"I know that picture." Rosemary smiled. "She was something else, all right. My father used to tell stories about her—he never really got over . . . it." She glanced down, plucked an imaginary bit of lint from her skirt. "He kept every letter she ever wrote him, which you're welcome to look at, as I said. My sister Florence said there were some journals, too, but I haven't a clue where they are."

Journals. Ellie kept her face expressionless with effort. The letters and photos would be an enormous help, but she hadn't even known any journals existed. "All right," she said, tamping down her excitement. "But . . . well, journals are an excellent source. If you could ask around a little, see if someone might know where they are, it would be an enormous help."

"I will."

Blue came in, carrying a thick paperback novel he'd obviously stopped to examine. Curious, Ellie tilted her head to see the cover. *The Nero Wolfe Omnibus*.

"Sounds like you two didn't need my introduction at all," he commented.

"No, sir, we did not," Rosemary said. "In my experience, two women very rarely need a man for anything."

Blue held up the can of lubricant. "Except for the

odd lock trouble." His hair, streaky like a lion's mane, fell over his forehead, and his eyes lit with the quick mischief that gave such an appealing aspect to his beautiful face.

Looking at him, Ellie suddenly realized there couldn't be many women who didn't give at least passing thought to the idea of him in her bed. It was an aura some men had, something that promised he knew where to linger and what to do.

Her gaze fell to his hands.

"You better watch out for this one, Ellie," Rosemary said, her voice only partly teasing. "Anybody tell you that yet?"

Ellie looked up at Blue. "I already figured it out."

Last night, Ellie had seen that he was attracted to her. Even when they thought they were being sly, men were not particularly subtle. It had made her nervous and she'd pretended not to notice. And then, when he'd been going through her CDs, she'd picked up a distinct sense of dismay or disappointment or something. He had walls. The charming Southern boy, the flirt and the tease, those were the man he put on show.

Looking at him now, she caught a hint of the other man. The one who drank late at night and found companionship in newsgroups. Lost, maybe. Definitely alone.

She sighed inwardly. Of course he was lost. Ellie had a brilliant knack for finding doomed and beautiful men, men who'd suffered every conceivable kind of abuse and disaster, men condemned to early graves from drink or hopelessness or an inability to bear one more thing. She didn't know what Blue's story was, but it was so obviously the same type that she felt a bite of annoyance at herself. The signs had all been there if she'd had bothered to take three seconds to see them.

After her last crash and burn—with a bass violinist with the Cincinnati Orchestra—she'd taken the oath: *I, Ellie Connor, do solemnly vow to date only sane, stable men from now on.* It was a vow she intended to keep.

She turned to Rosemary. "Would it be possible to set up a time when I might start reviewing those letters and pictures? It may take me several weeks. Will you be comfortable having me take them to my cottage, or shall I plan to work with them where they are?"

Rosemary looked troubled. "I would rather you didn't take them off anywhere," she said.

"Not a problem. I understand completely. When would be a good time?"

"I reckon you can work up there most any day. They're up in my attic. How about tomorrow? Meet me about seven, and I'll get you set up and you can work as long as you need to. My housekeeper will be there if you need anything."

"That would be wonderful." Ellie stood up and held out her hand. "I am so delighted I can't tell you."

Rosemary took her hand and inclined her head and smiled. "There are some others who might have stories about Mabel to tell. Why don't you come over here tomorrow night? We have a book group. I'm sure they'd love to talk to a writer, and there might be a couple of people who'll have some ideas and insights for you."

Ellie hesitated. She had a lot of work to do and evenings were prime time for her creative side. She had rules about keeping evenings to herself.

But then she thought of the women who would gather at such a meeting. Rosemary was of an age to remember the summer Ellie was conceived. There were probably others—and such an informal setting would be an excellent way to gather information without revealing anything of herself. "Okay," she said. "What time and where?"

"Seven. Right here." Rosemary turned and pulled a book off the shelf. "This is the book we're discussing this week. Take a look if you have time."

Ellie glanced at the cover, which had an attractive strip painting between the title and the author's name. "I'll try."

"That's all any of us can ask, now isn't it?

3

Outside, Blue still stung a teeny bit from Ellie's nonverbal but very definite rejection. Rejection of what? He scowled. Wasn't like he was making a play for her. Wasn't planning to, either. He liked women and they liked him back, and he didn't see anything wrong with a little light flirtation.

A nerve jumped under his eye and he blinked against it just as a voice sailed out a door as they passed. "Blue Reynard, if you walk by and don't stop to say hello, I'll butcher that hair of yours next time."

Tugged back to the normal world, he cocked his head and grinned through the screen. Connie was a balm for his wounded ego, and he found himself wanting to show Ellie there were women who didn't look at him like a cricket in the kitchen—nice music and all, but too much like a cockroach to bear inside.

"Well now, darlin'," he drawled through the screen door, "I was just lost in thought there for a minute. You know I'd never miss a chance to visit with my favorite hairdresser."

On the other side of a screen door, Connie Ewing braced a comb in a customer's hair and put a hand on her hip. "That's more like it."

Ellie had stopped beside him, and he touched her elbow in a directive gesture, opening the screen to let her go ahead of him into the shop.

The girl in Connie's chair squealed and covered her face. "Mother! You do this to me every time! Men should not be allowed in a beauty parlor!"

"*Salon,* girl," Connie said with the air of having said something a million times.

Blue chuckled and swung into the empty chair beside Connie's daughter. Shauna, not quite seventeen, pressed the plastic cape up to her face with a mortified groan. He tugged it down to uncover one green eye. "Boo."

She kicked at him and he swung away easily, laughing. On the other side of him was Alisha Williams. "Ellie," he said, holding out his hand to draw her over, "come meet Marcus's wife."

To her credit, Ellie didn't show even a flicker of surprise as she held out her hand to the tall, slim black woman with hair in braids to her waist—who was much younger than Marcus. "How do you do?" Ellie said.

"Nice to meet you," Alisha said. "Marcus told me you were coming to do a biography on Mabel Beauvais. I think that's real nice."

The woman sitting in Alisha's chair, an elderly black woman Blue didn't know well, whirled around. "Is that right?" she asked eagerly.

Ellie smiled. "Yes. Did you know her, by any chance?"

"Girl, I went to school with her!"

"That's terrific." Ellie shot Blue an open-eyed look, questioning, and he nodded. "Would you be willing to let me interview you?"

Blue, sitting to one side, saw the woman's face close. Instantly. Completely. "Oh, heavens, it's been such a long time and my memory isn't what it used to be. I don't think you'd find out anything from me that you couldn't get better from just about anybody in town."

"You might be surprised what you remember," Ellie said, her posture easy and unthreatening. "I'd buy you lunch at your favorite place in town if you'd just talk to me for an hour."

"Oh, let her take you to that little English tea place up in Tyler," Alisha said. "Have some of those little biscuits you like so much."

The old woman pursed her lips. "Well, I don't know. It's been a million years since Mabel left us. Don't know as I recall that much that would help." Cannily she added, "Do you like tea rooms?"

Ellie grinned, and Blue found himself noticing her lips again. A mouth in a million. He looked away, hearing her say, "Love them. Can I call you? Is it a date?"

"Let me think about it a day or two, sugar."

"All right. I'm staying at Blue's cottage, so you can reach me any time."

Connie made a purring noise. "Ooh, honey, you come on over here and tell me all about it." She gave a coy wiggle of her shoulders, a gesture she knew displayed her considerable bosom to good advantage. Blue grinned appreciatively and she winked at him.

"Does he leave his window shades open?"

Ellie laughed and lifted one eyebrow, leaning in close to say in a low voice, "I'll let you know."

"Good girl."

Blue shook his head, knowing Connie never meant a word of it. Although widowed three years before, she remained true thus far to her husband's memory. Not that the single men of Pine Bend weren't trying. Connie had been a bombshell every minute of her years on the planet. "Darlin'," he said now, "I keep telling you I'd be glad to give you a private viewing. You just say the word."

From beneath the plastic apron, Shauna Ewing moaned. "Will y'all stop it, please? My virgin ears are burning."

Blue lightly kicked her foot. She'd had a massive crush on him the year before, but had suddenly and abruptly gotten over it. Connie told him she thought Shauna had transferred the crush to somebody she met at camp, but the teenager wasn't talking.

Alisha spoke. "You ought to bring Ellie on down for dinner some night soon, Blue."

"I can do that."

Blue realized he was leaning back in the chair, watching Ellie. He found himself admiring the line of her cheek again, and frowned. It was one thing for a man to like the look of a mouth—natural to imagine all kinds of things in relation to mouths. Quite another ball game to start thinking a cheek was sweet. He jumped up. "I've gotta get myself to work, ladies. You can talk to Ellie tomorrow—she'll be at your book group."

"Will you?" Alisha asked. "I'm going. I'll pick you up if you want. It's on my way."

"Terrific. I'll look forward to it." She smiled in an open way. "It was nice to meet all of you."

Connie frowned suddenly. "You have any kin around here, Ellie? You sure look familiar."

Blue almost missed the flicker of alarm that passed over Ellie's face. In the next second it was gone, and she was shaking her head firmly. "Not that I know of." She lifted a hand. "See you all tomorrow night."

Ellie had a secret. Interesting.

Blue was quiet as they started back to Fox's Creek. Ellie picked up the fat paperback between them on the seat. "Isn't Rex Stout a mystery writer from the fifties or something?"

"Thirties." He paused at a stop sign and let an eighteen wheeler lumber by. "Have you ever read any Nero Wolfe?"

She turned the book over to read the back. "I've heard of him. A detective, right?"

A nod as he waited for traffic from the other direction. "Very colorful fella. He was my daddy's favorite, and I found a whole stack of them in his study when I was about eleven or twelve. Read them all, back to back." The road cleared. Blue shifted and gunned the truck across the narrow two-lane highway. "I thought Nero Wolfe was the greatest guy on the planet."

Ellie found herself loving the sound of his voice again, so musical, with its deep notes and slow pace. "Why?"

For a minute he was silent, and Ellie had the sense that he was deciding what was safe and what wasn't. "He's this really fat guy who sends out his people to collect facts about his cases, and he has a gourmet chef. He's kind of a beer connoisseur"—he shot her a sideways grin—"but the thing I loved was that he collected orchids. He has a plant room at the top of his house, and he spends two hours every morning and two hours every evening taking care of them."

She thought of the greenhouses. "What's the Ph.D. in, Doctor?" she asked. "Horticulture?"

"Close. Botany."

Ellie laughed, unable to help herself. "Really?"

A reluctant lift of one side of his mouth, a sidelong glance. "I know, I know. Geeky, huh? Everybody around here thinks it's a big joke, too. I just never got the hang of idleness."

"So are those greenhouses full of orchids, like Nero Wolfe's?"

He looked straight at her, the blue glittering. "Guess you'll just have to meander over and find out, won't you, Miz Connor?"

Now why did that sound so dangerous? She put the book down. "Guess I will."

If asked, Ellie would have guessed his degrees were in something esoteric and essentially useless—philosophy or history, perhaps. His posts had been brilliant and sometimes arcane in that way. She also would have guessed he made an art form of idleness, simply from the huge amount of time he seemed to spend in the newsgroups.

She shifted in the seat, crossing her arms. Figured. He wasn't just gorgeous. Not by a long shot.

They lapsed into silence as they drove down the badly paved road from town to his land. She stared out the window, trying not to imagine what a greenhouse full of orchids might look like.

Blue turned on the radio. A swing tune filled the gap between them with bright horns, and Ellie closed her eyes for a minute, seeing the desperate frenzy of dancers trying to forget a war swallowing up their loved ones half a world away. "Swing always makes me feel a little melancholy," she said.

"Sorry." He put a hand on the tuner. "I'll change it."

"Oh, no, that's not what I meant." She lifted a shoulder. "It was just a comment."

He nodded, settling his hand back on one thigh. Ellie thought about asking what made him choose a station with this kind of music over Top 40 or classical or whatever, but she kept her mouth closed on the words.

Pulling up in front of the cabin, he left the engine idling. "I'll drive you out to Rosemary's in the morning. It's kinda hard to find."

"You really don't have to do that, Blue. I didn't mean to come out here and eat up all your time."

"And I wouldn't let you. A little neighborly hand isn't such a bad thing, though. I'll be here at six-thirty."

Ellie nodded, deciding it wasn't worth an argument. "Thank you." She got out and watched him drive away, feeling a strange little knot in her chest. It was both lure and warning. Blue Reynard was a lot more than she'd bargained for.

But it wasn't in her nature to sit around brooding about such things. Instead, she let April out to run for a bit. While she waited, she poured a glass of tea and sat on the porch steps to keep an eye on her, bringing out one of the files of material Blue had left for her. Most of it was newspaper clippings from the thirties and forties, and Ellie felt a soft gust of gratitude that he'd gone to all this trouble.

She put the photocopied articles aside, anchored under a stone so the breeze wouldn't blow them away, and quickly glanced at the rest of the material: lists of blues clubs, possible contacts and where to reach them, the name of the local newspaper editor, a contact at the Church of God in Christ. The last one made her smile. From all Ellie knew of Mabel, church would not have been high on her list—but then, a lot of children first learned to sing in the local church choir.

The last item was a photograph, an eight-by-ten black-and-white glossy of the sort taken by wandering photographers at the clubs. A party of seven or eight sat around a table, dressed to the nines, hair slicked and tamed, teeth flashing in dark faces. In the middle sat a very young Mabel Beauvais, her eyes the focal point of the shot, long, exotic eyes, smoky and somehow hinting of secret laughter. She was wearing a dark polka-dot dress, rayon by the shine, which did nothing to hide her siren curves.

Ellie stared at it for a long moment, feeling the

same ache she'd felt the first time that she'd seen Mabel's picture. That secret laughter, that aloof amusement—there even when Mabel had been very young. How old was she in the picture? Eighteen, nineteen? Ellie turned it over to see if there was a label: Hopkins' Juke Box, November 2, 1939.

Not eighteen. Ellie turned it back to the front. Mabel was sixteen, and already had that look in her eye.

With a sigh, she got up and whistled for April, who came racing back through the tall grass of the field. It was time for the real story on Mabel Beauvais. Where had she gone? And why had she disappeared just when she was about to get all the fame and fortune every musician dreamed of?

Rosemary liked to take her lunch in Connie's shop. The two women had been knitted into a sometimes unwilling friendship by events neither of them had been able to control, beginning when the federal government had forced integration on the little town. They'd started high school together that year. Then, their boyfriends—Connie's Bobby and Rosemary's Marcus—had gone off to boot camp on the same bus. There had been a time in the early seventies when Connie was the only person in the world whom Rosemary felt she could share her terrors with, and vice versa.

But they'd drifted apart for a while after that, living parallel lives—getting married, having babies, and all that went along with that. Being well-raised, they'd taken their places in the community. They'd spoken, here and there, when they met in the street, but that was all.

Five years ago, the circle turned again, and they were widows within four months of each other, Connie first. When Rosemary's husband died, it had once again been Connie she could depend on to understand—not the grief, exactly, but the anger that came along with it.

Connie, who spent way too much time reading astrology magazines, claimed that their stars were aligned. Rosemary figured they were just unlucky enough to be victims of interesting times.

Today, Rosemary was more eager than usual to settle into the lunchtime gossip session. "Quiet here this afternoon," she said, closing the glass-fronted door firmly behind her to hold in the cool of the air conditioner attempting to lower temperatures generated by hair dryers and hot running water.

Connie was rolling a perm on Mrs. Jenkins, school board president, and the acrid odor of the solution mixed with nail polish the manicurist was applying in careful stripes to the tips of Alisha's very long nails. "I don't know how you do hair with those fingernails," Rosemary said with a shake of her head. "Or garden anything at all."

Alisha smiled her little cat smile, the one that was so annoying, and looked at her finished left hand. The one with the thick gold band Marcus had put on her finger. "I've had these nails all my life. They're like stone. I don't know how I'd function without them, to tell you the truth."

"So," Connie said from across the room. "What'd you think of that writer Blue brought around?"

"Seems real nice." Usually one of the younger girls would run out with their money to buy sub sandwiches or tacos from a stand near the highway, and today the job fell to Connie's daughter Shauna. Rosemary opened her purse and counted out four dollar bills to give to the girl, who was writing their orders down on an old envelope. "Get me the burrito today. And if you happen to see my son, tell him I'm going to be late for dinner."

"Will do," Shauna said, scribbling. She pocketed Rosemary's money and headed for the door. "He told me he was working till seven. We're supposed to go over our calculus tonight." She waved. "Be back in a little while."

Thinking of Ellie, Rosemary said, "I hate to see such a nice young woman fall to Blue's spell, though. You could already see it there in her eyes." She shook her head. "And she's just not his type at all, is she?"

"Not a bit," Connie agreed, "but I'm betting he'll have her in his bed inside a week anyway."

"Oh, I hope not," Alisha said. "He's such a dog."

Connie fitted a plastic bag over her customer's head. "That's not fair, Alisha. He's just had some hard knocks. His wife hasn't been gone that long. A man's bound to sow a few wild oats after something like that."

"It's been at least five years." Alisha put her hands side by side in front of her, narrowing her eyes to examine them. "Because I've been in town that long. Five years seems pretty long to still be wild out of grief."

"You know I'm very fond of him," Rosemary put in, trying to think of a way she didn't have to agree with Alisha. It pained her. Still . . . "Sometimes a way of living gets to be a habit."

Alisha snorted.

"I hate to see that sweet little thing get her heart broken." Rosemary paused. "She's not the least bit pretty, is she?"

"And skinny, " Connie added. She pursed her lips. "Maybe he won't even be interested."

"I thought she was cute," Alisha said. "She's got some color to her. I never do understand why men like those pale, pale girls."

Rosemary laughed. "Not all of them, sweetie."

Alisha tossed her braids. "Not mine, anyway." She grinned. "Oh, let's leave the poor girl alone. She didn't strike me as anywhere close to stupid, and it's not like you can't see Blue coming sixty miles away. A man like that . . ." She shrugged. "He was just born to be a dog."

"Dog is not the word I'd use." Connie said. She patted Mrs. Jenkins on the shoulder to direct her to a new chair.

"What then? What else can you call a man who runs through women like they're beer?"

Connie smiled. "He's a ladies' man, that's all. He likes women. They like him back. Nothing wrong with that."

Rosemary leaned back, crossing her arms over her chest. There had been a moment in the bookstore, when Blue had stood there with his hands at his side, looking at Ellie with a kind of winded look on his face. It made Rosemary think of Marcus, back in the days when he'd come back from war, torn up so bad he didn't sleep for months. "Maybe she'll just be a good friend to him," she said. "The man could use a friend."

They all fell silent, thinking of that. "Yes," Connie said. "That he could."

Ellie consulted her map and drove to the Stonewall County library. It was housed in an old brick building set in the midst of a small park. Long windows gazed blankly over the lush green lawn and tall trees that cast an agreeable depth of shade. It looked to Ellie just the way a library should, right down to the stone lions guarding the steps. A fountain chuckled to one side, and she glimpsed the shiny body of a goldfish in the pool beneath it.

She pulled open the long, heavy doors and was pleased to find the old library feel remained. In the smell, old glue and dust and bindings; in the waxed black-and-white floor; in the oak tables and chairs occupying a central aisle between the stacks. It even had a balcony, with a twisted iron railing, reached by a set of iron steps. A sign above the stairs said, "Reference."

There were few patrons about on a spring weekday—a mother and her toddler, an old man wheezing over the newspaper, and a skinny, bedraggled man slumped over a magazine. Ellie wound around up the circular stairs, then approached the trim woman behind the desk. She wore her glasses on a neon green rope around her neck, a color that did not go at all with the tailored shirtwaist dress or the soft blond wave. "May I help you?" she asked, her tone friendly.

"I hope so." Ellie took a list out of her satchel. "My name is Ellie Connor. I wrote you about doing some in-depth research here on Mabel Beauvais."

"Oh, of course!" The woman stood up and stuck out her hand. "I'm Mrs. Nance, the head librarian." Briskly, she pushed in her chair and gestured for Ellie to follow her. "I took the liberty of getting some material out for you—we're not computerized yet, so it can be a long job finding some of these things, and I thought you'd want to spend your time reading, rather than searching up and down all these dusty stacks."

Ellie blinked. "Thank you."

Mrs. Nance stopped in front of a long table where several kinds of books were sorted in piles according to size. She put her hand on a stack of enormous dark-bound books. "These are the newspapers. I got out some of the years I thought might be most helpful. These"—she pointed to a stack of soft-bound papers Ellie recognized as dissertations—"are a couple of doctoral papers I thought you might find interesting. I got one through interlibrary loan, but it doesn't have to go back for several weeks, and if you find it helpful, we can hang on to it a little longer."

Ellie, touched and pleased, smiled. "I suspect you have a teaching degree back there in your history somewhere."

The woman chuckled. "No, I can't say that I do. But I have read your work—the one you did on Laura Redding was especially wonderful—and I haven't ever had the opportunity to assist a writer before." She waved a hand. "Anyway, I'm very pleased that you're examining poor Mabel's life. She's the most famous person to ever come of Pine Bend, and we're proud of her. It's a sad story, and needs telling."

Intrigued, Ellie asked, "What do you find sad about it, Mrs. Nance?"

The lively brown eyes settled a little, and she looked off toward the long window. "Just that it was a hard time to be a woman, and even harder to be a black woman, especially a beautiful and talented black woman." With a small, puzzled smile, she added, "I guess it's the timing that's so sad. She didn't have a chance, not really."

Ellie nodded, oddly touched. "I agree with you."

"Well, listen to me talk! I'll let you get to your work. If there's anything at all you need, you just holler."

"I will." Inspired, Ellie sat down, took out her pile of blank index cards, her favorite rolling ball pen—black ink, never blue, which didn't look serious enough to suit her—and opened the first book of bound newspapers. Halfway through, a pale blue Post-it was stuck to a page, and Ellie turned the yellowed newsprint gently until she reached it. The tag was blank, but it was stuck to a story at the bottom of the front page:

LOCAL GIRL WINS PRIZE

Mabel Beauvais, daughter of Jacob and Marlene Beauvais, won first place and a $100 cash prize in a state gospel competition last Thursday. The fourteen-year-old, who has been a member of the Church of God in Christ choir since the age of five, sang "The Old Rugged Cross," which she said was her father's favorite. Mabel, who attends Carver School, said she plans to put the money away for college. "I'd love to study opera," she said.

Ellie noted the date of the paper and recorded the information, then took a second card and made a note to herself to check the possibility of a black girl studying opera in the late thirties—anywhere. Juilliard, maybe. She also noted the name of the grammar school. She liked being able to see the actual buildings that figured into a person's life. Seeing the way the neighborhood went together sometimes gave her insight she could never have attained another way.

By four o'clock, the light in the room had grown dim as the sun moved west, and Ellie's shoulders were tight with being hunched over her notes. Still, she had amassed two large stacks of cards—one with actual facts and dates, the other with reminders and questions she need to follow up on. She'd only managed to get through four years of primary newspaper material.

She stretched hard and wondered if she dared look up the papers from 1968, the year her mother had supposedly spent the summer in Pine Bend. It made her feel guilty to have an ulterior motive in coming here, especially when Mrs. Nance had been so helpful, but she didn't want to broadcast her private history.

It suddenly seemed futile and foolish to sneak

around. Rosemary and Connie—maybe even Mrs. Nance—were of an age to be able to answer Ellie's questions. It was quite possible one of them would remember Ellie's mother, Diane. All she'd have to do was ask.

But the truth was, Ellie wasn't entirely sure she wanted to claim her mother. She had no idea what kind of state her mother had been in while she lived in Pine Bend or who she'd been mixed up with. What if she'd been a crazed druggie, sleeping with a motorcycle gang or something? It was certainly possible.

Diane Connor had been beautiful, wild, and troubled from the moment of her birth. Her parents, in their early forties when she was born, were hard pressed to cope with such a rebellious personality. Nothing worked on Diana—she laughed at threats, ignored restrictions, even endured the rare whipping her father brought to bear in his old-fashioned, country way with stoic, unbreakable will. At sixteen, bored with school and her tiny western Louisiana town, she'd stuck out her thumb on the county highway and headed out of town.

The only thing Ellie had of her was the collection of postcards her mother had faithfully sent home once a week. There wasn't much on them in the way of news, nothing but the postmarks from various spots—Santa Fe and San Francisco, Atlanta and Washington, D.C., and an entire list of small towns all over the country—and a quick note, usually along the lines of "Hi. How are you. I'm fine. Traveling now with Luke, who has a motorcycle. Love, Diane."

At Christmas 1968, Diane abruptly came home, pregnant and broke. Her parents took her in, and she stayed just long enough to have her baby girl, to whom she gave the unlikely moniker Velvet Sunset. When Velvet, called Ellie by her grandmother after her favorite sister, was six months old, Diane's restlessness bloomed once more, and she was gone. Geraldine always had a faintly bewildered look on her face when she told her granddaughter about it. "One day she seemed to be turning into a normal young woman, sweet as she could be to her little daughter. The next"—a snap of her fingers—"poof, she was gone."

The second time she left home, Diane didn't bother with postcards. They didn't hear anything from her again until a Las Vegas police officer called with the bad news that Diane had been found dead of a drug overdose at a nearby campground.

It was hard, Ellie thought now, to imagine what kind of impact a hippie runaway, with flowing hair and gossamer clothes, had had on a small town like Pine Bend. What in the world had led her here, anyway? And what had made her stay for more than three months?

A man, obviously.

She glanced over her shoulder at Mrs. Nance, who was on the phone. Perfect. Ellie stood up and whispered loudly, "Mrs. Nance." When the woman looked up, Ellie pointed to the stacks. She felt guilty when Mrs. Nance nodded enthusiastically.

It was easy to find the newspapers, and as she ran her fingers over the years, she concocted a lie to cover her tracks if she had to: she'd say she was born in '68 and one of her hobbies was looking up the events of that year. It was only a small lie.

The newspapers were bound a year at a time. She pulled out the one she wanted, then also selected one at random from the forties, and went back to the table. Mrs. Nance was still on the phone.

Ellie stuck her index finger into the 1968 book and opened near the middle. July.

For one moment, she felt a wild sense of warning. Maybe there were things better left unknown. Maybe her mother had been ashamed of the man who'd left her pregnant. Maybe it was as bad as Ellie's worst imaginings—that Diane had been the companion to some biker gang. Maybe Diane had never named a man because there'd been too many.

No. Ellie's gut said it was a single man who'd held the wild child in place for a whole summer. And if she didn't at least try to find out who that man was, she'd spend the rest of her life regretting it. Taking a deep breath, she began to read. If she'd learned anything at all about historical research, it was that a person never knew where that perfect nugget of information would appear.

The big news that summer seemed to focus on three things: an embezzlement scandal, the disappearance of a young woman, and the war in Vietnam. Each week, an entire page was devoted to news of the soldiers in service, some in Okinawa or Germany or other names she'd almost forgotten. Most of the news came from Vietnam itself. Peter Stroo was having trouble with his feet again. Jack Mackey had done some R & R in Saigon, and he'd sent his mother a beautiful scarf.

Sitting in the placid library, with dust in her nose and sunshine on her neck, Ellie felt a queer twist on her time/space senses. Vietnam was a faraway event, a sad, terrible mistake. In the clips of her memory, it came tangled up with streamers of paisley scarves and images of girls sticking flowers in the ends of guns.

But here were the names and pictures of boys who were younger than she by a decade, writing letters home from a jungle so far away, writing to their mamas or girlfriends, and the paper printed the news with a grand sense of bonhomie that seemed more suited to World War II.

On two of those pages from the summer of 1968 were the inevitable notices, boxed and respectful: *Mr. and Mrs. Larry Needham were informed this week that their son, Bret, was killed in action on June 24.* There was also news of injuries, more frequent.

Feeling vaguely unsettled, Ellie put the bound book in the stack with the others she had been using this afternoon, and stretched. Mrs. Nance, as if waiting for her, took a heavy ring of keys from the desk. "Finished for today?"

"I am, thank you. Is it all right if I leave these here overnight? I have to meet someone in the morning, but I can come in after lunch. Will they be in the way?"

"Heavens, no. You can leave them there for a week. Nobody much comes up here."

Ellie smiled and lifted a hand in farewell. As she went down the wrought iron steps, she couldn't help wondering what her hippie mother had been doing in a town that so obviously supported the war. What could she possibly have found appealing about it? Another puzzle.

But it was one that would have to wait. All at once, Ellie was winded and tired, ready to lose herself in something else, something that wasn't a past filled with mystery. She wondered if there was a video store in town where she could rent a VCR and some tapes.

The idea held far more allure than it should have, considering how much work she had to do. She struck a deal with herself: if she worked every night this week, she could find out about a VCR rental this weekend, and take Saturday night off and pretend she was anywhere but a hundred miles from home, seeking answers she wasn't entirely sure she wanted to find. She knew what kind of movies she wanted, too—modern comedy, with no reference to wars or the past in any form. Movies lent forgetfulness. By Saturday, she thought she might need that.

The Lovers

The first time she ever saw him, he was laughing. Something about the sound rushed on her neck, like a breath of hope. It was a sound of unfettered happiness, pure pleasure, so fertile that she turned, urgently, to see who could laugh with such abandon.

And when she found him, the man who laughed like that, sitting in the dusk with his friends, he looked as golden as the sound. His hair caught the last of the evening sun, and it carried a red glimmer in the darkness that sparked like fire. And on his arms, the hair glinted in the same shade, making her think of Adonis. Wasn't it Adonis who ruled the sun?

She knew she was staring, but somehow, she couldn't make herself look away. He must have felt her gaze, because he turned his head and looked right at her, the smile lingering on his mouth, then fading. He looked away fast, but then looked back, and it was her turn to duck her head, glance away, ashamed that she should take even one minute of that perfect laughter from the world.

But when she looked back, unable to resist one last glance, she found him cutting the distance between them with a smile. As if he knew her. As if he'd been waiting.

For her.

4

Blue was tired. Sweat and dust had formed a kind of glue that cracked on his neck when he moved, and his arms were coated with mud. The sprinkler system for one of the greenhouses had broken a main pipeline this morning, and they hadn't discovered it until well past noon. He and Marcus had traced the break to a swampy spot behind the greenhouse, but sure as dawn, plumbing never went smoothly.

Marcus swore as his wrench slipped and he slammed his fingers between the lead pipe and the heavy tool. He shook his hand and glanced at the lowering sun. "We've done about all we can today, man. Let's just rig something up for the plants tonight and get on it first thing in the morning."

Blue nodded in defeat. "Got any ideas? You're the mechanical wizard around here."

"Not at the moment. I reckon you're just gonna have to keep an eye on the babies for tonight." He wiped a wrist over his forehead, leaving a smear of pale brown mud across his dark skin. "I'll run by Shumake's in the morning, pick up those joints."

"Damn." The babies Marcus spoke of were tiny orchids, part of the experimental work Blue was doing to find more efficient ways of germinating the plants. Conditions had to mimic the rain forest exactly for the research to be valid, and this might mean a setback of months. The thought of all the lost work depressed him. He propped his hands on his thighs. "It is what it is."

"Yep." With a groan, Marcus got to his feet and stretched. "I'm going to haul my ass home and take a shower. I got a meeting with the city council tonight about the memorial."

Blue nodded. "You on schedule for Fourth of July?"

"So far, so good." Marcus said. "I'll be glad when it's finally done."

"I bet."

"Yeah." Marcus stared off toward the horizon, his eyes far away, maybe on the faces that belonged to the names that would be carved into the memorial. One was Blue's brother, killed in Saigon in the last weeks of the war. "That woman just pulled up, if you're interested."

Blue looked over his shoulder to see Ellie getting out of her car, and a prickle moved over the base of his spine. He didn't get it. Four years and he'd only bothered with women when he got too horny to stand it anymore. Here came one so far from his type that she might have been a boy, and he'd been thinking about her, off and on, all day.

She didn't see them, and Blue did nothing to attract her attention.

"Let's get this done," Marcus said wearily.

"You go on. I'll take care of it." He'd be glad to have something to keep his mind away from . . . he rolled his head . . . things. Keep his mind off things.

"I'm not gonna argue. See you in the morning."

Blue didn't move for a long time, his body dead tired from shoveling wet earth out of the hole. The mud on his neck cracked when he shifted, and his wrists were thick with grime.

Only the thought of the plants withering got him moving. By the time he finished checking temperatures, adjusting the shades, and wetting down the inner walls of the greenhouse with a hose, he had no brain left. A good thing.

He deliberately did not look in the direction of the cabin, though he heard music playing, something soft and soulful, indistinct in the thickening evening.

As he came into the kitchen, his great-aunt Lanie rushed in from the other room. A tiny, thin woman with white hair, she wore a blue calico apron over her dress, and her long hands were knotted together. "I was just about to page you, honey," she said. "My cat needs to go to the vet."

"My cat, you mean." Piwacket had belonged to Blue's wife, and had been old even when they first married. Now she was seventeen and skinny as a wire. Like his aunt, who was just as skinny and just as old in human years. Both required a special diet and the odd trip to the emergency room but gave back a hundred times what they took. He couldn't really imagine his life without either one, though chances were good he'd have to part with one or the other before too much longer.

But maybe not. He'd been thinking the same thing for ten years, and neither showed signs of going anywhere yet.

Piwacket, in the universal language of sick cats, sulked under a coffee table. "Hey, darlin'," he said, and grabbed her by the scruff of the neck before she could run off. Her ears were hot, and when he pinched a fold of skin, it stayed stuck together. "Yeah, you've got to go in again."

Lanie had already dragged out the carrier and lined it with a bath towel that smelled of Blue. Piwacket had kidney disease—had had it for two years now, and routinely had to spend a night at the veterinarian's office, hooked up to an IV to rehydrate her.

Blue settled her into the carrier, and Pi glared at him through the wire mesh on top, but she seemed to accept her fate. "Did you call them yet?" Blue asked.

"No, but I'll do it now. They'll be gone before long if you don't get moving."

He kissed the top of her white head. "Thanks, Lanie. Go watch your soaps now, all right? I'll take care of my dinner."

"There's a salad in the fridge. Be sure and eat, and don't spend the whole evening sucking on a bottle of whiskey, either."

"Yes, ma'am."

• • •

Two hours later, with Piwacket safely hooked to IV tubes in her suite at the vet's—disgruntled but not particularly pissed—Blue finally got to get in the shower. He washed the grime of the day from him, threw on a pair of jeans, and wandered into the kitchen to see what Lanie had left for him. A Cobb salad. He pulled it out, decided he wasn't hungry, and poured a drink instead, bourbon over ice. From Lanie's apartment in the basement, he heard the television, and he eyed the bourbon guiltily for a minute.

Then added a jigger more whisky to his glass. There were days that warranted a good drink, and this had been one of them.

Turning to put the ice tray back in the freezer, he caught a blur of motion from the corner of his eye, and paused to look out the kitchen window. It faced the cabin, the greenhouses, and the open slope of field between them, and it was at the bottom of the slope that he'd seen movement. It was Ellie and her dog.

From this distance, he could make out no details of expression, but the game was as old as time. Ellie jumped and hunched and wrestled with the dog playfully, ducking and turning, running and stopping. April leapt and yipped, raced and jumped. Blue rubbed his ribs, sipping his bourbon, and watched them. In the gathering dusk, the woman's red shirt was bright, her black hair a blur, the dog a smear of black and white.

They both tired, and still Blue stood there, sipping whiskey in his bare feet. April slumped in the small space of grass fronting the small porch, and the woman collapsed beside her. There was more play, more subdued, as Ellie roughed up the dog's fur, then the dog fell against the ground, and the woman fell, too, resting her head on the black-and-white belly. Blue couldn't see her hands, but the angle of the red sleeve was such that he knew she put a hand against April's throat, rubbing distractedly as they lay in the grass. He thought of no-see-ums and mosquitoes, but if she felt them devouring her, Ellie gave no sign. They lay there, woman and dog for a long, long time. And only when they both got up and padded into the cottage did he take a fresh drink and a bag of potato chips into the den.

Automatically, he flipped on the television and fell into his favorite chair, a worn, oversized recliner that had been a fixture of the room as long as he could remember. It had been his daddy's chair.

In the flickering blue light from the television, he fell into a doze, then a deeper sleep. And as it often did when he didn't anesthetize himself, the dream came. A long, dim hall, with closed doors all the way along it. Blue felt a tight, bitter sense of frustration as he stared at all the doors. If he only knew which one to open. He tried one, and there was his brother. "Hey, Bruiser," Jack said, the spikes of his crew cut catching the light from the window.

Blue, with a sigh of relief, settled into a chair by the door. "I thought you were dead."

And then he saw that his brother *was* dead.

He bolted awake, spilling chips in a wide spray. For a long, panicky moment, he blinked into the darkness, the all-too-vivid picture lingering. God, he hated that dream. Every door, the same story. His mother. His wife. He wiped a hand over his face. At least his brain spared him his father.

Through the open French doors came music, floating on the currents of wind that blew up from the river. Without pausing for a second, Blue stood up and followed the sound like a sleepwalker, knowing even as he did it that it was the serenity of Ellie at play with her dog that drew him. He walked through the field in his bare feet, drawn by the mournful sound of a woman's voice, singing the blues. It was the only sound a man could bear at times.

The door was open to the cabin, and through the screen, Blue saw Ellie swaying to the music. She stood in the middle of the room, a piece of paper in her hand, as if she'd stood up to do something and had been snared by the music. And as if she had become part of it, she shaped it with her body, swaying, her shoulders and her head and her arms all moving gently, easily, on currents of dark notes.

He stood in the loamy soil and watched her, his hands loose at his sides, unable to move forward or move away, captured by the music and the peaceful heart of a woman he ought not want, but somehow did.

Ellie's head was full of images. She stood in the middle of the cabin and swayed with the music, letting the spirit of Mabel fill her. She was no longer herself, but sixteen and black and dancing in a blues club on the wrong side of the river. Her rayon dress brushed her summer-bare calves.

She reached for Mabel's laughter, trying to feel that spark, that vividness, but even with the music, and the dance, it did not materialize. With a sigh, she let her shoulders sag, and became only Ellie, and opened her eyes.

April sat by the counter in the kitchen, head up, ears pricked up, her tail swishing happily over the floor. Ellie turned. Through the time-blackened screen door, she saw Blue. He stood in the yard, an open shirt tossed over his arms, no shoes on his feet. Lamplight illuminated one cheekbone, one high arch of a bare foot. His lost, artless beauty stunned her.

He simply stood there. Ellie moved very slowly toward the door, and gently swung it open in invitation. She said nothing, only waited, until he took a step, then another, pausing at the stair. She nodded encouragement.

On the stereo, Sonny and Brownie's "Sail Away" began to play, smoky and slow, a song about seductive promises that could not be fulfilled. Blue looked behind her, seeming to awaken to where he was, how he stood there. He looked down, touched his stomach with the flat of a palm, looked back at her. "I heard the music," he said, his voice low and rough.

"Come in." She pushed the door wider, so there would be room for him to pass. "I still have some beer. I'll get you one."

"This is when I would go in and write you notes," he said, taking a step up to the porch. "This time of night. I'd go in and see what you'd been talking about and write to you."

Ellie smiled. "I wrote at night, too. I almost did tonight, and then I thought it would be silly for us to talk like that when you're only a little way up the hill."

"It's easier on the computer."

She felt his presence like the first low rumbles of a thunderstorm, a crackling along the hairs of her arms and low on her back. "Yeah," she agreed. "It is."

"Am I bothering you?"

Yes, she almost said. But she only shook her head and gestured for him to enter. He turned sideways to pass, and she pulled back as tight as she could against the doorframe, but his ribs brushed her breasts, one hand bumped her thigh, and he abruptly stopped instead of passing on through.

Acutely aware of the places their bodies connected, of his thumb brushing just below the joint of her hip, she dared not even take in a breath. She kept her head lowered, flooded with a wild sense of danger and embarrassment—why hadn't she told him to come in, like any normal person?—and the awkwardness she always felt when she first realized she wanted something.

The moment stretched, one second, two, five, until she was forced to take a breath, which moved her breast on his skin as she had known it would. His hand turned and his palm was against her thigh. She looked up at him.

He said nothing, did nothing, only stood there, touching her so lightly. A hint of bourbon came from him, and she thought he might be a little crazy. Maybe a lot. Maybe it had been a foolish thing indeed to accept his invitation to stay here, and even more foolish to let him in tonight, when whatever it was that made him seem okay was gone, and he was revealed for what he was: doomed.

Doomed, and he knew it.

She slipped away and left him standing there, and moved toward the fridge. April stood up and went to greet him, as calm as if he belonged here. Ellie opened the fridge and got out two beers. When she turned back, Blue was gone.

Instead of the relief any sane woman would have felt, she was conscious of deep disappointment. In a little rush, she moved toward the door, calling out his name as she went out on the porch.

"I'm here," he said, the voice dark molasses. "I needed a breath of air."

She gave him the beer and he took it, and the strangeness was suddenly gone. "I may not be bothering you, sugar," he said. "But I think you're bothering me."

Relief moved through her. "Sweet-talker," she said, and drank gustily, moving over to sit on the step, her back against the post.

He settled a few feet away, his back against the wall, his legs kicked out in front of him. "This used to be slave quarters," he said, and lifted his head as if he were listening. "My mama wouldn't come down here on a bet at night. She said it was haunted."

On the stereo, Sonny and Brownie sang about the seduction of African children to America, a poignant, mournful song that always made her feel emotionally wide open.

"No ghosts here," she said firmly, "but your house looks like it has at least a couple dozen."

"No doubt about that." There was no lightness to the comment.

"Any of them looking for you?"

"One or two. Didn't you see the one chased me down here tonight?"

"Oh, so that's what happened." She smiled through the darkness, and took a deep breath, smelling humus and the coppery hints of river water and a thousand notes of growing things. Overhead the sky was thick with stars, billions of stars that you could never see from the city. She had forgotten so much. "I didn't know I was homesick till I got here," she said quietly.

"Where you from?"

She started to answer, but he held up a hand. "No, let me guess."

"Go ahead."

He pursed his lips. "Can't be too far away. You try to talk real proper, but you can't hide all of it. Not Texas."

"No."

"Mississippi, then. Maybe . . . Jackson?"

"No and no."

"Hmmm." He drank some beer. "Not too much farther east. Unless, one of the Carolinas?"

Ellie laughed. "I notice you haven't been guessing places like Savannah or Atlanta or Charlotte."

"You're a country girl."

She knew he meant more than that—that her accent wasn't genteel enough for those places. For once, it didn't bother her. "That part is right."

"Okay, I give up."

"Sweetwell, Louisiana," she said.

"That's not but a hundred miles." He looked at her and she felt the questions he didn't ask. "So I wasn't too far off, after all. You pretty much are from around here."

"Sort of."

A small silence fell. Ellie listened to a lone cricket, whistling in the dark, and thought she heard water not far away. "Where is the river? I keep meaning to go look for it."

"Right behind those trees to the south. I'm sure April has already found it, but be careful. There's a lot of snakes."

"I'm not a city girl, remember?"

He nodded. "You have family back there?"

"My grandma."

"How about your mama and daddy?"

"Nope. My grandma's the only one left."

"That's unusual."

She shrugged. "I guess. They all died." That sounded so bald she smiled and added, "Happens to the best of us."

"Hmmm." He leaned his head against the wall, showing his throat in silhouette. "My folks are gone, too."

"Are you an only child?"

"Nope. Lost a brother in Vietnam." He drank some beer. "He's one of the ghosts up in that house."

"He must have been a lot older than you." She wasn't always the best with ages, but Blue didn't look to be much more than thirty-five.

"Seven years. We were both surprises."

"And your parents?" she asked. "Have they been gone long?"

"Long, long time." He took some beer and held it in his mouth a minute, pursing his lips around the taste like it held the pieces of a story. "My mama took Jack's death real hard. She had a heart attack the day of his funeral, and never really got over it. She died the next summer, and my daddy—" He sighed. "He didn't take both of them going like that well at all. He put a gun in his mouth the day after Thanksgiving."

His voice drawled out the story as if he were telling her about cutting grass evenly, and it made the horror all the worse. "How old were you?"

"Twelve at the end of it."

A thud bumped in her belly. Another winner here, all right. Her knack for finding wounded men had led her to abused and abandoned, but she didn't think she'd met one with suicidal parents before. "I'm sorry."

"Ancient history, darlin'. I don't even remember them, really. Lanie raised me. I survived." He looked at her. "Did your grandmother raise you?"

"My grandparents did. Grandpa died a couple of years ago, dropped dead of a stroke with his arms greasy to the elbow from the engine of his truck." She grinned softly in memory. "My grandma went out to get him for dinner and he had his cheek right on the carburetor, like he'd just gone to sleep with a lover. Still had a wrench in his hand."

The warm sound of Blue's laughter was more reward than it should have been. "He liked cars?"

"No, honey. You *like* chocolate ice cream. You *like*

your children. He had a fan belt in his chest, I swear he did. Never had clean fingernails a day in his life, but he could make just about anything run."

"Definitely a talent worth a pot of gold." He made a sound between a snort and a laugh. "Don't suppose you picked it up?"

"I can change my spark plugs, but that's about as far as I go."

"Too bad." He rubbed his face. "I've had one headache after another with machines lately." He put the empty beer bottle down. "Which reminds me that I have plants to look after. Thanks for the beer."

"You're welcome."

He moved into the pool of light coming through the screen, and it caught on the slash of skin showing between the flaps of his shirt. Supple skin, tanned dark even so early in the year. "Would you like to come see them, the greenhouses?"

He went down the steps, and paused. Ellie found her eyes on his lower belly, a vulnerable place on a man, where the skin curved downward. She wanted, suddenly and sharply, to put her mouth there.

She raised her eyes. "I'd love to see them, but not tonight, thank you."

"See you in the morning, then." He melted into the darkness, and Ellie caught sight of him again a few moments later, a shadow moving against the lights by the house.

Big trouble. She crossed her arms over her stomach, but didn't move right away, her eyes on the dark silhouette of him against the light.

If she were another sort of woman, Blue Reynard could have been a nice diversion. There were probably lots of women who could take a nice long sip of that sexy heat and walk away, and she had no doubt he'd happily put on his charming self to please Ellie if she showed the slightest inclination toward getting laid.

But she'd learned the hard way that she just didn't operate like that. She would start off telling herself it was just for play, the natural response of two adults who found each other attractive. She would almost certainly enjoy herself. In his cheerful moods, he'd be fun in bed.

Unfortunately, Ellie knew she wouldn't be satisfied with that. She'd start wanting to find out what made him tick. She'd feel resentful about being a notch on his belt. She'd start looking for ways to bind him to her—and then he'd bolt.

She thought of him tonight, looking crazy and lost and hungry. That was what she'd end up wanting—the heart and soul of him—and the wanting would make her crazy.

With a sigh, she went back inside. A man like that was nothing but trouble, and she was well past the age where trouble seemed romantic. Give her steady and practical any day.

But the cottage seemed very quiet now. The music had clicked off. Her notes were scattered over the desk, and she realized she'd worked for more than twelve hours today. It had left her faintly keyed up, restless, and she didn't want to plunge back into it.

For a moment, she thought of signing on to the

Internet. It was her usual method of unwinding. But knowing Blue wouldn't be there, that there would be no notes waiting for her, took some of the pleasure out of it. For months, they'd exchanged daily notes—sometimes long, sometimes just a line or two, and it was slightly disturbing to realize now that she'd come to depend on them. He'd become a steady spot in her world, with his wit and wild asides and flashes of genuine brilliance.

She was deeply tempted to follow him up to the greenhouse, to see what that place revealed about him. Instead, she fastened her hair on top of her head and headed for the shower, realizing only when she stepped under the spray that she was humming the soundtrack to her life again. Janis Joplin, wailing, "I need a man to love me . . ."

Corny. Very corny. She laughed and put her face under the water, washing away temptation.

Because she'd gone to bed so early, Ellie was up well before the sun even broke above the woods to the east. She ate some toast spread with home-canned strawberry preserves and drank coffee, sitting at the small oak table to rearrange her note cards, looking for some clue that might shed some light on Mabel's disappearance. There was nothing. On the surface, her life looked like a classic American rags-to-riches story: a young woman from a small town who had only her talent and determination, on the road to stardom. Mabel had never married, never had children, had poured everything she had and everything she was into her dream.

And made it—finally landed that contract that would have meant fame and real money.

Then disappeared off the face of the planet.

Ellie scowled and glanced outside. The sun was beginning to rise, lending the world beyond the cabin a rosy wash. Birds twittered in the trees. She listened, smiling, thinking of her grandmother shelling peas and calling out the names of birds: redbird, lark, robin, blue jay, wren, crow. Ellie could pick out the lovely sound of a blackbird, and a warbling sparrow, and the ever-present harshness of a magpie. Another made a series of high sounds that was almost like a dog whining. She didn't know what it was.

She glanced at the clock. Only 5:15. Blue wouldn't be picking her up for more than an hour. "Come on, April," she said, and grabbed her leash.

The dog's ears pointed straight up, and when she heard the rattle of the leash, she barked, once, sharply, and danced for a moment on her back paws. Ellie grinned and stepped out on the porch, closing the front door behind her.

The air was still cool, and laden with moisture that felt good on her face. A mist rose from the ground and made the bank of wild roses along the road look like a floating pink smear against their dark green leaves. The morning smelled of damp earth and water.

A path led from the drive in front of the cabin, branching out in three directions. One led to the house, another toward the road Ellie had driven down when she first arrived. The third led south, into a tunnel of trees, and Ellie opted to explore it.

Mindful of Blue's warning of snakes, she wore her boots and kept to the road so that April wouldn't inadvertently stumble into a nest. It was a narrow dirt road, divided by a line of grass, so it was used by some kind of vehicle, but Ellie would never have guessed from the landscape. Thickets of bushes and trees crowded right up to the edge of the dirt, and Ellie couldn't help but think of spiderwebs. She hated that trail of web over neck or arm or mouth. It wasn't so much the webs themselves as the thought of where the dislodged spider might have gone—like into her hair.

It was quiet and deserted, though once she glimpsed the roof of a structure through a break in the trees, with a line of smoke coming out of the tin chimney, but saw no visible access and assumed there must be another way in.

As Blue had promised, the path led to the banks of the river. It was a wide, slow-moving body of water, dark green in the early light. A figure sat in a chair on the bank about ten yards upstream, a man in a fishing hat with a line in the water. Out of respect, Ellie didn't let April off her leash as she'd planned. Instead, she simply led the dog to the edge of the river and held tight to the leash, letting the cool, mossy scent of water and forest and pine touch tiny, dry places on her soul and fill them. Birds sang joyously.

Abruptly, Ellie wished her grandmother were here. She thought of her chopping rhubarb for tarts, wearing a faded apron of the style that covered a woman's entire chest and shoulders and skirt front. No little froufrou aprons for Grandma.

It was the river and the early morning that brought it on this time. They'd always risen very early, like country people the world over, and often Ellie and her grandmother had left the house before sunup to pick berries or take a walk through the woods. Ellie learned to love the embrace of morning and nature, the uncomplicated peace of sitting on a riverbank, listening to the water and the birds. Her grandpa had liked fishing, but only rarely let Ellie trail along. With a fond smile, she crouched on the bank and watched the figure in the chair cast and reel with a deft, expert hand. As the light came up, she saw the figure was not male, as she assumed, but a slim, elderly black woman.

The woman caught sight of her and waved in friendly acknowledgment, then gestured for Ellie to come over. "Good morning," the woman said, tilting her head to look through the distance part of her bifocals. "You must be Blue's houseguest."

"Ellie Connor," she said.

"Nice to meet you. Gwen Laisser. Blue's daddy sold me that little bit of land you saw back there—oh, forty years ago, I guess."

Ellie nodded politely. "Fish biting this morning?"

"Not doing too bad. Got some bluegills for my supper, I guess, but I'm after a cat. You like catfish?"

"Oh, yes, ma'am, I do. Fried in cornmeal?"

"That's right." The voice was smooth and husky, tinged with a long, lazy drawl, soft on the *s* sounds.

April tugged at the leash, straining to smell something in a dip in the earth, and Ellie took a step to allow it. "My grandpa used to let me tag along with him every now and then when he went fishing," she volunteered. "I haven't done it in years."

"In my experience, folks have to get a little age on them before they remember what a pleasure it is."

Ellie chuckled. "Maybe so." She watched the water, watched the woman cast and reel, taking pleasure in the calm rhythm of it, and the soft, breathy humming that came from her, some kind of old gospel tune Ellie couldn't quite catch.

"I hear you're doing a biography on Mabel Beauvais," the old woman said.

"Yes. Did you know her?"

"A little." She looked up through glasses so thick they distorted her eyes comically. "How come you settled on Mabel? Not too many folks remember her anymore."

Ellie laughed softly. "Exactly what my editor said." She shook her head a little, and looked out at the moving water. "Truth is, I have no idea. Something in her face called to me, that's all. It just happens that way sometimes—some little thing snags your heart and you don't really have any choice but to follow."

"Is that right." Mrs. Laisser nodded. "I reckon I've felt that, once or twice." She grinned. "I will say old Mabel stirred this old town up good. She was really something, that girl."

A shiver moved on Ellie's shoulders. "Can you tell me about her?"

"I'll tell you what I remember. She was beautiful, but you already know that. What you can't see from the pictures is that she burned for her music. It was the only thing she cared anything at all about, from the time she was just a little bitty girl."

"Did you go to school with her?"

"I did. She sang all the time, too. We were jealous of her, you know, 'cause she got so much attention. And her daddy was a pretty well-to-do farmer, so she had better clothes than some of the rest, and a real haughty attitude."

Ellie laughed, wishing she had her notebook with her. "Mrs. Laisser, I'm used to writing things down, and I don't want to miss any of this. Would you mind if I came back another time with my notebook?"

"Not at all, child. Any time."

"How about going into Tyler for an English tea?" She smiled. "I met a woman in town, getting her hair done yesterday, who said she could be persuaded if I'd take her to tea. I'd drive."

"Who was it? You remember?"

Ellie couldn't think of the woman's name, but she described her. Mrs. Laisser shook her head. "No, I don't think so."

"All right, then. How about tomorrow morning, same time, same place? Do you fish every day?"

"'Less my knees are giving me trouble, I do. But I'm off to Dallas tomorrow for a little vacation. Be back next week early. How 'bout I stop by and let you know when I'm back?"

Ellie stuck out her hand. "That would be great. I'll look forward to it."

The woman put out a hand that had once been long and elegant but was now knotted with arthritis. "I'll leave you to it," Ellie said. "Good luck on getting some cat."

"Be careful around that man, now," she said with a wink. "He's plumb irresistible."

"Oh, we're just friends."

The old woman's eyes twinkled behind her thick glasses. "I reckon you aren't one of his girls just yet. But there can't be a woman born who can resist all that sad beauty."

Ellie chuckled. "Well, he's a charmer. But I'm immune."

The woman nodded cheerfully. "Bring a line some morning. I wouldn't mind it."

"Thank you. I will."

One of his girls. Ellie thought of him standing there last night, so oddly winded, thought of his gleaming flesh and the way he'd paused on the threshold, his hand against her thigh. Of course he had a horde of women. He probably couldn't help it. What else would a poor little rich boy do but drink and chase women?

He was sitting on her porch steps when she came back up the path, and before she could brace herself, a jolt of surprised lust shot through her. The morning sun brought out streaks of gold in the unruly length of his hair and gilded the hair on his tanned, strong forearms, and he looked, Ellie thought, imminently *climbable.*

"Hey," he said. "Brought you some coffee."

"I know I didn't spend an hour down there—have you been waiting long?" She took the offered mug, noting he'd doctored it with milk. She sipped it and found he'd also paid attention when she added too much sugar to her cup at Dorrie's Café. "This is perfect."

"I aim to please, ma'am."

"Am I late or are you early?" she asked again.

"I'm early." He dropped his head, examined a board on the steps. "Wanted to tell you I'm sorry about last night." He lifted his face, and sun struck the bright blue irises. "You must've thought I was ten kinds of weird, standing in the yard, spying on you like that."

Ellie lifted her eyebrows. "Well, maybe five kinds."

He grinned ruefully. "Anyway, I'm not dangerous. I don't want you to think you have to run off and find some other room in town. I won't bother you like that again."

"I didn't mind," she said, and hesitated. "But you know what? I can see there's this—" She closed her mouth, then started again. "You have a reputation, you know, being a ladies' man and all that, and God knows you have the gift, but I don't want anything like that from you. I like talking to you. I think we have a lot in common. But the last thing in the world I can do right now is get mixed up with some heartbreaker who makes me miss my deadline."

He inclined his head, a wicked smile showing those rich-boy teeth. "I have the gift, you say?"

She rolled her eyes. "Come on, Blue. Don't be that way with me. I don't need to flirt with you."

"Oh, we all need to flirt, now and again."

"Maybe you do. I don't."

He chuckled. "How about this, Miz Connor? Asking a leopard to change his spots is impossible, so you'll likely just have to put up with me flirting." His mouth sobered as he paused, and the gaze was straight and honest. "But I like your brain, and I like your company, and I really hate to ruin a perfectly good friendship with sex, being as sex is easy to find and friends aren't, so we'll keep it at that. You're free to roll your eyes and tell me I'm full of hot air, but I'm just not capable of talking to a female without sweet-talking her now and again, so you'll have to live with it." His eyes glittered. "Deal?"

Ellie laughed. "You're incorrigible." She stuck out her hand. "Deal. And I would appreciate it in the future if you buttoned your shirt when you came visiting."

His big hand engulfed hers and Ellie found herself noticing his square nails. Such a great hand, lean and well-shaped. Like the rest of him. She let him go.

"I'll try to remember." He angled his head toward the path. "Been down to the river this morning?"

"I was." Now that the rules had been laid out, she felt free to gesture for him to move over so she could sit down. "I met an old woman down there. She was fishing."

"Gwen Laisser. She's great. You'll like her." He straightened, attention caught by something in the fields between the house and the cottage. "Damn."

Ellie saw a scruffy dog racing down the path with full-tilt exuberance, ears blown back, tongue lolling. April got up and barked, protectively, but the dog was undeterred. It raced into the yard, going way too fast to stop, and barreled into Blue's knees.

"Sasha!" Blue said, reaching down to rub her head. "How did you get out?"

It was the same dog Ellie met the first night, the one Marcus called a "rat-dog," and with some justification. She was a medium-sized mutt with coarse fur and hints of terrier in the wisps of hair around her mouth. After greeting Blue, she moved to Ellie with a hopeful expression and sat down, still as she'd been wild, staring at Ellie eagerly. "What a sweet face!" Ellie said, and reached for her. "You're a cutie."

April whined, and Sasha jumped up to be examined. They sniffed and greeted, then apparently finding nothing objectionable, April made a playful bow and they were off, tumbling, wrestling, leaping in the dust.

"That's the most ill-behaved dog on the planet," Blue commented.

"Sasha, right? I think she's cute."

He sighed. "She's an escape artist. I really am beginning to think she knows how to climb fences."

"You know, if someone had asked me what kind of dog you'd own, I wouldn't have picked that one."

"No?" He looked at her lazily. "What would you have picked, Miz Connor?"

"German shepherd," she said. "Definitely. Something macho and beautiful."

"Well, I usually do like big dogs." He lifted a shoulder. "Sasha just showed up at my door one day. And well, let's just say I needed somebody right then."

Ellie decided she didn't want to know what demons had been bothering him when Sasha appeared. "April's happy. She can come visit me anytime."

"You want to leave April with her? They can play in the back, and April won't have to be lonely all day with you gone."

"All right."

"We'd best get a move on. Rosemary'll want us to be on time."

5

Rosemary's house was indeed hard to find, and Ellie was glad Blue had offered to drive her. They had to take the highway out of town, driving past vegetable stands, scattered businesses, and two churches before turning down a narrow road that branched off into the heavy woods every quarter mile or so. Blue chose this turn and that, using no marker she could discern—there were certainly no street signs—until he drove into a wide, cleared stretch of farmland. At one end of the fields, planted with what might have been soybeans, sat a three-story clapboard farmhouse, painted white, with a wide porch circling it on three sides. Ellie stepped out and smiled. "This looks like the house I grew up in."

"Yeah? Well, then you oughta have some idea what the attic will be like."

"Hot."

"That much for sure. We'll want to get done by noon."

A youth came out on the porch. "Hey, Blue."

"Hey, yourself, Brandon. You keeping out of trouble?"

The youth grinned. "More or less." Tall and athletic, he had the kind of fresh-scrubbed wholesomeness of country boys everywhere. "Did you hear I got into the Air Force Academy?"

"No! That's terrific, man. I'm not a bit surprised." He slapped him on the shoulder. "I know your mama is thrilled."

Rosemary appeared at the door. "Boy, don't stand around talking. Get that over to the post office and get to school."

"Yes, ma'am." He gave Blue a quick grin.

"Hang on." Blue put his hand on Ellie's shoulder blade and gestured with the other hand. "Ellie, this is Brandon, Rosemary's son, and one of Pine Bend's finest. Brandon, this is Ellie Connor. She's here to write a biography of your . . . what is she, your great-great-aunt?—Mabel Beauvais."

"Pleased to meet you." Brandon shook her hand with a firm, clean grip, and waved as he ran down the steps.

Blue turned to Rosemary with a grin. "That's a fine-looking young man. Lot to be proud of there."

"He's a good boy." She swung open the door. "Come on in. I'll get you settled, then I've got to git. Have to run by the bank before I open this morning."

She led them up a set of carpeted stairs that opened on to a wide landing, then circled up again and ended at a wooden door. "There's no air-conditioning up here, and it gets hot as Hades, so you need to keep this door closed, if you don't mind. I put a fan in the window, but mornings are the only time you'll be able to stand it."

"Okay."

The room was long and dim, with windows at either end. The accumulations of several lifetimes were tucked under the exposed rafters, old clothing and discarded toys and lines of trunks. Toward one end was one that had been opened, and Rosemary stopped there. "The letters and photos are in here. They're mixed up with everything. I managed to get some sorted out, but I'm afraid you'll have to sift through the rest. If you come across something you aren't sure about, just put it aside, and I'll be glad to talk to you about it later."

The familiar excitement rose in Ellie, and she gave Rosemary a reassuring smile. "I can't even tell you how grateful I am."

Rosemary patted her arm. "I hope you find what you need." She put a key in Blue's hand. "Lock the front door when you're done, please, sir."

"Will do."

"Am I going to see you at the meeting tonight, Ellie?" Rosemary asked.

"Wouldn't miss it for the world." She hesitated, unwilling to push, but dying of curiosity. "Did you find out anything more on the journals, by any chance?"

She snapped her fingers. "I forgot, sugar, but I'll call my sister this morning."

"Thanks."

Ellie and Blue settled beside the trunk and worked out a system. Since Blue knew more of the faces of the town and would more easily be able to weed out the ones that wouldn't mean anything, he volunteered to sort through the hundreds of photos stacked into piles, while Ellie concentrated on sorting out the letters from Mabel. There weren't as many as she'd hoped—a couple dozen—but Ellie was pleased with them anyway. She tried to resist actually reading any of them until later, but one date caught her eye and she carefully slid the old paper from the envelope.

"Listen to this," she said, and began to read aloud:

"'St. Louis, February 3, 1944

Dear Harry,

I'm sitting here this morning in my bathrobe, a cup of coffee in a paper cup from the deli around the corner that Mary brought up to me a little while ago and I can hardly tell you what I'm feeling. I sang last night. Now I know there's nothing new about that, I been singing every night, but it was different last night. I sang one of my own songs, and old Diamond Poco played guitar for me, and those folks went crazy! They hollered and danced and clapped so long I almost didn't know what to do. My heart almost exploded. Then a man from a record company came to talk to me after, and bought me supper, and I'm going over this morning to see the boss about maybe making a record!! Can you believe it?'"

Blue bent close to look over Ellie's arm at the letter, and a wisp of his hair brushed her jaw. It seemed curiously intimate, and she was suddenly aware of all her body parts—her shoulder blades and elbows—which immediately felt awkward. He smelled faintly of some exotic fragrance she couldn't quite name.

Briskly she read the postscript, "'P.S. If *anybody* can spare stockings, I sure do need them.' "

"Wow. That kinda gives me shivers." He reached for the letter and Ellie let it go, turning her attention back to the trunk. "I guess that's the appeal, huh? Makes it immediate."

"Exactly."

He handled the letter delicately. "She was so damned young. I always forget that part."

"The war was on," she said. "I never thought about what an impact that would have had on everything. Gas, rubber, tires, stockings. It must have been hard." She tugged a pile of blank note cards from her purse and made a note to check what exactly was rationed, and what problems that would have caused.

"It's a shame," Blue said, lifting his head. "She was so excited." A puzzled expression crossed his brow. "Doesn't make sense, does it? What could go so wrong she'd just walk away after she'd worked so damned hard?"

"I know." Her gawky sense of her own elbows faded, and she was only looking at the man who shared her passion for the blues. "That's the whole thing. Why?"

"Maybe somebody killed her."

"Most people think so. But where? How? There's no sign of it."

"It's a good mystery. Think you'll solve it?"

"I hope so."

"Maybe you need Nero Wolfe to help you."

Ellie chuckled. "The guy with the orchids?"

"Right." He gave her the letter back and turned back to sorting the pictures. Ellie finished going through her stacks of letters, then went through them again to set aside those from relatives during the same frame of years as secondary material. It was quite possible one relative had gossiped to another about Mabel.

While they worked, they talked sporadically. Once Blue nudged her and passed over a picture. "Look at this."

It was a photograph of a young black woman garbed in the heavy polyester style of the early seventies, standing with a man a bit older who had an Afro the size of a globe. Ellie chuckled. "Is that Marcus?"

"Sure is."

"Who is that with him?"

"Rosemary. They had quite the thing for a long time, evidently."

Ellie thought about the two, and realized they probably were close in age. "What happened?"

Blue took the picture back. "I don't know. Marcus didn't handle his war experiences real well. I've heard him talk about the wild times and I guess he raised some hell for a few years before Alisha, his wife, got hold of him. Rosemary was a good girl. Maybe she didn't like him acting crazy and cut him loose."

"Is Rosemary married?"

"She's a widow. Her and Connie—you met her yesterday at the beauty parlor—both lost their husbands within a few months. Both pretty young men, actually—neither one past forty-five. It was pretty sad." He lifted his head, tucked the picture into his shirt pocket. "That's when they got that book group going." He looked at the next picture. "You'll have a good time there. Bunch of wild women in that group. No guys allowed."

She riffled through a stack of letters from the fifties—too late for her purposes. "Sounds like fun."

He laughed softly and passed another picture over. "Oh, I'm gonna get him good. Look at this."

It was a group shot this time. Ellie could pick out Marcus—who was sticking out his tongue—and Rosemary. It was summer, in a park or someone's yard. Ellie smiled, only vaguely interested, and glanced it over.

And there, on the side, was a face she *knew*. Sudden heat burned the tips of her ears. On the sidelines, laughing and looking out of place in a flowing India cotton skirt, was a young woman. Not much more than a girl, really. She had tied her blouse beneath her breasts, and her long, long red hair trailed over her arms.

Ellie cast about for something to comment on. "When is this? Sixty-eight or sixty-nine? Seems like a very mixed group for the times." The words sounded calm and cool, expressing interest in a cultural curiosity, nothing more. She reached for the picture and he gave it to her. "The schools couldn't have been desegregated for more than a few years then."

"Hmm." Blue's mouth turned down at the corners. "Good point. I know when I was in school, we stuck to our own crowd. White with white, brown with brown, black with black."

"Yeah, me, too. And I'm way younger than you." She grinned. "I wonder why these guys aren't all divided up."

He inclined his head. "Maybe it *was* because it was just past segregation. Maybe they were idealistic. Wanted the dream to be real."

Ellie looked at him, thinking of her own high school. A small, rural Southern school, much like the one here, she was sure. There had been one or two very brave kids who moved between groups at that age, and there was never any particular hostility between them, but nobody even went to the same places after school. She'd lay money they still didn't, at least in her home town. Pine Bend was likely not much different.

Then she looked again at her mother's laughing face. "Who are all these people?"

"I don't know them all." He pointed. "Marcus, of course. And Rosemary. That's her sister, Florence, and Connie. This"—he pointed to a light-skinned black youth with his arm looped around Marcus's neck—"is James Gordon. He and Marcus were best friends from the time they were babies. He got killed in Vietnam. These guys, too. Bobby Makepeace"—he pointed to a boy with slightly rebellious hair the color of walnuts, who sported a small goatee—"was Connie Ewing's beau. And . . . I can't think of this guy's name. Big 4-H star—when he got killed, the newspaper put a big picture of him with this bull he sold for some kind of record when he was sixteen." His voice softened. "My mama cried."

"Who is this?" She pointed to the girl in India cotton.

"I don't know." He took the picture, narrowing his eyes. "There was a hippie bus that got stranded, broke down completely, outside of town that summer. I don't really remember a whole lot, but there were four or five of them that stayed most of the summer. My brother thought they were total trash."

In sudden horror, Ellie wondered if Blue's brother could have been her father. That would make Blue her uncle. "How old was he?"

"About . . . fourteen or fifteen, I guess."

Whew. "Hmm." She studied the faces carefully, trying to generate a lie that might sound plausible if he thought her interest was strange. "Is he in this picture?"

"No. He'd have been too young." He shuffled through a handful more, all taken the same day, and passed them over as he finished. "Oh, I bet I know what this was. The VFW hosted a party for the boys shipping out every summer. Potluck supper and a big keg of beer in the park. They did it up to the very end of the war. I went with my brother." He flipped through a handful more. "Yeah." He shook his head and held one up of a bunch of boys, including Marcus, the light-skinned kid who was his best friend, and three white boys. "Only Marcus and one other kid in this group came back." He raised his eyes. "And this is where the memorial is going up."

Oddly pierced, Ellie took the picture. "Poor Marcus." The boys looked up from a sunny day, with their whole lives ahead of them. Few of them were old enough for beards, and their bodies held that awkward thinness that boys seemed to hang on to so much longer than girls.

When Blue turned away to pick up another stack of pictures, Ellie pretended to be shuffling back and forth through the stack, and then as if she'd lost interest, set the first few down by her knees, using her index finger to separate out the one that had captured her mother.

"How sweet they all are," she commented, looking over his shoulder at the next shot. It was an ordinary run of photos, people eating, laughing, making faces, mugging for the camera in a dozen ways.

Blue halted his quick shuffling when he came to another of Marcus and his best friend. This one showed the two of them bent over their hot dogs, hair glittering in the sun. The photographer had captured an expression of secret amusement flashing between the pair of boys.

"They were so young," Ellie said. When she reached for it, he gave her the whole pile with a haste that made her glance up. "Is something wrong?"

"No." The word was heavy. "That's my wife." He grunted softly. "I forgot what a pretty little girl she was."

"Wife?"

"She died. Car accident five years ago."

Pierced, Ellie looked up. "I am so sorry. You haven't had the best luck, have you?"

A shrug, then a retreat. He shoved the pictures in her hands and stood. "I'm gonna go find us something to drink. Be right back."

She nodded, let him go without following him with her eyes, hungry eyes that would want to probe into those hurt places and find them, and—what? That was the thing. She never knew what she wanted to do with those wounded places in a man, but they always snared her. Maybe she wanted to put her hands on them, like an old faith healer, and draw out the pain.

It never worked. She blew out a sigh, shaking her head, and took the chance fate had offered to shuffle through the photos, looking for any that might show Ellie's mother again.

There were two. In one, she stood with another girl, dressed in the same hippie style. In the other, she was leaning over the table where Marcus and the boy with the walnut-colored goatee were playing a board game. Some other bodies were on the edge of the shot, and Diane appeared to be grinning at someone—but it was impossible to tell if it was the man with the goatee or someone just out of range.

The one with the goatee was Connie's beau, Blue said. If Diane had mixed herself up with him, that was all the more reason for Ellie to keep her secret a little while longer. She really didn't want to hurt anyone with this quest.

Feeling guilty—Rosemary had thrown open her home and Ellie was going to steal some of her photos—she tucked all three photos into her notebook, taking care to make sure they were secured. She promised herself she'd bring them back ASAP. It wasn't stealing if she brought them back.

When Blue didn't reappear, her curiosity led her to go through the stack more slowly, searching for the one of Blue's wife. In a picture of Marcus and his friend having a food fight, a little blond girl was laughing at the edge of the shot, and she showed up again in another one. Stringy long hair, scruffy-looking clothes, so skinny her knees and elbows looked like knobs. Not more than five or six—probably a younger sister of one of the others.

She heard his step on the stairs and wondered briefly if she ought to leave it alone. But when he gave her a Coke, she guilelessly lifted the picture. "She really was pretty. How long were you married?"

"Six years. I went to Ecuador to study orchids for my thesis, and she was waiting when I got back, all grown up and gorgeous." He looked at the photo, a rueful grin on his mouth. "She chased me my whole life, and I never even noticed till I came home."

"Were you happy?"

He nodded, slowly. Remembering. "All widowers were happily married, right?" He smiled, but the bleakness she'd glimpsed last night was there in his eyes again. He sobered. "Yeah, we were happy."

Ellie smiled, meeting his gaze calmly. "Good."

His mouth twitched. "Water under the bridge." He settled again. "We don't have much more time. Let's get busy."

Before Blue dropped Ellie off, he swung by the vet's to pick up his cat. Piwacket was fully recovered, by the look of her, her nose and ears pink once again. When he took her out of the cage, she gave him that deliriously pleased expression and tucked herself under his ear, trilling her happiness. The vet chuckled.

"What a cat." He gave Blue a bottle of antibiotics to offset the infection that had caused her decline this time, then his face sobered. "Blue, you know she isn't gonna last a whole lot longer. Some folks think there's a lot to be said for letting a cat be a cat—let her live life to the fullest at the end. You might think about that."

The familiar twist in his gut made Blue sharp. "She can be rehydrated every week if necessary, right?"

"She *can* be—"

"Thank you." Blue paid the bill, balancing Piwacket on his shoulder, the carrier in the other hand. At the truck, he opened the door and Pi leapt happily into the middle, greeting Ellie with a cheery bit of chat and settling in her lap for the ride home.

"What was wrong with her?" Ellie asked, lightly touching the shaved spot on her front paw.

"Nothing big," he said. "She has to have a special diet, low-protein, and some antibiotics to clear up an infection."

Ellie bent her head to Pi's nose. "Low protein? Tell him, Pi. Go ahead." She altered her voice to a high, sweet note. " 'Excuse me, Blue darlin', but cats are carnivores.' "

"I know." He grinned reluctantly. "But she has to have it, or she'll just keep getting sicker."

"Does she actually eat it?"

He paused. "Not very well."

Ellie chuckled and pretended to whisper. "Come see me, honey. I'll take care of you."

"No!" Blue scowled at her. "Lanie does the same damned thing. Would you give a person recovering from a heart attack a bunch of bacon?"

"Well, probably not. Unless they were a hundred and two and had been eating bacon all along."

"Piwacket isn't a hundred and two."

She touched his arm. "I'm only teasing you, Blue. It's sweet that you take such good care of her. I wouldn't really slip her anything forbidden." As if she spoke English, Pi trilled suddenly, as if saying, *'Please?'* They both laughed.

As they pulled out of the lot, Ellie said, "Blue, is there some way to drive through the black side of town on our way home? Maybe by the black school?"

He gave her a sideways grin. "Wouldn't have been no black school in those days, sugar. The colored school, maybe."

"Right." She smiled. "Will the cat mind being in the car longer?"

"Looks happy enough to me." Pi was settled serenely on Ellie's lap, purring loudly. "It won't take long, anyway."

Even now, the town was divided into two sections, black and white, without much crossover except at the edges, or in the case of land belonging to both black and white, as was the case with Gwen Laisser and Blue's family. Blue skirted a swath of farms, drove past the Dairy Queen and the Laundromat and the bowling alley, and turned on a narrow blacktop. He pointed toward a stretch of newly plowed earth, rich and dark. "Mabel's daddy owned about a hundred acres just over that rise. She'd have walked about three miles to school, down this road, and probably across those fields."

Ellie rolled down the window, letting in the thick midday air. Wind blew her hair back from her serious, intent face. Blue imagined she was imprinting details, and as if to give that theory credence, she inhaled deeply, lifting her nose like a dog scenting the air. He smiled.

"When she got through the fields," he continued, turning, "she would have crossed this bridge"—the truck rumbled over the wooden slats spanning a creek—"and then ducked under that stand of trees, cut through the alley there." He turned the corner and stopped in front of the school. "And she'd have been here."

The building had recently been turned into a clinic, but the general shape remained, a two-story stone building with long windows all the way across the front. Not much different from all the other buildings of the same age in town, though it lacked some of the more Gothic details.

Ellie didn't speak, only looked carefully at everything, across the road to the small cluster of houses that stood there, and back over her shoulder to the creek. Her hand moved on Piwacket's back, idly. "Mrs. Laisser said Mabel was kind of stuck-up," she said, suddenly, and flashed him that impish grin.

It changed her face, tilting up her eyes at the corner, exaggerating the slant of cheekbones, showing her good, strong white teeth. Blue found himself thinking about kissing her. He looked at her throat, at her hands on the cat, at her slim thighs, then back at that wide, pretty mouth, and narrowed his eyes.

She noticed. The smile faded, and her head dipped, letting hair fall down and obscure that pretty line of cheek.

Blue stuck his elbow out the window. Looked at the school. "I imagine she was. Stuck-up, I mean. Her daddy was the richest black man for thirty miles, and then she came up with that voice." He thought of the pictures. "Not to mention she was gorgeous."

Ellie laughed softly. "Yeah. Exactly."

He put the truck in first gear. "Seen all you needed, or do you want me to drive around some more?"

"We can go back now. Thank you."

"My pleasure, ma'am."

The Lovers

She lay next to him in the rumpled bed, lazy with sunlight that fell through the windows, drenching both of their naked bodies with yellow. He lay on his belly, the wrinkled sheet against his thighs, uncomfortable, but he was too sated to move, and gazed over the crook of his elbow at her. Light caught on the edges of her eyelashes, turning them white. Her skin glittered with beads of moisture, along her lip and cheeks, down her neck, along the smooth swell of one breast, in the shadowy hollow of her navel. His hand lay alongside her waist and he lifted it, brushing one finger over the strong rise of her hipbone, liking the powerful look of it, thinking a baby might one day rest there, a baby they made. He tried to think how her belly, almost concave now, would look swollen up with fruit from this, and his lips pulled into a half smile.

She opened her eyes and caught his smile and gave it back to him, her eyelids heavy, showing only a half moon of iris. Her lashes made spider leg shadows on her cheeks. "Penny," she said, and stroked his head.

He put his chin on his fist and put the other hand across her belly. His hands were big, like his father's, according to his grandmother, but there was room for all of it to fit across the cradle of bones. "I was thinking of babies."

Shock tightened her body. He felt something draw in under his hand, felt her fear. "Why?"

He looked at his hand, felt the smooth flesh of her belly against his palm, the brush of hair against his little finger, and imagined limbs, back, head, genitals all forming inside of her skin, some of him, some of her. But he had no answer. "I don't know," he said, and looked up at her, and surprised a wariness in her eyes.

"What would you do?" she asked, and he felt in her belly, and the faint tightness of her hand on his head, the unease in her.

He had not meant to drag real things, the outside, into this stolen, sacred time, and moved now to push it away. Rousing himself, he bent over her and pressed his mouth to her navel, then just below, where that body would grow, kissed her again. "I would kiss it every day."

She laughed, low in her throat, and curled up, ticklish after so much touching. He tumbled around her, joy welling in him, hot and sharp as they wrestled and tickled and teased, reveling in the slide of skin against skin, thigh to thigh, and arm to arm, the bump of a breast and the sway of his sex, and the brush of lips and hands and mouths. And he was whole, with her, as he never was when they were apart.

Whole.

6

Blue dropped Ellie off, got Pi settled, and headed off to the greenhouses, immersing himself in numbers and patterns and notations to get around the vague, sucking depression that had welled up in him when he saw the pictures. He wouldn't go back to Rosemary's attic again.

It hadn't just been the picture of his wife Annie that gave him this sense of sorrow, but all of it—Mabel and her sad story; Marcus and James and Bobby Makepeace and all those other young boys, bright and full of a life that would be cut short for most of them; thoughts of his brother, thoughts of how fast time went and how little joy he'd ever wrung from it.

He didn't know how Ellie stood it, delving into the past all the time for her work. He'd slit his wrists in three minutes flat.

When he heard her car on the road later, he found himself standing by the door, half-hidden in the shadows, to see what posture she held after a long day of sad stories. He watched as she stepped out of the car and went immediately to let April out to run. This time, they ambled down the road toward town, April leaping up every so often to lick her mistress's fingers, Ellie stopping just as often to bend her head into the heart of a rose. The flowers pleased her. She fingered them, trailed her palms over the sprays.

He thought of bringing her here, into the greenhouse, into this world he'd created out of his sorrow, but something made him shy away from that thought. It was enough to watch her and her dog, both of them so happy in the humid late afternoon, doing something so small as walking down a road next to a bank of blooming wild roses.

He bent his head and went back inside, to the comfort of notations and the pattern of observable results, to a world of flowers that had been blooming long before man walked the earth and would be blooming long after he was gone.

The Pine Bend Readers Group had been meeting every Thursday night for six years, growing from five members to nearly twenty, though it was rare for all of them to show up at any one meeting. The rules were simple: every regular had a chance to suggest a book in turn, and they read one book a week. No particular guidelines on what kind of books. Rosemary insisted that part didn't matter, so they read all over the board—mystery and bestsellers and literary and romance and even a bit of fantasy here and there. No one in the group was a big fan of science fiction novels, though they had read one or two, and none of them liked horror. Rosemary suspected men in the group might have shifted that balance a bit, but even if it was sexist, she didn't care. Women only. In her mother's day, women had come together over quilts and church suppers. Books, in her opinion, were just as good a reason.

Connie arrived at six-thirty, breathless as always. "Rosemary, you've got to try these." She flipped the covering from a tray of finger foods and plucked a huge black olive from the middle, offering it to Rosemary between the tips of her long, red-painted nails.

Agreeably, Rosemary accepted it. "Why, it's just cream cheese in the middle, girl. What's so exotic about that?"

Connie took one and put it in her mouth. "I never thought of doing it that way before. It's wonderful!" She closed her eyes as she chewed, and Rosemary thought for the millionth time that it was a pure waste that Connie Ewing would not even date. Tall and bosomy, she was still beautiful. Her eyes were long and blue, the mouth as pretty as a pear. Half the men in town had been lusting over her since she was twelve and grew those breasts and long legs to go with them, but Connie had given her whole heart at the age of sixteen, and when she lost him to Vietnam, that was that. Well, except her husband George, but that hadn't worked out all that well, considering.

"What did you do differently tonight?" Rosemary asked.

"Oh!" Connie put the tray on the table shoved over against the wall and turned around, straightening into a hammy pose. "I changed my colors. What do you think?"

"What colors?"

"Makeup, silly. Evidently, I was embarrassing my daughter." She gave Rosemary a rueful smile. "I just went a little lighter with everything, added some browns."

Privately, Rosemary thought Connie could go a little further in throwing out old styles. Her hair was tortured into an overblown nest that hadn't been fashionable for a long time, and her clothes were similarly outdated. "Looks good," she said, and meant it. "You have pretty skin." They set up the folding chairs. "Where's Shauna tonight?"

Connie waved a hand. "Off with that Kiki again. Seems like I never see her at all anymore."

"Get used to it, honey. It's only a year till graduation."

"I guess."

Rosemary's sister Florence came in, carrying a bottle of water and a plate of crudités. She'd been on Weight Watchers for more than a year and had lost nearly fifty pounds, putting her real close to her teenage weight. Right behind her came two other members of the group, Mrs. Nance, the librarian, and Lynette Cole, a middle-aged woman with brown hair and thick glasses. They put their dishes on the table and chatted, and a few minutes later, two others came in.

The first was Ellie Connor, the biographer. The other was Marcus Williams's wife, Alisha, with her waist-length braids and skinny thighs. Of course they'd come in together, Rosemary thought. Alisha had probably offered to drive when she found out Ellie was coming.

Still, it grated. Alisha. Always Alisha. She'd come to town one summer to take care of her grandmother, met Marcus, and set out to make him her man. Which might have been all right, except Alisha was way too young for him, and made him look a fool—laughing all over town with a girl practically young enough to be his daughter. Then she had those babies, boom, boom, like it was nothing. It had taken Rosemary seven years and more miscarriages than she wanted to remember to get Brandon.

Then Connie had hired Alisha to do the fancy braids and extensions and cuts all the young black women—though of course Alisha never said anything but 'African American,' which also annoyed Rosemary—wanted nowadays. Rosemary kept her hair herself.

Connie said Rosemary had a blind spot, and everyone else seemed to like the girl well enough, so Rosemary tolerated her. At least she hadn't brought her baby tonight. Sometimes she sat there and nursed right in front of all of them, hardly seeming to care if they saw her breasts.

Three others, young white women with children who had all joined the group in the past year, came in. Connie called them the triplets. They were all blond, young, and idealistic. One, a sweet little thing no more than twenty, was an aspiring writer who spent her spare moments typing a medieval mystery on an old typewriter Lynette had scrounged up for her.

Giving them a few minutes to fill plates and tend to their greetings, Rosemary spoke up when she found herself staring at Alisha again, laughing in the corner with Ellie like they'd been friends a thousand years.

"Why don't y'all come and sit down? I think this is about what we're going to have tonight." As they settled in the folding chairs, she gestured to Ellie. "I want you all to meet Ellie Connor. She's staying out at Blue's place, while she does some research about my aunt Mabel. She's a writer."

"Blue Reynard?" One of the triplets asked, her eyes widening.

Ellie smiled. "Don't tell me you have more than one Blue in town."

Connie said, "She means, 'Blue Reynard who should be on the cover of a romance novel, that Blue?'" She laughed when the triplet blushed. "They sent his picture to a magazine to be in a cover boy contest. He was fit to be tied when he found out."

"We didn't mean any harm," Triplet #2 said and leaned over the table. "You have to admit he looks like a movie star or something."

To Rosemary's surprise, Ellie's face went completely still. "He's very handsome," she said mildly.

"Handsome ain't the half of it," said Triplet #3. "My grandma used to say some men could set the streets afire, and that's the kind of man he is. Just looks like he'd know"—she wiggled a little—"everything."

Triplet #1 slapped her arm. "You're a married woman!"

"So? I have eyes, don't I?" She winked in Ellie's direction. "You let us know if you get to kiss him, won't you?"

"Nadine!" Alisha said. "You are a slut, girl."

Nadine laughed, unconcerned. "I'm just honest." She picked up the book of the week, a quirky women's fiction title. "And speaking of that, didn't you love this book?"

Alisha softened. "I did love it. She's very funny, too."

Rosemary leaned back as the discussion started, pleased that for once they'd found something to agree on. With so many different personalities in the group, settling on a new book every week sometimes ended up being a war.

Across the table, Ellie met her gaze, and Rosemary winked. The woman smiled.

And for the most fleeting of moments, Rosemary had a powerful sense of déjà vu. There was something about her face, about her smile, that so changed her appearance that Rosemary was reminded of someone. She tried to grab it—something about the tilt at the edge of her eyes, maybe?—but Ellie had turned back by then, and the déjà vu disappeared.

Funny little thing, Rosemary thought. She was small and strong and had that air of a survivor Rosemary always liked. Tough. Smart. But not at all pretty except the tumble of black curls she didn't do anything with. Flat-chested enough she probably didn't even bother much with a bra, and angular of face and limb.

It made Rosemary a little sad, because it was plain

the girl thought Blue was better than handsome, and she was definitely not the type he'd give much more than a charming smile to. Nadine over there, with her low-cut sundress showing her slim arms and a hint of cleavage, was Blue's type. So was Jewel, even if she was a little too plump. She had the right china doll coloring and the curves and the cluelessness Blue seemed to prefer.

With a twinge of worry, Rosemary hoped Ellie Connor wasn't building up some fantasy about Blue Reynard. Because the man would break her heart if she gave him a half a chance.

Ellie bided her time during the book discussion, and then waited while they decided on another book for the following week. The three young blonde women, plus the librarian and another woman, took their leave fairly early, and Ellie thought maybe it was over.

Instead, it seemed to be a signal to the others. They stood up, filled their plates, and settled comfortably in the best chairs. To gossip, she discovered quickly. They hashed over the week's events with the kind of old-fashioned relish Ellie had forgotten. It wasn't malicious, but she'd lay money few events went undissected by this group.

When the talk turned to the city council's final approval of a Fourth of July date for the unveiling of the Vietnam memorial, Alisha groaned. "I'll be so glad when that's over and done with!"

Rosemary lifted her chin. "It's important to us, Alisha."

"I know." She raised her hands defensively. "I'm sorry." She shot Ellie a sideways look, rolling her eyes.

Ellie smiled, but the chance was too great to pass up. "I saw some photos this morning of the boys who went to war with Marcus. There were six or seven of them. Both of you were in the pictures, too."

Rosemary sent Connie a worried glance, and Ellie looked at the hairdresser curiously, but aside from lowered eyes, could see nothing amiss. "That must have been the picnic we had for them before they left for basic," Rosemary said.

"That's what Blue thought, too." She leaned forward. "Is this a delicate subject? Should I leave it alone?"

"Not at all." It was Connie who answered. "That was a great day. I'll never forget it as long as I live." Her eyes lit with the memory. "All of us happy. Remember those girls? I thought the guys were gonna die over them not wearing bras." She gave a hoot of laughter. "Bobby kept wanting me to leave mine off—can you imagine? I'd've smacked myself right in the chin every time."

Ellie laughed.

"Yeah, Marcus tried so hard to pretend—" Rosemary glanced at Alisha and broke off. "I'm sorry," she said, and seemed sincere. "That's rude of me."

Alisha shook her head, unable to speak around the popcorn in her mouth. Finally she said, "I don't care about all that, Rosemary. I love hearing it." She lifted a shoulder a little shyly. "If you don't mind telling it."

"I'm confused," Ellie said. "Did I miss something?"

Connie answered. "Rosemary and Marcus Williams went together all through high school until he got back from the war. My boyfriend Bobby was in those pictures, too. A good-looking boy with a goatee? D'you see him?"

Ellie nodded and gave her a gentle smile. "I did. Very nice-looking."

"Well . . ." She shrugged. "He didn't come home."

"I'm sorry."

"I want to hear about Marcus," Alisha said.

Rosemary chuckled. "There was a couple of hippie girls in town that summer. Marcus was goggle-eyed over a little blond, though he acted real cool, I could tell." She frowned a Connie. "What was her name? Teeny little thing, never wore any shoes. Had about twenty yards of hair?" She poked Connie's arm. "You remember?"

"They called her Rapunzel. They were all crazy for her."

Ellie listened, half-frustrated, half-fascinated. A blond wouldn't be her mother. But somewhere on that day lay the secret of her father, she was sure. "How many boys were there that day?"

Connie frowned. "Let's see." She ticked off the names with her long, red-painted nails. "Bobby and Marcus, of course. And Rosemary's cousin James—"

"He didn't come back either," Rosemary said, and there was still a true grief in the statement.

"And then . . . must have been six or seven of them. Binkle and the boy with the 4-H ribbons—what was his name, Rosemary?"

"I can't remember. Oh—David. No, Dennis."

"Right. Dennis." She repeated the names, counting, and said, "That's it, I think."

Ellie did a name association to remember them all. Bobby Makepeace was easy in its irony. Binkle—tinkle. And a boy with 4-H prizes named Dennis. Blue had said something about him and a bull. It would probably be in the papers from the time.

A taut sense of anticipation moved in her, but mindful of Connie's connection to one of the possibilities, she wanted to take care in how much she revealed. "It seems so odd," she said. "So many boys going off to a very unpopular war suggests a patriotic town. Didn't the town hate those hippie kids?"

Rosemary shook her head. "It wasn't like that. They were so sweet. Most of them didn't stay but a week or two. I guess it was about five or six that stayed, a couple of guys and the rest girls. They worked around town, doing all kinds of odd jobs, and they didn't cause any trouble." Her eyes held a distant point. "I guess we felt like they brought the world to us."

"Maybe we should have listened a little harder, too," Connie said. "Marcus and Binkle were the only ones who came back out of that whole little group. And even Marcus . . . "

Ellie said, "Blue said it took Alisha to heal Marcus."

Alisha glanced at Rosemary, then at her hands. "He healed himself. It was just time, I expect."

"No, girl," Rosemary said. "It was you."

"He needed somebody who didn't remember," Connie said, "so he could lay it all down."

Immediately, Ellie heard a snip of a song: ". . . find the cost of freedom. . . ." She pushed it away. "It broke my heart to look at those faces this morning," she said quietly. "They were so young."

Silence fell, deep and fathomless. Into the stillness, Connie said, "I wish I'd listened to those girls a little more. They said we could all go to Canada. What would be different now, I wonder, if we had? All of us just run off in a group and stayed away?"

Rosemary shook her head. "Don't even go there, girl. I can't stand it." She sighed and stood up, looking at Ellie. "Sorry, honey. We seemed to have gone off track. You want to talk about Mabel?"

Ellie felt a pang of guilt. She had, after all, pushed them toward a discussion that pained them. "I'll wait."

Connie spoke suddenly. "I just got an idea! I think we should get all our pictures out, all of us, and put something together for that weekend." She paused, and spoke over a throat that was tight. "Not just remember the boys as soldiers, but as everything else they were? Like James was a musician and David was a rodeo star and Gary could dance like a wild man and Bobby—" She blinked tears back. "What do you think? I hate that all they are now is a name on a wall, dead soldiers."

"Connie, that's gonna—"

"I know. I know. I just think it would be good for us." She wiped her face with the heel of her hand. Ellie found in the mingled emotion and impatience a strange poignancy. "Men think of the death. I think maybe it's up to us to think of the lives."

Rosemary nodded once, then again, more enthusiastically. "I'll talk to Mrs. Nance. Maybe we can figure out a way to do a retrospective. She knows all those fancy scanning techniques—I bet she'll have some great ideas."

Their hands met, fluttered, caught, Connie and Rosemary's, and Ellie saw the strength they drew from each other, a bond forged in loss. She glanced at Alisha and they both stood to take their leave, saying hasty good-nights to the others, distracted by their plan.

Outside, Alisha paused. "Whew. *That* was intense!"

Ellie only nodded, feeling vaguely winded. After the long morning in the attic, she'd spent the afternoon piecing together the notes from three letters, and made an outline of the book the way she thought it would go. Then, worn by the rising heat, she'd fallen asleep in the wind of the box fan in the window and slept till dinner. It had not been a refreshing nap. She'd awakened cranky and restless.

On the way home, she commented, "Rosemary doesn't much like you, does she?"

Alisha chuckled. "You noticed, huh?"

"We saw some pictures of her and Marcus when they were young. He had a gigantic Afro."

"He told me. Blue ribbed him all day about it." She turned smoothly down what Ellie had come to think of as Rose Road. "I don't think Rosemary wanted him for herself, particularly, but it irked her that I got him." She grinned. "You'd think I was white, the way she acts."

Ellie laughed.

"I wish I could find some way to smooth it out," Alisha confessed. "I like the group and I don't have too many things to do—and somebody needs to be in there to keep them abreast of what's really going on in the world."

"Did those girls really send Blue's picture to a magazine?"

"Oh, Lord. He was furious when he found out—but it's true, what Nadine said. He's about twenty thousand times better looking than most of those cover models. He's too proud to do something as silly as a pageant, but I don't think they've given up."

Ellie tried to imagine him looking brooding and hungry on the cover of a novel, a beautiful woman in his arms. It wasn't much of a stretch. She said nothing.

"You like him, don't you?" Alisha pulled into the drive. "Blue."

"Not like that. We've been writing back and forth for almost a year. He's a lot more than the things those women were talking about." She paused, thinking of the sharpness of his mind, a sharpness he hid below that drawl and winks. "I don't think I've ever met anyone with quite that much brain, you know it? And man, he really loves the blues."

"You think?" She chuckled. "Where do you think that nickname came from?"

Ellie laughed. "Of course! I didn't think about it." She started to get out of the car. "Thanks."

"Listen, Ellie," she said quietly. "I don't mean to get in your business, but you should know that he's not—I mean . . . he's kind of . . ."

"Crazy?"

"Well, that too, but I mean a player."

A player. She hadn't heard that word in a long time. "Don't worry," she said with a grin, "I'm not looking for a man, and even if I was, he's really not my type."

"Good." She heaved an exaggerated sigh of relief. "One female to another, I thought you ought to know."

It had been a long day. Inside, Ellie took her shoes off and sank into the desk chair, automatically pushing the button to turn on her laptop. Rubbed her arches, then got up to feed April. The dog sprawled, practically comatose, against the wall, and opened one eye when Ellie came over to rub her favorite spots. "Sasha wore you out, didn't she?" April licked her muzzle twice, groaned softly, and fell back to sleep.

"I know how you feel," Ellie said, and yawned.

Taking a glass of tea back to the desk, she connected to her on-line service to make sure there were no E-mail messages from her agent or editor. While she was waiting for the files to download, she opened her notebook and carefully slid out the pictures she'd borrowed from Rosemary's trunk. Her mother was so young it was odd, but then, Ellie guessed she'd died young, too. Her mother had never even grown as old as Ellie was now.

It was an unsettling thought.

When Ellie had seen her mother's pretty, distinctive face and long red hair in the picture this morning, a strange arrow of grief had stabbed her. All these years, and she'd never missed this woman, who stared up out of the photo with an enigmatic expression. Why now?

Pushing the odd emotion away, she scribbled down the bits of information she'd gleaned from Rosemary and Connie and Blue, and tried to match the faces to the names. Since she'd only taken the photos in which her mother appeared, she didn't have all the boys' pictures, but it was easy to pick out Bobby Makepeace with his goatee, and Marcus and James. There were two other white boys, one very swarthy with a big smile, and a very skinny youth with the bandy-legged stance of a rodeo rider.

Ellie pursed her lips and picked up the photo of her mother smiling at someone—either Bobby or someone just outside the frame, and she heard herself sending up a little prayer. *Not Bobby, God. Please.*

And in truth, although she liked the look of the boy, liked his sunny smile and a certain brash sensuality she found appealing, his coloring was very close to Ellie's mother's—reddish hair, that milk white Irish skin, very blue eyes. If he was her father, Ellie was a genetic throwback.

The swarthy guy was a better bet. She wondered which one he was—Binkle or the rodeo guy.

She leaned back, chewing her lip. How would she piece this together without outside help? She didn't want it known that she was looking for her father. What if he was a family man whose wife didn't know about his liaison with a transient hippie girl? What if it was Bobby Makepeace, and Connie's heart was broken by a betrayal thirty years in the past?

No, for now, she'd do what she could on her own.

Her computer beeped, indicating waiting E-mail. Ellie punched the button without much interest, and went back to staring at the pictures. It beeped again almost immediately to let her know the mail was now downloaded.

Only one letter was in the box, from Laurence Reynard, Ph.D. With a smile, she clicked to open it. *Hey, darlin'*, he'd written, *why'd you have to have that picture so bad?*

Busted. Ellie tried to think of some lie, but couldn't come up with anything plausible. In sudden decision, she typed her reply. *It's personal, all right? I'll tell you about it when I can.* She hit a button to send it off, and put her feet up on the desk, memorizing the faces in the picture so she could spot them in the yearbooks at the library.

The machine beeped again, surprising her. Mail had come in from Blue. Grinning, she clicked it. *Why don't you come on up and have a beer with me? I was going to sign on and raise hell in the newsgroups, but I'd rather talk to a real person.*

Ellie hesitated. She didn't want to talk about the picture, and she wasn't completely certain she could trust herself to stay aloof from that charismatic sex appeal. *Are you properly dressed?* she finally typed.

The reply came back immediately. *Yes, ma'am. Buttoned all the way to the neck.*

She chuckled. *Okay. I'll be right there. Don't ask me again about the picture.*

7

Turning off the computer and the lamp, Ellie slipped on a pair of thongs and headed up the hill. The house glowed with lights, and as she started out, Blue turned on an outside light that made it easier, but it was still very dark, a kind of dark she'd forgotten existed. Crickets whirred in the grass, and cicadas answered from the trees, the only sounds for miles and miles, and the air was thick and soft against her face, smelling of earth and river and sky. She inhaled it deeply, pausing to catch the moment close to herself.

Peaceful. Life was so peaceful in the country. Not the actual lives—emotions ruled people no matter where they lived, so there was always some drama or another waiting to make things chaotic—but the details were easier. She could think better without cars racing and roaring and people shouting in the apartment overhead, and even little things like televisions and radios in an unceasing undertone of constant sound. She liked smelling air, not fuel, and loved the sight of the sky overhead.

A shadow startled her, and she made a sound of surprise before Blue caught her hand. "It's just me," he said.

For that brief second, she let herself feel his big, strong hand, rough from his work. Impulsively, she curled her fingers around his, and said, "You have one sexy voice, Dr. Reynard."

"Are you flirting with me, Miz Connor?"

She laughed softly. "Maybe so."

"Good. I like that." He walked up the path, hanging on to her. Ellie let it be. At the porch, he let her go, and gestured for her to take a chair. "I'm having bourbon, myself. What'll be your pleasure? Other than me, of course."

"I wouldn't mind a bourbon, if you'll walk me back down the hill."

"Careful now. I might take that as an invitation."

"You are amazingly arrogant, you know that?"

"Yes, I do. " She heard ice clinking in a glass and the quiet flow of liquid, and he gave her a glass.

"Thank you."

He settled on the step. "Not too many women drink straight bourbon these days."

"I don't very often."

"But you got a little off balance today, didn't you?"

She gave him a look. "So did you."

Quietly, he said, "Yes, ma'am, that I did. Guess we both have our closets full of skeletons."

"Most people do."

"You think so? I don't know. It seems like a lot of folks just get it right out of the gate. I see them in town, you know? Guys who've been making the right call since the day they were born, live quiet lives without a lot of turmoil, and just . . . keep it together. Never screw up their credit or forget to mow the lawn or leave a project half-done."

Ellie sipped cold fire from her glass and listened.

"You ever notice," he said, "that those people don't ever seem to have big traumas, either? Like their kids never have wrecks and their houses don't burn down. It's like they're protected with some big cloud of serenity."

"That's seeing it from the outside, Blue. Nobody gets through life without sorrow and loss. It's just part of the game."

He turned his face toward her, and in the darkness, Ellie could see no details, but she sensed his attention. "You really believe that?"

"My grandma always says there are green seasons." She tucked a foot up under her. "Times when everything goes on just right. Got money enough to pay the bills, and nobody dies and things are just the way they're supposed to be, most all the time." She paused to take another tiny sip. "But there are also gray times, when nothing seems to go right. You lose pets and people and have trouble with money."

"Not gray," he said. "Blue times . . . like when all the plumbing goes bad."

She chuckled. "Yeah. The gas pump goes out on the car."

"Stub your toe and get hangnails."

"Split ends and toothaches."

His laughter, low and rich, rolled into the night. "Lightning hits the modem. You ever have that happen?"

"No. I turn everything off in a thunderstorm."

"I do now. I had a whole computer fried one time."

"That's not gray times, that's foolishness."

"Well, I left it on when I went to bed. Maybe I'd been drinking a little."

"I get the feeling you drink a little quite a bit. Is that true?"

He didn't reply immediately, just shook the ice in his glass lazily. "Yeah, I reckon it is."

"Why?"

"Does there have to be a reason?"

Ellie shrugged. "I don't know. Maybe not. You just—well . . . never mind."

"Go on. I'm what?"

The darkness and the quiet made her bolder. "You're a puzzle, Dr. Reynard. Take those degrees of yours, for example."

"My degrees?"

She smiled. "Yeah, a big sexy Southern bad boy with advanced degrees in botany?"

"I'm good with things that grow. They never talk back, and if you lose them, you can always grow some more." He paused, gave her that faintly rueful smile. "If you take care of an orchid, it'll outlive you, and your grandchildren."

"You don't like losing things."

"No—though you'd think I'd be used to it by now. I've had my share."

"And green times? Have you had your share of those?"

He stood up and refilled his glass before he answered. "Yeah." The word was rough. "I kinda think I'd rather not have had them, though."

"If you meant that, you wouldn't have to drink so much."

He halted in the act of lifting the glass to his lips. Genuinely puzzled, he said, "Come again?"

"Never mind. It's none of my business."

"That's true, but you can't leave it like that. What do you mean?"

She looked out at the dark, listening to the crickets sing for one long moment. "You want the green times, but you're afraid of them, so you keep yourself safe behind the bourbon."

He gave a snort of laughter and tossed the drink back almost defiantly. "Bullshit. Not everybody needs to be carted off to AA. I drink because I like it."

Ellie shrugged. "You asked."

"So I did. And there may be a little truth in there, somewhere, much as I hate to admit it." He looked at the glass. "Or maybe it's just that drinking gets to be a habit. It does put up a nice little wall against things."

Ellie inclined her head. "What's the wall keeping out?"

He looked at her. "I guess I don't know anymore."

The bourbon was infecting Ellie's blood now, and she found she didn't want to go anywhere. She wanted to sit on this porch, with this man, drinking and talking in the dark, for as long as she could. "Tell me about a green time," she said quietly.

He turned his head and a wash of moonlight spread over his high cheekbone, over his jaw and mouth. "Those pictures today, that was a green time. My whole life was green then, had been from the day I was born. My mama always sang and danced and told silly jokes. My daddy was gone a lot on business, but he always brought us presents. We had three cats and two dogs, and a bowl of goldfish. My uncles came in and took me fishing. My brother was a pain in the neck, always calling me names, but Lord—I pretty much worshipped the ground he walked on."

Ellie smiled. "Pretty normal, I'd say."

"And there was Annie. My wife." There was the faintest ragged edge to his voice. "She used to hang around and drive me crazy back then—her folks had a place just on the other side of the river, there." He gestured. "But I even liked that, being the subject of hero worship, because it gave me somebody to be mean to."

"Poor Annie." Ellie laughed. "But I guess she won in the end, didn't she? She got you to the altar."

There was surprise on his mouth when he turned his face to look at her, then a perplexed little nod. "That she did. But by then, it was me doing the dragging." He swirled the bourbon in his glass, drank a little. The grin was broad when he spoke again. "She wouldn't sleep with me till I put a ring on her finger. Can you imagine? In this day and age?"

"She probably heard about your reputation, sir. Sounds like a smart woman."

"Who's been talking about my reputation?"

"Who hasn't?"

"Really?" He sounded offended.

Ellie laughed. "Blue, everybody I meet tells me more or less the same thing—everybody. Stay away from him. He's a dog. He's crazy." She paused. "You have a *terrible* reputation."

He put a hand over his heart, wounded. "Well, don't that beat all. I'm not that bad." He scowled. "And anyway, it didn't get bad till after Annie died, so she wasn't worried about that. *She* liked me."

"You can't honestly tell me your feelings are hurt?"

A single lift of a shoulder.

With surprise, Ellie saw that it was true. He was wounded by the talk, and for some reason she could not, or would not, name, it endeared him to her a little. "They all love you anyway," she said, and brushed her foot over his. "And I never listen to gossip."

The mouth lifted on one side. "Liar."

Ellie rocked a little, breathing in the night, thinking about what it might have been like to be a kid in this house. "You had a great childhood."

"I did," he said softly. "Now you. Tell me about your green time, Ellie."

His voice on her name made her imagine how it would be to have him over her, in her, and saying her name like that in her ear as they made love. She sipped her drink, surprised to find it gone. "Can I make another?"

"Let me get it."

"I can do it." She stood up. "I remember this one

summer. I was thirteen. My grandma had been working in a bakery, but she just up and took the summer off so I wouldn't have to go to my friend Jodie's house every day. I know now that Jodie's dad was having an affair and the family was none too stable, but my grandma just said she wanted to spend some time with me before I got too big to enjoy her company."

Drink poured, she settled back on to the glider. "We grew a gigantic garden that year. We always had rhubarb and peas and some corn, but this year, we planted everything you can think of . Watermelons and cantaloupe and dinner plate dahlias that were the talk of the town, I'm not kidding. It was hard work, and she made me weed even when I didn't want to, but boy—it was really something. The local newspaper, just a weekly, even came and took a picture of it." She sighed. "I never smell rhubarb without thinking about that summer."

Silence, easy as the humid air, settled between them. Ellie's thoughts rolled on in her mind. "The next summer was when my grandpa died. That's when the blue times came. For a while."

"How'd you come to be living with your grandma? Where was your mama?"

A prickle of alertness walked on her nerves. "She was just kind of unstable. I don't remember her at all. She was killed when I was two."

"What about your daddy?"

"Never knew him," she said carefully, and to be sure he didn't get suspicious, added, "I don't think she knew him. That was the free love generation, remember." She smiled to lighten the comment.

He stretched out his leg and put his bare foot against the top of hers. "Poor little Ellie. Now you're making me feel bad."

"How?"

"I think maybe you're right. At the heart of it all, I'm a coward. That's why I'd rather live in the plain times. Not green or gray. Just . . . plain."

His foot moved the slightest bit, and Ellie found herself wanting to kick off her thong and put her foot on his shin, just so she could touch him. She knew if she did it, he'd make the next move. Instead she said, "But without those bad times, we wouldn't have the blues."

"Wouldn't need them."

Ellie couldn't tell whether that meant he agreed or not. "And wouldn't that be a tragedy." It wasn't a question.

"You know, it really would be."

She pulled her foot from under his and stood up. "It's been a long day. I need to get some sleep."

"All right. Let me get my shoes and I'll walk you down."

"No, thank you, don't bother. It's not that far."

He moved closer, and Ellie smelled his skin, that faintly exotic odor that clung to him. "I'm not going to make a pass at you, if that's what you're worried about."

She bowed her head against that voice, feeling it run like a tongue down her spine. Ridiculous how she responded to him. She shook her head. "No, I'm not worried about that. I just don't want to put you out."

"No trouble." He ducked into the house, then stuck his head out again. "Seriously, wait for me, all right? It's too dark."

She nodded, crossing her arms as the screen door slammed behind him as if to literally get a grip on herself and the entirely normal but exceedingly dangerous rush of hormones he roused. She needed to keep her head with Blue Reynard or she was going to end up falling under his spell and into his bed—and she knew from experience she wasn't the kind of woman who could sleep with a man and just walk away.

What had he said this morning? That sex was easy and friends were hard. Which told her he *was* the kind of man who could have sex and walk away. He probably did it all the time.

Most men did.

And it occurred to her as she stood there in the soft night that he'd been warning her when he said that, and when he'd told her a leopard couldn't change his spots. It was his way to sleep with women he liked, natural as breathing, and he'd likely try to sleep with Ellie before they were through.

It was going to have to be up to her to make sure that didn't happen.

At two in the morning Blue finally gave up on sleep and got up, throwing on a pair of jeans. His dog Sasha eagerly joined him as he ambled into the kitchen for a glass of water, then went upstairs to the widow's walk on top of the house. It was an anomaly in this area, the legacy—like the lilacs near the back porch—of a bride from the northeast. It was also, aside from the greenhouses, one of his favorite places. He'd furnished it with a couple of chairs and a telescope and a CD player, hooked up by long, trailing lengths of extension cords, to a plug in the attic. Lanie swore he'd burn the house down one of these days.

Piwacket appeared, a tiny white ghost, and perched happily on the back of a chair. Sasha settled down with a sigh beneath Blue's right hand, and he kicked his feet up comfortably. It was a familiar scene. The night and the animals and the view of the stars.

He did not often sleep well. It wasn't, as the psychologists and school counselors had believed in his childhood, a result of the losses in his eighth and ninth years. And it wasn't the loss of his wife in adulthood. He wouldn't deny his psyche had probably been twisted by all that, but his insomnia stemmed from something else entirely.

Thinking.

As far back as he could remember, he had often awakened in the middle of the night with his brain on fire. The first time it happened, he was eight. That afternoon, he'd gone to the library with his mother. Because there was a hurricane forming in the gulf, he'd wanted to read more about them. He checked out a book on tornadoes, hurricanes, and hailstorms and read it in a single gulp. The idea of the circular motion of wind, and the patterns of high and low fronts, inflamed him and he spent the rest of the day trying to find someone to engage in a conversation about it. His mother listened, but she didn't seem to grasp the wonder he needed to get across. His dad was gruff. Lanie gave him the longest stretch of attention, but then she had to start fixing dinner.

Frustrated, Blue went outside and stared at the clouds, then wandered down to the river to look at the current, where the spiral pattern of life was repeated where the river dipped into a minuscule cove and circled around before it got out. In the woods, he spied the same pattern in the whorls of time on a tree stump. And in the evening, when the clouds rolled in, he watched them with rapt attention as wind stuttered them across the sky.

That night had been the first time. He'd awakened abruptly from a sound sleep, and it was as if he could see the entire structure of the universe—the galaxy and the stars reflected the water in the river and the circling structure of hurricanes and tornadoes. Wild with the excitement of his thoughts, he began the pattern that would weave throughout his life: he ambled outside to sit on the porch in his cowboy print pajamas and settled there to watch the rain pouring down from the sky. There in the midnight rain, he was free to let the thoughts go where they would.

Back then, he learned quickly not to talk about his dark-of-the-night thinking sessions. For one thing, he had a hell of a time getting anyone to grasp the big picture, no matter how many times he came at a concept. He could see a whole structure—whether it was weather or ecology or math—that simply made no sense to others. For another, he started to get a reputation for being downright strange.

In the ninth grade, two years after his parents had died, Blue was in trouble most of the time, headed for juvenile hall. But as if to make up for all the bad luck, he had one big stroke of good luck: he drew Florence Grace, Rosemary's sister, as his homeroom teacher.

From the first week, she seemed to get it. Not everything, but way more than he'd ever been able to get across to anyone else. She moved into action. Instead of *tsk*ing and shaking her head, she tried to find out what he could do. She fed him geometry, then trig, and had him in calculus in a single year. She hunted up experiments in weather and biology and botany for him to do on his own. She brought him biographies of brilliant scientists and thinkers who'd been tortured by their minds, as he was, and literature from every century, every kind of writer. Poets and dreamers, philosophers and novelists. She said she had no idea where that brain of his would lead, but the only way to find out was to learn as much about everything as he could until something clicked.

And Blue, starved for both attention and knowledge, consumed everything she gave him and more. That year, he spent as little as three hours a night sleeping. He read and pondered and experimented. Florence taught him to keep a journal and he often poured out page after page of speculation and observation.

She saved him. All he'd needed was tools, and Florence had given them to him.

These past four years, it hadn't been wonder that kept him awake. More often, he came here to escape the demons in his head, the ghosts that had chased him out of the house the night before. The ones that chased him up here now.

The ones that made him want to go down to the cottage and lie down next to that skinny woman with her wild hair and let that laugh roll all over him. What a great laugh she had.

Instead, he stayed where he was, head cocked back to the sky, a cat in his lap and a dog under his hand. He was an intelligent man; he knew the world was just sometimes harsh, but his luck with people had been pretty wretched by any measure. Marcus called him Job sometimes, as a joke that didn't really make either of them laugh. Blue sometimes thought he must have pissed God off in another life or been born under a bad star or something.

These days, he judged it safer to keep things loose and easy. As long as he didn't get too tangled up again with anybody, his life was pretty good. He had friends and a home and work and money enough to do pretty much anything he had a mind to do. When he got hungry enough, there were always willing women to warm his bed for a night or a week.

But now Ellie's words came back to him: *What's the wall keeping out?*

He frowned. Lots of people had taken him to task for his drinking the past few years—a comment here and there that made him understand folks thought of him as a hard drinker. Lanie hid his bottle when she thought he'd been hitting it too hard. Even Marcus, who was no stranger to a Saturday afternoon six-pack and always liked a nice bourbon at the end of the day, had commented once or twice that maybe Blue drank a bit too much.

But he'd never paid any of them any mind at all. Why did it matter what Ellie thought? She was a stranger, just passing through.

Still. He rubbed his ribs idly, unable to deny that her comments bothered him. It had bothered him that she'd known by his posts on-line when he'd been drinking. It bothered him that she thought he was hiding behind it.

Even if he was. Losing Annie so suddenly had ripped him to pieces, shredded his faith, his hope, his ability to believe in anything. There was a craziness in that kind of pain he didn't wish on anyone, and he'd been desperate to escape it.

He'd turned to his experiments, to the eternal flowers, and poured himself into building the big greenhouse, where he could mimic the Central American rain forest conditions as exactly as possible. He'd worked ten, twelve, fourteen hours a day, hiring Marcus to help him and bringing in crews to do the work they couldn't handle. At night, he opened a bottle of bourbon and anesthetized himself well enough to sleep.

A wall of work and bourbon. He'd erected it to let himself heal.

The answer surprised him, but it had the authentic ring of truth. He'd been flat-out unable to deal with his true reality, so he retreated into a world of flowers and bourbon until he could face it.

Was that such a bad thing? Wasn't there even

something like that in the Bible? That wine should be given to the grieving, or saved for the poor to make them feel better about their lot in life? Maybe. He couldn't remember exactly.

Sitting in the dark night, he thought maybe it was only bad if he didn't let go of habits he no longer needed. Maybe it was safe now to let go of the wall and face real life.

Maybe he'd give it a try, just to see. It was time. Maybe he'd even open his heart, just a crack, and see how it felt to really be attracted to a woman, not just sexually, but all the way. Maybe he'd kiss her and see what happened.

As if she heard his thoughts, Piwacket bumped her head against his chin, purring softly. He smiled and rubbed a hand down her bony back. "You like her, don't you?" He looked at the cabin. "So do I."

Something very like hope moved in him, refreshing and soft as a long cold drink of water. "So do I," he repeated.

8

Ellie kept her distance for a couple of days, unwilling to test her resolve about Blue Reynard's charm. She'd taken the old woman from the beauty parlor to tea in Tyler, but the interview had been less than satisfactory. Mrs. Porter wandered a little, touching only lightly on her memories of Mabel Beauvais before wandering down another path in her girlhood. The time spent was hardly a loss; Ellie had gleaned a basketful of details about a black woman's life in the thirties and forties and fifties that she'd be able to use in reconstructing Mabel's world. Still, Ellie was anxious to find more sources, and looked forward to Gwen Laisser's return.

In the meantime, her days took on a comfortable routine. Evenings were spent writing. Early mornings were given to research in Rosemary's attic, deciphering letters and taking notes on the material they contained. There wasn't much yet that she hadn't discovered in other sources, but Ellie's hopes had not dimmed.

Afternoons she spent at the library. Some of that time she was taking notes on the material the librarian had collected for her, but Ellie spent more of it on her search for her father. Finding the picture of her mother had given new urgency to the quest, and as she combed through the photos from the small high school yearbooks from the years between 1966 and 1969, she felt a humming sense of excitement.

In the photos she'd seen in Rosemary's attic, there were only three possibilities that Ellie could see. Two dead and one living.

The dead veterans were Dennis Nicolson, a skinny boy with a crew cut, the one Blue said his mother had cried over, and Robert Makepeace, Connie's beau. Ellie smiled at the name, wondering if it might have appealed to her mother the flower child. The last, and still living, possibility was Todd Binkle, a swarthy boy with big teeth.

Saturday afternoon, she had the second floor of the library to herself since the librarian was leading a children's reading hour on the lower level. It was busy, too, with a steady stream of patrons in and out all day.

Ellie availed herself of the archives happily. To be safe, she only took one yearbook off the shelf at a time, and kept its cover hidden in a sprawl of papers and bound newspapers and various other research materials.

She had two barometers to use at first: her mother's attitude and lifestyle at the time, and her own coloring, which had almost certainly come from her father. Diane had been fair, blue-eyed and redheaded. Ellie was dark-haired and green-eyed, and her skin tone ran to what her grandmother called "olive," though Ellie privately thought of it as sallow. Ellie's grandparents had also been fair and blue-eyed, though Ellie knew she'd inherited her grandmother's curly hair and strong, skinny body.

So first she looked at all three men in their senior yearbook photos, those carefully posed, well-scrubbed shots. They looked exactly the same—neatly cut hair and dark suits with ties and almost identical phony smiles. FBI candidates, every one.

Because it was a small school, she was able to find several pictures each of Crew Cut Dennis and Still-Living Binkle. Dennis had been a wrestler and a member of 4-H, and had scored a coup by selling his prize bull that year for the highest price any 4-H-er had ever gotten at the state fair. In the picture, he looked like a classic country boy—Wrangler jeans on his bowed legs, prominent Adam's apple in his skinny throat, a hunk of chew in his lip. Ellie narrowed her eyes. The coloring was almost impossible to decipher because of the black-and-white photography, but if Diane had wanted this kind of man, she would have found dozens just like him in her hometown.

Binkle was a little more promising. Even in the black-and-white photos, he was obviously swarthy. He showed up in the football and basketball team photos, and his physique showed his athleticism. He was good-looking, Ellie thought, but his class activities list also showed he was vice president, a member of the Young Republicans, Future Businessmen of America, dance committee, and chess club. A high achiever with a politician's smile.

Even if Diane had been captured by the admittedly sexy look of the boy, Ellie doubted he would have given her the time of day. She wrote a note to herself: *Is Binkle married? Does Blue know him? Look him up in the phone book; see what he does for a living.* Maybe if she could find out where he worked, Ellie could get a look at him in person.

That left Bobby Makepeace. Apart from the senior portrait, there was only one other photo of him, and there were no clubs or activities listed under his name. The additional photo showed him in a fringed jacket, grinning at the camera over a guitar. His hair was the slightly ridiculous Beatles style that had probably been very daring for this small town at this time period. He was piercingly handsome.

Ellie could see her mother liking a boy like this a lot. And she must have seemed like a fresh breeze to a rebellious small-town boy. She inclined her head, trying to see anything of herself in the face or the smile.

She took out the group picture again. There was Bobby Makepeace, between Connie and Rosemary, an arm around each one. His hair was a distinctly rusty shade of blond and red. If this was her father, Ellie was a definite genetic throwback.

Frustrated, she flipped back to his senior photo. Good bone structure, high cheekbones, a sensual-looking mouth. Ellie had the same kind of cheekbones, and her mouth was her best feature.

He seemed a likely candidate, and if she'd not met Connie, Ellie might have been tempted to ask some more direct questions of the townsfolk. Now it felt like a betrayal in some small way. Better to wait a bit.

She turned the page once more to look at Binkle, and she had to admit there was a lot more resemblance there. His hair was dark and a little curly, and there was in his face a Latin kind of angularity. She grinned to herself when she realized that instead of looking for similarities she was picking out differences. She didn't want this one to be her father. Funny.

People changed, though. He might have gone off to war and become a real person.

Idly, she looked at the opposite page and immediately picked out Connie's senior picture. Her hair was teased into a massive cone, and she wore white lipstick, and a sweetheart necklace hung around her throat. Then again, some people didn't change all that much at all. It amazed her how much Connie still looked like this. She'd aged very well.

Next to her was a face that looked familiar, a light-skinned black man with a mischievous grin. Taking the group photo out, she found him with Marcus—the other vet who'd died, James Gordon. Three boys from one high school class seemed like a lot. No wonder Marcus wanted a memorial—these boys were all from his graduating class.

Curious, she looked up Marcus's name in the index and found a long list of photos. The space for his senior photo was missing, but there were several others: Marcus in a track uniform holding a discus, and another with a ribbon around his neck. The caption said he'd taken state in the mile.

He was also in the group shot of student government, which surprised her a little, maybe because of the picture Blue painted of him later, as a troublemaker. But that had been after his tour.

The last picture of Marcus was in a group on the last few pages with simple captions of the student names. The one of Marcus showed him with James, both of them laughing uproariously.

Right below it was the one of Makepeace on the guitar. Ellie felt a soft melancholy creep through her at the sight of those two boys, James and Bobby, at the threshold of their lives, who'd died so far away.

Again it struck her how unreal Vietnam had always seemed to her. Not only unreal, but boring beyond belief—old and dusty and ancient, riddled with conflicts and strangeness that made no sense to her.

But the other night, with Connie and Rosemary, she'd felt the first flicker of reality as the past came alive, and as she peered at the old photos of boys long dead, it seemed she could almost hear their voices, hear the music and the war itself.

As a biographer, she'd often experienced this emotion—when a moment of history stopped being a fact on a page and lifted up, like a hologram, to show itself as whole and real and connected to everything else. Recognizing the feeling now, she let it grow, let the faces of Marcus and James and Bobby burn themselves into her mind before she deliberately flipped back to the one of Dennis the country boy. Remembering Blue's brother had also died in Vietnam, she turned to the index and looked up Reynard. He was in the ninth grade. A baby.

Hearing a step on the stairs, Ellie slammed the annual closed and hid it under her notebook. The librarian breezed by, gave her a wave, but didn't stop. Obviously, she was hurrying to the ladies' room.

As soon as she'd disappeared, Ellie rushed to put the annual back in place. Enough for one day. She had to concentrate on her book for the rest of the afternoon or she'd never get it done.

Still, as she dutifully made notes about Mabel's hometown life, the slight sense of melancholy didn't leave her, and the faces of the boys were burned into her mind.

As she was tearing lettuce for her supper, Blue showed up on her doorstep. "Knock, knock," he said through the screen. "Can I come in?"

"Sure. You want a Coke or something?"

"Anything cold and wet, darlin'," he said, coming in. "It's hot as hell today. I'm dying."

Ellie fetched a can of Dr Pepper and poured it into a glass with ice. He drank deeply, eyes closed, and Ellie allowed herself five seconds to admire him. Even in a T-shirt that had seen better times and after a long day's work in the greenhouses, he managed to look delectable. For one thing, the sleevelessness showed a lot of tanned arm and shoulder. For another, every inch of flesh was dewy with the humid air. For another—

Five seconds were up. She turned back to her salad. "What's going on?"

"Just thought I'd check on you. How is the research coming?"

She nodded without looking at him. "Good. I think I'm finally making some progress. Rosemary may even have tracked down the journal."

"That's great." He leaned on the counter. "I was thinking, if you wanted to come with us, Marcus, Alisha and I are going out to one of the blues clubs tonight. There's a bartender there I reckon would remember Mabel. She sang there once or twice, but more than that, he loved her. Want to?"

"Yes!" She didn't even bother to hide her delight. She grinned at him. "You didn't even have to throw in Mabel, you know. I'd have gone to hear the blues anyway."

He straightened, and moved ever so slightly closer, until there was only a hand's width of space between them. "Yeah?" He lifted an eyebrow. "What about Marcus and Alisha? Did I have to throw them in, too, or would you have gone alone with me?"

Ellie looked up at him, found herself snared by the angle of his tanned cheekbone, the shape of his mouth. "I don't know," she said honestly. "Probably it's better that they're going."

"I made the right call, then." He touched her shoulder with one finger, then stepped back. "I'll come get you around nine-thirty, then." At the door he turned back. "It's a black club, mainly, so you want to break out something fine to wear."

"Thanks for the warning." Ellie grinned. She knew just the thing.

Whistling to himself, Blue drove to Marcus's house. The smell of barbecue scented the air, and Blue went around the house to the tree-shaded back yard. A chow puppy leapt up as he stopped at the gate, barking happily at the visitor. A two-year-old boy, as plump and round as his dog, toddled over with the same cheery eagerness. "Hey, uncle!"

Blue came through the gate and knelt to scrub the puppy's belly, then roared and picked up the child. "Who's been eating all my porridge?" he cried.

James shrieked. "It was Daddy!"

"Yeah, and I ain't afraid of no giant." Marcus lifted his chin in greeting. "Hadn't had enough of me this week?"

"I smelled those steaks all the way down to my house." Blue lifted his eyebrows and put James down. "Tell your mama I need a beer."

"Walk when you bring it out, James. It gets shook up when you run."

Blue leaned against a tree. "What are y'all doing tonight?"

"Got no plans at the moment. What's on your mind?"

"I just told Ellie all of us would be . . . uh. . . going out to Hopkins' tonight."

"Is that right."

Alisha came out on the back step, wearing a filmy yellow sundress that made her look like a flower. The baby, Lena, was on her hip. "Hey, Blue," she said, and kissed his cheek. "You come for dinner?"

"I came to drag you out with me tonight."

"Really?" She perked up. "How about it, Marcus? We haven't been out in months. Your mama will keep the children. She told me earlier this week she hasn't seen them near enough lately."

"Fine by me," he said. "You know who's playing tonight?"

Blue shook his head.

"I can see, as usual, you got everything all planned out."

He lifted a shoulder. "It was one of those impulsive moments, you know. Pretty woman, opportunity, my mouth just opened."

Alisha frowned. "It's not Sheila, is it? That woman drove me crazy with her screechy laugh."

Blue chuckled. "Nope. Ellie wants to see the clubs, for her book."

The long dark eyes went cold. "You are a dog, Blue Reynard, and I like her, okay? So don't be playing any of your tricks. Just be real for once in your life."

"I'm not after her," he said, lifting his hand in a vow. "I swear it. She's just . . ." He shrugged. "She's a friend. That's all. I like her."

Ellie knew she wasn't beautiful. And it wasn't the delusional "my mouth is too full/nose too small/eyes too big" kind of not-pretty either, which she found ridiculous. It was her theory that every woman in America, maybe even the world, knew by the age of six who was beautiful and who was not. She was not.

Happily, she also cared very little about it. Her skin was good, her teeth were sound and she didn't have to worry about her weight, which all by itself seemed like a blessing big enough to offset just about any other physical flaw. She liked beer and doughnuts and chicken fried in bacon grease. It would kill her to subsist on what passed for food for most of the women she knew—women who repeatedly told her mournfully that they hated her. But Ellie figured it all evened out. She could eat what she wanted, but then, no man had ever stopped dead in the street to stare at her in longing, either. Her face wasn't beautiful and her hair was too wild and she didn't have the kind of curves that real men liked.

On a day-to-day basis, she didn't think much about how she looked. She wore a little blush to offset her sallowness, but her lipstick ran to Carmex and her wardrobe consisted mainly of wrinkle-resistant cotton-poly blends she could wash and dry at a Laundromat.

But there were times the girly-girl in her came out. A blues club where Mabel might have sung was definitely one of them. She'd learned what to wear to make the most of her admittedly small array of physical gifts—decent legs, good shoulders, and enough breast that she didn't look completely flat-chested in a tight dress.

She put some bad-boy rock and roll on the CD player as she showered and shaved her legs and plucked her eyebrows, singing along happily as she put makeup on her slanted eyes (a plus) and her almost sallow skin (a minus). The dress was as simple as dresses got: a plain black sheath with a nicely dangerous neckline over which her small helping of cleavage showed just a bit. Black stockings. Black high-heeled sandals. Her hair—since it wouldn't do a damned thing in all this humidity—she piled up loose on her head.

Dancing a little in the tiny bathroom, she added the final touch. The one really good feature she had was her mouth, and tonight she painted it scarlet. It did what it always did, made her eyes look smoky green and kind of mysterious, and her mouth downright dangerous. Pleased, she thought of Blue.

Which required walking into the kitchen to get a beer to calm her nerves and get her defenses back up. She was crazy to be going out with him, crazy to be primping to get his attention, but there it was. The reason she'd been so delighted at his invitation this afternoon was because she wanted him to see her, and dressing up was the only way she could do it without making an idiot of herself.

She'd gotten ready a little too soon. Nervous and keyed up, she jumped up, picked another CD at random and threw it in the player, then paced in time to the music.

Damn. At least be honest, Connor, she told herself. You want him bad. Stop pretending and just get it right out in the open. You want him because he's big and bad and gorgeous and maybe even partly because he's completely unattainable and everybody else wants him, too.

She sipped her beer, paced to the kitchen, then to the door. April, sensing her disturbance, lifted her head. "It's all right, baby," she said, pausing to pat her head—but carefully, so as not to get a slew of dog hair on her dress. "You got fixed when you were little, so you don't have to deal with any of this."

So just sleep with him already.

The voice belonged to the devil. Ellie knew it by the way it sounded so reasonable, so obvious. Just sleep with him. Have a nice fling and be done with it.

She took a breath, paced to the door and back, waiting for the angel voice, which would say something inane about virtue she could happily override. It never spoke up and after a moment, Ellie decided she'd killed the angel through neglect. Not that lust ever listened to the angel anyway.

But logic could work. Reasons to sleep with him: obvious. Numerous. Way too many to start thinking about ten minutes before she was going somewhere with him.

"Reasons *not* to, Ellie," she said aloud. Okay. Reason number one: He was wounded, somewhere deep, and she had a talent for falling in love with men like that. Falling in love with Blue Reynard would be a complete disaster. Not just because he'd love her and leave her, either, although that was a given.

But it would ruin the friendship between them, which was reason number two. She'd fall in love and then he'd start feeling trapped, then she'd get clingy and he'd have to duck out, and they'd never be able to sit on a porch in the dark again, or trade E-mails in the middle of the night.

She stopped pacing. The jangling tenseness of nerves along the back of her neck eased a little, and let in a picture of him laughing ruefully in the darkness, comfortable with her. Somewhere in the past year, she'd grown to value his companionship, his brilliant posts and wry attitudes. She had to admit she'd found it easier to be with him on-line, when she'd imagined him to be a burned-out Keith Richards look-alike, but that was life. He couldn't help how he looked, either.

His knock startled her enough that she spilled beer on her thumb. Licking it off, she called out, "Come in!" and put the beer down on the counter and picked up her purse.

The door opened. Ellie turned.

He filled up the whole doorway, looking clean and dangerous and sexy in a pair of jeans and a simple, plain white shirt he'd dressed up with a silver bolo tie. He stared at her, his eyes that pulsing, electric blue that was always a little startling. Winded, Ellie simply stared back, drinking in the sight of him.

"I'm sorry," he said at last. "I came to get Ellie. You know where she is?"

It was exactly the right reaction. Ellie laughed and spread her arms. "I guess that means you like it."

He lifted one eyebrow and looked at her, very slowly, from head to toe, lingering with proper appreciativeness at her neck and hem and legs. "Oh, yeah," he said, and put in just the right note of husky pleasure.

"You look pretty good yourself."

He winked. "It's a curse."

Ellie grinned. He let her pass, and she paused on the step to wait for him. He looked at her again, and shook his head. "I really can't believe how different you look."

"You don't have to flirt the *entire* evening, Dr. Reynard."

"Well, that's where you're wrong, Miss Ellie." He reached out a hand and wrapped one loose curl from her neck around his finger. "If I don't flirt, I might just have to act."

The very tips of his fingers brushed her nape, and Ellie had to fight to repress a shiver of reaction. "Bad idea," she said quietly.

He dropped his hand. "You're right. Let's go."

9

Hopkins' Juke Box sat amid a stand of pines near a bend in the river. It had been there since 1922, when an enterprising young man by the name of Lucas Hopkins decided it was time for his folks to have something of their own. He and his four brothers built it out of native pine, just one big, open room with windows to let in the breezes off the river and overhead fans to cool those inclined to dance or get hot over their blues.

What it lacked in decor, it made up for in atmosphere. Through the roaring twenties, it got a name for appreciative and generous audiences, and even big names stopped in for a jam session or simple night of communing with their roots. Through Prohibition, it thrived on bathtub gin and corn liquor, and came into its own in the forties and fifties, and now enjoyed the status of one of the oldest continually operated blues clubs in the region.

The parking lot tonight was already crowded to hear a local boy turned star who was dropping in for an evening.

Blue held open the door for Ellie, taking another deep breath of her perfume as she passed close by him. It afforded him a sweet view of the low neckline of her dress and the gleam of light over her shoulders, and then a particularly pleasant and lingering admiration of her rear end.

He liked women. Liked everything about them. The way they smelled and the way they moved, the look of their arms swinging when they danced, the shape of legs and hips and breasts, and the way they laughed and the little looks they threw.

He also knew he liked Ellie, but he'd originally been attracted to her mind more than her looks, although he'd grown to appreciate those, too. Tonight, she looked a whole lot different. He couldn't quite get over how different.

When they came up to the table where Marcus and Alisha were already seated, Marcus stood up and let go of a long, low whistle. "Baby, you do look good."

Alisha gave a little cry. "Ellie! You clean up like a diamond!"

Ellie, who had obviously been through this surprising transformation more than once, smiled serenely. "Thanks."

Marcus caught Blue's eye and lifted an eyebrow. Blue pounded a fist to his chest, like he was trying to get his heart started again after it had stopped. Marcus grinned.

Settling around the table, Ellie looked around with alert eyes. "This place is great! And Mabel really sang here?"

"She did," Blue said, and remembered to check out the bartender. "And we're in luck." He gestured toward the long bar, where several older men, all black, were hunched over their bourbons and gins and beers. Behind the bar, his arm propped up on the back counter, was a short black man with a goatee gone completely white and the belly of a drinking man. "That's Doc, behind the bar. He's been here since 1946."

"He doesn't look that old!" Ellie exclaimed.

"He's around seventy, I expect," Marcus said. "Came to work here when his daddy was killed in Italy." He looked at Blue. "Guess that would have to be around forty-four?"

Blue nodded. "I know he was a kid."

"The thing that makes Doc a good bet for you, Ellie," Marcus said, leaning over the table as he warmed to his subject, "is that he knew her. They were real close to the same age, grew up together. Then she sang here some. If anybody knew her, he did."

"Will he talk to me?"

"Any man in his right mind would talk to you, darlin'," Blue said with a slow grin. "Come on, I'll introduce you. You may not have much time tonight, since it's fixin' to get busy in here, but this way, you'll know who he is—and he'll know you."

She stood up with him, and they made their way through the close-packed tables and chairs. Blue put his hand on her back, right above the line of her dress, partly to get a guilty charge out of stroking the skin that was as supple as he expected, and partly to put his claim on her. A whole lot of appreciative male eyes watched her sidle through the chairs, turning this way and that, smiling her excuse-mes in the most natural possible way.

And in this, she surprised him. Some white women might have been uncomfortable in this crowd, even with him. There were other whites, but they were definitely the minority, a smattering of trophy girls with too much eyeliner and big hair, sitting in corners with dandies wearing a lot of gold. A few couples, in to hear the music, and some middle-aged guys who worked with black men at the lumber plant. One mixed couple, a black woman and a white man who had been married for more than twenty-five years, were regulars, and Blue lifted his chin their way as he passed.

At the bar, Blue and Ellie sat on stools, and Blue availed himself of the view of her upper thigh, encased in black nylon, exposed as her hem rode up. "Nice legs," he said.

She smiled. "You really are hopeless, aren't you?"

It irked him that no matter what he said, she wasn't about to take him seriously. To cover, he waggled his brows lasciviously. "Yes, I am, Miz Connor. You want some flirting lessons now?"

She inclined her head, and the red-painted lips pursed the faintest bit into a wicked, knowing smile. Her lids dropped seductively, exaggerating the tilt. "I think I know what I need to." She blinked, once, slow as a cat.

Just that fast, between one breath and the next, Blue got punched. "I guess you do, sweetheart."

Doc approached, saving him. "Blue Reynard," he

said in a hearty voice. "How you doin', man? Ain't seen you in here for a couple months." He gave Ellie an appreciative wink. "Guess I can see why."

"Doc, this is Ellie Connor. I think I told you I was writing to somebody who was doing a book on Mabel Beauvais. This is her. She's in town to do some on-site research, and I told her you'd be the man to talk to."

"Is that right." Doc's face sobered and he narrowed his eyes a little. "How come a white girl wants to do a story like that, you don't mind me asking?"

"Why not?"

Doc turned his lips down, nodding. "Fair enough." A man down the bar called for another drink. "Let me get you two something to drink and I'll be right back."

They ordered—Jack Daniel's for Blue. "Same for me," Ellie said. Blue grinned as Doc moved away. "Be careful, sugar. I might get you drunk and talk you into my bed."

"I'm a big girl. I can handle you."

"You sure can if you want to," he said, and laughed. "Sorry. That was bad, even for me."

"You should be ashamed of yourself."

"I am," he said and hung his head in mock shame.

When she laughed, he lifted his chin and for one moment, they were simply looking at each other. He saw reluctant appreciation coupled with careful reserve—she thought he was dangerous. A dog, as Alisha put it. "You're thinking of my reputation again, aren't you?"

"Maybe."

And maybe he was a dog. The reputation, after all,

did have some basis in reality, much as he hated to admit it. Maybe he was attracted to her not because of anything about her particularly, but because he'd lost his taste recently for bimbos and couldn't seem to work up enthusiasm for any kind of other connection with women. He picked up her hand and surprised himself by kissing the palm. "You're safe with me," he said.

"Am I?" The query was husky, musical, and made him look at her mouth, red and plump and tempting as sin itself.

"Well, maybe not."

Doc delivered their drinks and they pulled apart from the oddly intimate moment. "Now, then, young lady," Doc said. "What do you say we set up some afternoon meeting and you can ask me all the questions you want?"

"I'd love that. Lunch on Monday?"

"Sounds good. I'll meet you at Dorrie's Café at one o'clock." He gestured to Blue. "You can come, too, if you want."

Blue nodded at the oblique hint. Doc wouldn't be comfortable being seen having lunch alone with a white woman, no matter if it was thirty years past the civil rights era. He'd been shaped by his times.

"We'll be there."

Ellie loved the club, loved everything about it: the pine-paneled walls, the plain plank floor, the slightly out-of-season advertisements on the walls. She liked the customers, heads swaying, or bent in deep and serious conversations, or full of wild tales and head-thrown-back kind of laughing. She liked the smell of whiskey and cigarette smoke curling into the air. She liked the ceiling fans swirling the moist air around.

But most of all she loved the music. The blues always made her half-drunk anyway, and the band in the corner tonight was very good, a couple of vocalists, an electric guitar and a sax, some good drums. They played a wild mix of everything from Muddy Waters and Buddy Guy to John Mayall and Allman Brothers. They had no rules about era or exactly what qualified as the real thing, freely mixing harmonica and voice, rock and roll and Delta sounds in a full-throated combination that made the crowd crazy.

Drinking JD and water in her little black dress, smelling smoke and bourbon and Blue behind her, Ellie thought it was about as close as she'd ever get to heaven. She trusted her companions to know what the blues did to a person sometimes, and didn't even try to be careful or make conversation, she just left herself behind and went inside the music, floating, dreaming, smiling—even laughing sometimes. One part of her knew it was dangerous to let down her guard when she had so many secrets in her mind, and she was sitting with a man she wanted and should resist, so close she sometimes felt his breath sough over her shoulder or nape.

But the mood in the club was irresistible. The music, the sounds of low voices rolling over those notes, the bone-deep pleasure of it made every joint in her body soft.

At a break she turned with a faintly delirious smile to the others and saw by their faces that they were coming down, too, like the music was a drug. Alisha lifted her glass over the table and grinned. "Whew," she said.

"Amen," Ellie said.

Blue shifted beside her, his cotton shirt brushing her bare arm. "So, Dr. Reynard," she said, using conversation as a shield, "how is it that you came to be called Blue?"

When he turned his face to her, even in the dimness of the club, his eyes were almost unbearably bright, so beautiful it was impossible not to stare at them. A quiver of restlessness moved in her thighs. For the first time, she saw that his eyelashes were very long, and tipped with edges of gold that caught the light coming from the bar. He looked at her for a minute, his mind obviously not on the question, then he fiddled with his drink and looked at Marcus across the table. "I went crazy one summer, I guess," he said, and his mouth quirked.

"Naw, Ellie, he didn't just go crazy," Marcus said. He leaned forward and settled his elbows on the table with a kind of relish. Ellie thought of the picture showing Marcus at his Afroed, platformed best, and knew Marcus was about to get even.

Blue knew it, too. "Come on, man," he said, bowing his head with an abashed smile.

"You ever know a kid who went crazy for a song and played that song over and over and over and over until you wanted to kill him?" Marcus asked, ignoring Blue.

Ellie smiled. "Sure."

"Well, Blue fell out over 'Mannish Boy.' No matter what time of day or night—you may not know this, but the man never sleeps—you'd hear that song blasting out of the house, rattling the windows."

Imagining a young Blue, with hands too big for his body and not enough flesh yet on his ribs, dancing around his big empty house, pierced her. She grinned to cover it.

"It wasn't months," he said. "That was just the song that got me. I moved on in a couple of weeks."

"No, Ellie, it was months. Over and over and over and over. When he finally figured out there were a bunch of songs like that he might like, we about had a parade."

Blue burst out laughing, and the sound of it was even richer than his voice, and surprising in a way Ellie hadn't expected. "Lanie started calling him Blue and it stuck," Marcus said.

Ellie chuckled. "Wonder if the ladies at the Reader's Group know that story."

Alisha laughed. "I wonder, too. Oh, wouldn't they love that."

"Do you know *all* my embarrassing secrets?" Blue asked, pained.

"I don't know," Ellie said, lifting her glass. "Do I?"

He dropped his elbows on the table and leaned in close. "I guess you'll just have to spend some more time finding out."

The same light that had touched his eyelashes now caressed the line of his nose and fell into the dip above his top lip. Ellie straightened and tugged at the hem of her skirt. He caught the gesture and watched. "What about you, little girl?" he said. "Did you dance around to some song in your bare feet, singing into a lipstick?"

He said it quietly, that drawl like melted butter. She looked at her glass and shook the ice cubes down. "No," she said. "I was a lot older."

"Yeah?" One syllable that slid like a slow finger over the curve of her breast. "Tell me."

Marcus and Alisha had evidently exchanged secret signals, for at that moment, they both stood up. "We'll be back in a little while," Alisha said. "I see a friend of mine I want Marcus to meet."

Blue didn't even look up. Ellie nodded, then found herself drawn right back into that intense attention. Somehow, without her noticing, he'd moved his knee so that it touched the outside of her thigh. Somebody dropped some quarters into the jukebox and "Mannish Boy" burst into the room.

Ellie laughed as Blue shook his head over his shoulder at Marcus, walking away from the jukebox with a bland expression.

"In your bare feet, huh?" she teased.

He lifted a brow. "Enough about me. You were older," Blue prompted, touching one finger to her knuckles.

"I had a roommate in college who dated a blues guitarist," she said. "She kept asking me to go along, but I was studying all the time, you know, being a good student."

"What were you studying then?"

"Architecture, believe it or not." So many years

later, even Ellie had to smile at the absurdity of the choice. "I really loved music, but I couldn't *do* it, so I decided building things would be okay.

"But the college matched people up according to the interests and background, and I'd had a lot of training in various musical instruments, and put on my form that music was my number-one interest." She lifted a shoulder, remembering. "If you aren't good enough to land a record contract, or even be a studio musician or make a symphony, there isn't much open to you, you know? I couldn't really see myself putting on musicals with the fifth grade somewhere."

"Not real thrilling," he agreed.

"Right. But anyway, I drew this music major as my roommate, and it was a good match except that she was always wanting to drag me to this concert or that club." In spite of herself, Ellie was drawn back to that night. "I went to school in New York State, and it was cold, which I had a very hard time getting used to, and I'd flunked a math exam and was homesick and didn't even have a boyfriend."

He chuckled. "Nothing like eighteen."

"Exactly. So my roommate dragged me out with her and we went to see her boyfriend play. I mean, I'd heard blues before, but I wasn't really into them or anything. That night—" She broke off, remembering the pain that had gone through her when he started to play. "It was like the guitar told the history of the world, but especially my part." She shook her head. "It snagged me somewhere so deep I'd never be able to name where it was." She smiled. "You know who it was?"

His eyes glittered. "Tell me."

"Leroy Calhoun."

He tossed his head back, laughing again as he had a moment before, and his throat looked golden and vulnerable in the low light. Leroy was acknowledged to be one of the best blues guitarists in the country right now, and his style was a mournful, emotional sound that could make stones cry.

"Guess fate had plans for you," he said. "Did you change your major the next day?"

Ellie shook her head. "It took me another semester to figure out what to do, and I ended up changing schools so I could study music from an academic point of view. And even then, it was another couple of years before I figured out what I wanted to do—which was study the lives of musicians, write about them, for all the people like me who love music but can't do it."

"Like me."

Guiltily, she realized she hadn't given much thought to Mabel tonight, and looked around her, trying to imagine what it had been like in those days. Something looked familiar. "I have a picture of Mabel at about sixteen, in a club. Is this the one?"

"Yeah. Like Marcus said, she and Doc were good friends. He's probably the one who got her in."

Ellie put her hand on the table and wondered if it might once have felt Mabel's hand, thinking of the girl in the picture, so full of sass. "What could have happened?" she mused aloud. "I just don't understand how she could have made it to the very threshold of everything she'd ever wanted—and then just walked away."

"You haven't found anything in the letters?"

"Oh, I've found a lot of great detail about her life that I didn't have before, and I'm getting a fuller sense of her personality—but that's what's odd. Her attitude in the letters is exactly what I expected. She wasn't about to let anybody or anything get in her way, but it wasn't a hard-edged thing. She really had a sense of humor about everything."

"I really think somebody killed her."

"Maybe. But it seems like kind of a hard murder to cover up."

An edge of his jaw hardened. "Not in those days. Not a black woman. She could have disappeared anywhere, anytime in half a dozen states and nobody would even have blinked."

Ellie shook her head. "No. Not Mabel. By that time, she was becoming very well known, and she was especially beloved in the black communities she visited." She raised her eyebrows. "Not to mention, she didn't make a move without some gallant helping her do it. Men adored her."

"Maybe she ran off with some man, then."

"I don't think so, somehow. There's not really any evidence to show she loved any of those guys in return. Not a single name comes up in her letters more than once or twice." She turned her glass, puzzling over it. "My gut says she walked away. That it was her choice."

"But why?"

"That's the twenty-thousand-dollar question. I can't find *anything*. There had to be something, some trauma or secret or bad love affair. Something, you know? But I've documented all but about six weeks of her entire life, and there doesn't seem to be anything out of place."

Marcus sat down. "Those women can talk, man!"

Blue said, "When is the six-week gap?"

"In mid-fifty-two, a few months before she disappeared."

"That seems significant."

"Talking about Mabel's disappearance?" Marcus asked.

Ellie nodded. "Do you have any theories?"

"Marcus always has a theory."

"As it happens, I do," Marcus said, undaunted. "Think about it. When a man loses it, the thing that sends him over the edge usually has to do with pride or honor or some blow to his manhood. All those people jumping out windows when the stock market crashed, or when it comes out they've been wearing women's underwear for years."

Blue said, "What about over a woman?"

Marcus shook his head. "Nah." At the same moment, Ellie said, "No, a man tends to kill his woman."

"Right," Marcus said. "A man gets dramatic. But a woman, now—a woman punishes herself out of guilt of some kind, or love. I can't see that Mabel had anything to feel guilty about, so it almost had to be love."

Intrigued, Ellie leaned forward. "You think she was punishing herself?"

"What else?"

"You don't buy the theory that she might have been murdered, her body dumped and never found?"

"Nope. She walked around with a thirty-eight in her handbag, and she'd been all over the country for years in some very rough places. She knew how to handle herself." He gestured for a new drink. "I reckon something ate her up inside."

"I like that," Ellie said. "Maybe it was guilt *and* love—maybe there was a love triangle or something. Or she disappointed her lover so much that she caused him to do himself some harm."

"No way," Blue said. "Mabel had more men than she knew what do with. I could buy guilt on some other level, but not love. She wasn't the type."

Ellie smiled at the annoyed sound in his voice, and it occurred to her they were all talking about the long-gone blues singer as if she was a friend of theirs. She had that effect on everyone, it seemed.

Which was what made her such a good subject for a biography.

"Don't reject anything," she said. "If I've learned anything about piecing lives together, it's that nearly everyone has a weak spot, and something to hide."

Blue looked at her with an oddly serious expression. "I'll remember that," he said.

Ellie remembered the picture he had not asked her about.

"Maybe," he said, "Doc will know something."

"I hope so. Maybe I'll go back through my notes to see if there might be some possible hidden love affair, too. It makes sense in a weird way."

"I still say you're barking up the wrong tree," Blue said with a stubborn grin. "But it's your time to waste." He motioned to the waitress to bring them another round. "And I'm going to change the subject, since I don't want to get into an argument with a beautiful woman."

Ellie smiled. "Good idea."

"How's the memorial coming along, Marcus?"

"It looks like we're gonna make the Fourth of July ceremony. Slabs were delivered last week, concrete is poured, and they got the pavement up to build the park." His face showed a weary expression. "Maybe once it's done, things'll settle down around here. Connie Ewing gives me a dirty look every time I see her." He shook his head. "I really thought people would be glad, especially somebody like Connie. I wanted her to talk at the memorial, and she turned me down flat."

"Speaking of Connie," Blue said, "we saw some pictures at Rosemary's of a bunch of you having a picnic somewhere."

Ellie went still. She didn't even look at Blue for fear she'd give herself away, but she was grateful to him for bringing it up, for sensing that she needed answers that were found in those photos, and being kind enough not to press her to tell him. Under the table, she touched his leg and he put his hand on hers in acknowledgment. When she started to move away, he pressed her hand down on his thigh and kept it there.

"A picnic?" Marcus echoed, frowning. "Who was there?"

"You and James and Connie, Rosemary." He paused. "Annie, when she was about six." He glanced at Ellie. "You remember who else was in the pictures?"

Oh, he was clever. By forcing her to recount the ones she remembered, he would have a clearer idea of which ones interested her. "None of the names." She lied without a twinge of conscience. For a split second, she wondered what order to put the faces in, to conceal which ones mattered to her, then just blurted them out the way they came to her. "A guy with a goatee, a cowboy-looking kid, a woman who looked like a hippie, another black woman . . ." She shrugged, as if it didn't matter. "That's all I remember."

Marcus looked stricken. "That was the day before we left." Instantly, he looked twenty years older, his face drawing in, his mouth sober and sad. "Damn. I'd really like to see those pictures." As if remembering where he was, he lifted his head. "But it just breaks my heart all over again." With a smile that was both rueful and sad, he said to Ellie, "My best friend and I joined up on the buddy system. I came back and he didn't. Guess I never have got over missing him."

Under the table, Blue stroked her hand. "You never talk about him, you know."

"Don't I? Humph." A half shrug. "Knew him from the day I was born, just about. His grandma raised him, and she was meaner than a mad dog, so he camped out with me all the time."

"You loved him," Ellie said impulsively.

Marcus raised his head. "I did. But you know what? So did everybody else. He was one of the most genuinely good people I've ever known. And charming. He could have been president with all that charm." He seemed to drift a moment, thinking, then made a dismissive sound. "Water under the bridge now, I guess."

Blue said. "Why is Connie so mad? And why would you want her to talk, anyway? Her husband died of cancer, didn't he?"

"It's not about her husband." His mouth tilted on one side as he remembered. "You shoulda seen Connie in those days. Lord have mercy. She was built like"—he halted with a wry glance at Ellie—"a goddess and had this saucy little way and everybody for a hundred miles wanted her bad. But she'd been going with Bobby since they were twelve, and she didn't give anybody else the time of day."

"Which one was he?" Blue asked.

Ellie knew. The rusty-haired boy with the guitar and goatee. Bobby Makepeace. She worried silently that he might end up being her father. Or might not.

"Why did everyone join the Army?" she asked, then realized how it sounded. "I'm sorry. I didn't mean it like that. But when we were looking at that picture and half the boys in it were dead, it broke my heart." Delicately, she slid her hand from Blue's leg, and he let her go. "It seems like such a waste now."

"It was a waste, Ellie," Marcus said. "The only two in that picture that made it home were me and Binkle, the asshole."

Blue laughed. "Binkle, in case you're wondering, is a smarmy engineer who spent the whole war in Okinawa and now wants to be Mr. Patriotic and get misty-eyed over the whole thing."

The band was reassembling, and Alisha sat down. "Oh, let's not talk about the memorial tonight, please?"

Marcus picked up her hand and kissed it. "We're done now." To the others, he remarked, "Alisha's suffered through enough of it, trust me."

The band made noises and launched into sexy cover of "Mockingbird." Ellie closed her eyes. "I love this song."

"Me, too," Blue said. "Come on and dance with me."

She thought of all the reasons she wanted to. How good it would feel to be held, to feel his body against hers. She imagined what it would be like, swaying in the circle of his arms. With as much honesty as she could muster, she met his gaze. "No, thank you," she said quietly, and added an ego balm. "I'm not the greatest dancer."

He nodded. "Another time."

On the way home, Blue was quiet, and Ellie, dazzled and tired and maybe a little melancholy, simply let the wind blow her hair as she gazed out the window, smelling river and cow dung and pine. Again, the depth of the darkness struck her as they wound the tiny road back to his property. They didn't pass a single car, but then it was late, almost two.

He drove to the cottage and turned off the car. Into the silence came the whistling of a million crickets.

Ellie roused herself. "Thanks, Blue. I really had a great time."

"Let me get your door."

Before she could protest, he was out and walking around, so she gathered the shoes she'd slipped off, and waited for him to swing open the door. He put down a hand for her to grab. "Oh, I do love a gentleman," she teased.

He smiled, very faintly, but said nothing.

She gripped her shoes to her chest. "Is something wrong, Blue?"

A half beat more of silence, then, "Nothing a good sandwich wouldn't cure. You hungry? I could fix us some BLTs."

"Hmmm." Truth was, she was always hungry, and even more so after the long night after only a salad for dinner. She inclined her head. He had not made an untoward advance to her all night. She thought she could trust him, and there was something . . . lonely about him now. "As it happens, BLTs are my very favorite sandwich."

"Really? Is that a yes?"

His surprise and pleasure touched her. She nodded. "Will you wait a minute and let me change my clothes?"

"Sure."

It only took a few minutes to shimmy out of the dress and stockings—heaving a sigh of relief—and toss on a clean pair of shorts and a tank top. April sat in the middle of the living room when she came out of the bathroom, waving her tail hopefully. Blue stood over the desk, the picture of the group at their picnic in his hand. He put it down when he saw her, and Ellie expected a question, but he just said, "You ready?"

"Yes. Can April come?"

He grinned. "Sure."

It was the first time she'd been inside the house, Ellie realized, and it was a far more appealing place than she would have expected. Blue insisted she sit down at the table while he hustled up their sandwiches, and in her pleasantly inebriated state, she admired the cleanliness of the room with its painted-ivy border and white eyelet curtains. It was a cheerful room with a long line of windows down one side, but not quite the tastes she would have expected from Blue, who—by the way he moved—didn't mind spending time in the kitchen.

It was easy to admire him, too, tall and lean in his jeans and white shirt, his hair a little tousled and showing gold streaks from his outdoor work. There was, as far as she could see, not a single thing wrong with the way he looked. "You know," she said lazily, "you probably would have won that cover boy contest."

He shot her a devilish expression. "I'm real pleased to know you think so, Miz Connor. A man would be hard put to know what you thought about anything at all unless you told him."

That drawling, rich-boy bourbon voice pooled in her belly, but she tucked a foot up under her and lifted one shoulder with as much ennui as she could express. "You don't need me to tell you how gorgeous you are. I have a feeling every female in the world has been telling you since you were old enough to walk."

He chuckled, and added sliced tomatoes to the sandwiches he was building on toast. "Miracle Whip okay? Lanie won't buy mayonnaise, never has."

"Fine. Lanie is your aunt, right?"

"Actually, she's my great-aunt. My mother had an apartment built for her, in the basement so she could have some real sense of privacy, years ago when she lost her husband. She's pretty much looked after me for all my life."

"She took care of you when your parents died."

A nod. "Yeah. There was a night nurse, but Lanie was pretty much the one. When I went to college, she went to live in town, but after I got back from college, she came back here." He put the plates of sandwiches down on the table along with a jug of cold, sweet tea he poured into tall glasses of ice.

Her stomach growled in anticipation and she shot Blue a grin. "Looks great."

"Well, dig in, sugar. I'll wait for you like one hog waits for another."

It was a singularly pleasant meal. A breeze came in through the windows, cool as it would be for the next twenty-four hours, and the quiet eased her tense nerves. She liked the way he tossed tidbits to the dogs, Sasha and April, who both waited with ears alert and paws politely stretched before them, like matching statues, for those bread crusts. "Watch this," he said, and tossed a piece of tomato to Sasha, who caught it in midair, then settled and let it fall off her tongue to the floor. He laughed.

"That's mean," Ellie said, but she laughed anyway, and when April eased over to lick the tomato and slurp it up herself, she laughed even more. "The only thing she won't eat is potatoes. Not even French fries." To make up for the icky vegetable, Ellie tossed Sasha a tidbit of bacon.

As if she'd heard the food in the other animals' mouths, Piwacket raced into the kitchen, howling expectantly. Ellie started to pinch a tiny bit of bacon from her sandwich, then remembered. "She can't have even a tiny bite?"

Pi hustled over to Ellie's feet and meowed, then lifted on her back paws.

Blue looked torn. "It's really bad for her."

Ellie gave him an exaggerated frown. "Oh, just a teeny, teeny bit? Look at her! She's starving for it."

"I know how to please her." He rubbed the bacon along a corner of bread and put the bread down. She rushed over, gulped it down, and looked up expectantly. He chuckled. "See? Doesn't hurt her a bit."

"Okay. I didn't mean to intrude." Replete, she leaned back. "That was excellent, Blue. Thank you." Remembering something else, she said, "And thank you for leading the conversation with Marcus."

"Did you learn anything?"

"Yes." For a moment, she wondered if it might be okay to just tell Blue about her search for her father. He'd probably be able to help her. "Or maybe. I don't know."

He looked at her, patiently. The veneer of polish he'd put on earlier had worn off in the heat of the club and the long hours, and although he wasn't one tiny bit less beautiful, Ellie realized that it was a face she liked and trusted. "It's a silly little quest, that's all."

"Who's the woman in the picture? That hippie?"

Ellie let go of a breath and confessed. "My mother. But I'd appreciate it if you didn't broadcast that around. I'm sort of embarrassed by my need to find out about her."

"I won't say a word." To her surprise, he reached across the table and took her hand in both of his. "I bet your hands hurt a lot, with all the computer stuff you do." He rubbed a strong brown thumb over her knuckles with strong, decisive movements, and it felt so good Ellie heard herself half groan.

"Keep that up and I'm your slave for life," she said.

"I aim to please." He lifted his head, that astonishing deep blue of his eyes glinting, though he didn't smile. A lock of hair fell on his forehead and he didn't brush it away, just kept up the narcotically wonderful hand massage, rubbing away tiny pockets of weariness in her wrists and the heel of her palm, and all of her fingers, one by one. "Tell me about your mama."

Ellie didn't want to talk. She wanted to close her eyes and melt against him, close where she could smell that exotic odor that clung to his hair, and close to his buttery voice, and close to his mouth. He reached for her other hand and she gladly let him have it. "She was troubled," Ellie said. "A runaway—not because of a fight or anything like that. She was just restless, I guess, and somehow or another, she ended up here the summer before I was born."

His hands stilled for a minute. "Do you know who your father is?"

Ellie shook her head.

He went back to it, rubbing her fingers, his eyes on the horizon. "So you think it might be somebody there that day. At the picnic."

"Right." A little anxiously, she put her free hand over his, over hers. "Blue, I'm really kind of embarrassed about this, and I don't want people feeling sorry for me, and I really want the option of not revealing myself if it'll cause problems for anybody. Okay?"

He was close, and Ellie didn't know how bad she wanted him to kiss her until he did it, simply bent that much closer and put his beautiful mouth on hers with a soft, low sound. She didn't close her eyes at first, and it was the curve of black lashes against the bone in his cheek that she saw, close up and blurry, before the taste and smell of him surrounded her like the first threads of a soft, bluesy guitar starting a song.

His mouth. Full and skilled and right, somehow, and not too aggressive, because he pulled back fairly quickly and looked at her, those vivid eyes very sober. "I won't tell, Ellie. I promise."

But just then, she didn't care. She put a hand on that lean jaw. And he kissed her again, as if sealing it, and she didn't just let him. She kissed him back, stroking his jaw, his ear, his thick hair, feeling the curve of his skull and the warmth of his skin. He smelled of whiskey and the faint sweat of a long night. His skin would be salty.

But mostly, she was alive only at her mouth. It

went deep, that kiss, deeper even than Ellie had had the sense to expect. It was less a roar than a song that danced through her, igniting the nerves along the bridge of her nose and in her throat and the arches of her feet. She felt the exact second it ignited him, too. He tilted his head, and his fingers closed tightly around her head, and he made a soft, lost noise before he deepened it more, before he was kissing her with an almost savage edge. She wanted to bite him but settled for letting him pull her off the chair into the space he made between his legs. Distantly, she felt the slight sting of hitting the linoleum with her knee, but then there was only Blue's arms around her, and his chest and his legs and his mouth.

They kissed and kissed and kissed, their bodies pressed close, their mouths and tongues the only point of expression, kissed until Ellie thought she was going to faint from it, kissed until she felt even his body trembling.

When he slowed and pulled away, it took some time, as if they had to climb up from a deep canyon. When they reached level ground again, neither of them let go. Blue's hands slid down to link behind her neck, and he pressed his forehead against hers. He let go of his breath, and Ellie closed her eyes in her dizziness, holding on to his arms without thought, feeling the echoes of that kiss still rippling in her elbows and chest.

Even then, he didn't say anything, just raised his head and looked at her. Ellie felt his subtle trembling, felt her own faintness as she looked up at him.

"I guess you'd better go now," he said finally.

Ellie nodded. She hesitated, then touched the arch of cheekbone under his left eye with the very tips of her fingers. His skin was hot, a little flushed.

She pulled her hair off her face, and he helped her stand up. For a long, dangerous second, she wavered and felt him wavering, too.

Firmly, she stepped back. "Good night."

He swallowed. Put his hands in his pockets. Nodded. "Night."

10

Naturally, Blue couldn't sleep. After a half hour of trying, he got up, and instead of heading down to the porch, he carried a telescope up the stairs to the widow's walk.

The telescope was a good one, a present from his father, who had shown with that single gesture that he understood his son's questing need for knowledge. Over the years, Blue had sometimes considered getting a better one, but it wasn't like he was an expert on astronomy. It was just a hobby, and this scope was plenty for his needs.

From the roof, he could see over the treetops. The cottage crouched at the edge of the woods, and he thought of Ellie inside, asleep. He wondered what she slept in, and although he wanted to imagine her in some filmy negligee, he'd bet an oversized T-shirt was a lot more likely. Or some sensible cotton thing. Yeah. One of those sleeveless things with some little styling gewgaw on the straps, little cotton roses or something.

He stared at the little house, and imagined her lying on her back, a single strap falling down her arm, her black curls scattered around her sleeping face. He imagined himself coming into that darkness and settling on the bed beside her, and kissing the line of her neck, down to her shoulder. Imagined himself taking that covering off and putting his hand around her breast.

He took a breath, blew it out, rolled his shoulders a little, trying to dislodge the vision.

Man. What a kiss.

Sasha padded up the steps to join him, and Blue told himself to stop thinking about Ellie. He bent over the telescope, focusing on what looked like a smear of stars to the naked eye. Through the lens, they were sharp and crisp, a diamond cluster of seven. Unimaginably distant. He stared at them and felt the strain of daily life ease away as he imagined planets lit by a trio of suns. He wondered what it would be like to live on a planet with seven suns.

Straightening, he looked again at the dark sky. So far away. The universe was so huge it made him think that nothing was very important. He wondered if there was some baby being born right now that might one day be on a ship to those far-flung worlds. He wondered if they'd have time to send reports of what they'd found before he died.

Probably not. Maybe not even before his great-grandchildren died, though before he got to the great-grandkids, he needed to get to plain old children. It had been a great disappointment to him that he and Annie had had so much trouble conceiving. In the end, he'd given it up because it caused her so much pain. They'd only hesitantly begun to discuss adoption when she was killed.

Stealing back into his mind came the feel of Ellie, fitting just right into his arms. Kissing her had been almost like looking at the stars, a sense of quiet that settled him.

He looked back at the cottage. What would it hurt to just wander on down there, and knock on her door and let her open her arms and her bed? What would it hurt to lie next to her in the dark and breathe with her and sleep?

But he knew the answer. It might hurt her. It probably would. And he did have some standards. No, much as he wanted her, he'd have to just let it stand as it was.

With a shudder, he suddenly heard the course of his thoughts, from Ellie to the stars to children and back to Ellie.

Ellie. He looked down to the cottage and rubbed his chest.

Damn.

Marcus Williams was an early riser. He had been brought up on a farm in the farthest stretches of the county, and had learned to awaken before the cock crowed in time to do his chores before the school bus came and took him to the newly integrated Washington High School. His job had been to feed and water the chickens and get the eggs for breakfast.

As a young man, his habits had garnered him

plenty of ribbing from a more sophisticated high school crowd, but he'd managed basic training better than almost anyone had. Now, as he approached fifty, he found it a liability once again.

This soft early summer morning, he came awake to the sound of blackbirds in the trees beyond his window, their song melancholy in the faint gray before dawn. On a neighboring property, a cock crowed, and the sound penetrated the dreams of his wife, sleeping beside him. She stirred faintly, her ankle drifting over his calf as she stirred, breathed out heavily, and settled again into her deep nest of pillows.

Her skin was warm and soft against his, and he shifted to brush her long back with the tips of his fingers. She might wake up, or at least turn sleepily toward him, and they would make love in the slow and comfortable way of the happily married. Afterward, Marcus could get up and shower and make his breakfast, leaving the house long before she or the children stirred.

But this morning, she did not move, even when he brushed her nape and slid his open palm over the sleek dip of her spine. The children had been a handful the past few weeks, with colds and coughs and the crankiness that went with them. Marcus smoothed a handful of tiny braids back from her face, smiling over the sweetness of her sleep-slack mouth, and gave her temple a whispering kiss.

He got up and fixed his breakfast, turning the television in the corner to the morning news, listening to stories of hurricanes and strikes and faraway wars as he scrambled his eggs. A sober brunette delivered the news of a car bomb in Israel, and the storm expert came on to warn gleefully of the proper conditions for a series of tornadoes across the Midwest.

Through it all, through touching the warm skin of his wife, and while he smelled the savory ham Alisha nagged him not to eat, and while he shook his head over the bombing, was James.

It sometimes bewildered him, the way James came into his heart, into his mind this way, even after thirty years. The way his face would be as plain, the grief as sudden and piercing and fresh, as if it had all happened yesterday. This morning, he knew it was because they'd talked about him at the club last night and talked about the waste of the war.

Settling in with his plate and a cup of hot, fresh coffee, Marcus gave his attention to the news and thought about James in that nostalgic, happy way that sometimes came on him so early. Even so many years after, he could see the nappy head bristling with grass after a wrestling match. Hear the low softness of a chuckle as he acknowledged defeat or told a bad joke, as if he just naturally expected listeners to laugh along with him. Which they did.

After breakfast, Marcus walked, as was his habit, down the country roads to the center of town, where the new raw shape of the memorial was emerging. He'd fought long and hard for it, collecting details, comparing the service of Stonewall County vets to the rest of the country, appealing to patriotic hearts on the city council, focusing most of his efforts on a WWII airman and Binkle with his guilt. It worked, finally, and Binkle had cast the deciding vote. Marcus guessed that had earned the man a little respect.

It was nearly full day now, the sun peeking over the eastern forest in hazy arrowings of light that stabbed the still-raw ground where slabs of carved granite lay. There were three panels, to be fitted together when they were erected, and Marcus felt a pang as he bent to press the pads of his fingers to the triangular carving of names. James's was among them.

This morning, with a soft wind blowing over his face, it was easy to remember being ten, and fishing on the bank of the Cotton River. James had been raised by his grandmother, a woman as black and unyielding as a cast-iron skillet, and he ran to the freer world of Marcus's life—where there was a mother smelling of Tabu when she could afford it, and a bosomy grandmother who liked singing, and a daddy who took them fishing in the early mornings, and a score of children sleeping hurry-scurry in piles of cots and bunks and the odd double bed, sometimes four deep. No one minded one more child.

Marcus had four brothers and two sisters of his own, and had been raised with a changing array of cousins from his mother's large family. They came to stay on the farm for a month or a season or even for years unending, for a variety of reasons—a troubled marriage, or a job that forced a single parent to work late shifts, or a bit of trouble the child found in cities not as kind to black children as the country.

But from the first, James had been different. Special. Long before he met him, Marcus had felt sorry for the boy he glimpsed at the market or at church, his mouth turned down as his forbidding grandmother pushed or pulled or nagged him along to her bidding. To Marcus, it seemed plain the woman hated him, and he felt sad for any boy who didn't have someone to hug him regular. He couldn't see that prickly crow ever wrapping her arms around that boy.

He knew better now, of course. In her way, Hattie Gordon had loved her grandchild and wanted to spare him the same fate as his father.

Marcus no longer remembered why his mother had begun keeping James on a regular basis. The Crow had probably found work and James needed looking after. In those days, a neighbor had been a logical choice.

And from the first, when they were both five, James and Marcus had been inseparable. They chased crawdads at the river, and lay on the ground in sleeping bags, slapping mosquitoes, staring at the stars. They climbed trees and had pirate adventures in the forest. As they grew older, they talked about girls with a special code, and even when James, with his charisma and golden eyes and pale ocher skin, had proved to be the more popular of the two, Marcus never minded.

In all his life, he'd never known as unsullied a love as he'd known for James Gordon. He also knew, with the certainty of knowing he had a right hand or a big left toe, that James had felt the same way.

On this cool golden morning, having left his wife and his children asleep in the house they shared, Marcus touched the big letter J carved into black granite and felt a sorrow he would never reconcile. He lifted his head, seeing the slope of roofs covering the sleeping windows of the town. He was not alone in his lingering grief for someone lost to that faraway jungle. There was Connie Ewing, and Rosemary, and Blue.

Blue. On clear days, when he was really thinking, Marcus knew one reason he'd found friendship with a white man almost fifteen years his junior was his resemblance to James. Not color or age or background, but a certain blaze in the smile, a note in his laughter. Even the doomed look of his mouth sometimes of a summer twilight, and the lure he held for women.

Standing, he jingled his keys loosely in his fingers and let a small, quiet sense of pride move in him. Because Marcus had not forgotten, because he had worked to make it so, the memorial had come to fruition. Maybe, he thought, whistling as he headed to work, he'd think about getting something erected to remember Mabel Beauvais next. A room or two in one of her old houses, or a retrospective in photos for the library. Rosemary would be more than willing to help, he was sure—and with Ellie's biography coming out next year, it might be a sweet little tourist draw.

He laughed at himself. *Memorials Are Us. We remember so you don't have to.*

Ellie slept like the dead, and only awakened when April put her muzzle on the bed and whined right in her face, urgently. Groggy, Ellie opened one eye, felt the slight edge of headache at the base of her skull, and pulled the pillow over her head. April put her paws on the bed and slid her nose under the edge of the pillow, whining softly again. Ellie stuck out a hand and rubbed her ears, but the dog snuffled deeper, insistent.

"Okay, okay." With a sigh, Ellie got up and tugged her nightshirt down, then padded to the door and let April out to run. It was dark out, the sky hung with low clouds, the air thick with impending rain, and she glanced at the clock. Nearly noon. Amazing she'd slept so long.

Blue.

The single word whispered through her as she washed her face and started the coffeemaker. She leaned sleepily on the counter, her feet bare, her hair unbrushed, her shoulders weary with the long week.

Blue. Memories danced through her sleep-softened mind—his hair, his hands, his eyelashes, his laugh. And a wordless, sensory wash of mouth-tongue-hands-hair, something richer than the sum of its parts, that moved along her spine, across her scalp, in her thighs.

Blue.

Outside, it began to rain, just a few drips at first, plopping onto the roof of the porch and the dry ground, then more and more, very quickly, until the little cabin was awash with the steady, soothing sound. A sharp, urgent bark sounded from the porch and Ellie chuckled, going to the door to let April in. April hated to get wet.

But with the dog was the man. Ellie, still sleep-muffled, blinked at him for a long moment before she realized she was standing there in her nightshirt, an old Henley printed with cats. It covered her to her knees, sort of, but the fabric was ancient and she was suddenly acutely aware of her skin below it, of her nipples and the line of her underwear across her bottom. She had not brushed her hair.

And he did nothing to ease the situation, only stood there with the rain pouring down behind him, looking like the cover of an album, maybe something smoky and Southern, Allman Brothers with soul, in a pair of jeans and a simple white tank top and his hair loose on his shoulders and his jaw not yet shaved.

She didn't know whether to cross her arms to cover her breasts or smooth her hair back from her face, and without coffee, decisions came slowly, so she did neither, then tried to do both at once, touching the madness of her hair.

"I'm not dressed for visitors," she said finally. "Come back when I've had coffee and maybe I'll have a coherent word."

He didn't take the hint. Instead, he pulled open the screen door to let April in, and stepped inside himself. "You look just like I thought you might look in the mornings," he said, and his voice wasn't the teasing ladies' man tone, but something warmer, deeper. Hungrier.

A jolt of pure lust went through her, and she was more aware of her breasts than ever, but aware now in a good way, in a way that wanted those long-fingered hands on her. The yearning and her disappointment in herself came together, and she moved away, turning, pushing her hands across her forehead, catching her hair back at the nape of her neck. She held it there, out of her face, and felt more in control. "You want some coffee?"

"No, thanks. I want you to see something. Get dressed and I'll fix your coffee for you."

"It's raining."

His eyes glittered. "Yes, it is."

There was something thicker now between them. That kiss. She couldn't help thinking of it when she looked at him, and knew it must be in his head, too, and there was a part of her that wondered why they didn't just get on with it, because it was now perfectly obvious they were going to have sex. Now or later.

His jeweled eyes touched her breasts, her legs. He tucked his hands in his back pockets and inclined his head toward the bedroom. "Go on. Get dressed."

So she did and came back in a pair of jeans and the first T-shirt she'd been able to find, an oversized memento of a trip to Mexico last year. And a bra. Armor.

He was stirring sugar into a cup as she came out catching her hair into a ponytail with a scrunchie. It occurred to her as he put the big mug in her hand that, not counting seduction steaks and bottles of wine, she didn't think a man had ever prepared food for her. Certainly none of them ever fixed her coffee. "Thanks."

A soft smile. "Bit slow this morning?"

Ellie nearly denied it, but found herself smiling ruefully instead. "I guess I am. How do you do it?"

He winked. "Lots of practice. Besides, I let you do

my drinking for me last night. Didn't have but three bourbons myself."

"Mmmm." Ellie drank. "I didn't count."

"You ready?"

"For what? Do we really have to go out in the rain?"

"Trust me, you'll be glad. There's an umbrella in here somewhere. You can use that." He opened a closet and took it out. "Come on. You'll like this."

"All right."

And really, the air was lovely outside. Cool and gray and richly scented. Blue held the umbrella up over their heads and made small talk. He led them to the greenhouse. Even through the rain, Ellie saw the splashes of color against the walls, and she remembered something he'd said about orchids. Did she really, in her slightly off-center state, want to go in there with this man? She stopped. "What are you going to show me?"

A knowing shine lit his eyes. "You scared, little girl?"

"Maybe." Rain dampened his shoulders, made his arms slick, which made her think of licking him, which made her take a gulp of coffee. It scalded her throat. Better. "Wary is a better word."

He looked like he might kiss her, but something else came into his face and he only smiled, very softly. "You'll like this. I promise."

"Okay."

He led her to the door and pulled it open, stepping back into the rain so she had the protection of the umbrella. Ellie ducked her head and ran inside.

The smell struck her first—an unearthly, beautiful fragrance, exotic and deliriously sexy. Flowers, but not anything as simple or ordinary as roses or lilacs or even lavender; this was exotic, like rare perfume. In pure reflex, she breathed it deep, nearly tasting it, and found below the rich main note of flowers the earthiness of damp soil and the somehow soothing scent of water.

The smell of Blue's hair.

Then she registered what she saw. "Oh, my God!" she whispered, coffee held up but forgotten as her eyes lifted, higher and higher.

It was not like any greenhouse she'd ever seen. The light this morning was dim with the rain streaking the glass overhead in the giant, long room. Everywhere there were flowers, in a painter's frenzy of colors—white and yellow, red and hot pink, blue and purple and even green. Striped and spotted and fringed. They climbed the walls and bloomed from branches of trees, and clung to what appeared to be the enormous trunks of rain forest–sized trees covered with some kind of bark. "Are these all orchids?" she asked, and her voice was hushed with awe.

"Not all of them. A lot of them are." There was a kind of wonder on his face. "Cool, huh?" He took her hand. "But this isn't it, what I wanted to show you. Come on."

He led her down a graveled path, and she saw he'd kicked off his shoes at the door and now padded barefoot through the wonderland he had created. It was a dense, green world, with hidden treasures—Ellie glimpsed small pools and waterfalls, both small and large. Something flashed, then moved, and Ellie shied away with a little screech as a bird flapped out of its hiding place and landed on the path. "Birds?"

"Yep. They're rescues, mainly. Tropical birds taken out of the forest and sold to tourists who then don't know what to do with them. This guy is a flashy starling, basically."

Drawn by the commotion, another bird waddled out—a white pigeon with a bright red stain on its chest, as if an arrow had pierced it. Despite its exotic look, it waddled with the same aggressive stance as any city pigeon, and cooed loudly. "I guess Piwacket isn't allowed in here," Ellie said, laughing.

"Oh, no." He laughed with her, and drew her on, and now Ellie was genuinely curious. What could be better than just the greenhouse itself?

He ducked under a woven stretch of live plants and straightened, pulling Ellie behind him. "Ta-da!" He gestured with an open palm.

"Oh!" she cried. Looking up into the crotch of a "tree", Ellie saw the biggest, showiest flower she'd ever seen in her life. It was red, and at least fourteen inches across, with a showy lip in a paler shade. It bloomed in exuberance at the end of a long, thick stem. The leaves were plain, even ugly, but that flower was an astonishment. "It's amazing, Blue!"

"Told you." He grinned proudly, admiring the flower himself. "I've known she was going to bloom for several days, and this morning—boom. There she was."

"Incredible." Ellie turned in a slow circle, looking

at everything. The pools and waterfalls and trees and vines and flowers and leaves and birds, flashing in and out and making crying noises, and the rain pounding on the roof. A sudden welt of tears rose in her eyes, ridiculous and overwhelming. PMS, she told herself. "It's all amazing," she murmured. "How . . . ?"

"When Annie died," he said quietly, looking upward, "I couldn't sleep, couldn't eat, couldn't stand to talk to anybody. I had built this greenhouse, and Marcus and I had started some basic propagation experiments, but when Annie died, this is where I came." A sad kind of smile crossed his mouth. "It kept me going."

"Taj Mahal," Ellie said, and it made the tightness in her throat worse.

He lifted a shoulder. "Maybe."

Ellie blinked and moved to look closely at a string of flowers cascading in a graceful arch, red with white spots, and focused on something unemotional. "Do you export them or sell them or what? Why so many?"

"I don't sell them. People have been trying to convince me to, but I'm not a collector, exactly."

"What then?"

"Propagation experiments, mainly. Orchids are one of the most valued flowers in the world, and many of the most important species grow naturally in places we need to preserve—the rain forests, which are also one of the most economically distressed areas of the world." He spread his hands. "No big leap to think about using orchids to both preserve the rain forests and increase the economic base of poor countries. You follow?"

"Sure."

"The trouble is, orchids are notoriously difficult to propagate. They have millions of seeds, but everything has to be exactly right for those seeds to grow, and they have to have particular fungus to feed on, and even when you get a plant, it takes seven years to mature."

"So you must be very talented to have all of these flowers."

"Nope. They're hardy and sturdy and what they do is bloom. That's what they like. The problem is that the best method we've found so far to propagate them is by cloning, which requires a sterile lab and lots of equipment and specialized knowledge and doesn't do a lot to provide for the forests." Idly, he plucked a dry leaf from a plant nearby him, and leaned in close with a small frown. Evidently, whatever he saw reassured him. "So, what I'm doing here, basically, is reproducing the rain forest conditions as exactly as possible and trying to find organic ways to reproduce the orchids for a mass market."

"Had any success?"

His grin slayed her. Trouble, trouble, trouble. "You're looking at it."

"The big one?"

"Yes, ma'am. You know how much hotels and upscale restaurants would pay for flowers like that?"

His pride and pleasure were palpable. "Blue, that's great. I'm very happy for you."

"Enough to reward me with another kiss?"

It surprised her, coming from nowhere. But she realized it hadn't. His whole posture, his whole body language this morning said he wanted her. And, oh, God, did she want him. Especially now that she saw that his heart was made of flowers.

All the more reason to steer clear. Blue Reynard, with his music and flowers, and that smell of blossoms and earth in his hair, had the potential to make her previous broken hearts look like hangnails. "Oh, no," she said with the right note of mockery in her voice. "I'm afraid kissing a man in this environment would be much too dangerous, even for me."

He grinned. "Can't blame a man for trying."

"True."

His body relaxed. "You want the full tour?"

"Absolutely."

"All right." He took her hand. "And then maybe, a movie at my place? Lanie's home, so we'd have a chaperone."

"You've got a deal, Dr. Reynard."

11

Blue called to arrange for Ellie to meet him at noon on Monday so they could have lunch with the bartender from the Juke Box at Dorrie's Café at one.

Yesterday afternoon, they'd sprawled in a family room of his house, watching old movies on cable. Lanie, a funny, witty old woman, had sat with them, Piwacket in her lap, making risqué comments on the films. Ellie liked her. She was also grateful that the old woman had provided a distraction, for even with her presence, Ellie had been aware all day of the man sprawled across the couch or the floor or reclining in his chair. She noticed things about him she'd never noticed on another man—his cuticles, for example. His elbows, in need of a good dose of cream. His earlobes and the tops of his feet.

And he'd been every bit as aware of her. And it seemed they both found excuses to touch slightly. Sitting side by side, their knees the only contact. Handing off a snack, their hands tangled a little longer than necessary. She saw it happening, felt the fog of sexual awareness pressing down on her, and was helpless to stop it. But it was also so pleasurable in some ways that she didn't want to give it up. It had been so long and he was so different and—well, all of it.

Finally, exhausted by her week and the need to resist him, Ellie had taken her leave before dinner. Alone in the cottage with rain pouring down relentlessly, she'd read a novel and done her best to avoid thoughts of him.

This morning, the strange emotionalism was gone, and she felt like herself again. Now, on Monday morning, there was heat building over the fields as she walked the path up to the first greenhouse. Not even midday and already into the eighties. She'd piled her hair into a knot to keep it off her neck, but it never stayed, and bits clung to her damp neck and cheek.

She stopped a few yards from the door to the greenhouse, and took a breath. Flashes of those exotic, erotic flowers blinked in her memory, and she found herself remembering the taste of his mouth again. The smell of him, the feel of that kiss they'd shared in his kitchen Saturday night lingered on her nerves. It had woven itself into her dreams and made her restless, and now she couldn't think how to arrange her face. Or what to say.

"C'mon, Connor, act like a grownup, huh?" She marched the rest of the way and opened the door with firm purpose.

It was impossible to stay aloof from the splendor. She'd thought herself prepared, but the lush coolness within was so welcome she felt all the rigidness flow right down her spine and out of her toes, just like that.

And she'd thought it would be bright inside, now that the sun was out, but the vines and trees made it almost murky. She felt a draft on her ankles and wanted to take off her shoes to walk on the grasslike softness that carpeted the earth.

From amid the splendor stepped Blue, dressed for work in a white T-shirt and jeans that were sprinkled with soil. The sight of him sent a jolt through her, and a wash of memory—his mouth, that kiss—colored, not with the scarlet of desire, but somehow in shades of green and blue. Not a single word rose to her throat.

"Hi," he said quietly. His feet were bare again.

The spell broke and Ellie laughed. "I want to live in here!" She took a step, but something whizzed over her foot and she froze. "Was that a *snake?*"

"Just a little bitty lizard. I've thought about importing snakes, but they're a lot of work." He ducked under a branch and took her hand. He grinned down at her, and winked. "Lizards don't eat nearly as much."

The humidity glazed his cheekbone and his neck. His fingers slid between hers, tight. "How are you this morning, Miz Connor?" he asked. A huskiness marked the slow syllables. "Missed you after you went home last night."

"I . . . uh . . ." She couldn't remember, not with that thumb moving on her skin, not with all that skin gleaming. She frowned. "I read."

He loosened her hand. "Come on."

She followed him under the tangle of vines, along a

path laid in flagstone through the greenery, noticing that the little ponds littered the farthest corners and appeared at the bases of trees. They seemed to be networked in some way. "This must have taken a fortune to build. Did you get grants?"

He stopped and an odd expression crossed his face. "No need. I thought you knew." With a flipness that told her the subject made him uncomfortable, he said, "I got money to burn, sugar. My daddy came from real old money, and Mama was even more blue-blooded than him."

"Oh." Ellie stuck her hands in her pockets.

"Most people know. Didn't occur to me you didn't."

"It's not something you have to apologize for, Blue."

"Don't I?" He inclined his head. "It's not the blessing you'd think."

"I never thought it would be," she said honestly, and quoted, "'To whom much is given, much is required.'"

"I reckon." He glanced at his watch. "Hell, we need to get going. Let me change right quick, and I'll be ready."

"I'll wait at the house."

"No need for that. My truck is right outside. I keep some clothes in a room in here in case I get soaked."

Without further warning, he pulled off his thin shirt. He didn't pause, didn't wait for her to look, but Ellie did anyway, and a prickle went through her. His stomach was a work of art, as gleamingly hard-muscled as a picture in a magazine.

He balled up the shirt like every man on the planet, and carried it with him to a door she hadn't noticed between two tree trunks. Ellie watched him, her gaze on the dip of his spine. Her ears felt hot. "Be right back," he said, and ducked into the room.

The rat. Ellie whirled, putting her back to the door. She took a breath, trying to calm herself, but it only filled her head and lungs with the narcotic scent of flowers and earth that clung to him twenty-four hours a day. She paced and ran into a flower that looked exactly like human female genitalia. Turned again to see one that was a glorious shade of brown and copper, with a thick, brown stamen or pistil or whatever it was on an orchid. She covered her mouth and laughed.

Sex sex sex.

"What's so funny?" he said behind her.

Ellie turned and he was buttoning his shirt from the bottom up. The faintest hint of mischief danced in his eyes. She raised an eyebrow. "This is a den of iniquity, and you are the"—she struggled with a proper master for a den—"the ringleader."

He grinned lazily. "You should have let me know you had Victorian sensibilities, sugar. I'd have protected you." He fastened the last button and rolled up his right sleeve. "They didn't let Victorian women work with orchids at all, you know. They thought the women were too delicate to handle them."

"Is that right."

"It is." He finished the sleeves and stepped up. "You feeling overwhelmed yet?"

The answer was yes. The scent alone, in the air, in

his hair, was enough to arouse her, but in combination with his brilliantly blue eyes offering whatever would please her, and the temptation of that beautiful body—what woman would not be overwhelmed?

She swallowed, suddenly and deeply terrified. "Blue, let's not do this, okay? A little flirting, a couple of kisses, that's one thing, but I don't want to screw up this friendship. I like you, but I don't want to have sex with you."

"Yes, you do."

A tingling heat crossed her cheekbones. "I'm not saying I wouldn't like it. I'm sure I would. But it's just too complicated, and I'm not here for long, and—" She broke off, shrugged. "I don't want the complications in my life right now."

He touched her arm, drawing a finger from her shoulder to her elbow. "All I thought about yesterday was that kiss in my kitchen. Over and over and over."

She set her jaw, a sense of terror giving her strength. "You know what? I did the same thing. I thought about kissing you and how much I liked it, and how much I like you." A little unsteadiness crept into her voice, and she clamped her teeth together hard to control it before she went on. "I'm the kind of woman who likes to try to save a man who's drowning. And you're the kind of man who looks to a woman to hold on to. But the truth is, I'll start needing you to depend on me, and you'll hate it, and my heart will get broken, and then we'll lose what we do have."

"Is that what this is?" His voice was low, dangerous.

She met his gaze head-on. "Yeah."

He moved one step closer, his bare feet silent on the grassy ground. He brushed her cheek with his hand, and there was a perplexed expression on his mouth. "You're not my type. I like busty blondes who dress nice and don't make me think too much. That's what I was hoping you'd be like when you showed up."

"Wrong on all counts."

"Yeah," he said. "But it doesn't seem to matter. What I keep thinking about is lying down with you someplace where we wouldn't have to get up again for a long time. I can tell you I'll respect the limits you seem to need, but it would be a lie. I'm not even scared when you tell me you'd be clingy. I'm willing to take that risk." His gaze was straight and steady and almost too much to meet directly, and he lifted one hand to cup her cheek, very gently. "Maybe I'm just ready to come out from behind those walls, Ellie."

She pushed his hand away. "Maybe you are. But then again, maybe you're just bored, and I'm convenient."

"Ellie! Damn it." He frowned. "It's not like that."

"No?" He just didn't understand. "Well, it doesn't matter, because I can't sleep with you, no matter how much I'd like it—and I would. So stop teasing me and tormenting me and playing these games. Just be yourself."

"I *am*."

"Bad choice of words. Be straight with me."

A hardness she had not seen seeped into his eyes. "That I can do."

"Good." She looked at her watch. "We have to go."

• • •

The slanted parking places in front of Dorrie's Café were packed with pickup trucks and utility vehicles and anonymous white cars with various government agency designations stenciled on their sides. "Maybe this was a bad choice for lunch," Blue said, driving his truck around the block. "I should have remembered we'd have to be here early. Everybody comes here for lunch these days."

He rounded the corner again. A tall black woman with strong features was walking in the warm noon sunlight, and Ellie admired her calf muscles. Blue honked and stuck his hand out the window to wave at her. She inclined her head with a wry expression and wiggled her fingers, then shook her head.

Blue laughed. "You know you love me, sweetheart."

"Your mama!" she called back, but Ellie glimpsed the edges of a smile she tried to hide.

"That's Rosemary's youngest sister," Blue said.

"Ah. I haven't met her."

He pulled into a parking place near Rosemary's bookstore. "She works in the courthouse. We had a hell of a fight about that road out to Gwen's place a couple of years ago."

"Why?"

"Well, that's a story rooted in the sad old history of the county. After emancipation, that plot of land where Gwen lives was willed to their family by a guilt-ridden slave master who lived there."

"That would be your relative?"

He gave a nod. "It would. My triple great-grandfather, Ambrose Reynard. He was, by all accounts, a real bastard. Never met a woman he didn't seduce—white, black, free, slave, poor trash. Didn't matter. He scattered children from one end of the county to the other."

Ellie resisted making a comparison. Blue opened the door and held it for her, and he must have caught the wicked thought. "Don't say it," he said, and grinned. "Anyway, some of them got that land, but it was lost and the deeds were a mess. My daddy fixed it up with Gwen before he died."

"Is she related to Rosemary?"

"Not closely. Some kind of third cousin once removed or something like that."

"So she's related to Mabel, too?"

His mouth turned down. "I don't think so. Mabel was Rosemary's father's sister, right? This land came through their mother."

Ellie blinked. "Complicated."

"Just a normal day in the country, honey."

He held the door open for her and she ducked under his arm and into the low roar of Dorrie's. A country music song played cheerfully, adding a boisterous note to the rumbling of dozens of mostly men taking their midday meal. Two waitresses hurried among the tables, but took their time when they were actually talking to customers, stopping to make jokes and inquire after children. Ellie saw one waitress seat an older man with his buddies, and she took the salt shaker and put it in her pocket. The old man mounted a protest, but she could see he was pleased to be taken care of.

A man in a light linen suit, chewing on a toothpick, carried his bill to the counter. "Blue Reynard," he said heartily, smiling to show big white teeth. He stuck out his hand. "How you doin', man? I heard Stanford came out to look at that rain forest business of yours." Even as he spoke, his eyes strayed toward Ellie in the practiced crowd-roving of a born politician. He nodded at her.

Blue shook his hand. "How are you, Todd?" He gestured toward Ellie, shooting her a meaningful look. "Ellie, this is Todd Binkle. Todd, meet Ellie Connor, a well-known music biographer. She's here researching a book about Mabel Beauvais."

Binkle. Ellie managed to shake his hand—a stubby-fingered, but strong grip—calmly. "How are you?"

"Good to meet you." He had large eyes in a face that once had been sensual, but had grown heavy-fleshed and swarthy with middle age. His hair, cut a little long on top, showed the first silvery threads. Despite his name, he had a decidedly Mediterranean look, Greek or Italian, perhaps. "Are you here to do some research?" he asked.

"Yes."

"Is that right." His gaze was somehow compelling, the way he looked at her with what appeared to be genuine interest. In his yearbook photo, that directness had looked arrogant. In person, she found it appealingly inclusive. "You be sure and let us know when it's published, and we'll see to it that you get a lot of play around here. You think you might be able to swing back through and do a radio show one morning?"

"Todd owns the local talk station, in addition to being an alderman," Blue said. "He's always looking for ways to promote the city."

"That I am." There was no apology in the words. "If we want any say in what kind of growth is coming to Pine Bend, we can't sit back and let it happen. We have to call in what we want."

The hostess rushed over to ring up his bill. As he pulled his wallet from his inside pocket, Ellie spied a heavy gold ring set with an enormous diamond on his wedding finger. It didn't look like a wedding ring, but you never knew with men. A divorced or single man would suit her purposes better than one who was mar ried. She hated to think of upsetting someone's life with the pronouncement of, "Hey, guess what? I'm your daughter."

But with a strange sense of openness, she realized he really could be her father. And maybe it wouldn't be so bad. She smiled at him. "You're right about that, Mr. Binkle. And I'd love to come back when the book is published. Do you have a card?"

"Yes, ma'am." He gave Ellie an embossed linen business card that matched his suit. "I'll help you sell a whole bunch of books."

"Thank you." She noticed his eyes were green, like her own. "I'd be honored."

"Good to see you, Blue. Let me know what comes up with those experiments, all right?"

"Will do," Blue said. He waved at someone across the room. "Ah, there's Doc."

Binkle left and the hostess grabbed menus to seat Blue and Ellie.

"We're okay," he said to the hostess. "We're meeting Doc, over there."

"Y'all want tea or coffee?"

"Tea, please," Ellie said.

"Me, too."

"I'll bring it right over."

Quietly, Blue said, "He really is a contender, isn't he? Binkle, I mean."

Ellie raised her eyebrows. "Yeah. How weird."

He touched her arm, lightly. "It's all gonna work out just fine."

Doc stood up as they came close. "How you doin'?"

"Fine, Doc." Blue clasped his hand with easy grace. "Thanks for meeting us."

"My pleasure." As they settled in the booth, Doc said, "It's always a pleasure to talk about Mabel, you know. Not too many folks remember her anymore."

"Maybe the book will help revive interest," Ellie said.

He pursed his lips, nodded. "Tell me how I can help."

Ellie took out a steno pad she used for taking notes and glanced at the questions she'd put together yesterday. The waitress stopped by with tall glasses of iced tea and promised to be back in a few minutes to take their order. "Oh," Ellie said. "I guess I need to figure out what to eat. How are the cheeseburgers?"

"The burgers are great," Blue said, "but knowing you, it'll be the fries you want more of."

"Knowing me?"

"Yes, darlin'. Doc, you'd think she'd be a bird eater, wouldn't you? But she eats like a linebacker."

Ellie choked at the exaggeration. "Doc," she said, leaning over the table. "That is a lie."

"Good to see a woman eat," he said mildly. The benign dark eyes held a light of approval, but Ellie wondered if it was over her eating, or Blue's teasing.

"That's something you have in common with Mabel. She ate enough for three grown men and never did get even a little bit fat." With a fond smile, he leaned back. "I used to tell her she was gonna be big as a hog before she was through."

"That's exactly the kind of material I want," she said, and pulled the cap off her pen to scribble a note. "I haven't had much luck finding people who knew her well. Rosemary doesn't remember her very well."

The waitress stopped by and they ordered. Blue chuckled when Ellie ordered the cheeseburger and fries. She jabbed him with her elbow without looking at him.

Doc said, "You have any kin around here, Miz Connor? I keep thinking you look powerful familiar."

The question, coming so soon after meeting a man who might very well be her father, stopped her heart for the space of a breath. She pressed a hand to her breastbone, thinking it was the first time she'd ever known what it meant when she read, "her heart skipped a beat." Now she did. "No," she said, hoping no one caught her pause.

"Marcus said the same thing," Blue commented.

Ellie lifted a shoulder. "We all have a twin, they say." Carefully schooling her face, she looked at her notes, and made a decision. "Okay, Doc, I guess the biggest single thing I want to know is if you have any ideas about why she disappeared."

Bad move. Ellie watched as the weathered face visibly drew tight, closed. "I'm not willing to discuss that part."

He knew. The certainty prickled along the back of her neck, and tightened her stomach. But rather than alienate him, she simply nodded. "Okay, I can respect that." She put the notebook down and folded her hands on top of it. "Was she ever in love? My research shows that a lot of men loved her, but I don't see any evidence that she loved any of them back."

"We all loved her," he said, relaxing again. "She was a pretty woman, which you can tell by looking at the pictures, but it was more than that. It was like when she came into a room, you couldn't help looking at her." He shook his head, remembering. "Everybody. Old or young, black or white. Didn't matter. She just gave them that smile of hers, and they fell out."

For some reason, Ellie glanced up at Blue. He had that charisma, too. Even when he was sitting there quietly, one long leg cast out into the aisle because there wasn't enough room underneath. "I've heard that," she said, and gently restated her question. "Wasn't there anyone that caught her back?"

"There were a few she ran around with," he said gruffly. "With me, some. A fella out of New Orleans that sang. She ran with him for a long time, on and off." He twisted an empty sugar packet into a spike.

Ellie waited.

At last, Doc pursed his lips and let go of a sigh. "But there was one she really loved. Called himself Peaches." Old bitterness hardened his mouth. "Otis was his real name, and he wasn't nothing but a two-bit hustler bound for a bad end, but oh, Lordy, when Mabel got an eyeful of him, nothing would do but she had to have him."

Almost forty years had passed, but Ellie could see the name still sat like ashes on Doc's tongue. He lifted his glass and took a long swallow of tea.

"Why him, do you think?" she asked.

"I've wondered myself a thousand times. A lot of women liked him—he got over same way Mabel did. Charm like the devil's own snake, and a real snappy dresser."

"So, did he love her, too?"

"I don't know about love. They sure got together. Peaches bragged his way through half the country about Mabel Beauvais being sweet on him, though he knew better than to do it much around me. Oh, yeah, they were like a couple of minks for a while there."

Ellie scribbled as fast as she could. *Otis "Peaches" McCall*, she wrote in her spidery long hand, and commented aloud, "A man brave enough to call himself Peaches had to be pretty sure of himself."

"That was a name some woman hung on him and it

stuck. He didn't do nothing about it. Used to brag about being sweeter to eat than a Georgia peach."

Blue laughed out loud. "Bold SOB."

Doc scowled. "Maybe I shouldn't have told that to a lady. Sorry."

"Oh, no!" Ellie was still making notes, but she waved her hand eagerly. "This is great material."

"Don't go makin' it sound like she was some fast woman or something, now, because she wasn't. Till she met that fast-talking weasel, I don't know that she ever slept with another man."

Ellie nodded. Privately she thought that was doubtful, but Doc obviously needed to remember her a particular way. "My goal isn't to write an exposé," she said. "I'm just trying to find the real woman, the flesh-and-blood person who wrote all that great music."

The waitress delivered their order, still steaming. Ellie's stomach growled at the food on the heavy ceramic plate the woman set in front of her, piled with curly fries.

Blue leaned close. "How are you going to talk and eat and take notes at the same time?"

She lifted her hands and wiggled her fingers. "I'm ambidextrous," she said. She doctored the burger with ketchup and mustard, then cut it in half, salted the fries, and positioned her notebook on the table beneath her right hand. Taking up the hamburger in her left hand, she said, "So when did she meet him?"

Doc laughed, showing big teeth that were only faintly yellowed with age and tobacco. "You're something, girl, you know it?"

"Thank you."

He cut into a small steak. "They met in fifty-one, and might have gone a long time, 'cept Peaches got himself shot one night outside Hopkins'."

Ellie's nerves stilled. "Shot? When?"

He frowned, and his mouth worked. "Musta been about fifty-two. Summer, 'cause I remember it was hot."

"Who did it?"

"Never really was decided. A lot of men in that club that night had good reason to kill him. Somebody waited in the trees just outside, and shot him clean through the heart. He died before he hit the ground, and no amount of screaming by any woman could bring him back. We all figured it was Jake Horace. He'd been threatening for better than a year, and Peaches still wouldn't leave his woman alone."

"Was Mabel with him?"

He shook his head, chewing his steak. Ellie availed herself of the opportunity to eat some of her own food, and when the first fry, hot and salty and perfectly cooked, hit her tongue, she let go of a small noise of approval. "You were right," she said, offering Blue one.

He took it and grinned. "Usually am."

Doc spoke. "Mabel was out of town when it happened, but she was there by morning."

"Do you know the exact date?" Ellie said, pen poised.

He narrowed his eyes. "Must have been around July."

"Fifty-one or fifty-two?"

"Fifty-two."

Ellie looked at the facts on the page. Three months later, Mabel walked off a Dallas stage and was never seen again. She chewed on the inside of her cheek for a minute, trying to decide if she ought to pursue that angle or let it go.

Blue took the decision from her. "Hell, Doc, that wasn't but three months before she disappeared. Looks pretty cut-and-dried—grief stole her music."

Carefully, Doc put down his fork. "It might look that way, son. But with God as my witness, that wasn't the reason."

"You know, but you're not telling," Blue said.

"That's right. And more than that, I'm not ever telling."

"Can't you at least tell me why you don't want us to know?" Ellie asked. "It's the most tragic mystery I've ever come across in my career."

Even after forty years, his eyes looked dangerously misty. "It was that, all right."

"You loved her."

"I did, Miz Connor. From the time she was a little bitty girl until this very day. She deserved somebody who'd take care of her secrets. That somebody is me."

The Lovers

The night was thick as gauze and hot as bathwater; the forest dark and mysterious. It frightened her a little, but she knew where she was going.

A hand shot out and snagged her off the path, and she

cried out her surprise until his mouth came down on hers, hungry and rich, making her swallow the fear. They fell backward into the space beneath the spreading boughs of a pine tree, where a blanket had been carefully spread.

"You think of everything," she whispered.

"I missed you," he said, kissing her mouth, deep, then her face and her eyes. His hips pressed against hers.

"Me, too." She put her hands around his head, and pulled him to her, kissing him. Then she pushed him over and straddled the straining thrust of his member, pressing herself to it. "Let me show you," she said and wickedly, slowly, unbuttoned her blouse to reveal her breasts, unbound. He made a sound and reached for her as she shucked the shirt off her shoulders, arching her back to press her heat against him below and her breasts into his palms. She cried out when he sat up and hauled her close, trembled at the feel of his hands sliding down her naked back, pushing away the elastic of her skirt and her panties. She sobbed her need when he freed himself and urgently plunged, joining them. The tangle of her clothes, and the rasp of his jeans against her knees only added to the sensations, but nothing, nothing could compare to the taste of his mouth against hers, the restraint of his tongue flickering on her lips as he held himself there, deep inside her. He lifted a hand, groaning as he stayed there. "I love you." He moved and panted the words against her breasts. "I love you, I love you, I love you."

And when the edge of separation was spent and they lay panting and slick with heat and sweat, chests skidding together, he held her tight. "I can't stand this."

She buried her face in his neck and kept back her

weeping, and to stop herself from begging him not to go, she said the only other words she could summon. "I love you," she whispered. It didn't say nearly enough. They were easy words, tossed around for Cokes and shoes. They could never express the swell of light just thinking of him brought to her chest, the pained and joyful depth of it.

He lifted his head and put his hands on her face and kissed her softly, gently, slowly. "We'll find a way," he said.

She let him believe it, just as a thousand generations of women had before her. "Yes," she said. Because she loved him. Because he needed to hear it. Because it would break his heart to know the truth and have to make another choice.

Because she loved him, she would spare him.

12

Blue spent lunch in a state of restless anticipation, as half-drunk and silly with infatuation as a boy. He'd forgotten how much fun it was. Next to him in the little booth, Ellie smelled of fresh shampoo and coffee. Her thigh rested against his own in perfect innocence and temptation. As she and Doc talked, Blue watched her quicksilver expressions rush over her features. He admired the smoothness of her skin. Thought about twirling a black ringlet around his finger. Mainly, he thought a lot about kissing her.

Trouble was, she was all worried about his reputation. He frowned into his glass of tea. How'd that happen, anyway? He'd have to have a talk with some of the womenfolk around here. In the meantime, he'd just show Miss Ellie Connor he wasn't a dog at all. He was proud of himself for sticking to light drinking at the blues club, and yesterday, he hadn't been tempted to find the bottle even once. So far, nothing terrible had happened.

Outside the restaurant, strolling down the sidewalk back to his truck, he said, "So, you think Binkle might be the guy?"

That faint hesitation. "I don't know. And worse, I have no idea how to find out, without asking people who might have known my mother." She looked a little green at that thought. "I really don't want to do that yet."

He paused on the sidewalk to look at her. "You know, I'm sure all of them would be happy to help you. I'm not sure I understand why you want to keep this so quiet."

She bowed her head. Scratched at a mark on the sidewalk with her toe. "I don't know." She glanced over her shoulder and stepped close to let a woman pass. "It's complicated."

He took her arm and directed her to a quiet bench set beneath a pecan that shaded the cars. "How 'bout here?"

"Maybe I don't—" Her dark brows came down. "It's a lot easier to do this stuff on-line or something. Let me just do it that way."

Blue had never seen her so uncomfortable. Her body was poised on the edge of the bench, her purse held in her lap, her face turned away. There was some deep truth about Ellie Connor in all this. And because he was infatuated, because there was no other person on the planet he'd rather have been with in that moment, he said, "I'd like to hear it from you. On-line is okay, but it's not real life, is it?"

She scowled at him. "You're a pain in the butt, Blue Reynard, you know it?"

He laughed. "Yes, ma'am."

Lacing her fingers together, she sighed and said, "Everybody else in school always had a mom and a dad. It was a little town, nobody got divorced or anything. And there I was, living with my grandparents, and everybody knew my mother had run off and come home pregnant. It was embarrassing."

"You had nothing to do with that."

She made an annoyed sound and gave him a "get real" look. "You've lived here all your life. You know better than that."

He lifted a shoulder in concession.

"It did not *help* that my legal name is Velvet, and every year somebody would find out," she said with an air of long suffering, but he also heard amusement creeping into her voice, "and there would be a few days when everybody went around calling me Velvet Condom." She didn't quite smile, but her nostrils flared.

Blue roared.

"Oh, sure. Go ahead and laugh," she said, but she was grinning.

He forced himself to stop. Put his hand on her arm. "Velvet, huh?"

"It's even worse. Velvet Sunset. How's that for the ultimate hippie name?"

He grinned. "Poor Ellie."

"Yeah, yeah. Anyway, the teasing wasn't that big of a thing. Kids do that, and I sure wasn't the only one. But some of the mothers and teachers felt sorry for me." Her eyes narrowed. "I hated it. Like there was something wrong with me because I couldn't name my father."

She didn't look at him as she talked, and Blue saw a high peach bloom on her cheeks, not a full blush, but a heat of strong emotion anyway. And he understood her self-containment was hard won, understood how threatening it would be to have to reveal too much too fast. "All right," he said. "I get it."

"Do you?"

His smile this time wasn't all that amused. "It wasn't that different for me, Ellie. My daddy shot himself, and I lived in that big old house with my aunt, and they were all just sure I was on the fast track to hell."

"Of course." Now she did look at him, her hazely green eyes deep. Connecting. The little thread of commonality wound around them, pulling them closer, and Blue was glad of that much, anyway.

He stood. "Come on. We've both got work to do today."

As they passed Connie Ewing's shop, he saw Connie, Rosemary, and Alisha eating lunch out of paper bags. He waved.

Rosemary shouted. "Blue, come in here."

He halted on the sidewalk and grinned. "You promise I won't get infected with girl cooties?"

"I don't know," Connie drawled, eyeing him from head to toe. "I might have to tie you down and uh . . . give you a haircut."

"Bawdy wench." He grabbed Ellie and held her in front of him, as if to ward them off with one of their persuasion. "I've got my protection today, now. You can't hurt me."

Ellie shook her head, and he suspected she was

rolling her eyes in the general direction of Alisha, who grinned.

Low in her ear, so no one else could hear, he told Ellie, "You have one fine rear end, woman."

"Quit," she said briskly, and slapped him away, sliding to safety in a beautician's chair nearby Alisha.

Connie chuckled and patted the seat nearby her with a coy wiggle of her shoulders. He grinned appreciatively when she patted his leg and gave him her most predatory smile, making her eyes tilt in blue splendor. "We've been talking about you, sugar."

"Uh-oh."

"We're going to have a potluck tonight, to put together a photo display for the Fourth of July festival," Rosemary said. "First of all, I want you to get those pictures out you've been promising me for two weeks so we can get them mounted."

He winced. "Sorry. I keep forgetting." He looked to Ellie. "You think you can remind me when we get back to the house?"

She nodded in an oddly grave fashion.

"Second," Rosemary continued, "I want you to fry a big batch of that chicken and bring it over, so you can help."

He glanced at Ellie again, and her eagerness to be included was painfully visible to him. Her eyes pleaded with him silently. "All right," he said, looking at her for a long moment, then back to Rosemary. "I can do that. What time?"

"Sevenish, I guess. Maybe it'll have cooled off by then."

"I'll be there."

"You'll come, too, won't you, Ellie?"

"Sure, if I won't be in the way."

Blue couldn't resist needling her just a tiny bit. "I thought you worked in the evenings."

She blinked slowly, making him think of a cat. "I can make exceptions sometimes."

"Oh, that reminds me," Rosemary said, putting her napkin on the table. "I'll call my sister Florence right now to see if she knows where that diary might be."

"That would be wonderful," Ellie said.

In the truck a few minutes later, Blue put the key in the ignition and paused. "You owe me big, Connor."

She inclined her head. "You're right. And my debt keeps mounting, doesn't it?"

It was his moment to say he could think of ways for her to pay him back, a moment to make some light comment. But he snagged in those big, deep eyes and thought of a little girl in a rhubarb garden, pulling weeds. "Just make sure you spell my name right in the acknowledgments."

"Would that be B-L-U-E?"

"L-A-U-R-E-N-C-E," he replied, and started the truck. A bright swing tune filled the cab, and he reached to turn it up. "I love this."

"I still say it's weird you like swing so much."

He stretched his hand along the back of the seat, preparing to back out, and looked over his shoulder. A stream of cars, diverted from the memorial construction, passed the end of the tailgate. While he waited,

Blue said, "My mama loved to dance. This was her favorite, and she used to dance me all over the house."

A genuine smile of wonder bloomed on her face, and Blue thought it was one of the things he liked best about her. She loved life and everything in it. "Can you dance swing?"

"A little," he admitted, "But don't tell any guys, okay?"

She chuckled. "Cross my heart and hope to die."

His thumb lay close to the back of her neck, and a curl hung over the nape, escaped from the prison of the ponytail. He brushed her skin, lightly, musingly. Her reaction surprised him. She glanced down, a pale stain of pink on her chin and ears, and below the thin T-shirt, her nipples rose the faintest bit. Electrifying.

"Ah, Ellie, damn it." With a quick gesture, he threw the truck into gear, wrapped his hand around her neck and kissed her before she could object.

She still tried. He heard the slight, soft yelp and took it in his own throat. Thirty-six hours of thinking about touching her rushed to the nerves in his lips, and down his neck and into his buttocks as their tongues tangled. And in a split second, they were back in that place their first kisses had created, a land of their own, a place he didn't recognize but wanted to stay in. She wasn't coy with him. She opened her mouth and kissed him back with the same kind of hard, deep need he felt himself.

Breathing hard, he lifted his head. "If you really think we're gonna get out of this without falling into bed, you're not the woman I suspect you are."

She closed her eyes, which only made it worse. "I don't know what to say to that."

"Don't say anything. Maybe you should just trust me."

Her smile was soft, but maybe kind of sad. "If I did, I wouldn't be the woman I think I am."

"Touché." He let her go. Put his hands back on the steering wheel. He felt her, all through him, on his mouth and in his belly, and all the way down his spine. God, he'd forgotten how it felt to want somebody so much. "Ellie—" he began, and halted. "I'm not who they say I am."

"I'm not worried about them, Blue."

"Then what?"

She stared straight ahead. Shook her head. Finally lifted a shoulder.

He let it go.

Rosemary happened to be watching through the windows when Blue kissed Ellie in the cab of his truck. There was a sun glare right down the middle of the windshield, so she saw it happen in pieces. A conversation, then that abrupt, sudden move, and a kiss—Lord have mercy—a kiss to curl your toes.

Behind her, Connie said softly, "Like they'd eat each other up."

"What?" Alisha rushed over, peered out, and swore. "I'll kill him dead if he isn't nice to her."

Connie drawled, "Oh, I'm sure he'll be plenty nice. You won't hear her complaining any time soon."

"Connie, not everything is about sex," Alisha said

with exasperation. "I'm talking about her getting her heart broken. I already warned him once. And her, too, for that matter."

"Not everything is about sex," Connie agreed, her mouth sober as she looked out the window. "But that's what Blue Reynard is about."

Rosemary met Alisha's gaze, and for the first time, she didn't see a young, slim usurper, but a woman in her own right, with her own plans and views of the world. "I like him," Alisha said quietly. "I just don't think he's much of a catch."

"You're right," Rosemary said, and touched her arm, once, briefly. "But there isn't much you can do to stop a runaway train. And that one's gone clear off the tracks. We just have to wait for the wreck, be there to pick up the pieces."

Ellie took April for a quick walk to the river, half hoping she'd run into Mrs. Laisser. But the post-noonday sun was hot, almost oppressive. Even the river seemed as if it were running sluggishly, and of course there was no sign of anyone around. Ellie let April snuffle in the undergrowth for a while, and stood slapping mosquitoes and gnats from her sweaty skin as she thought about Binkle.

Standing there in Dorrie's Café, talking to the flesh-and-blood man who'd aged from the face in the yearbooks, had been a strange experience. She'd seen, in his dark hair and large eyes and overly full lips, ghostly images of her own features. His hair was cut short enough it was impossible to know if it curled, but the color was definitely black as Ellie's.

April lapped at the river. Ellie leaned on a tree and gazed at the feathery branches of a pine, glistening under the weight of sun and wet air. When she'd originally seen the pictures in the yearbook, she had not been able to imagine her wild mother finding anything remotely appealing about Binkle. And yet, today, in his wealth and ease of bearing, in his seemingly genuine interest in people, Ellie had been surprised to find herself reconsidering. If he'd had half that self-assurance as a youth, he had probably been quite appealing and persuasive indeed.

And the truth was, her pool of possible fathers was pretty small so far. She might be able to find out more tonight. It was entirely possible that Diane had fallen in love with someone who had been camera shy, or had been working that day. Any number of things.

Still, Binkle was a strong possibility, and she felt an odd mix of hope and trepidation.

"Get to work, Connor," she said aloud. And didn't move. Looking over her shoulder, she could just glimpse the roof of the big house, and thought of Blue with flour scattered over his forearms as he battered chicken pieces for the dinner tonight.

Just before he dropped her off, he'd taken her hand. "Do me a favor," he'd said in that deep, slow voice.

"What?"

"Don't go into that house and start thinking about me or us or anything else, all right?" His mouth was sober. "Just let it all be."

Ellie had nodded, but how did a woman put such a thing out of her head? How could anyone put Blue Reynard on full-stun out of her head? Coming across the cab, his mouth parted just enough that she could see the edges of his front teeth and the pinkness of tongue, and then that tongue was in her mouth and his hair touched her face and his finger dug into her scalp—and any reason she might have had to not kiss him just disappeared. Poof.

For three days, her nerves had been prickling at the slightest provocation—a drop of water on a wrist, or the brush of grass over the sole of her foot. Her dreams had been taut and steamy, full of images of limbs and mouths tangled.

Stop it.

The heaviness of the heat finally drove her to whistle for April, and they lazily made their way back up the track. It was almost oppressively quiet. No birds moved in the trees or called out greetings. Nothing rustled the leaves. Even the insects were still.

It took Ellie back to her childhood, to summer days that seemed to stretch for a thousand years ahead of her, long dull still afternoons spent seeking some relief, at the creek or in the deep shadows of a tree. She'd been a terribly solitary child, she thought now, and wondered if Blue had been.

As she rounded the last stand of trees before the cottage, she spied Marcus and Blue standing by the big greenhouse. Her steps slowed. By their gestures, they were discussing some problem, and Marcus took a sheet of paper Blue gave him, pulled his keys out of his pocket, and waved lazily. Blue picked up a box and carried it into the big greenhouse.

Ellie thought of the cool, soft air inside that long structure, thought of the shadows and the smell, and her feet moved of their own accord away from the stuffy cabin toward the greenhouse. Toward Blue.

As she neared the door, she heard music. She paused at the door, listening. Pachelbel's Kanon—which had to be one of the loveliest, if most overplayed, pieces of music in all of time. If she'd had any doubt about entering, those notes erased it. She opened the door and stepped over the threshold.

Inside, the sound engulfed her, poignant and sad, and so fitting to the Taj Mahal aspects of this place. She closed the door behind her and walked in a few steps, but when she didn't immediately see Blue, she stopped to absorb everything. The music swelling up, the dazzlement of pink vines overhead and the relief of the coolness within after the heat outside, and the smell of earth and blossoms in the moistness.

She stepped close to a trail of pink and white orchids of the sort found in nurseries and corsages, and tried to inhale a scent. There was none, but the flowers were beautiful anyway, and she lifted a finger to touch one of them.

Suddenly, from overhead came a soft sound, a hiss she couldn't quite recognize, and then there was water—rain—falling in a gentle mist all around her, cooling her overheated skin, dampening her hair. She lifted her face to it, laughing softly. Had she ever been in such a place?

She moved on the path, ducking under branches and low-lying trees, following the graveled path past small pools of coppery water and birds fluttering their wings in the shower, winding by orchids shaped like spiders, and like trumpets, and like strange, unearthly beings. Some were huge, some were tiny, some were beautiful, some were not.

At last she caught sight of a jeans-clad leg through a break in the denseness, and she ducked under a vine, her mouth open to speak her pleasure. In that moment, the Kanon finished, and the world was eerily silent for the space of five or six breaths. Ellie found herself poised, feeling the exact angle of her elbows and knees as she moved beneath the vine, aware of her heartbeat in her ears and the soft sound of air in her nostrils.

Bach came on the speakers, a joyous and yet mournful piece, the best of the violin concertos, at once a celebration and a moan—the mix of joy and sorrow found in every moment of every life. She stood up, tossing loose hair from her face, and saw him.

She halted, silent. For Blue stood in a sort of clearing against a backdrop of riotous orchids, his arms outstretched, his head thrown back, the shower falling silvery over his face and neck and arms, wetting his shirt and his jeans and his hair. On his face was an expression that could have been deepest sorrow or deepest joy. Or maybe reverence. It was even possible to imagine he was weeping, moved to joy by the music, as she was.

And in that instant, she knew. She knew. There was no other man on earth like him. No one with exactly this combination of joy and passion and sorrow, this mix of lost and beautiful, this heart of music and flowers.

Think, she told herself. Think what it will be like when he starts pulling away, when you find out you can't save him from himself. When you have to get in the car and drive away and go back to your old life.

But it was like trying to imagine the last day of camp on the first day. You knew it was coming, but it was a long way off, and in between was so much to anticipate that it was impossible to even consider skipping it. He was more beautiful than anything she'd ever seen, standing there amid his flowers.

As she stood there, stricken, she must have made some small noise, for he turned, and lowered his arms, and his chin. His face was wet, all those planes taking the light. He didn't smile, only looked at her soberly, his eyelashes spiky.

Then he simply reached down, crossed his arms and took the hem of his shirt in his hands, drawing it off in one smooth motion. He dropped the tangle of fabric on the floor and held out an arm to her. Her gaze caught on the line of his lean waist, then on a rib, and—

Naked. She just wanted to be naked with him. Here. Her feet moved, and she reached for the hem of her own wet T-shirt, and drew it off, and dropped it. The rain wet her face and her breasts and she felt it collecting, then dripping from her hair to her shoulders.

He took a step and captured her, his arms slid around her, wet skin skidding, sliding, and Ellie felt a buzz beneath her skin as she raised her face to look at him, at Blue, before he took her chin in his hand and kissed her roughly, with no elegance, only a thick thrusting claim, and she opened to it, just as inelegant, letting him in, following him back, sucking hard at his mouth. He made a noise and pulled her hard against him, and they rubbed together instinctively.

She put her hands around the edge of the waistband of his jeans, all the way around, feeling the elastic of his underwear, and for some reason she couldn't name, it send a wildness through her, that single detail. She wanted to rip the offending fabric from him, touch all of him with all of her, and she bit at his mouth, and put her hands around his buttocks. His hands moved, too, moved on her back, down her sides, and his mouth—oh, his mouth! He kissed and sucked and slid and devoured, every infinitesimal movement an expression of purest need.

Blue wanted *her*.

It sent a kind of violence quaking through her, and she broke away from his kiss to reach between them, water streaming down her face, and unbuttoned his jeans. He sucked in his belly to make it easier, his hands moving down her shoulders, her back, until he found the clasp of her bra and unfastened it. Ellie straightened her arms and he skimmed down, and it fell between them. She kicked it away and pulled his hands up to her breasts. The flesh of his palms was slightly rough, but his mouth, when he knelt to put it on her nipples, was silky and hot, and she closed her eyes with a sharp exhalation, tipping her head back to the shower falling over them. Her hands slid on his muscled shoulders, slid to his neck, into his hair.

He raised his head, putting his hands on her shoulders. Ellie looked down, and managed the unfastening, and started to push away the fabric, but the feeling of his eyes on her face, and his silence, unnerved her for a moment. She halted, and raised her eyes, thinking suddenly that he might not want to make love in here, that it was, after all, his Taj Mahal. "Would you rather go to the cabin?" she said.

A soft laugh. "No." His thumbs moved on her neck, and his eyes touched her lips, her hair. "I just want to look at you." His hands slid downward, took her breasts in his palms. He bent his head to kiss her collarbone, and his tongue lapped the water beaded there.

Of course he would not rush. He never rushed. And he didn't now. He took his time exploring, tasting the round of her shoulder, the breadth of her ribs, the weight of her breasts. Ellie closed her eyes and put her hands in his damp hair and let the need build.

"You're made like a tiny little doll," he said, and fell to his knees so he could kiss her belly. She bent slightly over him, clasping his head to her, and touched his beautiful shoulders, and his hair.

He groaned suddenly, his hands still and tight on her thighs. His head fell, damp, against her belly.

Dazed, she said, "What is it?"

"Shit." He fell into a sitting position and took her with him, pulling her hard into his lap so that she straddled him and their upper bodies slid close and held. Ellie noticed the shower had stopped. "I'm just wondering how I got so lucky and so unlucky all at once."

"Unlucky?" She blinked.

He sighed. "I don't have a condom."

She drooped against him. "Damn." With a sense of embarrassment, she hid her face against his shoulder. "Well, I feel dumb."

"Dumb?" He shook his head. "Oh, Ellie, please don't. I've been dying to make love to you. Don't change your mind now." He bent, suddenly, and kissed her neck, and opened his mouth on the place, just below her ear, that made her crazy. "Please," he said in a rough voice, "don't change your mind. I want you so bad." His hands tightened. "Tonight, okay? I have a whole seduction planned. Wine and music and candles." He lifted his head, and the blue of his eyes was extravagant, intense, irresistible. "Please."

She forgot embarrassment, forgot that she was a skinny, unbeautiful woman, forgot that he was dangerous and lost, and let the yearning hold sway. Keeping her eyes open, she kissed him.

"Tonight," she agreed. His chest hair, crisp and soft at once, brushed her breasts and she pressed her hips against his arousal. "But I can't tell you how disappointed I am. If anyone finds out, your reputation as a dog is going to be seriously damaged. What kind of Lothario doesn't have a condom at the ready at any moment?"

He laughed softly, and put his hands on her breasts, lightly stroking. "I promise I'll make it up to you."

Reluctantly, Blue let her go, and although he kept meaning to turn away to let her manage the awkwardness of putting herself back together in some privacy, he couldn't seem to keep his eyes off her. She moved without self-consciousness, standing up, bending over to pick up the sodden mess of her little bitty bra. She took one look at it, shook her head, and stuffed it into the pocket of her shorts, then walked the few steps to the shirt and bent to pick it up. One soft white moon of breast swayed forward with the action, and he wanted to kiss it, touch it. He touched himself, pressed hard to ease the buttons closed on his jeans. And still he watched her.

Her back was curved and smooth, her skin as flawless and beautiful as the orchid petals all around them, her shoulders narrow, the collarbone prominent but not bony, which maybe he'd expected. She raised her arms over her head to put the shirt back on, and all that wet flesh glistened in the low light.

He closed his eyes, counted backward from ten. When he reached one, he took a breath and blew it out, then opened his eyes. She'd pulled the shirt over her head. The fabric was wet and clung to her nipples, the highest point on her. Blue couldn't help himself. He snared her by one wrist and bent down to put his mouth on that pointed crown, because he could, after wanting it so long, because he thought it would remind her, and because he wanted to hear that soft gasp of surprise and pleasure that she gave. But though he did hear that sound, it wasn't all. She raised a hand and cupped him, stroked him, through his jeans.

Agony.

"Tonight," she whispered, and danced away,

almost running through the greenhouse away from him, leaving him counting again. Backward from a hundred.

It didn't help. He found a dry T-shirt in the workroom, tugged it urgently over his head and grabbed his keys from the hook by the door. He wouldn't embarrass her by going anywhere in town, which meant a twenty-mile drive into a neighboring little town, a hole in the wall that at least had a grocery store and pharmacy. As he paid for the economy-sized box of Trojans, he caught a sideways look from the clerk, and realized he must look like a wild man, his hair damp and messy, his jeans wet, his shirt dry, his only purchase the giant box of condoms.

He chuckled, which turned the speculative look on the clerk's face to one of alarm. Blue took his change and jumped back in the truck and raced back to Pine Bend and Ellie, praying urgently that she would not change her mind.

He drove to the cabin and leaped out, into the sunlight and the heat. He slammed the door behind him and walked through the hot dust. "Ellie!"

13

Ellie had showered the heat of the day from her, and shaved her legs and dried her hair, unwilling to let it lie, damp and annoying, on her neck the whole day. It was impossible to even think of working, so she put on a lightweight robe and stretched out on the bed beneath the fan. She'd been lying there about five minutes when she heard Blue's truck outside.

She jumped up and looked out the window, laughter rising in her chest when he leapt out of the truck and cried her name, a package in his hands. Giddy, she went to the door just as he landed on the porch, still barefooted. April started to wiggle, making a whimpering noise of greeting. She barked, once, pointedly, lifting a paw as if she'd open the screen door herself, then pushed at it with the same paw. The dog looked back at Ellie, as if to say, well, get up already! He's here. He's *here.*

"I know."

Blue stood beyond the screen, his head cocked so

his hair fell in a tumble nearly to one shoulder.

He simply stood there, holding his hand to the screen in deference to April, who wanted to lick it but didn't much like the taste of weathered wire. Behind him was the strong clear sunlight of midafternoon, a time when children screamed and splashed at the local pool, and bank tellers were making change. She'd imagined loving him in darkness, with a little bourbon and music to blur the reality. Not sober, in daylight, making it impossible to excuse her actions later.

But looking at him, she noticed that desire didn't need night or liquor or even music. "Condoms, I presume?" she said through the screen door, nodding at the box in his hand.

A vulnerable little flush crawled up his cheeks, and Ellie felt her heart catch. He looked wild, barefooted and his hair wind blown, and his jeans still wet, and a sudden tentativeness on his mouth. "You didn't change your mind already, did you?"

Ellie pushed open the screen door. "If you aren't naked inside ten seconds, I swear I'm going to explode."

He laughed, relief and the same giddiness Ellie was feeling. "Yes, ma'am."

He came in, pushing the box at her. She shook the bag off of it and got a fingernail under the flap, then turned and closed the wooden door for privacy. Her heart was still racing and uneven, and her hands were shaking a little as he shucked the shirt and shimmied out of his jeans, and turned to face her, naked and beautiful and slightly abashed.

The box in her hands was forgotten as she admired him, the long legs dusted with hair that took gold sparks from sunlight pouring in through the windows, and the flat lower belly, and the aggressive slant of his swollen organ. She smiled and went toward him, feeling that curious mix of fondness and protectiveness naked male aroused in her, and put her hands on that funny flesh. She pressed the condoms into his hand.

"My hands are shaking," she said. "But if you get one out, I'll be more than happy to adorn you."

He tore the box open, and little foil packets spilled all over the floor. He laughed, taking one of the few left in the box and dropping the others as he leaned close to her. "Now you." He untied the robe, bending his head to kiss her at the same time. He pushed the fabric off her shoulders and Ellie dropped her arms to let it slide off.

Oh.

Naked.

With Blue.

She closed her eyes and pressed close to him, her breasts against his chest, her arms around his back, his hairy thighs against hers. She opened her palms wide on the silky flesh of his back and felt his organ nudging like an ungainly animal into her belly until he reached between them and slanted it upward so he could press closer.

She rubbed her face across his chest, kissed the dip in the middle, and touched his nipples with her tongue. Sunlight blazed against her eyelids and silence was the only sound. Silence and breath and the wet sound of her mouth.

"God, Ellie," he said, and his hands were in her hair. He kissed her lips and eyelids and cheeks, his mouth wet and hot and hungry. And always that nudging, thick against her belly. She wrapped her hand around it, and felt the jump, and Blue made a sound in his throat, and she opened her mouth and took his tongue, her fingers moving lightly, then not so lightly.

Finally she broke away, panting, and pushed a little against him, pointing wordlessly to the bed, taking his hand, pulling him behind her. When she was about to lie down, he said, "Wait."

She turned toward him, only dazedly aware of sunlight streaming in around them, pooling over their bodies. He was gilded with it, his shoulders, burnished in a round arc, the hips narrow, his organ heavy between lean thighs. But it was his skin that drew her hand, supple, smooth, perfect. She skimmed her fingers down his throat, over the curve of his arm, as he stood, only looking at her.

"You're so gorgeous," he whispered. His hands cupped her breasts lightly, and lifted them, and there was an expression on that artful face that made her feel lost and pleased. She felt her orientation shift; a dizzy sense of growth pushed through her, as if she were Alice in Wonderland after one of the magic pills. She did not mind when he knelt before her, and opened his mouth and touched the very tip of his tongue to one nipple. The sight stunned her, his hair falling in gold and brown around his face, her white flesh against his darker fingers, that red tongue flickering over the pointed copper.

Everything in her went still as she watched. His mouth, full lips so beautifully cut, closing around her, hot and wet. His eyelashes, gold-tipped and long, fell in arcs across his cheekbones, and his wild hair tumbled around her fingers. Ellie swayed.

He skimmed a hand down her belly, between her thighs, and still Ellie watched, feeling him with one part of her while the other part watched in breathless wonder. He was beautiful, his back gleaming in the sunlight, and he kissed her all over, suckling and stroking until Ellie could no longer stand up. Even then, he simply settled her back on the bed and kept stroking, sure and strong, light and teasing, all with such intense enjoyment she felt like a queen, like Mabel, and when she came, she moaned with such depth that she might have been embarrassed, but then Blue was over her. He tore open the condom package with his teeth and one hand, and Ellie took it. "Allow me." She slid it on, then pulled him back to her, wishing for a moment that it could be bare flesh that slid inside her, but he fell on her, his tongue swirling into her mouth as he arranged her legs and plunged in with a wild noise of deepest pleasure, Ellie still pulsing all around him and shuddering from her shoulders to her hips.

And then he was rough, as if he could not help it. His hands dug into her buttocks and lifted her close, and his teeth bruised her lips and she thought she could feel his plunge to the bottom of her ribs. When he came, he roared, like a lion, his hands so tight, her legs so close around him that for the first time she understood what union meant.

They collapsed together, sweating, breathless, and did not speak as heartbeats slowed, as trembling finally ceased. Ellie's limbs felt weighted and gilded, and she touched his hair where a band of yellow light fell through it. He kissed her wrist. Ellie didn't want him to move, but eventually he shifted, slid sideways and lay beside her, his hand across her belly, his forehead pressed lightly into her shoulder.

She simply drifted, closing her eyes, feeling air across the damp places on her skin, and sunlight on her toes. His hand was big and covered her from hipbone to hipbone, pelvic bone to rib. She sensed him looking at what he touched, felt the small, exploratory movements of his fingers, a millimeter here or there.

"Your skin is like orchid petals," he drawled, his voice quiet.

Ellie smiled, but didn't open her eyes. "From any other man, I'd think that was a practiced line and laugh at you, but I reckon you have a good acquaintance with orchids."

"They're cool, though. Your skin is warm."

She laced her fingers through his hair, silky and thick at once, let it trail across her wrist, twined some around her ring finger. He would break her heart, eventually, but there wasn't much to do about that now. Maybe it would be worth it. She pressed details of the moment into memory so she could take them out and admire them later. His hip against hers, the feel of his skin, the sound of his breath.

His hand slid down a little, brushed her thighs. She felt him lift on one elbow. "You always so quiet?"

"Mmm." Lazily, she opened her eyes. "Who needs words?"

"Maybe I do," he said, a perplexed little frown creasing his forehead.

She shifted, turning on her side. Looking at him made it harder to stay aloof, because there was vulnerability in his jeweled eyes and on his jaw. If she thought of him as a rascal, a ladies' man, a rake, she could keep her distance.

But there he was, an all-too-human man who had once been a boy who'd lost his family, and a teenager who played a single song so often and so loud that it earned him a new name, and a man who'd built a Taj Mahal of flowers because his heart was shattered by grief. She brushed a lock of hair off his forehead, stroked a line of gentleness over the side of his face. "I don't mind talking," she said quietly.

He closed his eyes for a moment and pulled her closer to him. "Oh, Ellie," he breathed into her hair. "It's been a long time since a woman got to me."

"Yeah?" she chuckled, pulling back a little instinctively. "Well, you sure got to me, Dr. Reynard. Lord have mercy." She clutched his arms in mock horror. "This doesn't mean we have to give up tonight, does it?"

"Hell, no. Got lots of condoms," he said with a chuckle, and gestured to them, scattered all over the floor. "Be a shame to waste 'em after that emergency trip to Hector."

"You drove to Hector and back that fast?"

"I did." Laughter shook his shoulders. "Oh, they'll be talking about me for months."

Ellie got a sudden picture of him, wild-looking, barefooted in some tiny little grocery in Hector, and laughter welled in her, too. "You were quite a sight on my front porch. Did you go in the store without your shoes?"

Amusement overtook him, and he turned to her, shaking, laughing against her neck. Nodded.

"Condom emergency," she cried, and they clung to each other, giggling like teenagers, and then one would slow and the other would start to say something, and they'd be off again, laughing so hard they had tears streaming down their faces.

Finally, they slowed, and Blue took her into his arms. "Whew."

"Don't say anything more," Ellie cried, feeling the edge of hilarity still ready to spill out any second.

"You, either."

Finally calm, she sighed softly, entirely too pleased at the way her head fit in the hollow of his shoulder. "You have to promise this won't ruin our friendship, Blue. I couldn't stand that."

"Why would it?"

"You know better than that. Sex ruins lots of great friendships."

"Not sex that good."

She turned her head. "It's not the sex. It's all the bad feelings that come after." She sighed. "You may as well understand right now that I will fall in love with you—but you don't have to feel bad about it. When it comes time to go, I'll keep my dignity and I swear I won't slobber on your shirt." She smiled softly. "Or at least not much."

"Ellie—"

"You don't have to say anything back. I just wanted it out on the table." Earnestly, she looked at him. "Promise, Blue. We have to stay friends."

He cupped her head and kissed her, deep, stirring up the low thud of desire again. She made a soft noise and he let her go. "I promise."

"Thank you." She slid her body against his, skin to skin, and it didn't take him long to stop talking and start kissing. And this time, it was Ellie who led and Blue who willingly followed, and at the end of it, they slept, tangled, in the stuffy heat of afternoon.

Blue awakened to a feeling of sweat and disorientation, groggy from the heat and humid air. He didn't like sleeping in the daytime. It left him dull-witted and vaguely headachy.

As he surfaced, he felt female flesh against his hip, and the soft weight of breasts against his forearm. He smelled the shampoo Ellie used on the hair tickling his nose. Dizzy in the heat, or maybe because of her skin pressed against his, he shifted.

He didn't get up. Because he wanted to lie here and look at her, take her in, before she could raise up those defenses again. Even her honesty was a defense, a way to keep him a little apart from her. In sleep, the intensity of her waking expression slid away, leaving that sinful mouth parted softly. She tucked a curled wrist under her chin, and the other arm was flung out to the other side of her body, as if to keep her bearings in the wild sea of a double bed.

Her skin glowed with lovemaking and laughter and the dewy air. He caressed the delicate collarbone and the line of her shoulder with his gaze, touched breasts that were startlingly lovely, shaped in twin pears with a crown of unusually dark cinnamon. Slid his gaze down her hip, her thigh, the delicate line of her ankle. Her skin was exquisite, creamy, but not as pale as he'd thought. Against the white quilt, she was tawny with pearl.

His gut ached as he looked at her, smelling their lovemaking on his hands and her skin. A low headache pounded in the back of his skull from sleeping in the heat, but that didn't stop him from swelling, once again, as he thought of what they would do tonight.

There wasn't time now for more, but he lifted on his elbow and kissed her shoulder, opening his mouth to taste her skin. The act sent electric shocks from the tip of his tongue to the tip of his member, which leaped in eagerness. She made a sound, and stirred, arching up a little into him.

Her cheeks flushed with pleasure as he ran his hands over her body. "We have to go," she whispered, but he felt the thready speed of her heart as he kissed her. A lost kind of heat flooded through him and he moved against her thigh, kissed her mouth.

And forced himself to stop. "Tonight, you'll be in my bed."

"What about Lanie?"

"Darlin', she's old, but not stupid. If she hears us, and that's a big if, she'll just chuckle to herself."

"Ew. I don't know if I like that. She'll think of me as one of your girls."

He shook his head, considered, then told the truth. "I don't bring women up there. We come here."

A troubled expression crossed her face, but he kissed her to keep any words from coming between them. "I just want you to sleep all night with me. I hate this bed."

She laughed. "All right."

The sun was low by the time they got to Rosemary's, and Ellie stopped for a moment to admire the low gold light falling on the fields around the house. Peaceful. It made her wish for a home of her own and a garden to tend and suppers to get ready. The thought gave her a little pang.

"Blue Reynard," Rosemary exclaimed when she opened the door. "You didn't bring me *Popeyes* chicken!"

"I got wrapped up in something," Blue said. "Sorry."

Ellie willed herself not to look guilty as Rosemary gave her the eye—or maybe she was just looking at her curiously. She caught Blue's eye by accident, thought of the condom emergency, and had to swallow hard against laughter. Her words came out in a breathless rush. "Hi, Rosemary. I'm afraid I'm not much of a cook, but I brought some potato salad from the grocery deli."

Rosemary looked from one to the other, and Ellie wondered if their wild afternoon was stamped all over them, visible in the swelling of their lips and marks they'd made on each other. Even just standing next to him, she felt a silvery pulse beating between them, winding round her throat, his hands, limbs, as if their cells could not abide the division between them.

But if anything showed, Rosemary didn't let on. "I'll forgive you this once. Come on in and get something to eat. We have a lot to do tonight."

Leading the way to the wide, old-fashioned dining room, Rosemary waved to the rest of the group. "I think you know everyone."

Ellie nodded toward Connie, and Alisha and Marcus on the other side of the table. Mrs. Nance, the librarian, waved cheerfully. Her glasses hung on a bright pink string today. Florence, her plate filled with fresh veggies and a little piece of meat, smiled. "Hi, Ellie. Good to see you again. Have you met my nephew Brandon?"

Ellie smiled at the tall, strikingly handsome youth. "You're the one going to the Air Force Academy."

He grinned. "And you're the one writing the book about my great-aunt Mabel."

"Yes."

From the kitchen came a small, dark-haired girl, about fifteen or sixteen. She carried a big pitcher of tea. "Bragging again?" she said to the boy.

"I don't have to brag. I got my mama to do that for me."

The girl grinned and put the pitcher on the table. "Hi," she said to Ellie. "I'm Shauna, Connie's girl."

"Shauna has been accepted to Tulane, University of Colorado, and *Yale.*" Florence said, winking at her son. "I brag for everyone."

"Oh!" Ellie blinked. The girl was older than she looked. "That's terrific. Have you decided?"

"CU," she said. "I think I'd like to live in the mountains, and it would be nice to be not too far from somebody from home." She grinned at Brandon. "Even if he is obnoxious."

Blue chuckled. "Ellie learned a thing or two about winters when she went to college. You might want to ask her about it."

"That's true," Ellie said. "Be sure to take warm clothes you can wear in layers."

"I will, thank you. Did you like it, snow and winter?" She lifted a shoulder. "I'm looking forward to it."

"I learned that I'm a thin-blooded person," Ellie said as diplomatically as possible. "Snow is pretty, but I only like it through a window." She smiled. "A lot of people fall in love with it."

"It'll be nice for us," Connie said. "We can drive up to see y'all at once, and have somebody to travel with."

"Everybody, get you a plate and let's get the food done with. I have a gazillion pictures for us to get through, and I don't want to be at it all night."

They filled Chinet paper plates with chicken and Jell-O salad whipped to a froth, two different kinds of green salad—"the spinach salad only has a very light vinaigrette dressing," Florence said—and baked beans and potato salad.

"I'm starving," Blue said, low in her ear.

She allowed herself one quick smile at him. "Ditto."

As they ate, Rosemary explained what their purpose was. "Most of you know Marcus has been working for more than three years to get the Vietnam memorial approved. On the Fourth of July, we'll have the official unveiling—and Mrs. Nance is going to help us to put together a photographic retrospective to hang in the library. What we need to do is find as many pictures as we can of all the vets, living and dead, and arrange them into groups, so she can have them mounted and displayed."

She passed out duty assignments. It appeared to Ellie that most were given according to class: Connie and Marcus would work on the classes of sixty-eight and sixty-nine, which were by far the largest; Florence, the oldest of them, took everything before; Rosemary and Blue took the rest. Those unfamiliar with the faces would help the others.

The photographs everyone had brought were divided into neat stacks around the room, keeping them separated. "When you find a picture you want, mark the back with the owners' name so we know how to credit them. Y'all okay with that?"

A murmur of assent. "Please," Rosemary said, "be real careful about keeping the various piles apart. No one wants to lose any of their own pictures, or mix them up."

Ellie felt a jump of excitement when Marcus said, "Ellie, you mind helping us? Alisha's got an uncle in Florence's group."

"I'd be happy to."

The table was cleared and wiped down, and coffee set to brewing in the kitchen. Then the various groups clumped at different spots along the broad table, with piles of photos. Ellie moved to sit beside Connie, who looked grim. "I'm going to get a drink of water," she said, and her chair scraped loudly as she jerked away from the table.

Bewildered, Ellie looked at Marcus. "Am I intruding?"

He shook his head. "No. This is hard for her." Flipping through the photos in his hands, he drew one out of the rusty-haired, goateed boy. "This is Bobby Makepeace. And Connie has never really said a proper farewell," he added as she returned.

A look passed between them. Connie glared. Marcus met the anger with patience and a lack of apology. "He didn't join," Connie said to Ellie. "He got drafted, and he couldn't get out of it, and his daddy would have killed him if he'd gone CO." A glance at Ellie. "Conscientious objector," she explained. She picked up the photo, and her mouth, the lipstick carefully repaired after supper, was tight. "I tried to get him to go to Canada. I'd have followed him to Antarctica. China. Anywhere."

Ellie saw Marcus put his big hand on her shoulder, saw the slight release of tension in Connie's body. "It made me so mad when they granted amnesty to all those people who ran to Canada. Not mad at them. Mad at Bobby."

"That's natural," Marcus said.

"I know." Lifting her chin, she pulled a pile of photographs over. "Let me show you who we're looking for, Ellie, so you can help."

There were twenty-three veterans between the two classes. Some of them Ellie recognized. Some she did not. Connie found a representative photo of each and placed them in a row across the top of their area for reference. "I guess we'll just make a pile under each one, huh?"

A little overwhelmed, Ellie stared at the group. Technically, *any* of them could be her father. She ruled out the obvious noncontenders: nine black men, five very fair types—if her redheaded mother had borne a child with a fair man, Ellie would almost certainly have been blonde—and three hee-haw types, including Crew Cut Dennis, who had been in the original photo Ellie had stolen from Rosemary's trunk.

That left six, minus Bobby Makepeace. Five. One was Binkle. Of the other four, one was dead in Vietnam, one in a car accident. One ran a co-op grocery business in Dallas. The other one was Connie's late husband.

That startled Ellie. She glanced at the photo and saw there was genuine possibility there. Binkle was swarthy but thick-featured, a trait Ellie didn't share. Surreptitiously, she looked at Connie's daughter. "Does she look like your husband?"

Connie's face softened. "Spittin' image. She got his green eyes. Did you notice how pretty those eyes are?"

"I did," Ellie lied politely. Her own eyes were green.

The piles began to accumulate. Marcus and Connie shared memories of everyone, of high school, and Ellie liked the way the memories eased the lines in

Marcus's face, put a twinkle in his dark, usually serious eyes. He had big white teeth and a robust laugh that infected listeners with a need to at least smile.

"Oh, now look at that," Connie said. "Remember that old bus? What a wreck it was." She turned the photo so Ellie could see a faded color photo of an aged school bus painted with flowers and peace signs. Brightly colored curtains hung in the windows. "This is the group we told you about, the hippie kids. They never did get the bus going again. It just died right there alongside George Reed's pasture. He finally had it hauled off a year or so later."

Ellie chuckled. "This is almost a joke to someone my age. That such a thing ever existed."

"Oh, it existed." Connie flipped through the pictures, and handed one over. "These were some of the kids. Most of them took off pretty fast, hitchhiking or what have you, but the driver of the bus and a couple of girls hung around most of the summer. You remember, Marcus?" She gave him a picture, too. "What was that girl's name?"

Two girls, with the hipless bodies of adolescence, stood in front of the bus, arms around each other. One wore shorts and a halter, the other a filmy skirt and blouse. Both were barefoot. Ellie flipped it over. "'Diane and Suzie,'" she read aloud.

"We didn't call her Suzie, though." Connie grinned at Marcus.

He grinned, shot a half-abashed look at Alisha, and said, "Rapunzel. She had the prettiest hair I ever saw."

Ellie looked at the photo, and the woman did have

the kind of hair that would loan itself to such a nickname. Yards and yards of thick blond hair. The girl herself was nearly lost in it. "I always wanted hair like that," she said. "So I could toss it around."

Connie laughed.

"The other one was Diane," Marcus said, slow, like he was remembering. "She was a sweet one. Kinda lost." He plucked a picture out of the pile, gave it to Connie. "Remember?"

Ellie had been listening to them discuss other remembered figures for a couple of hours, but it was oddly eerie to hear her mother's name on someone else's lips.

"Yeah, she was real nice," Connie said and handed it to Ellie, a casual gesture of inclusion. "Made me jealous she was so skinny. Rosemary, you remember her? Diane?"

"Sure."

"What was her last name?"

A tough flutter of heartbeat lodged at the center of Ellie's chest, and she stared down at the picture, praying they would not remember.

"I don't remember. Something Irish. It went with that red hair."

Connor, Ellie thought. Conn of the Hundred Battles.

Blue spoke up, his voice carrying an odd note. "Can I see it?"

Ellie tried not to look at him, not to meet his eyes, but she failed.

"A skinny girl with an Irish name, huh?" He took

the proffered photo. "Cute." He passed it back to Ellie, his eyes direct as lasers. "Maybe O'Skinny?"

The rest of them laughed, but Ellie was suddenly aware that nearly everyone in this room had known her mother. Talked to her, seen the way she moved and the way she laughed and heard her voice.

It made her so deeply, unbearably sad for a moment that she felt actual tears well in her throat. She looked down at the picture, at the young woman with her clear white skin and turned-up lips, her breasts free beneath an Indian cotton blouse. Oh, Mama! she thought. Why'd you go away so fast?

And it occurred to Ellie that she wasn't looking for her father at all. With movements as natural and calm as she could manage, she put the picture down. "Where will I find the bathroom?" she asked Connie.

"Right back there, honey. Take a left at the kitchen and you'll see it."

Marcus found the evening painful, which surprised him. He'd been looking forward to it for days. But somehow, it wasn't as pleasant to wander down memory lane as he had expected. It was piercing to see the gap between what they'd been at eighteen and what they'd become.

Some of it was good, and he managed to get Connie smiling a bit, teasing her about the ways the boys had fallen down behind her. She saucily tossed her head, and informed him they still did, thank you very much. But he knew she had the same lump in her chest that was crowding out his pleasure in the task.

On the other side of Connie, Ellie was quietly intense. Her curly hair was loose around her face, but that didn't hide the telltale marks on her: a beard abrasion, faint but distinct at the edge of her jaw, and one small love bite, low on her neck. She avoided Blue's gaze, but there wasn't anyone in the room who couldn't feel the heat moving between them, or failed to note the way Blue teased her, tried to catch her attention, tossed little bits of paper at her, like a boy with a crush.

The loving had done good things to Ellie. She had a kind of heated glow, almost visible, that obscured the sharpness of her features, made a man look at her smoky eyes and plump mouth. She was focused on the task, very seriously picking out photos to go with the faces of boys she'd never met.

But as they were winding down, Connie made a ribald comment about one of the girls, and Ellie let go of a surprised hoot of laughter that was bawdy and deep. Her face tilted into an exotic arrangement of cat-slanted eyes and slash of cheekbones, her teeth white and large, with one front tooth just a little bit lapped over one next to it.

Recognition struck him like a donkey kick. No longer déjà vu, no more niggling doubt. He knew that tooth, that deep laugh. He knew that careless shrug and the loping, loose walk.

For a moment, he simply stared, unable to quite take it in. Winded, he put a hand to his chest and wondered if he would have a heart attack, wondered if all the work on the memorial had finally just unhinged his brain.

But now that he suspected, it was more amazing that he hadn't put it together before now.

Abruptly, he stood, moving clumsily in his panic. "I just remembered I have to get something done by morning. Alisha. Let's go."

His wife looked bewildered when she glanced up, but she took one look at him and nodded. Sometimes, he got overwhelmed with war images, and she probably thought that was it now, considering. She made their excuses and joined him in the dark car. She didn't say a word or push for more than he wanted to say, or sulk because they had to leave. As he started the car, she simply put her hand on his leg and gave it a squeeze. They drove home in silence.

14

As Blue and Ellie were getting ready to go, Florence rushed to the door. "Hold on, Ellie! I almost forgot to tell you—the journal is ruined. Mildew got it, and the pages are all stuck together. I'm real sorry."

Ellie covered her pinch of disappointment. "That's too bad. You can't read anything?"

"Not a word. I threw it in the fireplace."

"I'm disappointed." She suspected it hadn't been ruined at all, but a decision had been made to keep it private. "But I appreciate the effort, anyway."

Blue touched her nape lightly, brushing the hairs that grew there. "Let's go," he said, and his voice rolled down her spine like sunlight. Which made Ellie remember how his shoulders looked with that glossing of butter yellow sunbeams this afternoon, and her hips went soft.

She raised her eyes. Let him see her hunger. "Let's do."

He took her upstairs to his bedroom, which was rumpled and smelled of him, and threw back the covers and fell down on the bed. "Come here," he said in that bourbon voice, his mouth cocked in the slightest and most promising of smiles. Ellie went, and he enfolded her, tangled their arms and legs together, and kissed her deep, as if he were drinking life from her lips.

And she let herself go, let herself accept the masterful craft of a ladies' man, the shuddering, exquisite, almost painful depth of pleasure he delivered. His big hands were gentle and urgent by turns, and he laughed when they almost slipped off the bed. He could chuckle when he was in her, and he held her tightly afterward.

Ellie, who had never been pretty, lay on his rumpled bed in a room lit with a single fan light on the wall and felt as gloriously, sensually beautiful as a Titian model. Her body ached in places, rubbed raw, and the muscles in the backs of her legs and her shoulders held a faint tremble of exertion. But her skin tingled and her bones were liquid with satisfaction.

Laughing low in her throat, she turned to him. "Lord have mercy," she breathed, and put her hand on his round-muscled upper arm. "You are a master of your craft, an artisan of the highest measure, a king of the bedroom arts."

"I think I like it when you get around to talking," he said. He opened his eyes and gazed at her soberly, the blue of his eyes an almost painful shade. "It's not me, sugar. This is not standard operation." He brushed her nose with his thumb. "We've got one hellacious chemistry goin' here."

Because his beautiful mouth was so close, because it was so easy and she'd thought of it so often, she put her hand on his cheek and kissed him. He closed his eyes and responded with the same gentle sweetness she gave, and it sent a tiny arrow through her chest. She settled back on the pillows with a sigh.

Lazily, he moved a foot over her ankle. "Tell me how you came to be so interested in music, Miss Velvet."

She laughed. "Don't even go there, Larry."

"But you are kinda velvety. I like it. Though I guess I can understand why you wouldn't like Velvet Condom." He started to laugh, ducking his head into her neck.

Ellie felt the giggle rising and halted it. "Don't get me started again."

"Music," he prompted.

"Oh, yeah. It's simple. I know you'll find this hard to believe, but I was the homeliest child on the planet."

"No, I can believe it." He rubbed her stomach with a grin.

"Thanks." She rolled her eyes. "Way too much hair, big nose, skinny as a rope." She shuddered. "Needless to say, even without the Velvet angle, I was not invited to be a member of the popular crowd."

"Okay."

"So I took up music. I sang in the choir and I played instruments and traveled with the marching band."

"Ewww. Doomed yourself to eternal geekhood with that, didn't you?"

"Yep. But it was good for me in some ways. I got to travel, go to these competitions in big cities and stay in big fancy hotels with the other geeks."

"What'd you play?"

"Oh, a little of everything. Took piano lessons from the time I was about six, started with clarinet in third grade, got hot for the cello in middle school, and switched to saxophone for most of high school. Oh, and I sang alto at church and school."

He lifted his eyebrows. "You said you don't have any musical talent."

Ellie laughed. "I don't! I can carry a tune and I can play okay, but I just was not born with the music gene. I love it, but love does not a musician make." She looked up at him, liking the way light shone through a fall of his hair around his face. "How 'bout you?"

"Same thing, really. Not the geekhood—*I* was cool, you know."

"No. I bet you were one of those loner rebel types. Black leather and cigarettes."

A twinkle lit his eyes. "Yep. James Dean, all the way. The trouble was, I really liked school, and it was the only thing that didn't bore me out of my mind, except music. Rosemary's sister Florence turned me on to Bach when I was about fourteen, and I made my way through the Great Composers series then. I knew I had no talent, but it still made me happy."

"The Great Composers, huh? I got them through the piano." She rolled her eyes. "Some are definitely greater than others."

Suddenly, her stomach growled. Loudly. She laughed. "I guess I worked up an appetite."

"You? Hungry? What a surprise." He chuckled, and put his hand on her tummy. "I'm starving myself. Let's go see what we can find."

He stood up and stretched, and Ellie lay where she was, admiring his lean, long form, the high round of his rear end, the molded shape of his legs. He tossed her a long shirt to put on and dragged on his jeans. Ellie slipped on the shirt and padded with him down the stairs.

It wasn't until they got to the kitchen and Sasha whined at the backdoor that she realized she'd forgotten April. "Blue, I have to go let April out! She'll be dying."

"All right." He grabbed a bag of chocolate chip cookies from the cupboard and drew a glass of water for each of them, handing Ellie hers. "Let's do it. She can come back here." He bent and kissed her, once, and opened the door. "I want you sleeping in my bed tonight."

"I can't go out like this!"

"Sure you can. Nobody around for miles."

She laughed. "If you say so." The tails of the shirt covered her to midthigh. "But I don't have tough feet like you. What about stickers?"

"No stickers in that field." He held out a cookie, backing away as if it was a lure. "Come on, little girl."

"All right." She followed him out into the pure, unbroken stillness of a country night, with a billion stars twinkling in the very dark sky. She breathed in, deeply. "I had forgotten how much I loved the country," she commented. "I love the quiet so much."

"Me, too." He offered the bag and Ellie took a handful of cookies out. "The whole time I was a kid, I couldn't wait to get somewhere else. When I got out there, I found out cities just aren't my style."

"I like cities. I like the movement, the energy, but I like this better. You can always drive into a city for a fix. It's harder to do it in the reverse."

"I keep wondering what'll happen to Brandon Grace. Going into the Air Force, that's brave—and there's a commitment, too. He won't be able to just come home."

"He sure is cute," Ellie commented. "He looks like Tupac Shakur with hair."

Blue laughed. "You're right. Never noticed before." He gave her a look. "You like rap? Seems a little off your usual style."

"I make it my business to pay attention to the music world." She munched a cookie, and thought about it. "I can't say I like a lot of rap. The critics are right—a lot of it is misogynistic and violent and antisocial. But the best of it is an anguished kind of poetry that's very powerful. I really took it personally when Tupac got himself killed. Cried my eyes out."

"I'm surprised, Miz Connor. He was a two-bit gangster."

"Maybe." She shrugged. "He was also beautiful and young and very talented. Some of his songs . . ." She trailed off as they reached her porch steps. "Sorry. Don't get me going on him. It's still a sore spot."

"You have a soft spot for dead musicians in general, I guess."

Ellie inclined her head. "Maybe so."

From within, April barked sharply, and Sasha, who had come along, barked back, leaping on the door to scratch eagerly.

Blue opened the door and April sprang out, rushed for the grass, and squatted with an almost audible sigh. "I'm sorry, baby," Ellie said, and gave her a cookie. "Blame Blue. He distracted me."

April gulped the cookie, licked Ellie's hand and raced up the hill with Sasha, tumbling, bumping each other, racing back and forth. "Dogs have great body language," Ellie said.

"They do. Very physical." He looped an arm around her shoulders, and to her amazement—she would have thought some heat might be dissipated by now—Ellie felt an immediate response, one that deepened when he turned to her in the cool air, and put his arms around her and kissed her. His hands fell wickedly and pulled up the tails of her shirt, and the night touched the back of her thighs along with his fingers. "I like physical."

She reached between them and unfastened the ties to his robe and cupped his organ in her hands. "Me, too," she breathed. "But I swear if we have sex again, I won't be able to walk for days."

"Ditto," he admitted, and took her hand instead. They walked a little ways, and he said, "Your mama was sure pretty."

"She was." The sorrow from earlier welled in her

throat again, and this time Ellie didn't have to fight it so hard, so the sense of loss didn't seem so intense.

"What happened to her?"

"She came home at Christmas, had me, then took off again when I was about six months old. My grandma said she was really sad the whole time, and she wasn't surprised that the next thing anybody heard about her was when a cop came to the door to ask my grandmother to identify a photograph of her body. She overdosed on heroin."

"Ah, man. That's sad."

"I've always wondered what made her so unhappy." She shook her head. "There's nothing to really account for it, you know?"

"There's not always a reason for things," he said. "You're a historian, so you want answers, but that doesn't mean they're always there."

"I know, but I can't help looking."

"Lucky for me." He took her hand, and led her back to the house, where they ate and talked of other things, then wandered back to his bed for a very, very gentle last round of making love. She slept curled into the cradle of his arms.

The days after that first night spun together like the tigers Sambo tricked in one of Blue's favorite stories from childhood. He let himself fall into the gildedness, into the orchid-sleekness of Ellie's body curled into him, the velvet sound of her voice in his ear. At night, he slept hard, the sleep of a man at peace.

Mornings, he made coffee and sent her down the

hill to work because he didn't want to get blamed for her missing a deadline. Even the mornings seemed unreal, soft as a tiger's fur, and sometimes there was a mist rising up from the ground that swirled around her knees, making her look like a ghost floating toward the cabin his mother had believed was haunted.

It was on one of those mornings that he was simply standing on the kitchen steps, watching her go, that Marcus came up, carrying a green metal thermos filled with the coffee and chicory Alisha made. Blue watched until the last of April's white tail disappeared into the cabin, and only then turned to admit Marcus to his world.

There was soberness on the mouth framed with its graying goatee, no smile in his eyes as he stared at the cottage. Blue almost thought there was anger on his face. After a minute, Marcus looked at Blue. He said nothing.

They went to work. All day, Blue waited for Marcus to make some remark about Ellie spending her nights with him, to comment on the fact that Blue had taken a lover again after a long time, and maybe ask what that meant to him. Marcus didn't hold back. He had opinions on everything and he expressed them.

But not this time. He said nothing until Ellie was coming back up the hill at the end of the day. Her hair was smoothed back tight from her forehead, caught in a ponytail at the back of her neck, and it showed off the perfect shape of her head and her small ears and the clear, high brow. Blue halted, watching her with that hot twist in his chest, looking at her long legs below the wrinkled khaki shorts, and the straightness of her shoulders below her plain shirt. It surprised him anew every time he saw her, that stab of a hot poker right through his breastbone. She felt like summer, like sunlight.

Too late, he realized he wasn't alone this time, and a man didn't like to think his expression showed what was in his mind. He tapped his shovel on the ground and glanced at Marcus to make sure he hadn't seen.

But Marcus, too, had stopped, and he didn't notice Blue because he was watching Ellie, too. Watching her approach with an expression of such raw pain that Blue could only call it stricken.

A flash of jealousy burst in him. Had Marcus wanted Ellie for himself?

No. The man had been crazy in love with Alisha since she appeared in Pine Bend, and that had not changed.

Blue nudged his friend without really knowing why, except he didn't want Ellie to see that expression.

Marcus, jarred from wherever he'd gone, looked up briefly, then bowed his head. "Alisha sure is fond of that little white girl," he said gruffly. "Told me to tell you to bring her for supper soon." He paused and gave Blue a faint smile. "She also said she'll kill you dead if you break her heart."

Blue nodded. "It'll be the other way around this time, Marcus," he said quietly, and stepped forward to greet Ellie, take her hand, draw her back into his world.

Camp: golden days overlaid with a kind of honeyed brightness. Silvery nights spent entwined and laughing and talking.

Maybe because she was so eager to be able to enjoy the nights, Ellie worked by day, and she found a new inspiration and enthusiasm for her project. She lined up interviews with a baker's dozen of elderly Pine Bend residents and spent three days solid driving around town to talk to them—and the results were better than Ellie had expected. People remembered Mabel vividly, remembered the first time they heard her sing—in church as a nine-year-old, belting out "Rock My Soul" to a stunned congregation at the Church of God; at a school program when Mabel was twelve; at Hopkins' one hot summer night in 1943.

It was great material, and one hot afternoon more than two weeks after she'd started sleeping at Blue's house every night, Ellie transcribed the notes carefully to index cards, letting the visions of Mabel move through her while a CD of her music played in the background. Ellie hummed along, making a mental note to seek out stories from more whites. The accounts she'd collected thus far were heavily weighted to the black, and that was fine, but Ellie wanted the white side of the story, too. How had the other half of the segregated town felt about Mabel Beauvais? How soon had they known the little colored girl with the big voice would be a star that would put Pine Bend on the map?

She still hadn't had a chance to talk to Gwen Laisser, the woman she'd met on the river. Blue said she often left town for fairly long stretches. The truth was, Ellie was compiling enough information she didn't strictly need Mrs. Laisser's tale, but she had liked the old woman and wanted to get her memories down.

Ellie yawned. Afternoons were tough. She grinned at that and looked up at the big house. She wasn't sleeping as much as usual, after all.

The phone rang. Startled from what had promised to be a lovely daydream, Ellie answered. "Hello?"

"Well, I guess you're still alive, then, if you can answer the phone."

"Grandma!" A teeny stab of guilt pricked her. "Hi!"

"Hi, yourself. Do you know it's been nigh on a week since you called me, girl?"

"No way!" Ellie swiveled in her chair to look at the calendar. "Oh, wow. You're right. Sorry about that. I've been up to my elbows in interviews. Time got away from me. Is everything okay?"

"Fine. Got the corn planted and cut some fresh rhubarb for pie this morning. How's the book going?"

"Pretty good. I'm not sure I'm going to get to the bottom of Mabel's disappearance, but it'll be a good book anyway. She was really something."

"And your other search?"

Ellie sighed. "I don't know." She thought, suddenly, of Connie's husband with the green eyes. She hadn't looked him up yet, and to remind herself to do it on her next trip to the library, she scribbled a note. "I haven't been following up those leads much. I did see some pictures of Mama, though. And some people here do remember her. It felt kind of . . . odd."

"Don't let it break your heart, sweetie. It's all water under the bridge."

"I know. You been walking every day? Taking all your meds?"

"I have. Doctor dropped the blood pressure pills to one a day."

"That's great!"

A pause. "And how's that man?"

"What man?" Ellie asked, biting her lip, then couldn't quite pull it off. "Blue, you mean?"

"Blue? Is that his name? Oh, brother!"

"It's a nickname, Gram. He loves the blues. That's where it comes from."

"Not another musician! Don't you ever learn, child?"

Ellie let her grandmother hear her exasperated sigh. "He's not a musician and it's not like that."

"Girl, you think I can't hear the sloppiness in your voice when you say his name? I wasn't born yesterday."

Ellie laughed. "Okay, okay! He's gorgeous and doomed and I'm trying to keep my distance, but it's not easy. This time, though, I promise, I'm grown-up enough to manage a broken heart."

"I see." There was disappointment in the word. "Well, do you know when you might be coming home?"

"Well, I'd like to get a few more interviews, and give it a little more time to see if I can get someone to tell me what happened to Mabel. Somebody knows, but I haven't been able to get anyone to crack yet. Maybe another couple of weeks. Not much longer than that."

"All right. Keep in touch, huh?"

"I will. I promise." She hung up the phone, feeling faintly hollow.

A broken heart.

Somehow, over these magic days, she'd managed to keep that reality at bay. It was just so easy to be with him, to laugh with him. He was smart and funny and good-looking and wry, and they shared spectacular sex. Sex she would never forget. Wild or tender, intense or lazy, it didn't seem to matter. They matched.

Nice try, Connor.

Oh, all right. She tossed down her pen and went to the fridge for some tea. It wasn't just great sex. She knew about that physical connection; she'd found it once or twice before. Some men—especially the kind she tended to be attracted to, the artists and musicians and lost souls of the world—were just born knowing how to please a woman, and Ellie had been lucky enough to find them.

This was . . . different. When she was with Blue, she found no need to erect walls against him, to be anyone but herself—the plain, unadorned Ellie Connor. She'd never felt that freedom with anyone before this, and she realized, dropping ice into her glass, that it had started way before she arrived in Pine Bend.

It had started with the E-mails they'd exchanged, and grown with their shared taste in music, and through the friendly debates they'd engaged in, and on through to the surprise and delight of discovering that he laughed—at the same moment and with almost the same level of amusement—at the exact same things she did.

And it was all of that, all those moments and other things they shared, that made the sex so much more than just fantastic orgasms. All those other moments added to and underlying the pleasure of pressing naked against him, and kissing him.

"Damn it." She put her hands on the counter and took a breath. How long had it been since she arrived to find a hard-drinking, wild-loving, lost, and beautiful man sitting on his porch? Three weeks? Four?

People didn't change that fast. He might be feeling infatuated and happy for the moment, the darkness diverted by a new love affair, but how long would that last? The problems weren't solved. He still drank a little more than she liked, though she had to admit it was quite a bit less than it had been. He didn't get drunk, but he didn't seem to like to face an evening without a drink or two. Did that mean he had an alcohol problem? Or not?

She had no idea. She did know he was self-destructive. Or was he? She thought about the way he'd been with her, so funny and warm and sweet. She thought, too, of the way he'd taken his grief and built that beautiful world of orchids, and of the way he was using beauty to try to find economic answers for people in faraway places. That didn't seem destructive.

Frowning, she took a long gulp of sweet tea and put the glass down. On the stereo, Mabel sang a moody blues song about lost love, and it felt like she was singing Ellie's future, that future that would not contain Blue.

But why wouldn't it? Maybe he wasn't as lost as she had originally thought. Maybe he was just now emerging from a long tunnel of grief and he was ready to love again.

Maybe.

"Oh, Ellie, stop rationalizing." She did this every time. Convinced herself for a month or a season that *this* lost man was different from all the others. *This* one could be saved. All he needed was love—her love, of course—to make him whole.

Such a seductive scenario. And just as doomed as it was every other time. No one could be saved by anyone outside themselves. No one.

Bowing her head, she allowed a little honest sorrow to fill her, make her ache. She wanted Blue to be saved because he was so different from anyone she'd ever met. She wanted him to thrive because he had so much to give. And selfishly, she wanted it because it would mean she could stay.

With a faint smile, she shook her head and moved back to the desk, ready to dig back into work. The only way she was going to get out of this with her sanity intact—the heart was already doomed—was by recognizing right now that this small, beautiful time was all there would ever be. She could keep Blue as her friend if she was firm and strong, if she promised herself to walk away with dignity and honor the minute the research was finished.

Because the first vision she'd had of him was the true one: Blue Reynard was lost, and she couldn't save him. And she'd learned enough to know that she couldn't bear to stick around and watch him self-destruct. The minute she finished her research, she had to go.

15

That night was the first one since Ellie started sleeping next to him that Blue had his dream. They'd had dinner with Lanie in town, and Blue had sensed a distance in Ellie through dinner, a faint aloofness that he put down to the visibility of the three of them out in public. Maybe it embarrassed her a little, or made her self-conscious. Lanie sure enjoyed it, and after a while, Ellie seemed to relax over a steak and a glass of wine.

But later, she still seemed kind of vague, and for the first time, they didn't make love. Blue showered and came into his room to find her sound asleep. He crawled into bed next to her warmth, but didn't wake her.

Thunder wakened him, thunder and a wild wind howling around the eaves. Dry-mouthed, he woke with a start, thinking immediately of tornadoes. It was that time of year. Ellie slept on, oblivious. She slept like she ate, as if she were ten and played outside all day.

Gently, he slid away from her, pausing to pull the sheet back over her shoulder so she wouldn't get a chill. Snagging his jeans from the floor where he'd dropped them, he went to the hall and put them on. The dogs followed him downstairs, nails clicking on the wood. He turned the television on to the weather channel, and while he waited for the local news, collected bourbon and one of the good crystal glasses from the sideboard in the dining room. He poured a drink, listening with half an ear to the rain, counting beats between flashes of lightning and the thunder that followed.

No warnings on the television, and the lightning was still pretty distant. Safe enough.

But now he was awake. He turned on the stereo, quiet as a whisper, so he could hear it through the window that opened on the porch, then carried the bottle and glass outside, holding the door for the dogs. Sasha dashed out, but April hesitated, looking over her shoulder toward the stairs, then at Blue, undecided. "She's safe, baby," Blue said. "You can come out with us."

Rain fell in steady sheets beyond the porch. A crack of lightning burst over the air, and on its heels came a boom. He raised his brows. That wasn't too far away. April whined softly, leaning against him. "Don't like storms, baby?"

Licking her lips, April lowered her head as if she felt guilty. Mist blew on him, cool and sweetly scented, as Blue poured himself a stiff drink. The grass shone pale gray in the cool light, and around the perimeter of the land, the forest crept right up to the fences. As a boy, he had imagined the trees tiptoed forward when no one was looking. It was well past midnight, and there were no sounds but the rain on the land.

There was only Blue and bourbon and the hole in his gut, that empty, empty hole that sometimes seemed it would suck him in a piece at a time if he weren't vigilant. It ached tonight, surprising him with fresh violence after a few weeks of quiet.

He tossed back the whiskey in one hard swallow and felt the burn all the way down his esophagus. It flowed right into that black hole in his belly, and blurred the edges. He poured another.

Sasha slumped with a sigh and went to sleep behind him. April lifted her nose to the night, scenting something Blue couldn't identify, then as if sensing Blue's mood, she wandered over, and settled with her full weight against his calf, looking out at the night with him.

"Damn, you're a good dog." Blue settled an arm around her, grateful for the company. Her fur was thick and soft under his hand, and he simply ran his hand through it, over and over. April lifted her head backward and planted a polite lick to his chin.

The music ribboned out behind him, a drifting blues song that brought his sorrows to the surface. He sipped his bourbon, and the laughing face of his wife was in his mind. He tried never to think of Annie. Ever. When he gave all her things away the day after the funeral, folks said it was healthy that he did that. That he accepted her death with such calm sorrow.

But the truth was, he just couldn't stand to run across something accidentally. A scarf left on a chair. A pillow with her smell on it. A pair of shoes kicked under a table. He'd lose his mind if he didn't get it all out of the house.

Her parents took care of the funeral and the autopsy—multiple head and chest trauma; a trucker short of sleep had run head-on into her car as she returned from a trip to Houston to see a cousin—pretty self-explanatory, in Blue's opinion, and the coroner agreed. And to avoid thinking of what that meant, from letting his mind give him pictures of that car and his wife, he scoured the house for her things and put them all in boxes and put them outside.

When that was done, he took all the pictures he could find, from childhood on, and put them in a box and carried it to the attic. It was nearly two years before he dated another woman, and that only out of pure physical need.

Which was how things had been till Ellie came, small and intense and smart, and stirred up his libido and his life, making him feel again, waking up the dead spots he'd thought safely buried. In the first giddy rush, there had been no room for the warning pinpricks he felt in him now, points of pressure where the dam might give way if he didn't stand guard.

He could name them by their colors. That red one there. Anger. Anger so hot and red he couldn't bear it. Anger that after everything that had been taken, God had had to take his wife, too. Anger that he could never seem to hang on to anything he cared about.

The blue-green pinpoint, piercing his appendix or thereabouts, that was sorrow and fear, that was the color of the light in the hallway of his dream, where no matter which door he opened, he found some dead loved one.

And the rosy yellow was the one that scared him most of all, the one he was out here drinking, trying to drown. Because that one was love, pushing through in a dozen places like some wild weed, taking everything over.

He swore and poured another, but the more he drank, the brighter the pinpricks grew, until he was winded and afraid. "Damn," he whispered, and bent his head to the soft fur of the dog standing sentinel beside him. "Damn," he repeated softly. Just damn.

He'd discovered what the walls were keeping out.

When Ellie awakened, Blue was not in bed. That was not unusual. It was true he didn't sleep much, and he often rose before she did. But the morning was rainy and dark, and she wished for his body next to hers. She rolled over and tucked her face into his pillow instead, smelling him in the fabric.

And with a shock, she realized this was what it would be like . . . in some not-too-distant future. Waking alone again, with only memories left of him, and not even a pillow smelling of his hair.

Slowly, she rolled on to her back and looked around the room. It was both simple and complex, both bright and filled with odd, very dark shadows, like the man himself. A tumble of discarded clothes were piled on a chair; in the mix she saw her favorite shirt, a dark blue cotton that pointed out the ruffian blond streaks in his hair and the devastating blue of his eyes. A flash of him in that shirt, his elbows braced on his knees, a wicked twinkle in his eyes, passed across her vision, sending a fierce wave of emotion through her.

She thought, too, of the way his face looked when he was in her, how it took on that strange, serious expression, haunted and hungry. And all she could do was touch his head, circle him more tightly, pull him closer, whisper his name.

And she thought of the lonely sound of music she heard sometimes late at night when she woke up and he wasn't in bed.

"Damn," she said aloud. She'd gone and done it. Fallen in love, hard, with a man who had lost so many pieces he would never be whole. And in this still, rainy morning, she could taste what it was going to be like to leave him behind.

As if he'd heard her stirring, he appeared suddenly at the door. For one moment, he simply stood there, his arms loose at his sides, and she saw a haggardness in his cheeks. She simply gazed back at him, letting him choose, one more time, what he would do.

Without saying a word, he stepped toward the bed, shedding his shirt and letting it drop on the floor. Then he climbed next to her and knelt over her, a knee on either side of her body, covered only by the sheet. She felt a catch in her throat at the strange aura coming off him, anger and heat and need, and she didn't move.

He stared down at her, then suddenly bent and kissed

her with what she might have labeled violence in another man, his big hands tight on either side of her head, his tongue a claiming thrust—as close to a cry as she ever heard from him. There was bourbon on his lips. She thought of him sitting on his porch that first night she came here, the darkness on his cheeks, the danger in his eyes, and she'd known then that it would come to this.

She lifted strong arms to his wrists, not to pull him away, but to brace him as she sat up, the sheet coming off her body. She wrapped her arms around him, meeting his despair with love. Even as she did it, as she tasted the bourbon on his tongue, she knew they were acting in accordance to the script she'd told him they would act out—she was trying to save him from himself, and he was clinging to a woman because he didn't know how to get himself out of that place alone.

But even that couldn't change it, couldn't change the landscape where they went together, a world as green and blue as a Scottish tartan. He made a soft choking noise when she gripped a handful of his hair and held it tight while she kissed his beautiful throat and his eyelids and his rough-stubbled cheeks, pressing her small body into his large one. It was she who freed him, who invited him, wordless, to take her in whatever way he needed, and met his roughness with her own strength. She gripped his shoulders and hung on, one hand still tangled in his long hair, as he took her with rough cries, his hands hard on her shoulders, his mouth on her neck.

And when he was at last still and weak against her, she said nothing, only stroked his head, his shoulders, and he simply put his face into her hair and kissed her ear, once, fiercely.

Ellie held him and closed her eyes so she'd always remember, and hoped that some of her love was leaking from the pores of her skin, pressed in so many places against his own, and that it could seep back through his and mend the shredded heart that he protected so fiercely.

Unsettled by the morning and the sense that somehow, everything was suddenly going to come undone, Ellie could not sit in the cottage and work. Heading out in the heavy rain, she went to the library, and found it deserted except for a plump, white-haired volunteer who said Mrs. Nance had gone to visit her niece for a few days in Austin.

Ellie thanked her and made her way upstairs, shaking rain from her hair. A good many of the bound books still sat on the back table Mrs. Nance had set aside for her, and the sight made her feel guilty.

This morning, she'd resolved to give the mystery of Mabel's disappearance another week. If she couldn't find out by then what had happened, she'd write the book without the information, leaving it the poignant mystery it was. It was a way to focus and set goals.

But first she took out the yearbook to look up Connie's husband. Ewing. She didn't know his first name or how old he was, or if he had a dozen brothers, but she started with the yearbook she'd been using, the one with Marcus and Connie and Rosemary in the senior class.

No Ewing at all. Not in the senior class, not in the junior. But on the freshman list, she found a photo of an awkward girl with truly awful, insanely curly hair listed as Tina Ewing. She wore cat's-eye glasses that obscured the shape of her face, but Ellie felt a little thrill of excitement looking at that hair.

Leaving the book on the table, she went to the stacks and took out the yearbooks for the years just preceding the one she'd been using. She found him in the graduating class of 1966, member of the last class at Washington High School that was segregated.

She carried the book back to the table. His hair was in a crew cut, so it was impossible to tell if he had the same curly hair as the girl Ellie assumed was his sister. But he had the kind of high, broad cheekbones and straight aggressive nose that spoke of Native American blood, and a certain intensity of expression that made her think he might have been the sort of dangerous guy her mother tended to like.

He was a genuine possibility. She looked up activities and other activities and found that he'd been an athlete of some talent—one photo showed him in a football uniform, helmet under his arm, still glaring at the camera. Another showed him in a skimpy basketball uniform. The uniform cracked her up—in comparison to the baggy long shorts that were worn today, these looked positively scandalous. But it showed the shape of his body, long and lean and strong. Almost too thin.

She made black-and-white copies of all the pages, then put the yearbooks all back on the shelf, tucked the loose copies into her notebook, wondering how to handle finding out more. She could come clean and just ask, of course, but that led back to Connie—and her daughter Shauna. How would they feel about it? At least Ellie knew for sure that Connie was otherwise involved at the time, with Bobby Makepeace. And George was dead, so it couldn't hurt him if Ellie was his daughter.

No, she still didn't want to go public. Not just yet. There was another meeting of the book group in a couple of days. She'd ask Connie about her husband then, see if she could glean some more information first.

"Get to work, Connor," she said to herself.

Mabel.

Thinking about it yesterday, Ellie had come back again to the six-week gap in Mabel's life. She had begun to think that Mabel had despaired through that period and had somehow gone somewhere to lick her wounds. What would have caused that? The collapse of the love affair with Peaches McCall.

But she was here today on a hunch that had come to her between sleep and wakefulness, holding Blue's body close to her own. She wanted to read the accounts of Peaches's shooting.

There were only a few paragraphs. He'd been a criminal, and a black one at that. In the fifties, the paper would not have felt compelled to say much about his passing. It was described as a drunken argument that turned fatal.

Ellie frowned. Hadn't Doc told her that Peaches had been shot outside the bar? Noting the names in the article, she closed the book and went back out in the rain to the small police headquarters. A sergeant on duty, tall and trim, with steel gray hair and dark eyes, listened to her request with the skepticism of an officer of the court toward a civilian, but in the end, he let himself be persuaded, and led her to a file cabinet. "We don't have too many homicides around here," he commented, tugging the drawer open. "And ninety percent of those are some jealous lover killing a rival or whatnot."

Ellie nodded. "I suspect this was in the same vein."

"Likely was, ma'am." He flicked through the files and pulled out a very thin one. He opened it. "Yeah," he said, glancing over the report. "Not a lot here. Got ambushed outside Hopkins' on July eleventh, 1952. A Saturday night. Shot clean through the heart. Dead before he hit the ground, probably."

"Did they find a weapon?" Ellie asked.

He scanned the report, flipped a page up, *tsked*. "Doesn't look like it."

"Can you tell me what kind of gun killed him?"

"Looks like a small caliber. Real close." He frowned. "Humph. Must have been somebody he knew, then. Somebody he probably thought would be glad to see him."

Ellie kept her face straight. "Was there anyone with him when it happened? Any witnesses?"

"A whole passel of 'em, looks like, but nobody was talking. There was no arrest."

Ellie went back out to the car and put the key in the ignition, then sat there, staring at the rain-blurred world with a sense of doom. "Ah, Mabel," she said aloud. "What am I going to do if you killed him?"

There was no way to find out this afternoon. Alisha had invited her and Blue to come over for supper before the reading group. The thought gave her another wave of uneasiness, and she still didn't start the car.

She felt, today, as if she'd been asleep these past few weeks and had awakened from the enchantment this morning. Suddenly, the deadline seemed pressing, and she realized she had made no progress at all toward figuring out who her father was.

And the truth was, sooner or later, she was going to have to go back to real life. On to the next project. Get on with her life.

A truck passed by in the street, spraying water over the side of her car, and Ellie realized she didn't want to go anywhere. It was like the night on Blue's porch. She'd wanted to sit there and drink bourbon and listen to him all night long, suspended in possibilities.

And now she wanted to just stay right here, in this small space of time in her life, when she was in love with a man who needed her, who made everything in her shout out loud.

But sitting there in her reliable-for-travel Buick, she realized it was more than that. She didn't want to leave this little town that made her feel like herself again, where she'd made connections that somehow went deeper than usual for no particular reason she could discern.

She didn't want to leave Pine Bend with its painful

history, or Rosemary or Connie or Alisha and Marcus. If she hadn't allowed herself to get mixed up with Blue, she might have been able to stay, but as usual, she'd shown a genuine brilliance for making bad decisions.

The rain pounded down on the roof, and she flashed on the way Blue had stood in the doorway this morning and the taste of bourbon on his mouth. That was really at the root of all this soul-searching today, and if she were honest with herself, she'd admit it.

The descent had begun. Blue would let her go.

With a sigh, she started the car. If she had to leave town in a couple of weeks—and she doubted very seriously that it would take any longer than that—she might as well enjoy what time she had left. Because this was as green a time as she'd ever known. It would be a shame to waste it brooding.

16

It was still raining when she got back to Fox's Creek, but it had slowed to a friendly drizzle that made the world seem cool and the greens greener. Ellie let April out to run, and stood on the porch, waiting for her to come back.

On the hill, she saw the dark tall figure of Marcus, silhouetted against the whitish walls of the greenhouse. His truck was parked nearby, but the space where Blue usually kept his was empty.

She was moving up the hill before she really acknowledged to herself that she was going to do it. Wet grass slapped at her ankles and she had to duck her head against the soft rain. She whistled for April to follow her.

Marcus caught sight of her—she knew by the break in his steady movements, a half-second halt between starting to bend and actually doing it, but he didn't straighten and wait for her, just kept up with what he was doing.

"Hey, Marcus," Ellie said.

She half expected him to pretend he hadn't seen her, make some polite exclamation of surprise. But that wasn't his style. He stopped long enough to acknowledge her with a nod. "If you're looking for Blue, he ran to the hardware store. Be back shortly."

Ellie had believed she was coming up here to ask him some questions about Mabel, ask his opinion, maybe, on whether he thought Mabel could have killed Peaches. But standing there, she knew she wanted to clear the air. For a minute, she simply watched him in his steady rhythm, his competent hands pulling grass from the edges of the wall.

"Something on your mind?" he asked.

She took a breath. "Yeah. I guess there is. Blue said we're going over to your house tonight for dinner, and well . . ." She stuck her hands in her pockets. "I guess I just wanted to tell you that's not necessary. You don't have to be polite to me or whatever it is. I can see that you kind of have a problem with"—the words threatened to jam, so she rushed it all out—"Blue and me, um, hanging out while I'm here, and I don't pretend to know why, but you always seemed pretty friendly before so you must have your reasons, and I just want to tell you it isn't necessary"—she took a breath—"to act like you like me." She pulled a lock of hair from her mouth. "Or whatever."

He had straightened as she talked. "Finished?"

She nodded.

He wiped his hands on a red rag. "I like you fine, Ellie. I like what you've done to that man, too." He lifted a brow. "One of y'all is going to end up with a broken heart, I reckon, but that's just how life goes sometimes." He scowled. "Not that Alisha sees it that way. She likely won't let Blue back in her house once you've gone."

Ellie frowned. "Then why—"

He held up a hand. His gaze was direct and serious. "Is your mother Diane Connor?"

"What?" A fist clutched her heart. Surely Blue hadn't betrayed her? No. The minute the thought appeared, she knew it wasn't that.

He cocked one brow, waiting.

It was impossible to lie, looking into those dark, sober eyes. Ellie nodded—and realized how he'd known. "Rosemary's house that night, right?"

"Yeah. Why would you tell everybody you're here to do a book on Mabel?"

"I am! Trying to find out"—she lifted a shoulder, suddenly humiliated to admit that she didn't even have a name for her father—"what happened to my mother here was just too tempting."

"Happened?"

Ellie took a breath. "She came home pregnant. Never said who the father was. My father."

A charge sizzled in the air for a moment. Ellie finally looked up and noticed a strange, guarded expression on his face. "You're looking for your daddy?"

"Pitiful, isn't it?" A loop of hair, frizzed in the damp, fell on her forehead and she pushed it away. "Did you know her?"

"A little. Why don't you just ask her?"

Ellie realized that he had no way of knowing the rest of the story. "She died when I was two. It hadn't become an issue yet."

"Died?"

Ellie nodded.

"Hell. I'm sorry."

Blue's truck sounded on the road. Ellie glanced over her shoulder. "Marcus, you wouldn't happen to know who it might be?"

A single shake of his head. "Can't help you there. I reckon if you're meant to know, the good Lord will figure out a way to tell you." He pursed his lips, touched that goatee with two fingers. "You might want to wonder why your mama wouldn't tell. Could be a good reason she didn't want you to know."

He knew. Ellie felt the certainty from her crown to her toes. "Maybe you're right," she said. "Thanks."

Everybody had their secrets. Marcus, too, it seemed. But as she dashed back down the hill, she realized that Marcus was protective of Connie. Which lent even more weight to the possibility that George Ewing might be her father.

Interesting.

Blue awakened in the stillest part of the night to find the bed empty beside him. For a moment, befuddled a little by the bourbon he'd drunk at Marcus's, he thought Ellie had already left him, and he put a hand out, thinking of her. The bed was warm. She'd probably gone to the bathroom.

On his pillow, Piwacket stirred, bumping her cheek against the crown of his head, and he smiled, moving his head a little. "Silly cat," he said, and raised a hand to gently rub her bony back.

When Ellie hadn't returned in five minutes, then ten, Blue got up and put on his jeans, picked up his cat, and went looking for her. She wasn't in the kitchen, though he saw evidence that she'd made a cup of tea. He checked the porch. Empty. He peeked out the kitchen windows, but the cabin was dark.

Finally he let Piwacket settle around his neck, purring into his ear, and climbed the steps to the widow's walk on the roof.

Ellie didn't hear him at first. Blue stood in the doorway, stunned all at once at the sight of her. She wore only one of his shirts, and it rode up on one side, showing a stretch of hip, obviously bare. Her hair was swept into a careless knot—how often had he seen her do that, take that thick, curly hair and twist it all up into a Wilma Flintstone bump on top of her head?—and as always, curls had sprung free to fall on her brow and down her neck, and the sight gave him an instant swell of lust, a need to spread his palm over that bare hip, brush his mouth over the turn of ear hiding beneath a single lock of dark hair.

Her face wore a pensive expression, very sad. "Must be deep thoughts," he said, settling in the chair opposite the one she sat in.

She smiled faintly, turning her head in greeting, but the rest of her body stayed lax, her legs propped up on the railing, her arms akimbo. "Some," she admitted. "This is a very good spot to sort things out. It all looks manageable from here."

Piwacket deserted him for Ellie, sidling around the dogs to leap into her lap. "Been slipping her liver?" he asked.

"I wouldn't do that." She bent and put her face to Pi's neck. "You are the sweetest thing."

Blue wanted to ask what things had seemed unmanageable till she came up here, but thought she'd get around to it if she had a mind to. He put a bare foot on her chair next to her bare hip, a soft, pleasant electric charge, and leaned back, resting his head on the railing to look at the sky. "Feels nice out here," he said.

"Mmm."

They sat in the quiet and the dark a long time, not speaking. Blue let his thoughts wander, filling his eyes with the sight of the stars. "I had one of those stars named for my wife," he said. "You know those things where you send in sixty bucks and they send you a form with the star and the name?"

"Did you? That's a sweet memorial. Which one is it?"

He turned his head. "Can't see it right now. Below the horizon."

Funny how it didn't hurt to think of her, not with his foot pressed warm into Ellie's leg, not with the night and the cool washing over him and a low sense of arousal warming his sex.

He thought of dinner at Marcus and Alisha's. Ellie loved the children, and played rambunctiously with them, a fact that made Alisha love her even more.

James cried when it was time to go to bed, wanting to stay up and play with her some more, and Ellie had gone in with Alisha to read a book. He heard snatches of it—she read *The Black Snowman* in a lilting voice and waited as Alisha read *Owl Moon*.

But all through dinner and into the companionable time afterward when they all sat out in the backyard, surrounded by citronella torches to keep mosquitoes at bay, and listened to the roar of cicadas and crickets, there had been a funny sense of strain between Ellie and Marcus.

"What's with you and Marcus?" he asked now.

"What?"

He lifted his head, wanting to see her face. "You heard me. Y'all are either having wild sex when nobody's looking—which, frankly, I like to pride myself you'd be too tired to do with me around—or you're hiding something else."

"What are you talking about?"

He laughed softly, and reached out to put his hands on her ankle. "C'mon, Ellie. You think I'm blind? You were so polite with each other it was like a Jane Austen novel." He raised his voice to a falsetto. "'Mr. Williams, would you be so kind as to pass me that pitcher of tea?' 'Why, certainly, Miz Connor, I'd be honored to pass you the tea.'"

Ellie laughed. "You're imagining things."

"Liar, liar, pants on fire." He slid his foot up higher on her hip, and the shirt revealed more thigh. "Can't be a surprise party, seeing as I don't have a birthday till August."

"It figures. August. I should have known you were a Leo."

He grinned. "Don't change the subject." Using his toe, he pushed the shirt up a little more, showing an intriguing glimpse of darkness. "This is about whatever secret stuff you've got going on here."

Ellie grabbed the hem primly and yanked it down. "Maybe." She frowned. "Blue, do you think Mabel could have been the one who killed Peaches?"

He inclined his head. "You are *so* transparent, Miz Connor." He managed to get hold of the hem of the shirt in a good grip with his toes, and pushed hard and quick, showing a lot more than hip. "Mmmm." He wiggled his eyebrows. "What else you got under there?"

"You have a one-track mind, Dr. Reynard," she said, grabbing his foot with a laugh and shoving it off her chair.

"Yeah?"

"Yeah." She dipped her head, throwing him a sloe-eyed glance that sent bolts of heat over his skin, and he found himself poised at the promise in her voice.

With a smooth gesture, she crossed her arms, grabbed the tails of the shirt, and skimmed it off over her head. Then, with a wanton gesture that nearly took off the top of his head, she dropped it over the railing and leaned back. "Better?"

He didn't move, letting the prickles of desire, the building thud of heat fill him entirely. Moonlight made sharp shadows of her body, a deep smoky half circle beneath the plumpness of each breast, a small pool of dark over her belly button, an inviting geometric in the shadow of her thighs. "Is this a plot to distract me?" he asked and his voice rasped.

Her lids fell, languidly, and her nostrils flared, and he knew she was dying for his hands on her. But her voice was arch and cool and she let her arms fall sideways, like a woman in a Maxfield Parrish painting. "I don't know. Is it working?"

A swath of light made her throat creamy. Her nipples, aroused and exaggerated by the angle of shadow, captured his gaze, and he touched his lips with his tongue, knowing she was watching. A faint shudder moved under her skin, rippling against his leg where it touched hers. "Yeah," he said. "It's working."

Blue moved, pushing her legs apart to kneel between them, thrusting his sex, tight below denim, against the nakedness of hers before settling his mouth on her throat. With a wicked depth, she laughed and wrapped him close, putting her hands in his hair to pull him up to kiss her. "You are so easy, Blue Reynard."

"Just me, huh?" He grasped her buttocks in his hands and pulled her tighter against him, resisting her kiss, holding his mouth so close his lips tingled with anticipation, so close their breath hurried from one to the other. Against his bare chest her breasts were a hint and a swell, an agonizingly pleasurable jolt, and even through his jeans, he felt the eager pulse of her against him.

Their gazes tangled, and it seemed they were poised, right there, for a long, long time, breathing together in anticipation of a kiss, her hands tight in his hair, his tight on her rear. And the roar of need was so good, he let it dangle, slipped his tongue out and flickered it over her plump lower lip. Then again, on the top. She arched a little, pressing her breasts into him, wiggling, and he groaned, feeling a bolt of heat up his spine.

He kissed her, all at once, opening his mouth to meet hers, open and starving, and pulled her into his lap so he could put his hands on her breasts, loving the cry she made when he pressed up into her. She made a helpless sobbing noise and bit his lip, power suddenly in her arms. Taking her weight on her knees, she broke the kiss and fumbled with his zipper—then halted. "Condom?"

"In my pocket." His voice was husky. "Right . . . front."

"Oh, I do like a man who is ready." She stuck her hand in his pocket, and somehow those fingers were wandering, all over. "Funny, I can't seem to find it."

"Well, I'll just have to be patient, then."

"Ah, here we go." She tucked the packet between her lips, and started what she'd begun, which was peeling off his jeans. He helped her with the jeans, kicking the fabric away so that they were both naked under the starry sky. "Allow me." Ellie tore the package with her teeth and put the condom in her mouth.

He did. But when she raised her head, eyes heavy-lidded with both amusement and desire, he took her arms. "Not yet, sugar. I'm so easy and all." Sitting up, he pulled her arms behind her back and settled her in his lap, lightly, and put his head down, suckling her nipples hard, wondering if she could come with just this.

She made a muffled, laughing sound and spit out the condom. "Trying to choke me to death?"

He chuckled and touched her with the slow, long strokes she liked, and lifted his mouth to her lips, bracing her in the crook of his elbow as he kissed her and stroked her and as she began to come, he plunged. Deep. Hard. And held her there.

Dizzy now, but loathe to end the time, he kissed her and kissed her and kissed her, breathing her breath, touching her hair, her back, her breasts, until his strength to resist was gone, and she moved against him and kissed him, holding him deep, and he was lost, lost in a reeling wholeness.

When it was over, he fell backward, gasping and weak, and Ellie fell over him, her body limp against his, her head in his shoulder. "A person could die, having an orgasm like that," she said.

He brushed his hand through her hair. "You're so easy, Ellie Connor."

She laughed.

Ellie slept later than she intended, waking up in a pool of sunshine that made her conscious of the sticky sweat collecting on her neck and arms. The old house was poorly air-conditioned, and heat gathered on the upper stories, never entirely dispelled. She took a cool shower and washed her hair, tying it into a tight knot on top of her head—not the most flattering style, but by far the most practical in the heat.

When she got to the top of the stairs, she heard

Lanie down in the kitchen, singing "The Old Rugged Cross" along with the radio. Ellie halted, embarrassed. She usually left before Lanie came upstairs, and now she didn't quite know how to manage the situation. She was glad she'd opted to shower here rather than at the cottage, as if the water would somehow wash away the scarlet bravado of her seduction last night. Still, it was very weird to have to face the old woman when she had very obviously spent the night.

No way around it.

Taking a breath, she started down the stairs, with Piwacket, April, and Sasha trailing behind her. Ellie let a blue-edged memory creep back into her mind, and a ripple moved down her spine. Whew. What a night!

At the foot of the stairs, she realized she'd left her watch on the nightstand. Patting her bare wrist, she whirled to go back up. All three animals froze in place, waiting to see what she would do. "Excuse me," she said to April, pushing by. Sasha, panting, didn't move, and Ellie shoved by her as well. Piwacket tripped along ahead, tail high, glancing over her shoulder to make sure she had the location right. They all went into the bedroom, followed her to the bed, then obligingly followed her out, down the hall, down the stairs. Flanked by the faithful, she said, "Honest, guys, I could have done it by myself."

"Land, child," Lanie said as Ellie and her entourage came into the kitchen. "Don't they half drive you insane?"

Relieved at the ordinary greeting, Ellie just shook

her head, smiling ruefully. Piwacket trotted into the kitchen and meowed urgently at Lanie. It was the yelp of a cat that knew and expected something, and Ellie opened her mouth to protest as the thin frail white woman bent to put a dish of all-white tuna down on the floor for the tiny, frail white cat.

Lanie straightened and caught Ellie's glance. She lifted her chin. "Soon as he'll let her go, she's ready. In the meantime, I'll be dadblamed if I'll let her starve to death." She narrowed her eyes. "Don't you go tattling on me."

The cat wolfed the food, making a low noise that was somewhere between a purr and a meow. Ellie made a motion of zipping her lips and throwing away a key.

"You hungry, girl?"

"Oh, no. I'll just grab some cereal at the cottage."

"Don't be silly. Skinny thing like you? Besides, I've seen you eat, child. Sit down and keep me company while I fry us some eggs." She glanced at Pi. "In *bacon* grease. Doctors want to ruin every tiny little thing."

Chuckling, Ellie moved to a cupboard and took out a mug—her favorite, made of blue ceramic with stars painted over the outside. She was in the middle of pouring her coffee before she realized how proprietarily she had moved in this kitchen, like it was hers. And as if to underscore the realization, Lanie said, "Hand me a spatula, child."

Ellie reached in the drawer and pulled it out, feeling a faint sense of hollowness in her chest. She stood over the sink and sipped some coffee, trying to warm the cold spot, but through the windows she could see the rain-forest greenhouse with hints of bougainvillea pushing pink against the roof. She thought of Blue, coming up the path later, humid skin smelling of earth, and his hair carrying hints of exotic flowers.

She closed her eyes.

"Pretty isn't it?" Lanie said. The sizzle of eggs hitting hot grease punctuated the room, as homey a sound as . . . home.

"It really is," Ellie said quietly. "I didn't know I missed being in the country so much. It makes me feel peaceful to be here." Or maybe it wasn't the country so much as Blue, making her feel so good.

"So marry him."

"What?"

"You heard me. Marry him. This old house fits you like a glove. And I think the ghosts must like you, too. Ain't heard a restless one since you been here."

"There are ghosts?"

"Land, yes." She flipped the eggs. "Over easy good for you?"

Ellie nodded.

"Family ghosts, mostly, I reckon. Always are in a place like this. I don't know how Blue stands to have his computer in the very room where his daddy shot himself." She slid eggs on a plate and gave it to Ellie. "Sit."

Taking the heavy china plate edged with silver, Ellie obeyed. She put a napkin down for both of them, and swung backward to reach in the drawer for silverware. And paused. She'd done it again.

Lanie plopped her own plate on the table and sat

down. "You one of those women who don't want to tie herself down?"

Ellie picked up her fork, wondering just exactly how to navigate this minefield. "No," she said carefully. "I always figured I'd find someone eventually. It just hasn't happened."

"Well, why not Blue?"

She pursed her lips, wondering how to answer. "You know I'm crazy about him. Everybody knows." She poked her egg yolks and watched them spill over the whites. She shook her head, raised her eyes, and said as honestly as she could, "I can't save him, Lanie."

"A good woman can do a lot in that direction, though."

"No. A man saves himself. And if Blue can't, if he doesn't find his way through all that despair that still haunts him, he'd shatter me. Not just my heart. My life. The lives of any children we'd have. All of us would go down with him—and the horrible part of it would be him seeing that, and being unable to stop it."

Lanie said nothing. Very precisely, she cut a triangle of egg, set her knife aside, and lifted the egg to her mouth. Like a cat, her mouth motions seemed out of proportion to how much food she had taken.

Worried she'd offended the woman who was, for all practical purposes, his mother, Ellie added, "Have I made an enemy of you, Lanie? I'd hate that."

"No, child." She put her fork down. "I reckon you're right. I wish you weren't."

"Me, too, Lanie. More than I can say."

"Too bad," she said. "It was worth a try." She

glanced at Piwacket, her nose and ears bright pink as she cleaned her paws. "Fact is, we're both hanging on till he's got somebody else to hang on to."

"You're not *ill?*"

Lanie waved her hand. "Oh, I've been sick for years. Like that cat—I have the sugar, and heart pills and blood pressure pills and lately, some other things I don't even want to know what they're for." She waved the subject away. "Neither of us is in imminent danger of keeling over, though. We'll hang on."

Ellie chuckled, relieved when the old woman took up her fork again. "So how you doing on that biography?"

Relieved to change the subject, Ellie said. "Making progress. I'm just about finished with the research, except for a few interviews. Do you remember anything about her?"

"Well, sure I remember her. Our times weren't like y'all's, but it's a small town, and we all knew each other, colored and white." She swept a pile of crumbs from the oilcoth. "She was about twenty years younger than me, so I was old enough to pay attention to all the little things they printed in the paper. I always have wondered where she got off to."

"You ever hear any gossip about what happened?"

"Oh, sure. Everybody talked about it. Some said it was murder. Some said she had a broken heart or she had a baby or that she killed her lover and couldn't bear what happened, so she just lit off into the world."

"Killed her lover?" Ellie narrowed her eyes. "Had a baby? Do you think it was true?"

"I don't know. Any of it could be, or none of it." She blotted her lips. "You oughta go talk to Doc, over to Hopkins'. He was always crazy in love with the woman."

"I have." She sighed and put the plates on the rack. "He's willing to talk about her, but not anything bad." She smiled. "And I assume having a child out of wedlock would have been considered quite scandalous."

"Oh, yes."

A blast of inspiration struck her, and goosebumps rose all over her skin. "Oh!" she cried. "Of course!"

Lanie chuckled. "What is it?"

"There's this six-week gap in her life that has been driving me crazy." Lost in thought, a sense of excitement rising in her, Ellie sightlessly picked up her plate and carried it to the sink. "It never occurred to me how different things were on this level. If she'd been pregnant out of wedlock, it might have hurt her career if people knew she'd had a baby." She stopped, staring into space, where all the pieces fell, like the cards in a computer game, into their places. "If she was pregnant, she would have had to hide it, and she would have had to go somewhere to have the baby."

"No doubt about it."

She dashed over, dropped an impulsive kiss on Lanie's head. "I have to go." She squeezed her shoulders. "Thanks so much!"

The Lovers

She liked to watch him in sleep, when all the masks and danger fell away, revealing the true man. And it was rare that she had the chance, the chance to look at him so freely while he was unguarded. He was careful that way.

But just now, he was fast asleep, stretched out like a cat in a puddle of sunlight. A black cat, he'd say if he were awake. A jaguar. And he'd pose and pounce and make growling cat noises in her ears and gnawing cat bites at her neck.

But black wasn't the word. Not even his hair was really black. Very dark brown most of the time, but at moments like this, each infinitesimally small curl captured a beam of gold light and cast it back to the world, making his head seem as if it were haloed. Or shaped with an aura of gold, like one of those old medieval paintings.

His eyelashes and brows . . . she propped her chin on her hand and considered. His eyelashes embarrassed him. They were so long they fell like fans on his cheeks, making his sleeping face look like a child's. They always said that, that lashes and sleep made a man look like a child, but in his case, it was because of those very long, very dark lashes. They were, perhaps, very close to black.

Not his flesh. The smoothest skin she'd ever seen, almost completely hairless—arms and legs and chest and chin—and not a nick or a scar. But no one, no woman with half an ounce of brain, could ever mistake that smoothness for anything but pure maleness. His limbs were long and sleek, without a pucker of softness anywhere, just smooth graceful lines of work-born muscles in his arms and down his back and thighs.

Sometimes she wondered if she would love him if he looked another way, but it was impossible to imagine him in another body, with any other face. She yearned to make love to him, to that body, because it belonged to him. Looking at him gave her pleasure because he was beautiful, but also because that face and that body contained his heart, his soul. She reached out now and curled her hand around his ankle, wanting that small connection.

It must have awakened him, for he reached out one strong, elegant hand and put it against her head. "Come here, baby," he said. "Let me hold you."

Gladly she moved into the circle of his arms, and nestled into the curve of his shoulder. He kissed her head and settled his cheek against her hair, and fell asleep again, holding her.

17

Ellie took time enough to change clothes, though it was fairly difficult to find anything clean or unwrinkled enough to wear. Someday, she really had to think about doing some real laundry, rather than just a load here and there. The only thing left was a sleeveless cotton shift in blue calico that she'd never much liked—but it packed well, and with a jacket, it could look professional, so it was a mainstay.

It was too hot for the jacket today, of course, and she settled for rubbing lotion on her arms, noticing for the first time that she had really not acquired much of a tan thus far this summer. Over her hair, she dithered, and finally just left it in its little knot on top of her head.

As she drove to Hopkins', it occurred to her that the dithering was due to nervousness. What kind of customers would be there in late morning? Anyone? Did Doc work in the morning?

She slowed. Maybe she should have called first.

Mellow out, Connor, she told herself wryly.

What's the bottom line here? The worst that could happen—the very, very worst—was that Doc wouldn't be there, or he'd refuse to talk to her about Mabel if he was.

But, in her heart, she had to admit it was a little intimidating to go there by herself. A black club in a town she didn't know well. It was one of those unspoken rules of culture in America: One waited to be invited to country clubs, to uptown society dinners, and to any spot run by and frequented mainly by another ethnic group. Walking in uninvited meant you'd probably get an icy stare or two.

Okay. She took a breath and let it go. Perfectly understandable reason for feeling nervous. She was allowed to feel it, she just couldn't let it stop her. By the time she reached the gravel parking lot, she was ready to go to bat as Mabel's biographer. To write this book, she had to have more answers.

There were three other cars in the small lot. Not so intimidating. She parked in the shade of a tall pine and turned off the engine. Before she got out, she looked at the place through the windshield, trying to shed herself, to see the place the way Mabel might have. The last time she'd been here, she'd been so dazzled by Blue's physical presence that little else had made an impression. Even now, thinking of the way he'd flirted with her that night made her smile. It had all started right there. With the blues winding around them, binding them together.

Get to it, Connor. With a sigh, she grabbed her purse and notebook and got out of the car, and paused again to let her imagination soak up whatever details it chose. It was humid and hot as she crunched over the gravel. Birds and wind made the only sounds. She tried to put on the Mabel persona, see the scene through the blues singer's eyes.

Mabel would have been wearing silk, or maybe rayon, the old kind that needed an iron every three seconds. No stockings. High-heeled sandals—she'd had a taste for vampy shoes, which showed off her pretty ankles. Ellie felt her body ease a little, into a more natural gait. Yes.

The oak tree arching over the roof, casting deep shade over the entrance and a grassy meadow to one side, would have stood then, though not quite so thick. From the meadow, a well-worn path led into the forest. Mabel would have known where it led.

Ellie stepped into the shade, and with a ripple of sudden awareness, she realized Peaches had been shot right here. Within a couple feet of the door. Someone he'd known had come up to him and shot him clean through the heart. She closed her eyes and tried to sense any lingering trace of that sudden violence, but there was nothing but the brush of wind against her elbows, a gust that loosened her hair and pushed curls over her face. From within came the sound of music.

Hoisting her bag over her shoulder, she pushed open the door like a professional in pursuit of answers.

Coming as she did from the bright day, she was blinded. She heard the door shut behind her, deepening the gloom, and for a moment, stayed where she was, blinking to clear her vision. The jukebox was playing

Jonny Lang's cover of "Lie to Me"—not exactly a good sign—and somewhere in the back, someone clinked glassware. Ellie could make out the red tubing around the jukebox and the blaze of brighter lights around the bar. Still mostly blind, she headed toward that beacon of light—and instantly cracked her shin hard against a chair.

"Shit."

"Hurt enough to suit you?"

Ellie rubbed the place. "Marcus?"

He laughed, so amused it annoyed her. "Hang on, little girl. We'll come rescue you."

"I'm fine," she said, and straightened. Her eyes had finally adjusted. Doc stood behind the bar, heels of his hands propped on it, his face closed as she approached. Marcus sat on a stool, a cup of coffee before him. At least he was a point of friendliness, although Ellie had the sudden distinct sense that she was about to be played like a fiddle.

The only other person there was a small black woman somewhere between fifty and seventy. Impossible to tell. She wore a pair of thick glasses that distorted her eyes and effectively hid the upper half of her face. As she came closer, Ellie recognized her. "Hi," she said. "We're neighbors. We met one morning on the river—you were fishing."

"I remember."

"Mrs. Laisser?"

"That's right." Her voice was low and calm. "Please call me Gwen."

Ellie smiled. "Gwen it is." She turned to Marcus. "I didn't see your truck out there."

"Nah, I came down from my mama's. She sent some beans down to Doc here."

A little pause. Ellie felt the awkwardness of them calmly waiting, all three of them, to state her purpose. "I came to talk to you, Doc, if you can spare the time."

"About Mabel, I guess."

Ellie nodded.

"I done told you all I know already."

"Yeah." Ellie pursed her lips. She felt Gwen's eyes on her from one side, and Marcus's from the other. "I know. Um. The thing is, I still have big gaps I need to fill in. I came up with a couple of theories I wanted to ask you about."

He gazed at her steadily with flat eyes.

"Please," Ellie said. "It isn't my intention to smear her. But I can't possibly write this without knowing the truth. She was a great singer and songwriter, but more than that, before all that, and through it, she was a woman, and what happened to her in her life made a difference in what she wrote. If I don't know who the woman was, how can I write with any authority about her music?" She took a breath, and repeated, "Please. I need your help."

Doc pursed his lips, considered. Capitulated. "All right." He gestured for her to sit.

Marcus moved his knees and Ellie settled on the vinyl-covered stool. "They're kind of sensitive questions," she said, glancing toward Mrs. Laisser.

Doc remained stone-faced. "You can speak freely here."

Taking a breath, Ellie folded her hands on top of the

bar and leaned forward. "There are a couple of gaps—and they're important. Whatever happened during that spring and summer of fifty-two must have led her to leave everything behind." She pressed the fleshy parts of her thumbs together hard, for courage. "Two questions. Did Mabel ever have a child?"

Ellie was watching carefully, but it wouldn't have taken a trained observer to see the pain that flashed over Doc's face. He shook his head. "What you want to drag that up for? Why you want to dig in her secrets and make her look bad?" He slammed his hand on the bar. "Folks need to know what she did for music. All the rest don't mean nothing."

In spite of his outrage, Ellie felt a flare of exhilaration. He hadn't denied it. And since he was riled up anyway, she tossed out the second question. "Was it Mabel who shot Peaches?"

Doc made a noise and walked off, muttering to himself. He picked up a bar towel and wiped the far end, shaking his head. Ellie, defeated, started to move. Marcus put his hand on her arm. "Give him a minute."

And sure enough, he came back down to her. "I just don't know why you keep poking around in all this. What does it matter, now?"

Reaching deep, relying on instinct, Ellie responded with as much earnestness as she could. "Because music doesn't just appear in the world. It's the musicians who make it live. It comes from the soul. What Mabel knew and who she loved and what happened to her made a difference in her music."

He lowered his eyes, and Ellie pressed on. "I'm telling you honestly, from the bottom of my heart, that I don't write to expose the seams of a musician's life. I write to illuminate the music that came from them."

She leaned forward. "Mabel is so special, and maybe some of those things you're hiding from me made a difference that I'll be able to understand when I get ready to write about those songs she wrote before she disappeared. They're so rich, as rich and beautiful as any music I've ever heard. I'm here, Doc, because I love those songs, and I don't want her contribution to be lost in time. Can't you understand that?"

Reluctantly, he raised his eyes, and Ellie saw a glimmer of respect there. "Doc, I need to know why she walked away, and I think you're the only one who knows."

Silence. Thickest right in front of her. The mulish silence of a man protecting a woman. Ellie glanced at Marcus, who shrugged a little, commiserating with her. "Well, you know where to find me if you change your mind," she said, and slid off the stool. "She must have been one hell of a woman."

She headed for the door.

"Young lady." It was the woman's voice.

Ellie turned.

"Hold on, and let me walk you out." Mrs. Laisser made a move to get off her stool, but her feet didn't quite reach the floor. Marcus reached out and helped her down, and there was nothing frail about her step. When she got to Ellie, she said, "Come on."

Ellie followed her out to the lot. The woman didn't

speak for a minute, then she lifted her head. "Doc won't ever give you anything true. Men never did understand Mabel Beauvais," she said, finally. "This is a woman's story, and if you want to find out what happened to her, you're gonna have to talk to the women who knew her."

"Well, that's what I've been trying to do. And yet none of them seem to know what Doc knows." She hesitated, then plunged forward. "How well did you know her, Gwen?"

"As good as anybody, I expect." A slow, almost sad smile. "I can tell you one thing that Doc just can't bring himself to say: That woman loved Peaches McCall, heart, soul, and bone. And he made a fool of her."

Ellie nodded. "That's what I thought." She inclined her head. "What was he like, Peaches?"

The smile was somehow young. "Honey, there wasn't a woman in this town that didn't at least think once or twice about that man's hands on her. He just had that scent about him, you know? And a way of looking right into a woman's eyes that—" She broke off, shook her head. "You know what I mean. He liked to set the streets afire."

A vision of Blue rose before her, loose limbs and sultry eyes and that deadly, sexy smile. "Yes."

Gwen moved a step away. "You oughta go talk to Peaches's mama. Hattie Gordon. Tell her I sent you."

"Thank you." As Gwen started to back away, she said, "Will you still tell me what you remember, now that you're back?"

"If you don't get what you need from Hattie, I will." She smiled. "You're a pretty brave girl. I like that." She lifted a hand in farewell, and headed back inside.

Marcus had to take his mother in to the doctor and run some errands for her, so Blue spent the morning taking soil measurements and making notations, all the while thinking about Ellie.

Ellie, with her life story nearly as sad as his own, and that bright strength running through her. He wished he could give her the name of her father, a gift, but it was easier said than done without betraying her secret. And whether he thought she ought to keep it or not was beside the point. She'd trusted him with it, and he'd keep it until she gave permission to do otherwise.

So he tried to puzzle it out on his own. Reaching up to pluck a dead blossom from a cattelya, he reached back to think of the hippie kids who had been in town that summer. He remembered it pretty well, considering he'd only been eight or nine at the time.

The bus had driven into town like something right off TV, as surprising and thrilling to a small boy as a movie star walking the streets. He and his buddy Delbert had taken the path by the river up to the spot where they had been stranded, there in Reed's west pasture, and spied on them through the trees. The bus itself was a marvel, painted with flowers and peace signs and butterflies, and Blue loved the look of the people who got off it, too. Loved the long strands of tiny beads they wore around their necks, and their long, wild hair, and the colors with which they adorned themselves. He liked their sandaled feet and bare torsos, and once—shocking and electrifying—Blue and Delbert had watched the two girls bathing in the river, purely naked right outside. With a faint smile, he wondered now if one of them had been Ellie's mother.

He'd loved them. And for years after, his main goal in life had been to grow up and "be a hippie," an ambition that made his father choke in disgust, and his brother turn red-faced. It didn't change Blue's mind any, but he did learn not to try and imitate those bird-of-paradise people around his family.

Standing now in his greenhouse in his bare feet, he supposed there were people who'd say he'd done just that. What grown man spent his time barefooted in a wild world of flowers, playing with lizards and bugs, trying to find ways to feed people who had trouble feeding themselves? He chuckled as one of those lizards scurried across the arch of his foot.

Sometimes he guessed things just worked out, in spite of everything.

And in a single moment, between taking a sample and standing to put it in the plastic rack, Blue was swept with a sense of such pure contentment, such expansive rightness, that it nearly made him dizzy. All the things that normally troubled him in that vague, sad way seemed to disappear all at once. He had no wish to be anywhere but here, in this day, with his work and his friends and his house.

And Ellie.

Ellie. Wanton and wise, funny and so deadly earnest, sane and secretive. Just the thought of her made his skin ripple, and he could close his eyes and feel her hair against his face.

In that light-struck state, it didn't even scare him to understand he'd fallen in love with her. Way in love. A having-babies-and-dentures-in-the-glass kind of love. It didn't scare him because that's what a man did, finally—or at least a lucky man, anyway—fell in love. Fell in love and took a mate and settled in and had some babies to cuddle who turned out nothing like you expected, but as long as they were happy, it was okay. The circle turned, and sometimes there were sad stretches, but then it turned again, and there was a green season once more. And usually, everything was all right in the end.

Oh, yeah.

He sort of swelled with all this, as if he were filled with helium, and without a second thought, he put down his samples and went to the house to change his clothes. Piwacket followed him hopefully up the stairs, and he remembered he hadn't given her pills this morning. "Oh, you hate me for this, don't you?" he said, and patiently gave her the tiny yellow pill, stroked her throat until she swallowed, then let her go. She blinked, purred for a second, and jumped down to run down the hall to his study. Silly cat. She'd sulk under the desk for an hour or two, and that was fine.

In the meantime, he had some shopping to do. Whistling, he splashed cologne on his jaw, combed his hair, and set off for town. He didn't want Miss Ellie Connor going anywhere. Nowhere at all.

• • •

Ellie found Hattie Gordon listed in the tiny Pine Bend phone book. Standing at a pay phone outside a convenience store in the sun, she dialed the number and remembered, wiping sweat off the back of her neck, why she didn't like Southern summers all that much. A woman answered curtly, as if the phone had called her from some pressing task.

"Mrs. Gordon," Ellie said, "my name is Ellie Connor, and Gwen Laisser told me to get in touch with you."

"Go on."

"She said if I wanted to learn more about Mabel Beauvais you'd be the one to ask."

"'S that right." It wasn't a question.

Ellie pressed on. "I was over at the juke joint this morning trying to get Doc to tell me—"

"Doc! Have mercy. That man always was so love-blind he'd never tell you a damned thing." The swear word, mild as it was, shocked Ellie faintly, and she realized she hadn't heard women around here swearing at all.

"Exactly," she said, dryly. "So will you tell me?"

The silence went on so long Ellie said, "Mrs. Gordon?"

"You say Gwen told you, huh?"

"Yes."

"All right. C'mon then. You might not like what I got to say, but you can come hear it anyway."

Ellie carefully followed the directions Mrs. Gordon had given her, and was happily surprised to find herself exactly where she should be at the end of the notes.

The house was set back from the road, a couple of miles upriver from Hopkins', a small farmhouse made of weathered gray wood. Laundry flapped in the breeze, sheets and towels and the underwear of a large woman. Pigs in a spotless pen lazed in the afternoon sun, and when Ellie slammed her car door, a dusty black dog got up from a patch of shade to come over and nose her knee. Ellie patted his head, expecting someone to peer through the screen door, but no one did, and she climbed up a set of steps to a porch furnished with chairs and tables and pots of red geraniums, vividly bright against the uniformly worn colors around them. She knocked on the screen door, trying not to appear as if she was peering into the room within.

"It's open!" came a voice from the back.

"It's Ellie Connor, Mrs. Gordon."

"I said it's open, girl. C'mon back."

Gingerly, Ellie swung open the screen, and stepped into the cool, bright living room. It was furnished with overstuffed chairs, the backs covered with crocheted doilies in a raised-rose pattern. An antique floor lamp stood beside a chair, and one wall was entirely covered with pictures, generations of family photos.

Ellie paused in front of the photos, too curious to help herself, trying to pick out the infamous Peaches from the dozens of men on the walls. "You sure have a handsome family," she called out, and they were—a rather light-skinned lot, with large, soft-looking eyes. There were wedding and baby photos, school pictures and boys in uniform. Ellie halted in recognition at one of them, and made a soft sound of dismay.

"That's my grandbaby James," Mrs. Gordon said, wiping her hands on her apron. "Died in Vietnam."

"I've seen pictures of him," Ellie said, and turned. The woman was short and round as a dumpling, with deceptively unwrinkled, very dark skin, a darkness that made her pale brown eyes seem uncanny.

"That's his daddy, there. They called him Peaches." She pointed at a black-and-white of a man in a loose, forties-style suit, obviously at a party of some kind. He had a twenty-four-karat smile and the broad-shouldered, loose-limbed height that was made for a suit like that. He had his arms around a woman on either side, and Ellie saw that he was everything Doc had hinted—and more. She didn't want to be drawn to him, didn't want to like the sensual face, the knowing eyes, but even in a photo, there was so much charisma he was hard to resist.

"Peaches?"

"That's what they called him. I named him Otis, after my daddy, since his own was a good-for-nothing gambler who ran out on me." She lowered her girth into a chair. "Got me a good man second time around." She pointed to a sober, kind-looking man. "Too late to save Otis."

Ellie took her cue, and settled opposite. "I've seen pictures of James before, him and Marcus."

"Marcus." She spat the word. "Wasn't for Marcus and his big dreams, James would never have joined no white man's army."

Ellie remembered Marcus telling her that he and

James had joined the Army on the buddy system. Remembered, too, how his eyes clouded with grief when James was mentioned. "I'm sorry," she said. "He looks like a very nice young man."

"He was," she said, and even so many years later, there was still pain in the loss, a pain Ellie hadn't heard over Peaches. "Good as the day is long, I swear he was. Not like his daddy—nor his mama, either."

"Pea—er—Otis wasn't a good man?"

The tight mouth drew up even more into a grimace. "Lawsy, no. Cut from the same cloth as my good-for-nothing husband, was Otis. Couldn't do a thing with him from the time he was ten years old." She sighed. "I loved him, you know—you can't help but love your children—but that woman hadn't shot him that night, some husband would've had done it sooner or later."

"A woman shot him?"

The scowl deepened. "I thought you knew all this."

"Some of it. Not that."

She inclined her head, suddenly changing direction. "Child, you sure look familiar. You got any people around here?"

She'd heard the question so often, she said automatically, "Not that I know of." With a shrug, she added, "I just came here to do this book."

"A *book?*" The scowl came back. "Gwen know you're doing a book?"

"Yes."

The pale eyes measured her, unblinking. Ellie tried

very hard to appear earnest and honest. "You gonna write all of it—the bad and the good?"

Ellie quelled her impatience. "I just want to figure her out, first. If you have anything you don't want me to write, say so, and I'll leave it out."

"No, child, you don't understand. I *want* it all in there. She killed my son."

Even though she'd been expecting this, Ellie felt a ripple of sorrow or dread or something go through her. "She did?"

"She sure did. Right in front of a dozen folks on the front steps at Hopkins'. Bold as you please." Mrs. Gordon warmed to her subject, using her hands to spin out the drama. "Dressed herself up in a red dress, with red shoes, and had her hair done perfect that afternoon—Luerelean Williams did it herself and told me about it, said Mabel had the *works* done that day, fingernails and toenails, and course they were glad to have her there—she spent more money in one day than most folks in those days had in a year. Mabel brought in a hat she'd bought in Memphis, a red hat, and she matched her nails to that color, and then went over to the drugstore and got herself a lipstick to match, too."

Ellie let herself be drawn into the story. She could see Mabel doing something like that. "She dressed herself up to go kill him?"

"She was a vain one, Mabel Beauvais. Folks always talk about how she could sing, but it was the way she looked that drove the menfolk wild. That's what made her so mad about Peaches taking up with Marcia Talbert. She had to have everybody's attention on her, all the time, and she made damned sure she got it, hell or high water."

"I got the impression, from several people, that Mabel was deeply in love with Peaches."

Mrs. Gordon lowered her eyes to her hands, contemplating them for a moment. "I reckon she was." She looked at the picture of her son. "But that don't change the facts. She dressed herself all in red, and went there to find him. She waited out there in the parking lot until he came out, then took that gun from her purse and shot him, close up—I imagine he was trying to sweet-talk his way out of it, and with Otis, that meant putting his hands on a woman—right through the heart." Staring sightlessly to that night long ago, she said, quietly. "Dead before he hit the ground, the doctors say."

Ellie thought of a dozen things to say, but opted instead to remain silent and let the story roll out in its own way.

"Mabel put the gun back in her purse, got in her fancy car, and drove away. And nobody ever saw her again after that. Just—gone. Left her child, left her mama, left everybody, and just disappeared." She humphed. "Typical."

"Left her child?" Ellie asked, careful not to put too much excitement into the question.

"Can you imagine? And we never heard a word from her, either. Till the day he died, James asked about his mama, and what could I tell him?"

Half-dizzy with this last revelation, Ellie took a deep breath. She took out her notebook and started scribbling as fast as she could. "Tell me about that, about Mabel having the baby," she said.

And Mrs. Gordon talked. The sun moved, making the room dark, and Mrs. Gordon led Ellie to the kitchen, where she dished up plates of spaghetti thick with fresh sweet peppers and chunks of tomato, and from a simmering pot on the back of the stove, greens—"You ever had greens, child?" "Yes, ma'am"—and all the while, the woman talked. She told a riveting tale, moving back and forth in time, full of side trips and asides and rambling descriptions. Ellie scribbled notes as fast as she could, exuberant, giddy, and thankful.

Finally. *Finally.*

By the time she left, with a bag full of leftovers—she really did love greens and ate them with her usual appetite, which delighted the old woman—it was nearly sundown. She still didn't know where Mabel had gone, but at long last, she knew the whys, and the details. She urgently wanted to get home to her notes and her computer. In this mood, she would work all night—and it was about time.

She didn't see Blue's truck, and was about to write him a note when she caught sight of the hood coming up the road. She settled on the back porch steps to wait, and grinned when he pulled up. "Hey, good-lookin,'" she called.

He jumped down, trailing dogs from the cab, both of whom rushed up the hill to greet Ellie, tongues bobbling. Blue grinned, ambling in his usual way behind them.

Sitting there, with her arms crossed on her knees, Ellie was struck with him. Just *him*, all rolling, sexy grace and leanness, his hair shot with gold. It was still hard to believe that smile was for her.

All at once, work didn't seem that important. He had a bag of groceries and his jaunty good humor said he would cook for her. The idea of sitting in the kitchen, drinking a beer while he played music and chopped things and teased her, was a thousand times more appealing than going off to her little cottage alone.

But this would not last. Work would. And after such a long struggle to piece together the missing bits of Mabel's life, Ellie couldn't afford to squander all the raging creative energy she felt. She needed to pour all this heat and emotion into her work. It would be wasted on sex.

And yet, he was temptation made flesh. He put the bag of groceries down on the step and took her hand, tugging her to her feet, then wrapped his arms all around her, hips nestled close, and kissed her. Deep. Those knowing lips and teasing tongue, the muscles in his back shifting under her hands, the way they did when he was over her, in her. "Mmm," he said, a long, low, satisfied sound. "I've been thinking about that all day." He shifted his body, rubbing them together playfully, and put his forehead against hers. "You were such a wicked thing last night that I've been thinking up questions for you to avoid all day."

He smelled like the air here, and the greenhouse flowers lingered on his skin, and Ellie leaned in close, letting him want her, impossible as it was, letting herself want him back.

"Uh, Blue," she said before she could weaken.

He slid a hand under her shirt and his palm ignited tiny nerves across her belly. "Mmm-hmmm?"

"I have to work tonight."

"Tomorrow."

She turned her face into his thick hair, let the roughness of jaw graze her brow. "No, tonight."

"Aw." He raised his head. "Really?"

"Yes. I learned so much today." She let it fill her. "So much."

The blue eyes twinkled. "Have dinner with me first and tell me all about it. I got everything for chicken."

Something warm and deep pushed at her then, making her lean forward and put her hands on his lean cheeks, and tilt forward to kiss that beautiful mouth, very gently. "You know something, Blue Reynard?"

"What?"

She almost said, *I'm so crazy in love with you I can't breathe*, but instead said, "You are the sexiest man God ever made."

Something funny—hurt—crossed his face, so fast it was gone in a blink, quickly replaced with that sly, knowing smile. "Told you so."

She laughed.

"All right, then." He let her go, smoothing a hand down her arm. "I'll let you work. Come find me when you're done. You know the way."

"You might be asleep."

"Darlin', you know I never sleep." He lifted one

wicked brow. "And even if I am, you can surely think of some way to wake me up."

Ellie laughed. "All right."

He waved and walked by her, a little stiff across the shoulders, she thought, like he was self-conscious or a little hurt. Then her eyes fell to the jeans-clad hips, high and lean, and a tactile memory of that flesh against her palms rose up to tempt her—and she had to wonder if she'd lost her mind.

But Gwen's voice came back to her—*And I'll tell you one thing that Doc just can't bring himself to say: That woman loved Peaches McCall, heart, soul, and bone*—and Ellie told herself to hold the lust, the longing. Feel it. Because Mabel was all around her, pressing in, her voice a soft, throaty croon of longing.

Use it. Ellie turned, whistled for April, and hurried to her notes, to her book, to her work.

18

Since the night she'd first slept with him, weeks before, Blue hadn't been alone at night. He carried the groceries inside, putting the chicken and salad into the fridge, the tomatoes on the windowsill. The rich red of the fruit slowed him for a minute. It reminded him of rubies, the rubies set in a soft line across silver in the ring he'd bought this afternoon. He'd spent a lot longer trying to choose it than he'd planned, dithering between these rounded rubies in a faintly medieval ring or the square-cut emerald in white gold. He didn't know why it had to be color for her. Didn't know why silver, either. In sudden worry, he pulled the jeweler's box from his pocket and looked again. Tension eased. It was beautiful. Right.

And one day's delay was no big deal. Ellie was passionate about her work, and he'd sensed the undercurrent in her—the conflict she felt over whether to stay and spend that passion on him or give it to her work. He'd ached to coax her to give it to him, but in the end had tried to be graceful. She didn't—as Annie sometimes had—show up all bored and lonely, and want him to stop in the middle of some experiment. He wanted to give Ellie the same respect. She'd said she worked evenings, and she'd shifted her habits for him all these weeks.

Still. He clicked the box closed and wondered what to do about dinner. About the long evening ahead. Sasha came running when he opened the back door, and he fed her, then prepared a plate for Piwacket and called her.

She didn't come. A stab of worry went through him and he called more loudly, going to the kitchen door, listening for her reply. When she still hadn't appeared, he took the stairs to the study and peeked under the desk. She was there, curled in a ball, and she lifted her head when she saw him, yawning. Relief washed through him, a flood of cool against the heat of worry.

He picked her up, so tiny and thin she was nearly weightless, and she curled into his neck with a purr, her body warm against the hollow worry in his chest.

It struck him that he was expecting to have to pay for all this—the joy he'd found with Ellie. While he went around feeling good and happy, there was an apprehensive part of him that was waiting for the other shoe. When would he pay? And how much?

Piwacket lifted her head and gave his ear a moist bump, trilling softly. Blue held her and wanted to believe that her long, happy old age was a sign that things had changed in his life—that he wasn't Job, being tested, or a man living under a curse. He wanted to believe he would be able to enjoy this, but in the dark, with rain beginning to fall outside the windows, he could not quite shake his worry.

Lightning cut across the sky, followed by a sharp clap of thunder that sent Piwacket flying from his arms to her hiding place under the desk. She glared up at him, and he chuckled. "I know you find this hard to believe, but I'm not in charge of the weather." If a cat could have rolled its eyes, hers would have rolled then. Blue grinned, and tugged playfully on her tail, his apprehension dissolving with the storm.

A little superstition wasn't surprising, given his experience, but it would be crazy to let it run his life.

All through the night, he rattled around his house. He settled first in front of the television, and surfed for an hour through fifty-seven channels before he got bored with it, and went upstairs to the office where his computer was. He signed on to the Internet and searched for something that might interest him, and finally broke down and opened his E-mail, hoping for a note from Ellie.

It gave him a funny sense of déjà vu to find one and feel the pleased surprise, just as he always had before she arrived, all angles and toughness, in his real life. He opened the message.

B—

I'm sitting here, with Mabel's song—the one song, not all of them—rushing through me, pouring through my soul, through my bones, and I finally get it. "Hearts and bones and blood in a tangle . . ." It makes so much more sense now!

I have so much to tell you, but for now, just this: She loved Peaches McCall with everything in her.

It has taken so much work to get to this point this time that it's all the sweeter. This is why I do this—this feeling right here, when it all comes together and I feel like I am that musician. For just a little while, I can feel what it might be like to have the gift of music in me, feel it being born into the world through me. Was it Salieri who said, "Music is the language of God"? That's what I think. There are many beautiful things in the world, but music is the highest, most beautiful, purest of all.

I do sometimes wonder why musicians seem to have to suffer more than most people. Ever noticed that? They have to pay such a high price for the gift—even now, in our own times. Even the ones who get to be more or less happy and live long lives somewhere pay some huge price for it.

But you know what, Blue? To have music in me like it was in Mabel, like it was in John Lennon, like it is in Eric Clapton, I'd pay that price. I really would.

Ah. You know what I mean. I don't have to say it to you. You know.

Thanks for being understanding about my need to come here alone tonight and work.

Love, Ellie

Blue stared at the note, blue letters against a white screen, his heart full. Then he hit the Reply key.

> Ah, Ellie, I think I fell for you the first time you posted like that in the blues group—nobody captures that spirit of musicians and their power like you do. Is it wrong to ask if I can read the book before anybody else? I'm dying to see what you've done.
>
> See you in the morning, darlin'.

He smiled to himself, patting himself on the back for being so mature and letting her do her thing. Then, because he couldn't stand to leave it like that, stop talking to her, he opened a second window.

> P.S. What I'd really like to be doing now instead of typing notes in the dark and drinking bourbon and getting annoyed with the idiots in the newsgroups (don't these people have lives? g) is kissing you.
>
> I'd like to hear a knock at my back door and I'd like you to be standing there naked, and I'd like to answer the door naked, and then I'd like—oh, I bet you can figure out the rest.
>
> Tomorrow, sugar.

He sent the mail, then went to stand by the window. It offered a slightly different view of the cottage than the kitchen window, but through the rain, he could see lights glowing in the cabin.

He missed her. He wanted her. His life, which had been acceptable before she appeared, was empty and boring without her. Piwacket trilled around his ankles and he picked her up, idly rubbing her skinny shoulders as he mentally planned his proposal—for Ellie, it should be something beautiful and romantic. Something that would make her get all choked up and teary, that she could tell her friends about for forty years. In his mind, he saw it all—a granddaughter with Ellie's eyes, saying, "My grandpa's the most romantic guy in the world."

Oh, yeah.

Ellie was still lost in the book when the sun started coming up over the eastern trees, staining the sky a soft purple first, then lighter and finally giving the world a hard wash of red. She blinked and stretched her shoulders, realizing for the first time that she'd been up all night.

But what a night! Wandering over to the fridge, she took out a gallon of tea she'd made a day or two earlier and took a long swallow. Across her shoulders, she could feel the strain of such a long stretch of writing, and her eyes were grainy from a lack of sleep, but there was a jumping kind of restless giddiness, too.

She glanced at the desk, with the piles of paper piled up beside the small, efficient printer, and felt a soft dizziness. She lifted the mouth of the tea jug to her lips again and the moisture wet tissue long dried, forgotten, and it tasted as good as anything she'd ever known.

Finally—finally—Mabel had come to her last night. Ellie had played one song over and over, a song Mabel had written, then sung, with a kind of whispery brokenness Ellie had always loved: "Hearts and Bones," a ballad of lost love that must have been written for Peaches.

And it was Blue who had made it come home for Ellie, Blue with his seductive mouth and lost soul, that irresistible combination. Mabel, as Gwen had said, must have felt much the same for Peaches, and unlike Ellie, had believed it was a true and honest love.

In her slightly light-headed state, she glanced toward the big house where Blue probably slept right now. It was so easy to imagine him there, tangled in the humidly softened sheets, his long limbs and dark, smooth skin; his dangerous mouth slack in sleep, his lost soul hidden as it always was, behind a defense of wry beauty.

The work she'd done tonight was very good. She knew it, deep. Knew it from the way Mabel had just simply come alive for her during the long, quiet midnight hours when the rest of the world slept.

But there were questions remaining. Ellie had figured out the why of Mabel's disappearance—it was a method of atonement. Because she'd sinned so mightily, she gave up one of the things she cared most about: her music.

Undressing, Ellie wondered about Mabel's son.

Not many women could just walk away from a child. And by all accounts, Mabel had been quite fond of children. It didn't make sense that she'd just leave her baby with his grandmother and disappear, not even to atone for killing his father.

Wearily, she sat on the edge of the bed, aware that her thoughts were beginning to chase each other like squirrels, round and round and round. Enough. She closed the blinds to darken the room and fell on top of her covers, too tired to even take a shower.

She awakened, minutes or hours later, to someone's pounding on the door. It took a few minutes, given her disorientation, to discover the source of the sound, and even then, she simply rolled over, feeling the sweat gathering against her neck and along the length of her upper arms. She grew aware of the sound of a hard rain pattering, slapping, pouring on the roof and windows, and, befuddled, realized that it had been thunder she heard. Close and loud.

But no. The knock, very distinct, came again.

"Just a minute," she called, when it became clear whoever it was wouldn't go away. She stared at the ceiling for a minute, blinking hard, then swung her legs over the side of the bed, found a wrapper to put on, and padded to the door. She glanced at the digital clock on the desk as she passed: 1:10. A normal time to be awake if you belonged to the normal world, but for Ellie it meant she'd been sleeping for exactly four hours and twenty minutes.

She swung open the door and glared. "What is it?"

Then she saw who it was. "Marcus? Is Blue okay?"

"He's fine." The shoulders of his shirt were wet. "I just wanted to talk to you for a minute, if you have it."

She frowned, peered behind him at the downpour. "Man, it's really raining hard." Which made his presence on her porch seem even stranger. "C'mon in." Ellie left him to follow her, and headed for the coffeepot, which she'd prepared to start automatically. "Give me a minute, all right?" She rubbed her face and headed for the bathroom. "I don't wake up without coffee."

"If this is a bad time—"

Ellie waved it away. "No problem." She gestured to a chair. "Have a seat. I'll be back in a second."

She washed her face and tried to find something to wear—the laundry problem again—and settled for a pair of moderately wrinkled shorts and a black tank top that was ninety-seven years old. When she returned, the pot was half-brewed, and she poured a cup from the middle. "Want some?" she asked.

Marcus shook his head. "Ellie, I really didn't mean to intrude. I can come back."

Ellie cocked her head. Curiouser and curiouser. Marcus was perched on the edge of the chair, his hands twisting a tube of paper between his knees. He looked ill at ease, even a little apprehensive.

And he'd come through that hard rain to talk to her. She carried her coffee to the table and sat down. "Did you find something out about Mabel? Her disappearance?"

He pursed his lips, twisted the paper a little tighter,

as if to hide it. "No." He raised those sober dark eyes and said abruptly. "It's about your father."

Ellie blinked. Straightened. "Oh."

"I knew your mama," he said at last. "She was as lost and sweet as any girl I've ever known, before or since, but she fell in love that summer she was here. Put a light in her."

"Who, Marcus?" Ellie leaned forward and winced a little. "I bet I guessed, though: Binkle, right?"

Marcus laughed. *Really* laughed. "I gotta ask why you settled on him."

"Don't laugh. I was very methodical. There couldn't be that many, right? So it was a process of elimination. He's dark. My mama was as fair as morning, and I had to get it from somebody." She frowned. "Or Connie Ewing's husband, maybe. I saw a picture of him, but haven't managed to explore that angle much."

His eye twinkled. "Your mama wouldn't have come within twenty feet of Binkle. And George Ewing was already in Vietnam that summer."

"Oh, of course." She nodded, still fuzzy from too little sleep and the abrupt awakening. Outside, a bright flash of lightning made the windows bright, and she mentally counted the time until the thunder came, distant and low. She was aware, faintly, that her heart was skittering a little. "Then who, Marcus? I really can't even imagine who else."

Marcus bowed his head. And she thought for a minute there was dampness in his eyes. "You look just like him. I don't how I missed it for so long." Another beat of hesitation, and he reached into his shirt pocket and pulled out a photograph. "He's dark, all right."

Ellie took it with a hand that trembled faintly. "Oh, my God."

It was the same photo she'd seen a dozen times, in the yearbook and in Rosemary's attic and finally on Hattie Gordon's wall yesterday. "James Gordon?" she said aloud, and her voice was very soft.

"I didn't know how you'd take it, Ellie, or I'd've told you the night I figured it out, over at Rosemary's. And there're other people involved."

Her lungs felt pinched, airless. Ellie stared at the sweet, laughing face, and felt the strangest sorrow wash up through her throat. Into her eyes. "I can't believe it," she said quietly, and stared at the uptilted corner of his eyes and touched the corner of her own. The photo trembled in her hands. "I do look like him," she whispered, and the tears rushed up through her mouth and washed down her cheeks and she had no idea why it *hurt*.

"I don't know why I'm crying," she said to Marcus, but that only made it worse. She put the picture down and put a hand over her mouth, trying to catch some of it. "Everyone who knew him loved him so much," she said. "You and his grandmother . . . the way she talked about him yesterday, you could tell she missed him still, all these years later."

He took her hand across the table. That giant and somehow elegant hand. "Your mama loved him, too. And he loved her back, Ellie." His mouth worked. "He didn't know she was pregnant, or—" He bowed his head. "I don't know. I don't know what might have been different. It wasn't easy, you know. He was shipping out, and she wanted him to go to Canada. . . ." He shook his head. "Wish he would have."

"When did he die?"

"June third, 1969. I wrote your mama. She must not have got it. I never heard from her."

"Oh, I think she did." The first wave of sorrow had eased, and Ellie felt only sad. "She left when I was six months old. That would have put it right about the time you wrote. Oh, my poor mother!" New tears, new grief, swelled. "It must have been terrible for her." She took a breath, stared at the picture. "I never considered him." She looked up. "I'm kind of shocked. Is it okay to say that?"

He gave her hand a squeeze. "Yeah."

She took a breath, let it go, tried to get her mind around this new information. Would Blue mind? Would it make a difference to him?

"I reckon you'll want some time to let it settle," Marcus said. "You want to ask me anything, you know where to find me."

Ellie nodded.

But as he stood up, the ramifications of James Gordon's being her father bolted through her. "Oh, my God, Marcus! That makes me Mabel's granddaughter!" She laughed. "How amazing."

But it also seemed sad. So very, very sad. And overwhelmed with all of it, Ellie put her head down on the table. "I'm sorry," she said, covering her face. "I think I might be pretty tired." She took a breath. "I never knew my mama, you know? And I thought I came here, looking for my father, and I did, but it's been finding my mother that's making me sad." Looking at him, she said, "They loved each other?"

He looked, for a single moment, like he might cry right along with her. "More than I can put into words, Ellie," he said soberly. "Like that song Mabel sings."

Ellie closed her eyes.

He touched her hair. "Get some sleep, girl. Let your heart come to terms with it."

Ellie nodded. Raised her head, pressed her mouth together and tried to wipe away her tears.

There was deep graveness on his face. "You're all any of us have left of him, Ellie. Lot of people are going to be happy to know it when you're ready to tell them—there's so much of him in you." He ducked his head and turned away. "You want to talk, you know where to find me."

"Marcus," Ellie said.

He turned back.

"Thank you."

A single nod, and he was gone.

After he left, Ellie simply sat there at the table, the photograph in her hand. A sense of unreality gripped her—after not knowing for so long, it seemed impossible that the puzzle should be solved. That she should know. Have a face, a name, a person.

That it should be this person. James.

She stared at the high slant of his cheekbones, Mabel's cheekbones, and touched her own. Touched her hair, which had always been the bane of her existence, so wild and curly and uncontrollable, and realized why. She touched her mouth, which had been her only good feature, ever, and remembered the photos she'd stolen from Rosemary's attic. She got up and scrambled through the mess on the desk to find them. There were James and Marcus, arms looped around each other's necks. And in the other, there was the whole group of them, including Diane, who was obviously staring right at James. Next to them was Rosemary.

Rosemary, who was . . . what? Mabel's niece, which would make James her cousin. And Ellie was her second cousin. Which made Florence and Brandon her cousins, too.

She'd never had a cousin. Never had much family at all.

Would they mind?

In a daze, she stood up and went to the small bathroom and stared at her face in the mirror, feeling as if she'd never seen it before. The same high forehead, the same tilted green eyes, the same mouth and chin and teeth. It was a face she'd thought, all of her life, was black Irish. From her grandpa. Connor. Conn of the Hundred Battles, he always told her. She'd based an entire framework of heritage on being Irish. It wasn't something she thought about every minute, or even once a month. But it was there, always.

And of course, it still was. She could still claim those people who'd crossed in desperate hunger to come to the promised land where they might finally have enough food in their bellies. The stories her grandfather had told her always made her so proud.

But there was more now on her face. In her bones. Other sea crossings. Other stories.

Now that she knew, it was apparent in a thousand small details of her person. How was it *possible* she'd never noticed? That not one person in her entire life had taken her for black, or mixed race?

A voice from *The Point* came to her: "You see what you want to see."

Right. She looked hard into her eyes and wondered how this made her feel. To be suddenly black. She wasn't sure. Wasn't sure if it was pleasant or unpleasant. If it scared her. If suddenly, now that she knew, other people would know, too. And would that make any difference to her?

Would she feel different, now, walking into Hopkins' by herself? And if she did, wasn't that kind of a falsity?

Stop.

Abruptly, she shook her head and moved into the small bedroom area of the cottage, feeling overwhelmed with the revelations of the past twenty-four hours. Too many. She'd done too much thinking.

Right now, she needed to do something physical. With a burst of energy, she grabbed the duffel bag from the corner on the floor and started shoving clothes in it—underwear and socks and T-shirts and shorts, then hauled it outside, getting soaked in the process, and dumped it in the back seat of the car. April watched curiously until Ellie picked up her purse, then jumped up in a rattle of rabies tags. "Come on," Ellie said. "Let's get some clothes washed."

The Laundromat was located in a small strip mall at the edge of town, and it was fairly busy this time of day, even in bad weather. Ellie wiped rain from her face with a sleeve and nodded to the young mothers keeping watch over tumbling loads, and found a free washer toward the end. Only half of her clothes fit into one, and for a minute, Ellie felt flummoxed, trying to decide how to handle the dilemma. She needed to wash *everything*.

An older woman on the other side of the bank of appliances said, "I'm about to finish up with this one, hon, if you need it."

Ellie glanced up, nodded. "Thanks."

Get a grip, Connor. She took a deep breath and separated out the darks from the lights, started the load of lights on this side, then carried the duffel around to the other machine and started shoving them in, and rooted around in the bag to make sure she hadn't missed anything.

Only a box of tampons and a spare comb rattled around in the bottom, and Ellie poured in detergent, stuck in the quarters, and started the second load. She wasn't about to wait around, going crazy in the hot, noisy building, so she flung the bag over her shoulder and stood at the windows, looking for someplace to while away a half hour. A Dairy Queen perched across the parking lot. If they sprinted, they wouldn't get too wet, though April wouldn't like it much.

Perfect. "Let's get some ice cream, April. Vanilla for you. Maybe a root beer float for me."

April lowered her head and followed Ellie out, giving

her a miserable look when they stepped out into the rain. And there, with rain falling on her head, Ellie froze.

The tampons in the bottom of her bag. They were still there, instead of being moved to the bathroom at some point, as they should have been.

A cold wash of terror made her feel slightly nauseated. God, how long had she been here? She counted back, thinking of the day she looked at the calendar in the cottage the first night she came. Five weeks. Almost two months. How was that possible?

April barked, sharply, and Ellie realized she was standing in the rain like a crazy person. "Come on, baby." They dashed for the shelter of the DQ and stood beneath an overhang to shake themselves off.

When had she and Blue first made love? More than a month? Maybe a little more than that. Or a little less.

No. She shook her head, sensibly. They'd used a condom every single time. Well, except once. *Every* time. None had ever broken or come off that she could think of.

The thought eased her mind. Often when she traveled, she'd had an extra period. She'd decided a long time ago it was some kind of urgent message from her body to hurry up and settle down, get with it. She'd almost taken it for granted. She couldn't remember ever skipping one, but it was the flip side of the extra, she supposed.

Nothing to worry about.

She ordered a giant root beer float for herself and a scoop of vanilla in a dish for April, and carried both over to one of the tables under the awning. And worried.

The thing was, when there was an extra, there was no question about what was happening. With a skipped cycle, however, how could you know? Especially if you'd been having wild sex for—

Her heart squeezed.

In the end, she knew what she had to do. There was another teeny little town about ten minutes up the road. She'd go there, to some anonymous drugstore, and buy a pregnancy test. No way she'd go into any store in Pine Bend for it; everyone in town would be speculating by nightfall.

Intolerable thought.

It was probably nothing, she told herself. Nobody ever got accidentally pregnant when they were being careful, not in this day and age. She'd never even had a scare. This would turn out to be nothing, too.

But all the way down the road and back, she remembered little things that scared her. The depth of her sleep. Her need for naps. Her voracious appetite, big even for her.

Most of all, she thought of her easy tears. She wasn't a weepy person. She just didn't think it ever solved anything. She didn't cry over milk cartons or Hallmark commercials on television. She'd never shed a tear at a movie in her life, and even at her grandfather's funeral, when she knew she'd miss him like crazy and she'd never see him again, she'd only cried a few tears.

She didn't like to cry.

And yet, over the past couple of weeks, she'd been sniffling over everything.

Doesn't mean anything, one part of her said. She'd

been immersed in the emotional and passionate tale of a woman who'd loved and then lost everything. She'd gathered the tales of boys killed too young in Vietnam, and watched those they'd left behind struggle—even so many years later—with the notion of their loss. She was half in love with a man whose life had been so rife with losses that his best friend called him Job.

Half in love? echoed that cynical little voice.

She narrowed her eyes and ignored it. The *point* was, there were plenty of reasons to feel emotional and weepy.

But when she got the kit to the cottage, her hands were shaking. Deliberately, she set the small paper bag on the counter and went back out to get her clean, folded clothes.

The test blared at her from the counter. She couldn't stand to wait for morning, and she growled, then carried it into the bathroom and paced around while she waited for the signs to appear. Yes or no.

It didn't take long.

She stared at the plus sign for a long, long time, unable to summon a single reaction. Then, without even knowing she was going to do it, she walked across the room, picked up the phone, and dialed her grandmother.

The line was crackly with distant lightning, and Ellie wondered, as she listened to the phone ring, if this storm stretched as far as her grandmother's farm. It rang four times. Ellie was about to hang up when Geraldine picked up. "Hello?" She sounded impatient and breathless.

"Hey, Grandma. Did I bring you running?"

"Ellie! I was just in the bathroom." She gave a soft hoot of feminine laughter. "I've been thinking about you all day, sugar. How are you?"

Ellie closed her eyes at the swell of relief in her, and leaned her forehead against the wall. "Well, it's been a long twenty-four hours. I'm pretty beat."

"You don't sound good at all. You been eating right?"

"I have," she said, straightening. "Listen, I just called to tell you I'm almost done here and I'll be home to see you sometime tomorrow evening. Might be late, though, so leave a light on."

"Tomorrow?" Happiness lightened her voice. "Ya'll getting this storm? I don't know if you oughta be driving if it's still this bad. They had a tornado over in Carthage, and we've had the sirens on and off all day."

"Hmmm." Ellie peered out the windows. "It's raining pretty hard, but I haven't heard anything else. I'll keep an eye on the weather, but otherwise, I'll be there."

"Give me a call and let me know when you're setting out. I'll fix you something and leave it on the stove. You still have your key, don't you?"

"Yeah." Ellie felt a sudden push of tears. "I have so much to tell you, Grandma."

"I'll look forward to it, sweetie. We'll have a nice long gossip."

"I can't wait."

The decision made, Ellie felt shaky and completely exhausted. She turned the ringer off the phone, and stripping off her dirty clothes, she showered, then fell, barely dry, into her bed. She thought about turning the box fan on, to cool her overheated body—a body, she thought just before sleep overtook her, that had another one in it. How odd.

Just as sleep edged over her brain, blurring everything, just as her muscles were falling slack—finally—a thought bolted through her. She opened her eyes and rolled over, a rush of adrenaline making her heart race. "Oh, my God," she whispered aloud.

She tugged on clean clothes, scrabbled around looking for an umbrella she'd seen in the closet, and rushed out, walking purposefully, her head down against the rising wind and wet. Through the trees and rain, she glimpsed the tin-roofed house she'd seen a dozen times. She'd never tried to get to the house itself before, but there had to be a way. Gwen got to the river somehow.

Ellie walked to the place where the chair had been set up, then walked along the bank until she spied a raked path that curved around a live oak hung heavily with moss. She ducked under it, getting even more soaked in the process, then hurried up the path.

It opened up on a small garden, planted with squashes and corn and beans—Ellie was in the backyard. She stopped for a minute, and pressed a palm to the spot just below her ribs, a place that almost hurt with anticipation.

The back door was propped open beyond a screen door, and Ellie called out in warning. "Mrs. Laisser!"

She skirted the garden and called out again, "Gwen! It's Ellie Connor."

The woman came to the door holding a dishtowel. For a long moment, she simply stood there, her hands wrapped together under the fabric, her face showing nothing. Then she seemed to come to some decision and pushed open the door.

"Come on in, Ellie. I been expecting you."

19

As Blue cooked in anticipation of Ellie's coming over, he felt restless and edgy, a state he blamed on the storm. All around there were tornado warnings, and although they didn't seem to hit around Pine Bend too often, he was worried about hail and what good-sized stones might do to the greenhouses. He'd built them from reinforced glass because they did sometimes get some hellacious hail, but you could only prepare so much.

Allowing himself a good belt of bourbon, he turned the small television in the kitchen to the Weather Channel to keep an eye on things. The bourbon eased his worry, and he battered the chicken pieces and set them to frying, then sliced tomatoes, red onions, and cucumbers and mixed them with a vinaigrette heavy with herbs that Lanie had taught him to make. He made a pitcher of iced tea and made sure there was ice, then called down to the cabin.

No answer. With a slight frown, he glanced out the

kitchen windows and saw her car was in the driveway. She was probably just sleeping after staying up all night, and he'd leave her to it. On the Weather Channel, they reported tornado watches for a neighboring county, but it looked like Pine Bend would escape. Lots of rain and wind, but not even hail warning. He flipped it off and turned on the radio, where he'd hear weather warnings, but could also get some music as well.

Gwen stood aside and let Ellie pass. "You hungry, girl?"

Thinking of her day, Ellie couldn't remember when she'd last eaten, except the root beer float at the DQ. The kitchen she entered smelled of fried meat and onions and made her mouth water, but she didn't want to overstep her bounds. "No, thank you," she said.

But as if to make her a liar, her stomach growled. Loudly.

Gwen chuckled. "Go on and sit down." She nodded toward a table shoved against the windows on one side of the room. "I don't cook a whole lot no more, since it's just me, but I lost about ten pounds a couple months ago and the doctor took to nagging me so much I promised I'd make a real supper at least a few nights a week."

Ellie settled on the edge of the chair. Her heart kept up its thready, excited rhythm, and it had been going for such a stretch now that she thought she was probably flushed the color of roses. Outside, the rain poured down, the gray sheets making a cave of the homey kitchen, a place of shelter and protection. "Mrs. Laisser—"

"Not yet, honey," Gwen said abruptly. She put down a plate of golden fried pork chops and piles of stuffing. "It's nothing but Stove Top, you know, but I like it a lot. You want some corn?"

The food smelled so good she nearly swooned. "Let me help you somehow."

"Don't be silly." Taking a pair of tongs from a drawer, she pulled out a steaming ear of corn and put it on Ellie's plate. "There's butter on the door of the fridge if you want."

"Thanks."

Gwen filled her own plate and sat down with Ellie. "You don't mind if we say grace, do you?"

"No, not at all." She bent her head dutifully.

"Will you do me the honor?"

For an instant, Ellie couldn't remember a single one of the prayers that had been drilled into her since childhood, but then there was one on her tongue, "Graciously heavenly father, for what we are about to receive we thank you. May it nourish our bodies, Amen."

Gwen was smiling when Ellie lifted her eyes. "That was nice." She lifted a sharp knife over her chop. Then she took a deep breath and said, "Now, what was it you came over to talk to me about?"

Ellie pressed her lips together. "I went to talk to Hattie Gordon yesterday, and all of her stories helped me pinpoint almost everything."

"Mmm." Gwen gestured. "Eat while you talk, child. What'd you figure?"

"I think Mabel gave up her music to atone for the sin of killing Peaches," she said, rubbing butter over the corn, "I even think I know where she went."

Gwen lifted her head.

Ellie took a bit of the corn and it exploded into her mouth, all sweet crispness and salt and butter and she gave a soft cry. "Oh, that is so good!" She took another bite, and another, aware of Gwen smiling at her, but suddenly so hungry she was almost faint. Taking a moment to blot her lips, she explained, "I worked all night and I don't think I had much to eat yesterday either."

"Merciful heavens," Gwen said softly, "you are so much like him."

"Him?" Ellie echoed, but she knew. She knew.

"Marcus told me he was over to talk to you this afternoon."

Ellie carefully wiped her fingers, and a strange heat, anger and hurt, welled up in her. "I can understand everything," she said. "But not why you left your child."

Mabel Beauvais took off her glasses, the big lenses that obscured the still-classic line of her cheekbone and the unmistakably beautiful eyes. Few wrinkles marred the tawny skin. "An eye for an eye," she said with a sigh. "I took her son, so she took mine."

"Oh, of course," Ellie whispered.

"I wasn't thinking clearly, you know?" She rubbed the bridge of her nose. "I think about it all now and it seems like another person lived that life, loved that man, and hated him so much she could shoot him. I just couldn't think straight for loving him. I hid away and had our son and he wouldn't even marry me. Made me bear that *shame*—" She took a breath. "And I left James with his grandma, trying to think what to do . . . "

"Did James ever know you?"

Mabel/Gwen picked up her fork and eyed the contents of her plate with little interest. "Not as his mama. I didn't come back here for a couple of years, and by then, there wasn't much left for me to do but just be the neighbor lady. She gave me that much, anyway."

"Eat," Ellie said, and touched her hand.

The old woman raised her eyes, and there was sorrow in them. "I saw it the minute you walked up to me on those banks. You walk like him, have a lot of his same movements. And you really have his laugh, and his smile—that little overlapping tooth, that's your daddy's." She stabbed a triangle of meat and ate it. "When I saw you at a distance, it like to give me a heart attack."

Ellie shook her head, all that emotion welling up in her throat again. She poked at the food on her plate. "I can't quite take it all in."

"Guess you got a little more of a story than you bargained for, didn't you?"

Ellie let go of a helpless little laugh. "You could say that." She ate some of the stuffing, the tension easing out of her. "And we need to talk about that. About what you want me to write, and not write."

"There's plenty of time for all that, sugar. For now, let's just eat, shall we?"

• • •

Blue was putting the last of the fried chicken in the oven to keep warm when the sirens went off—tornado warning. The sound went through him like an electric shock. He opened the door to the basement. "Lanie! You hear that?"

"Get down here, child."

"I gotta get Ellie. Sasha!" his voice was harsh, and the dog came skittering around the corner. "Go," he said, and pointed. "You got the cat?"

"She's in my lap. Hurry up!"

To keep the dog in, Blue closed the door to the basement, and without bothering to grab a coat or umbrella, he slammed outside—into a storm that had suddenly grown very loud and fierce. The wind nearly took him off his feet, but he staggered and leaned down hard into it, his clothes and hair soaked in seconds as he ran down the hill. He cried her name before he was on the porch, "Ellie!"

Inside, April barked, and Blue opened the door without worrying about a knock. Agitated and nervous, April barked and whined and licked his fingers, as Blue cried out Ellie's name again. She must really be exhausted.

But she wasn't there. He looked in the bedroom and saw only the rumbled bed. He even looked in the bathroom, thinking in his panic that she might have hidden in the shower when she heard the sirens that were bleating their warning into the roar of the storm.

On the counter was a pregnancy test, and he reached for it when April barked, sharply, urgently, and he raced back out. Be stupid to get himself killed in all this over something he could just ask her about.

"Come on, baby," he said to April, and they raced back up the hill to the house, and down into the basement, just as the hail roared into the clearing, unbearably loud, banging and crashing. He and April ran into the small, heavily fortified room that was used as a storm shelter, and closed the heavy door. Lanie sat calmly in her chair, crocheting by the light of a lamp at her elbow. She lifted her chin. "Towels right there behind you."

Shivering in reaction, Blue wiped his face and hair and grabbed April before she could shake herself, rubbing her back. The smell of wet dog filled the small space. "She wasn't there," he said, and let the dread fill him. "God, I hope she's somewhere safe."

April whined. Lanie kept crocheting. "You said she was raised around here, and she's not a stupid woman. She'll know what to do."

He jumped up and paced to the wall. Back again, ears straining for the sound of the storm. Even here, it was loud, a roar of rain and wind and hail. He perched on the edge of the cot, April on his foot, shivering, and listened to the metallic sound of hail striking things. Impossible to tell what things. Or how big the hail.

"Doesn't sound loud enough for a tornado, does it?" he said to Lanie.

"Hard to tell from here, son." She peered at him. "Nothing you can do. Don't get yourself all worked up."

But somehow, he knew: Here was the other shoe.

Not Ellie, he begged the heavens. Just not Ellie.

Outside, the storm roared and pounded. A sudden crack, and then a series of smaller cracks and bangs and roars, made even Lanie turn pale, but they only looked at each other and didn't say a word.

April whined. Blue prayed.

Ellie panicked. Gwen opened a trap door in the kitchen and pointed for her to go down first. She took one look at that dark, spidery hole and just shook her head. "I can't!"

Gwen took the broom and went first, her movements urgent as the sound of the storm intensified around them. Then she grabbed Ellie's ankle and said, "Come down here now."

Ellie went, shuddering. Squeezed into a small shelter with Gwen, she kept her knees to her chest, her hands over her ears, rocking back and forth, her heart pounding with terror. Every few seconds, she was sure she felt a spider crawling on her back, and slapped at the imaginary creature with a little screech.

"I hate this, I hate this, I hate this," she said. She couldn't stop thinking about April, who would be frantic by now, barking and whining. Ellie tried to tell herself that dogs were smart, that April would have dived right under that heavy desk when the hail started, and would do her whining from beneath it, so she'd be safe enough even if the walls came down around her.

"Don't fret too much," Gwen said. "We get the warnings all the time, but almost never have the real thing. Think about that cabin you're living in. Been standing there for more than a hundred and fifty years."

Finally, finally, the sound of the storm lessened, and it was only a soft, pattering rain. The siren shut off, leaving the world almost preternaturally quiet. By the time they crawled out of the shelter, covered with dust and trailing spiderwebs, even the soft rain had stopped. In silence, they walked to the door to look outside.

"Will you look at that!" Gwen cried, like a girl, and pushed by Ellie to open the screen door and pick up a ball of hail the size of a baseball. She laughed. "You ever see hail this big before?"

Ellie shook her head, following more slowly. There were hundreds of the ice balls on the ground. Not all were the enormous size of the first, but many of them were at least as big as golf balls. They covered the ground like snow, mixed with piles of shredded leaves, broken branches, and even—Ellie stared in sick surprise—a whole complete tree, uprooted and flung across the back garden like a twig. "Was it a tornado, then?"

"I don't know." Gwen bent and picked up another giant ball of hail. "I'm going to stick these in the freezer." She straightened. "You can run on and see about your dog. Come back later and we'll have ourselves a real talk."

Ellie looked at her, and remembered all over again . . . remembered everything. Too much. Feeling a little winded, she nodded. "I will."

"Look out, now. Gonna be lots of tree branches loose."

"I'll be careful."

She started at a careful walk over the soggy, littered ground, leaping over the smaller branches, going around the bigger ones. Lots of tree branches. Thick mud sucked at her shoes. Puddles soaked her to the knee. Water dripped from the branches overhead. Everywhere was pulverized greenery and muddy debris, the exhaust trail of the storm.

Ellie couldn't run. It was impossible. But the need to run, the anxiety over April, the need to see what lay beyond the thick trees in that clearing where the cabin and greenhouses and big house stood, made her heart hurt. She found she was stumbling, and realized she'd had only three or four hours' sleep in the past thirty-six hours, and in that thirty-six hours, she'd been slammed with one revelation after another.

At least she was too far gone for hysteria.

Finally she came close to the end of the woods, and leaped over the last hurdle in her path, and ran, stumbling, toward the clearing. The house on the hill showed first—looking sound and stable and eternal against the heavy gray sky. Some of the windows were broken on this side, and there was a confetti of pink and purple petals scattered over the grass, but it looked fine otherwise. As she stared at it, hurrying, she tripped on a tangle of cardboard, flung there by the winds, and nearly went down on her face.

"Get it together, Connor," she breathed, and straightened.

A sharp, glad bark reached her ears, and Ellie looked up to see April hurtling down the road, her tail high. She barked, and barked again, and rushed to shove her nose against Ellie's hand. Her fur was wet, and she stunk like wet dogs the world over, but Ellie was so relieved she fell to the road on her knees and put her arms around her, gladly accepting the return kisses and licks and dog-nose nudgings. "Oh, I'm so glad you're okay."

Everything would be all right. The house showed no real damage, so Blue was okay, and April was fine. Anything else was manageable.

Or so she thought until she came around the bend fully and saw Blue. He stood on the edge of the grass, his arms loose at his sides, his face a pure, even gray, as he looked in the direction of the greenhouses.

She felt a lump in her throat and looked. But it didn't look as bad as she expected after seeing his face. There were broken panes, but not nearly as many as she would have expected from hail of that size. "Blue!" she cried, and rushed over to him. "Is it destroyed? Are your experiments ruined?"

He shook his head. "No. Maybe some. I'm amazed."

He sounded like he was in shock. Dull voice. Looked it, too. His hair was wet, and his clothes, and his mouth was strangely slack. "Your color is kind of bad. Is Lanie all right?"

"Yeah. She's fine."

She put a hand on his arm, leaning close in concern. "Were you hurt?"

"No." He swallowed. Pointed toward the cabin. "Look."

She turned. A tree, the tree that had given shade to that porch, and kept the roof cool for probably thirty years, had come down sideways, catching the northwest corner of the building. The whole cabin had simply caved in under the weight. She could see the bed, the coverlet soaked, showing beneath the trunk of the tree.

A wave of nausea struck her. "I was sleeping there."

"Yeah." He sounded so casual.

"How did April get out of there alive?"

"I got her earlier."

And one more thing. "Oh my God, Blue!" she started at a run. "My notes! All that work!" She slipped in the wet grass, and landed on her rear end, hard. It was the last straw. She burst into tears.

But her distress seemed to wake up Blue, because he was suddenly there, his arms around her, his head in her shoulder. He picked her up. "You're exhausted, Ellie," he said. "I'm going to put you to bed."

"But my notes! My computer!"

"I'll take care of it. You made hard copies of everything. It'll all be okay."

Miserably, she closed her eyes. She hadn't made a copy of the work overnight. Not a single tiny bit of a copy. But there was no more room in her for a single new shred of emotion or revelation or anything else. Like a child, she let herself be carried to bed, her clothes stripped off and her body dried with a fluffy towel. He tucked her in and kissed her forehead. "Don't worry, Ellie, I'll find your stuff. Just sleep."

And then she remembered all the things she hadn't told him—about Mabel and Peaches and about James and about herself. And . . .

Sleep sucked her under.

20

Blue went back outside, intending to see what he could get out of the cabin or at least look inside the greenhouses and see how much damage had been done. But when Marcus drove up fifteen minutes later, Blue was still standing in the grass, conscious of the cold gathering down his back, somehow unable to decide which task to tackle first. Greenhouse, he'd think, then think about taking a step that way, and then decide, no—cabin first.

"Hey," was all he managed when Marcus came up the hill. He thought about asking if everybody was okay, but Marcus wouldn't be here if they weren't.

"Everybody okay here?"

Blue nodded.

"Been down to check the damage?"

He shook his head.

Marcus spied the cabin. "Jesus! Was Ellie in there?"

"No. She went down to see Gwen."

"Is she in the house?"

"Yeah."

Marcus stood there another minute, then walked up to the house. Blue didn't turn. Didn't move. Went back to trying to decide between the greenhouse and the cabin.

Marcus reappeared, a bottle of bourbon in his hand. "I know you been giving it up, but trust me, you need a drink." He took a swig straight from the mouth and gave it to Blue. "You look like shit, no offense."

Blue took the bottle and drank. Liquor burned his tongue, his throat, settled hard in his belly. It gave him room to breathe, which he did, then drank again, deep. He gave the bottle back to Marcus so he wouldn't be tempted to more. "Ellie's worried about her book. I gotta see what I can dig out of there."

"All right, man." He screwed the lid on the bourbon. "Let's do it. Been in the greenhouse yet?"

He shook his head. "Not yet."

"Doesn't look too bad." He whistled. "Tornado did touch down over in Hector. Took out the grocery store, I heard."

They walked down the hill. Blue stopped in the yard of the cabin, and stared at the crushed bed beneath the beams of the roof. Abruptly, he turned and threw up the bourbon he'd just drunk.

It didn't help. His body roiled with nausea, and he stayed bent, his hands on his knees, his eyes closed, waiting for it to go away. "She stayed up all night. I don't know what made her go to Gwen's." The rest was unspoken. What if she hadn't?

Marcus was silent for long moments. Slowly, the nausea faded and Blue straightened. He looked at the bed, the muddy quilt, to test himself, but the illness had passed.

"You all right now?"

"Yeah. Let's see what we can get out of here. She's worked her ass off on that book."

It turned out to be a fairly uncomplicated procedure. Because the tree had come down on the northwest corner, the bulk of the damage was on that side. The front window over the desk was broken, and held jagged teeth of glass, but a beam had landed on the edge of the heavy desk and had offered some protection. The laptop was cracked, and the pile of papers were damp, some smeared, but they were able to get them without much trouble. A box of index cards and spare disks had been protected by plastic cases. "Well, I don't know if anything is coming off the laptop, but the rest is all right."

"Hold on," Marcus said, and reached one more time through the jagged glass, straining to reach a folder at the edge. He pulled it out and flipped it open. "Pictures."

Blue nodded. "Let's take these to the house and go on over to the greenhouse, see what we can do." His mind was clearing a little now. "You sure Alisha's all right with the children?"

"I'm sure. Hardly even hailed over there."

Blue looked over his shoulder once more at the destroyed cabin, thinking about the box he'd seen in the bathroom, and his eye caught on the bed again. He looked away quickly. One thing at time.

It was close to midnight before Blue and Marcus finished at the main greenhouse. The damage within had been minor—some broken glass, some plants with hail trauma, but nothing that should interfere with the experiments. The reinforced glass had paid itself off with one storm.

Hail had not been as kind to the other two, and the bulk of the work they did was moving tender baby plants from the cold greenhouses to the big one. Some of those experiments would have to be started again, but they'd been talking about rebuilding the smaller houses, anyway. They were old and needed replacing. He might even put in a lab.

Lanie had taken the chicken out of the oven and left it on the table, covered with a thin white dishtowel. "Eat," said the note she'd scrawled. But he had no appetite. To keep her off his back, he took a breast from the plate, tore pieces of meat from it, and fed it to the dogs, who waited with polite, bright eyes at his feet. Even Piwacket got a teeny bit. He threw the bones in the trash and thought about having a deep slug of bourbon, but his stomach rejected the idea.

He went upstairs, the dogs trailing behind. At his bedroom door, he stopped, his heart suddenly pounding with something very like terror, and the nausea rolled in his belly again. With his hand on the door, he paused, resting his forehead on the door for a minute. His body settled, and he went in quietly. In the light from the door, he could see Ellie's form. One calf hung off the bed.

A waft of scent enveloped him, not a perfume, but the essence of Ellie herself, her skin and soap and hair, all of her, and it struck him in the solar plexus with a sensation like pain.

She lay on her belly, arms and legs flung out, hair scattered in dark ringlets across one cheek and the curve of her shoulder. She wore not a stitch, and her flesh was more beautiful than any sight he'd ever seen, smooth as pale butter—her curved back and finely made limbs, and the lush, perfect roundness of her buttocks. A dewiness lay over the swoop of her spine, and it was there that Blue put his mouth, unable to resist. He knelt beside the low bed and began at the nape of her neck, brushing aside the small soft scatters of hair so he could kiss that first set of bones. Lightly, closing his eyes, breathing in the smell of her skin, he followed the line downward, to the hollow just above her perfect rear.

She stirred slightly as he trailed his fingers over the round of those hips, down the backs of her thighs. Stirred and shifted, turning in sleepy confusion, not anywhere close to awake, but her hand moved to his hair, then went lax, a gesture of purest trust. Blue stared at her a long time, drinking in the angle of her chin, the moon of a breast, and he gave in to the need rising from some deep place inside of him. He slid out of his shirt and his jeans and lay down next to her, flesh to flesh. Ellie stirred, awakened, startled a little. "Blue?"

"Sshhh," he said. "Go back to sleep."

And she did. He simply lay with her, holding her, and wanted to weep.

Ellie did not know what time it was when she finally awoke. It was dark and still beyond the windows, and for a long moment, she simply stayed where she was, content in the comfort of the bed. She rolled over and stretched hard—then everything rushed in again—everything. She sighed.

A noise in the other room brought back a vague memory. "Blue?"

He came from the bathroom, clad only in jeans. His hair was tousled, as if he, too, had slept, and she felt a soft rush of yearning to have him close by her. "How you doing?" she asked sleepily.

He lifted a shoulder, and there was still that same dullness about him that she'd noticed yesterday. Shell-shocked. "All right. You?"

"Wasn't anything wrong with me a good night's sleep wouldn't cure." She held out a hand. "Come here. You look awful."

But instead, he only sat on the edge of the bed. "Ellie, do you have something to tell me?"

She frowned, thinking there was a lot she needed to tell him. "What do you mean?"

"I saw the box in your bathroom yesterday when I went to get April. Well, I went to get you, but—" He sighed, wiped his face. Weariness lay on his back, in his face, like a shroud.

"Box?" Memory dawned. The pregnancy test. *That* damned box. She sat up, bringing the covers with her, and touched his back. "That'll wait, Blue. It's been a rough couple of days. Why don't we just let everything alone for right now?"

"No. I don't want to do that."

It worried her, the dull roughness in his voice. "Blue, did you sleep?"

He dropped his hands. Shook his head. "But I didn't drown myself in a liquor bottle, either." He said it like it wasn't much of a victory.

"Lie down."

"No . . . I'm—not right now." He looked over his shoulder. "It's not you. I just don't want to sleep yet." He paused. "I want to talk about the box."

With a groan, she squeezed her eyes shut and rolled over, pulling a pillow over her head. Damn, damn, damn.

She felt his weight come down on the bed beside her. Then that big gentle hand on her back. "Ellie?"

With a sigh, she pulled the pillow from her head and looked up at him. "Fine," she said with annoyance. "But you're going to find out everything the way I did. It was one hell of a day."

"All right." He settled, and at least one whole leg was on the bed now. "Tell me."

Feeling vulnerable, she wrapped herself firmly in the covers and tossed tangles of hair from her face. "Are you ready for this?"

Still nothing was revealed in the dark smoothness of his face, or the liquid blue eyes. He nodded slowly.

"Let's see . . ." she held up her hands and enumerated the points on her fingers. "First, I found out that Mabel killed Peaches—and that she did have a child.

You know who?"

"No, who?"

"James Gordon."

His eyes widened, showing the first glimmer of emotion she'd seen. "Holy shit."

"Exactly." She went back to her fingers, halted in sudden fear. "This is where it gets kind of hard, okay?"

"Spill it."

"I found out who my father is."

"Ellie, that's great! Who?"

Ellie raised her eyes, and a strange sense of sadness overtook her again. "Marcus came over yesterday. He brought me a picture."

Blue's eyes narrowed, realization dawning on his face. "James," he said.

She nodded slowly, watching his face to see if she saw any flickers of rejection. There was nothing, one way or the other. "How'd Marcus know?"

She lifted her shoulders. "I told him about my mother one day. He acted so strange when you and I started sleeping together that—" she broke off. "Long story, but basically, he'd put it together before that. He seems to think James and I look alike."

"You do." Blue sounded a little strained.

She bowed her head, waiting.

"Ellie," Blue said. "What about the box?"

She took a breath, couldn't find any words. Nodded.

"Oh, man."

"I don't know how. We were careful." She shrugged. "But—facts are facts. I'm pregnant."

He stared at her, dismay plain. Very slowly, he

closed his eyes, and stood up, turning his back.

"Blue, don't do this. That's not fair."

"It's not you, Ellie. I swear to God it isn't."

"Oh, really!" Deeply wounded, she flung the covers from her. "I'm not asking anything from you, okay? You don't have to worry about any of that." From the floor she grabbed her shirt, and shorts, and flung them on, her hands shaking with humiliation and embarrassment. "I don't know why I thought you were different. And I don't even *want* to know if this is because you've found out that my father was black—"

"Ellie, for God's sake!" he reached for her suddenly, managing to catch an elbow that she yanked away. "You know better than that."

"I thought I did." She stared at him, willing herself to hang on to whatever teeny bit of dignity might be left to her. "Let's just let it all go right now, Blue. My book is done. The storm took my room, and obviously whatever we had is over. So let me just get in my car and go. You don't have to ever think about any of this ever again."

"No!" He lunged, and they tumbled sideways together on to the bed. "You listen to me now." He pinned her arms when she struggled, and she glared at him, but even in her anger she saw the grief in his face. Why grief? What had he lost? She stopped struggling.

"I love you," he said, and she thought he might weep with that admission. His eyes were an unholy shade of bright blue. "That night I was going to cook, and you wanted to work, I was going to propose. I had a ring and everything."

Ellie made a sound.

"Just listen," he whispered fiercely. He let her go. "I can't do it." He swallowed hard, looked away. "I saw that cabin, and I knew I couldn't do it again. Not again. I can't."

She rose up on her knees and pressed her mouth to his lips, tasting his terror and his grief—it was Ellie he was losing, and it did matter, and he would miss her forever, just as she would miss him—and she let her tears fall on his face since he couldn't seem to get to his own. "Oh, Blue."

He broke a little, pulling her close. His face, damp with her tears, burrowed into her neck. "I wish I was braver, Ellie. But just you alone was more than I could stand to think about losing—you and a baby. That's too much."

She clung to him, unashamed of the tears that poured down her face. "I love you," she said quietly.

"I know." His grip was so tight she almost couldn't catch her breath. "I'll make sure you don't want for anything."

"Thank you." She pulled away, wiping her face, and looked for her shoes, half-blind. He didn't move as she put them on without socks. "I'll call you and tell you where to send my stuff."

"Ellie," he said urgently as she went to the door.

She stopped, waiting, looking at that beautiful face that she'd known from the beginning had held doom in it. Doom for him. Not for her. As long as she got out of here right now, she'd get over it. What she could not do was sit here with him and watch him self-destruct.

"Don't say anything, Blue. I know where you've been. I know why you can't do this." Weakening, she put her hand on his face, kissed his beautiful mouth one more time. "In time, we'll be friends again, and you won't have to sit around waiting for that other shoe to fall."

He swallowed.

"But," she said in a stronger voice. "I'm not waiting around for you, either. Just so you know. I'm not going to pine. I'm not going to kill myself out of grief. I'm going to go home, have this baby, and cry a lot while I get over you, but I'll be looking from the corner of my eye for the man who's going to love me."

"I do love you."

"I know," she said, and felt stronger. "Just not enough."

He let her go. Let her walk down the stairs, and through the front door, and get into her car. He didn't even follow her out, or watch her go from the door. Ellie whistled for April, and managed to drive all the way through to the other side of Pine Bend before she had to pull the car over and let some of her grief out. April whined next to her, licked her arm on the steering wheel, and shifted foot to foot in distress. It finally made Ellie laugh a little, and she gave her face to be licked. "Thank you," she said. "Too bad men aren't as reliable as dogs."

April barked once. Ellie put the car in gear and headed east. Toward home.

Rosemary opened the container with her tacos and salted them. Connie's shop was quiet in the aftermath of the storm. None of them had been hit hard, though there were a lot of trees down, and Connie had to have four windows replaced at her house. In Rosemary's half of town, the storm had never been that bad to begin with—a lot of heavy rain and wind, which had played havoc with her roses, but not even hail to speak of. "Where's Alisha?" she asked.

"Had to run her baby to the doctor for some shots, then take him over to Marcus's mother's house." Connie picked at a burrito. "Not like we have much business today. Everybody's busy with the cleanup."

"Only be a few days, I'm sure. Not like Hector." Word had come in that Hector was hit hard. It made her sad to think of those people without their homes, but nobody had been killed, thank God. She picked at her own food—her appetite was not exactly huge either. "I think I need to make some ice cream this evening."

"Oh, now that sounds real good. And some cold watermelon."

"Mmm. And some cold fried chicken."

Connie grinned. "We're planning a picnic."

Alisha burst in the door. "Oh, my God," she said, breathlessly. "You are not going to *believe* what I have to tell you." She pushed the door closed and locked it, turned the Open sign to Closed.

"What do you think you're doing?" Connie said. "Turn that back, right now."

Alisha shook her head, waving a hand with iridescent blue nails as if to underscore the point. "No, y'all have to hear this all the way through."

"What?"

Alisha sat down. "I just came from talking to my husband. Blue's there, fit to be tied, pacing up and down one greenhouse to the other like a caged cat." She touched her throat, jumped up. "I have to have something to drink."

"Alisha!" Rosemary said. "Sit your skinny little rear in this chair and tell us what's got you so excited before we both bust."

"I am, I am." She carried a cold can of Diet Pepsi back to her chair, brushed a braid from her face and smiled. "Ellie's gone."

Connie and Rosemary spoke in the same instant.

"What?"

"Why?"

"I don't know, exactly. Marcus is *so* pissed, so it's something Blue did. They were having a big fight when I walked in, yelling like I've never heard them yell."

"About what?" Rosemary asked.

She widened her eyes. "I don't know. I didn't quite get it. But, listen, this is the good part." Her voice quieted for drama. "Ellie was here to do the book on Mabel Beauvais, right?"

"We already know that," Rosemary said with a scowl.

Alisha arched a brow. "She was also here looking for her father."

Connie sat back, mouth faintly open. "Her father?"

"This is so good!" Alisha laughed with excitement. "You know how she was asking all those questions that night at our reader's group, about the kids who went to Vietnam? She was trying to figure it out then, who might be the right man."

"Oh, my God," Connie said, and sat forward. "I knew she looked familiar! Oh, my God."

Rosemary felt a slow, soft build of dread. "Who was her mother?"

"One of those hippie girls. I don't know which one."

A burst of pain broke in Rosemary's chest. "I know which one," she said, and tears welled in her eyes. "It was the redhead. Diane."

Both Connie and Alisha turned to her, alarmed. "What's wrong?"

Rosemary covered her mouth, amazed at the wave of feelings that could still come over her like this, thirty years later. The quick, deep sword of loss. She pressed trembling fingers over her mouth and looked at Connie, who would know. "I kept thinking . . . I did know until . . ."

She stood up, walked away, struggling to control herself. She turned and looked at Connie. "Ellie's daddy was James Gordon," she said, and couldn't stop the tears quick enough. Connie was there, offering her broad shoulder, taking Rosemary into her arms.

"Oh, honey," Connie breathed. "It's all right."

To her credit, Alisha was silent a long time. When

Rosemary finally lifted her head and took a deep breath, Alisha said, "I don't understand what just happened, but I sincerely apologize if I upset you."

Rosemary blotted her eyes. "No, girl, it's not you. It's just the way life is sometimes. James was my cousin."

Alisha frowned. "But why—"

"He just wasn't like anybody," Rosemary said, and had to stop when the visions of him came too fast. James laughing, that crooked tooth in front showing. Those golden eyes dancing. The gentleness of the way he looked out for children and stray dogs and every sparrow with a broken wing. "If I tried to put it in words, it would sound too corny, so I won't. He was as good a soul as God ever made, and there wasn't anybody who knew him who didn't wail when his body came home."

Connie took Rosemary's hand and squeezed it.

"It was so plain he was *smitten* that summer," Rosemary said. "And when we found out it was with some little silly white girl—it made us all kinda scared for him. It wasn't like now. And we all worried that she'd just prance on out of here, and leave him all brokenhearted. Which she did."

"She loved him," Connie said. "She begged him to go to Canada, but he thought that would be cowardly, so he went to Vietnam anyway."

Rosemary felt a little dizzy with the idea of that poor girl going off—who knew where—to have that mixed baby by herself. "It couldn't have been easy for her."

"Marcus said she's dead, too," Alisha said.

Rosemary shook her head. "I wonder if Ellie even knew she was black?"

"Never seemed to think so," Alisha said. "And it's just as plain as day when you know." She fell silent. "I guess it was women like her that used to 'pass' in the old days."

They were all quiet for a moment. Then Alisha shook herself. "I forgot the best part! Gwen Laisser—"

Rosemary raised a hand. "Don't say it, girl." There was steel in her voice. She shook her head, and her finger, for emphasis.

"What?" Connie said. "That's not fair!"

Alisha folded her hands, looking at Rosemary, who turned her head to look at Connie. Connie who'd been at her side for going on thirty years, who'd shared the loss of their loves to Vietnam and then their husbands, who would share the empty nest in a couple years more. Connie who'd known James, and now Ellie, and maybe deserved a little something for all of that.

"Connie, I'll tell you, but you have to swear on Bobby Makepeace's grave that you will never tell a soul."

Bewildered, Connie raised a hand. "I swear, Rosemary. On Bobby's grave. What is it?"

"Gwen Laisser is James Gordon's mother. And her real name is Mabel Beauvais."

Connie's mouth and eyes made perfect circles of surprise. Then she laughed. And laughed. "Oh, my God! That's perfect. Perfect." She settled and shook her head. "Boy, Ellie got a little more than she bargained for, didn't she?"

Alisha leaned back in her chair and took a long swallow of soda. "I wonder what Blue's gonna do?"

"Do?" Connie echoed.

"If he lets her go, he's the stupidest man on the planet."

"Or the scaredest."

"Most scared," Rosemary said. She pursed her lips. "I really thought he was in love this time, to tell you the truth."

"Maybe he doesn't want black babies," Alisha said. "He seems liberal enough, but it's different when you think it's you."

Rosemary frowned. "Maybe. I don't see that with him, though."

"No, me either," Connie put in. "How did you hear all this, Alisha?"

She grinned. "I eavesdropped!"

All three of them laughed at the brazenness and the confession. Rosemary stood and walked over to the sink, running the water cold to splash her eyes. "If that man has the sense God gave a monkey, he'll go right after her and bring her home."

Connie lifted her head. "Funny, isn't it? How her mama came in and stirred us up all those years ago, and now it's Ellie who did the same thing?"

"This time, though, we're gonna take the gift God gave us," Rosemary said, blotting her face. "I wish to hell we'd listened to Diane Connor when she was here."

"Don't say that," Alisha protested. "Things happen for a reason."

Rosemary and Connie both snorted at that. "Live a little longer, sugar," Connie said, getting up. "Then tell me that again." She reached for her purse. "Come on. We need to see a man about a girl."

21

Ellie drove straight through to Sweetwater, right through the Big Piney Woods, across the Sabine River, into the lush, overgrown county of her birth. It wasn't yet noon when she drove down Main Street, and she got stuck behind a green tractor for five blocks before her turn, so she had plenty of time to absorb the sights.

After her time in Pine Bend, Sweetwater suffered in comparison. Though small, Pine Bend had made an effort to keep up with the times, draw new business and industry, keep growing, by hook or by crook, in whatever ways they could. On the surface, they were much the same: the café with wide windows with trucks in front; the shoe-repair shop, the big courthouse in its nest of lawn and trees.

The differences were more subtle. The fashions in the window of the single clothing store were ten years out of date. The Rexall had a sign for a circus seven seasons before in the window, and the barbershop still had a twirly pole. The sun beat down like an iron, and Ellie felt that the trees themselves were sagging.

It was better when she turned off to go down the road that led to her Grandma's house and left the withering town to drive under a thick tunnel of trees joining arms overhead. Here and there, she glimpsed fields of soybeans or corn, then the creeping growth took over again.

Sixty acres of land was cleared around Geraldine Connor's house, so Ellie saw it a long time before she was actually there. It sat, stolid and stable, in the midst of a rose garden, the flowers in full, glorious bloom against the dark-gray house. Down a long drive was the triple garage that had been her grandfather's pride and joy, every cinder block square of it placed by his own hands. It was as ugly as ever, though Ellie smiled to see someone had painted black-eyed Susans on the side facing the house. Probably Geraldine herself.

As she turned into the graveled drive that wound around the neatly clipped lawns, Ellie felt something in her just give way. One minute, she was fine, the next, it seemed like too much effort to keep her foot on the gas. She slowed and stopped, and just sat there for a minute, breathing it in: home.

She visually touched the tiny details that made it so, one by one: the plastic daisies with spinning petals that lined the porch; the battered, peeling milk box by the back door; the fan pattern on the wooden screen door that was repeated on the eaves of the porch itself. With a sense of relief she got out of the car, smiling at the plethora of roses blooming like a catalogue picture in the hot morning, feeding bees by the dozens, who made a soft, blurry counterpoint to the noisy silence of a summer midday.

Geraldine banged out of the house, wearing a pink calico apron over a pair of slacks and a tank top that showed her goosey arms. "Ellie!" she cried. "You're so early! I haven't barely got anything done yet for your visit."

"You know I don't care, Gram." Ellie put her arms around the slim shoulders and breathed in her scent of Jean Naté toilet water. "I just had to come first thing this morning."

Geraldine pulled back, tilting her head down to see through the distance portion of her trifocals. "You in trouble?"

Ellie lifted her arms, let them fall back to her sides. "In a word, yeah. In the very old-fashioned sense of the word."

A depth of sadness Ellie would never have expected crossed her grandmother's face, making her look suddenly very, very old. "Oh, honey," she sighed. "That town is a curse to my daughters."

Ellie burst into tears.

"Come on, darlin'," Geraldine said. "Let's go make us a glass of tea and you can tell me all about it."

Blue sat on his porch, his feet braced on the railing. Over the tops of his toes, he could see the last rays of daylight fading, till the whole world was engulfed in grayness. In one hand, he held a glass of bourbon, the bottle handy on the floor by his chair. In the other hand, he held a fat cigar, purchased for this very evening at the liquor store.

He heard a step on the path and didn't turn, knowing it would be Marcus. It was. "Evening," he said, and sat down in the rocking chair. "Mind if I have a little taste of that whiskey there?"

"Depends on what you're planning to say to me. I've already been visited by the furies, and you yelled at me this morning, and Lanie had my ass about ten minutes ago."

"The furies?"

"Yeah. Connie, Rosemary, and Alisha. Who seem to think they know me better than I know myself."

"Hmmm." Marcus went inside for a glass and poured himself a drink, then took his time settling in. After several savoring sips of the bourbon, he said, "It's that curse, right? You think you're living under some cloud that'll bring bad luck to anybody you care about."

"Yep." He lifted the glass, took a long swallow.

"Well, Job, I can't say that I blame you."

"Thank you." A burn started in his gut as everything came rushing back in—that bed, destroyed under the weight of that roof. His flesh rippled. "Why don't you just get on with it, get it out, and we can drink in peace and quiet. I figure I've earned a good drunk, and don't intend to stop till I'm there. You can join me or not. Up to you."

"All right, then," Marcus said. "Here's what I came to say: Sooner or later, you got to face your own life."

"Well, funny thing is," Blue drawled ironically,

"that's just what the hell I was doing, Marcus, my friend. Exactly what I thought. Right when I thought life was just gonna be the same thing, day after day after day, fate sends this—*woman* to me to turn everything upside down, make me feel and think all over again that maybe normal folks would just get over the past and get on with things." He pulled the ring case out of his pocket and shoved it at Marcus. "I was going to ask her to marry me, believe it or not."

Marcus took the case, opened it, and whistled softly. "Beautiful. Good choice for her, too. I don't see her in diamonds."

Blue looked over. "Yeah, that's what I thought, too. Good." Then he scowled and rocked forward, his feet coming down hard on the wooden floor as he reached for the bottle. "Makes no difference now."

"I don't know why not," Marcus commented mildly.

"I don't expect you to." He paused. "You know, she didn't even really fight me. Just kinda left."

"Hurt your feelings, did it?" Marcus shook his head. "You're just being your usual, pigheaded self, Blue. Man, listen—the girl had one shock after another, the kind of things that turn you upside down, things none of us usually ever have to think about." He rattled the ice in his glass restlessly. "Then you throw her out. You're a fool."

Blue stubbornly looked at the trees at the edge of the clearing and thought about what work he'd do tomorrow.

Marcus stood. "I give up. You sit here and feel

sorry for yourself if you want. I'm going home." He took the steps and said over his shoulder. "To my woman."

Blue couldn't even summon the profane response he knew Marcus expected. *My woman* gave him too clear a picture of Ellie, curled in sleep, that wild hair all over the pillow. It made him think of her laughing in his kitchen, and teasing him in her country drawl that she tried to make fancier for him.

And all of that just gave him a hole in his gut, a hole he poured bourbon into. He hadn't slept in a long time, and the bourbon was making his head heavy. Wearily, he stood up and went upstairs to his bed, where he fell face-first, blotting out the vision of a woman with plans for his workday tomorrow.

Bourbon and orchids. They'd built a wall for him once before. They could do it again.

But an hour later, he had to admit it wasn't working. God knew he was tired enough. The bourbon should have shoved him over the edge. But each time he closed his eyes, his brain coughed up a parade of flashing disasters, things that had happened, things that could happen, things he couldn't prevent. When he found himself imagining the animals getting hit by cars though there weren't even any cars in the neighborhood, he gave up.

Out of habit, he turned on the computer and while it booted, went downstairs for a cup of tea. It was odd not to have April trailing him around, and a tiny stab of regret stuck him.

He shoved it away, blinking quickly to keep Ellie's face out of his head.

The chicken on the table mocked him and he sat down, finally a little hungry, while he waited for the kettle to boil. It was damned good chicken, and he devoured the first piece, then another, in the time it took for the kettle to whistle.

It made him a little sad to think of the way it should have gone with this chicken. It had been for Ellie, because she liked his cooking so much. And he'd planned to bake the ring into a biscuit, which was why he still had it in his pocket. He touched the lump against his thigh, and felt the hollow sense of loss.

He knew he was on autopilot, and knew everything would make sense when he finally got some sleep. He was smart enough to know he was shaken by the force of that other shoe. A storm of biblical proportions, warning him away. What man in his right mind wouldn't panic?

From the cupboard, he scrounged up a bag of cookies, and added a generous measure of sugar to his tea. The chicken had only pointed out to him that he was starving. For good measure, he also got a chunk of good cheddar from the fridge, and carried it all back upstairs with him. Piwacket, awakened by the racket, followed him, trilling happily at the smell of the cheese. He gave her two very tiny crumbles, one at a time, and opened his E-mail program, watching as the files loaded. The first was one from Ellie. Seeing her name there gave him a terrible jolt, almost as if she were dead, writing from the grave.

She'd sent it the night before last, in answer to his request to read her book. *I'd be honored to have you read the book, Blue,* she wrote. *In fact, I was going to ask if you would read what I've done. I'd love to have your feedback.*

He stared at it. The last message in the queue was also from Ellie. It had been posted just a few hours before, and he wondered how she'd done it. Her laptop was still here, and it was broken. He opened it, his heart pounding in anticipation.

My grandmother's address is RR #31, Box 12, Sweetwater, Louisiana. I wasn't thinking very clearly this morning, but I'm in a panic about the book and all my notes, and it would mean a lot to me if you'd box them up and send them by overnight mail to me.

Ellie

That was it. He realized he'd been holding his breath, hoping for—what? He didn't know. A sign, maybe.

But the note gave him something to do, anyway. He went downstairs and got the box of notes, manuscript pages, and disks, and carried it upstairs with the laptop. First, he put the manuscript pages in order. A lot of them were damp and smeared, but most were fairly readable, and if worse came to worst, she'd at least be able to have them scanned to disk. The note cards, protected by the plastic box, were fine, and he checked the disks in his own hard drive to make sure they hadn't been damaged. They were fine, too.

Last, he turned on the laptop. To his amazement, it made the small humming noises and little buzzes that indicated it worked. The LCD was cracked, and when the files came up, there were little lines of distortion running across the screen, but it was still readable.

On the screen was an icon showing Mabel at maybe twenty or twenty-five, laughing, and a text box said, *Hearts and Bones.* Blue clicked on it, and a word processing program opened to a file. *Chapter One,* it said.

He began to read, but just as he started into it, the doorbell rang. Startled, he looked at the clock and realized that it wasn't even ten o'clock yet. It had just been such a long day it only felt late.

It was Gwen Laisser standing there on the back steps, wearing a light silk coat. "I been over to Hopkins'," she said with a tight mouth. "I saw Marcus there. What'd you do with my granddaughter?"

Blue knew he hadn't had much sleep, but this did not compute no matter how he came at it. "I'm sorry, I don't get it. Who do you want?"

"You got so many girls now you can't keep 'em straight?"

"You mean Ellie?"

"I do. Where is she?"

He still didn't get it. "You want to come in? I don't think I know what's going on here."

She pulled off her glasses. "Blue Reynard, I can't believe you're that blind, and I know you're not that stupid. You mean all this time, you didn't know?"

"Know?" He shook his head. "Gwen, come inside. I don't know what the hell you're talking about, pardon my French." Wearily, he left the door open and went into the kitchen. "I got some chicken here, if you want some."

It hit him. He lifted his head and looked at her, and all the pieces fell together.

She shook her head at the expression on his face. "You really had no idea. I thought somebody would have told you sometime or another, seeing how you were so fond of her. Mabel. Me."

"Mabel Beauvais." He stared at her. "All these years, you've been living right here." Another piece of the puzzle fit together. "And Ellie is your granddaughter."

"That's right. And she is the only thing I've got left, son, so I want you to sit right there and listen to me."

He sat.

"I feel for you, child," she said. "I really do. And I know you think you're living under some curse, and I reckon I know a little about that kind of thinking myself. But I want you to think about those deaths in your life. God's not out to punish you. Your mama was close to sixty and smoked like a fiend from the time she was ten years old, so it was no big surprise she had a heart attack. Your brother went to war, and that surely increases the chances of dying young. Your daddy put a bullet in his head because he couldn't stand all he'd lost. The only person you lost through no fault of her own was your wife. It was sad, Blue. It was terrible, and we all cried right along with you."

"Don't," he whispered.

"Don't you don't me," she said. "Get up off that whiny butt of yours and go after your woman. Marcus told me she's gonna have a baby, and I'll tell you now you haven't seen any misery in your life if you don't get that baby born in this town where we can all enjoy it. Including you."

He looked at her, and couldn't decide whether to laugh or cry. "I can't believe I've been mooning about Mabel to you all these years."

She cracked a smile, and in it he could see that devastating young woman with so much fire. "Did my heart good." She poked at a piece of chicken and picked it up when it didn't jump off the plate. "And I reckon it was you that the good Lord used to set everything to rights here. You see how that happened? He figured you'd suffered enough, Blue, and sent you a woman."

He bowed his head. And unashamed, he wept. Someday, he'd sing the blues again. Life was just like that. But it wouldn't be today.

Ellie and her grandmother talked for hours. Talked about the book, and the surprising outcome. Talked about the town of Pine Bend, and finally, finally, Ellie eased into her search for her father.

It was past midnight, and Ellie felt guilty, but her grandmother showed fewer signs of weariness than Ellie felt. They had eaten and cleared the dishes, and sat now at the kitchen table, with a bowl of peanuts in the shell between them. Geraldine loved peanuts and had passed the pleasure of them to Ellie. She cracked one now, and thought of George Washington Carver, and it seemed odd that she could somehow claim him a little bit now. One of her people.

Or was that pretentious? Just because her father was black, because her blood connected her to that vast, loose "people" in America, what connection did she really have? None in her history. In her head, she was as white as she ever was. If her father had turned out to be an Italian American, would she run out and try to learn Italian? Or cook pasta?

A little thrill went through her, though. One person she could claim was Mabel Beauvais. Imagine!

"What is it, Ellie? You've been drifting off all night. Are you thinking about that man?"

"No," she said softly. "I'm thinking of another one." She opened her purse and took out two photographs, taken from Rosemary's trunk, and put the first one down. It was the one of Diane laughing at the edge of the picture, staring at someone just out of sight. "I found this when I was looking for material on Mabel," she said.

Geraldine made a soft noise of pain, and picked it up. "Ah, she was such a pretty little thing. I never did know what to do with her." She looked up expectantly, waiting for the other picture. "And you found your daddy, didn't you?"

Ellie swallowed, and put down the picture of Marcus and James mugging for the camera. "The one on the left," she said. "James Gordon."

Geraldine only nodded. "You look just like him."

"Aren't you even surprised?"

Geraldine pursed her lips. Shook her head. "Not really. Your mama wouldn't say, of course, but I had my suspicions all along."

"You *did?*"

"You don't have to sound so shocked—I mean, she came back here, silent as a prayer, and wouldn't say one word about the father of her child. And she just cried and cried when you were born, like her heart would break. I figured you must favor him."

"You never said a word."

Geraldine put the picture down. "What would have been the point, Ellie? Your mama was gone. I had no idea who your other people were. You were stuck with us, in a little town, the illegitimate child of a girl who never did get a thing right. It was gonna be hard enough without me adding something that was only a suspicion. And your grandpa flat-out refused to see it." She looked at the picture. "He was a fair enough man, for his times, but it would have broken his heart to think his daughter had—"

Ellie nodded. Her grandfather had been a product of his times and his culture. He would never have used profanities, either in public or private, and he'd never discriminated against anyone over their color, but he wasn't comfortable with a heavily integrated world. He had liked that the diner on Park Street was where the old white guys ate, and that the "colored" guys liked the one on Market.

"It wouldn't have made any difference over him loving you, child."

"I know."

"So, did you get to meet him? Does he know he's your daddy?"

Ellie glanced up, that quick slice of sadness going

through her solar plexus again. "No. He died in Vietnam. She tried to get him to go to Canada, but—" She shrugged, feeling suddenly weary. "So, maybe it was all for naught."

"No. You know. That's something." She gave a little cackle. "And now that baby won't be such a shock. I did worry about that a little, that you'd end up with a child that was a big surprise to you."

Ellie laughed. "Oh, that could have been kind of interesting to explain."

Beneath their giggles came the sound of a rumbling engine, and headlights suddenly flashed through the kitchen windows, making big squares of white light on the walls. "Who the devil could that be?" Geraldine said, and jumped up.

A door slammed and then the engine and lights died—Ellie stood up, too, thinking it was weird that those sounds should come in that order. Without a hint of expectation, she stood up, too, and they both went out on the porch.

The motion-sensitive lights on the back porch suddenly flicked on, showing the big black truck Ellie had grown to know and the shadow of a man behind the wheel. It also illuminated a man coming toward them, a man who looked rumpled and tired, his hair tousled, as if he'd been sleeping, his chambray shirt wrinkled, his feet bare. "Ellie, damn it," he said in that bourbon drawl, and stopped, his hands on his hips.

"This is him, huh?" Geraldine said, leaning in close.

"Yeah." She couldn't quite take it in. "Blue, what are you doing here?"

"You know," he said, and came forward till he was standing at the foot of the steps. "I can't really answer that question." He turned his attention to Geraldine and held out his hand. "How are you, ma'am? You must be Grandma. I've heard a lot about you, but Ellie never let on that she got so much of her beauty from you."

Geraldine snorted at this extravagance, but Ellie could tell it pleased her anyway. "You must be Blue."

"I am. And I've been a real jackass."

"So I heard." Geraldine said.

The teasing left his face. "Can I talk to you, Ellie? I wouldn't blame you if you want to make me wait, but we've driven for a couple of hours, and I'd like to have five minutes, anyway."

She nodded.

"Y'all go ahead," Geraldine said. She lifted her hand to the man in the truck. "You there, come on in and I'll fix you something to eat."

Marcus stepped out, and slammed the door firmly. He mounted the steps and nodded toward Geraldine. "Thank you," he said. "I need to call my wife, too, if you wouldn't mind loaning me your phone. I'll call collect."

"That's fine. Come on."

Marcus looked at Ellie and lifted his eyebrows. He touched her shoulder on the way by.

"Wait a minute. Grandma, this is Marcus Williams. He's the other man in the picture I showed you."

Geraldine cocked her head. "Is that right?"

They went inside, leaving Blue and Ellie on the

porch. He still stood on the ground. She still stood on the porch. She looked at his feet. "When are you ever going to grow up and wear shoes like a normal person?"

"I was in a hurry." He lowered his head. "Ellie, I lost it when I saw that cabin. It scared the shit out of me, and I panicked."

"I know."

"I've got your stuff in the truck if you want it, but"—he took a breath and reached into his pocket—"I kept thinking I wanted you to have something you'd remember always. Something that you could tell all your girlfriends and our grandbabies about to show them how romantic their grandpa was." He looked at the case in his hands, then at her. He looked tired. There were lines along his mouth, and hollows below his cheekbones, but his eyes were clear. "But here we are, and all I can think is that it's been a million years since I felt so good, since I woke up in the morning and felt happy." He swallowed, and she would have called his body language shy in somebody else. "I just want to marry you. I want to have ordinary days. I want babies. I want to laugh with you and listen to music and hold hands."

"No sex?"

He blinked, and it was then that she realized he was dead on his feet. She laughed. "Blue, darlin', how long has it been since you slept?"

He rubbed his forehead. "A really long time."

"I figured." She came down the steps and held out her hand. "If the word sex didn't catch your attention, you're a long way gone."

He didn't move, only looked at her, her hand in the air. And then, he kissed her, the kind of hungry, starved, lonely kiss of a man who was sure everything was lost. She put that flying hand on his shoulder, and took the box from him. He simply collapsed around her, his head on her shoulder, his arms tight. "Ellie, I didn't even know how lonely I was before you came."

"Me, too, Blue." She kissed his cheek, and laughed softly. "Would it be okay if you took that ring out of the box so I could see it? If you really don't want to put it on my finger, that's okay, but I want to see what you picked."

"Oh! Yeah." He took the box from her and opened it, shyly. "I didn't see you in diamonds, Ellie. There's so much life in you, like rubies."

Ellie got blurry eyes as she took it out of the box and started to put in on her finger. "No," he said, "Let me."

It fit perfectly. She admired it with a faint smile.

"Do you like it?"

"Yes. It's beautiful." She flung her arms around him, carefully, because he was so fragile and so tired at that moment. She closed her eyes and smelled the bourbon on him, and the orchids in his hair, and the scent of earth on his neck. When she opened her eyes, he was still there. "I can't promise to live forever."

"Me, either."

"It's not always going to be wild passion and nights on the roof."

"Once in a while on the roof is all a man needs."

Ellie held on, irrelevantly thinking about the endless circle that was a ring. Or maybe it wasn't irrelevant at all. Somehow, the circle had turned and taken her to Pine Bend, where she had needed to go.

Somehow, she loved him. And somehow, he loved her back. All the excuses and defenses she'd used to shield herself fell away. She raised her eyes. "I fell in love with you the minute I first saw you, Blue." Her voice was serious. "And every day that went by, I loved you a little more. That scares me to death."

He touched her cheek. "Green seasons, Ellie. This is one for us now. When it comes time, if we have to, we'll sing the blues." He paused. "I'll sing them for you if you sing them for me."

And Ellie hated to cry, but there was no stopping her tears over that. "Okay," she said, and holding the ring tightly in her palm, she flung her arms around his neck and let him catch her close. He hugged her, tight, and Ellie buried her face in his shirt, suddenly faint from what she'd come close to throwing away.

After a long moment, she caught her breath and said, "I warned you I'd end up slobbering on your shirt."

"And I told you then that I wasn't going to mind." He kissed her, sealing it, kissed her and kissed her and kissed her, and Ellie felt lightheaded with it, with all the things that had happened to her since she'd come down the road and seen the finger of God above the trees.

"That's enough, you two," Geraldine called from the kitchen. "Come on in here and act like civilized people for ten minutes."

Ellie didn't think Blue would be awake for ten more minutes, but she'd find him a comfortable place to crash. She tugged his hand, but he held back for a minute. "You didn't tell me about Gwen," he said.

"I forgot."

"She threatened my life, by the way."

Ellie laughed. "Really?"

He nodded, looking at the house. "That's gonna be the most spoiled baby that was ever born."

"There's worse things."

"Yeah," he said, and allowed himself to be pulled toward the house. "I reckon there are."

The Lovers

June 4, 1969

Dear Diane,

I am sorry to tell you James died yesterday. This envelope was in his pocket, ready to be mailed to you. I thought you'd want to have it.

Marcus
Williams

June 2, 1969

Dear Diane,

I got your letter a few days ago, and I just want you to know how much it meant to me to get it. To know you're doing okay and the baby is so sweet and that you can take good care of her until I come home.

All I can think about now is how much I love

you. I thought it would get better, you know, after I hadn't seen you for a while. I thought I could stop thinking about you. But I dream about your smile. It wakes me up and I just ache to be with you, and then I'm remembering all those days we did have, when it was just the two of us, alone and naked and in love. I think about it a lot. I think about that wholeness, and I know it made you mad, but I'm so glad that time made a baby. If love makes children, ours should have made twenty.

Make sure she isn't afraid to be who she is. We'll take her someplace that it won't matter. Where she'll never be ashamed to be our child, but will wake up every day being glad.

I love you, Diane. I could say it, write it here, a thousand times and it wouldn't be enough. I felt you coming my whole life, and there you were, right in front of me, and I knew the first minute I saw you. The very first minute. You knew it, too. Take care of yourself for my sake. I can't stand to think of anything happening to you. I love you.

I love you.

I love you.

Kiss Ellie for me. (Sorry, I have to agree with your mama about Velvet. Let's call her Ellie.) Tell her that her daddy loves her.

I love you.

James

22

Fourth of July dawned as wet and sloppy as any day Connie Ewing could remember. She woke up to rain patting against her windows, and the sound made the knot in her ease a little bit. She'd always thought of Bobby dying on a rainy day like this. He'd loved rain, and it made her happy to think it might have been raining in the jungle the day he died.

But the weather made the group a more somber one than Connie had hoped. They held up their umbrellas, wishing for everything to be over, moving from foot to foot, trying to be respectful, but all looking forward more to the coffee and potluck coming after than they were for this.

Well, maybe not everybody. Rosemary stood arrow straight beneath her black umbrella, her face closed and quiet, her shoulders rigidly straight under her dark dress. Next to her was Gwen, all dressed in black. Connie wished she still sang—it was a day for the blues, somehow. Especially those long, deep, mournful notes Gwen had done so very well.

Marcus sat under the awning, dressed in a dapper black suit, along with Alisha and the boys, all shined up like new shoes. He was the master of ceremonies, of course. It was his project, this memorial, these heavy black slabs of sorrow that would help them remember.

Remember.

Connie spied Blue, finally, and he was dressed up, too. Formally, which she'd never seen, and next to him was Ellie.

Ellie, James's girl. It was so plain, now that she knew. It had to be hard for Gwen and Rosemary and Marcus to even look on that face. Hard, but joyful, too. Connie watched her as the names were being read, one after the other. Forty-two of them. Ellie stared hard at the stage, her face wet, and plainly not from the rain. She and Blue held hands, tightly.

Connie stood there even after all of it was done. Shauna had offered to stay, but Connie sent her on. "I'll come on in a minute," she said, and Shauna left her to it.

With a small, pierced breath, Connie moved close to the slab and put her fingers on the name. Robert Makepeace. Bobby.

She closed her eyes and called up a picture of him that day, that day they'd all been saying their good-byes. A sunny summer day, so much unlike this one, and the whole group of them waiting at the Greyhound station—Connie and Bobby, Rosemary and Marcus and James. She tried to remember seeing Ellie's mother there, that little slip of hippie child, and she could see them there, both girls, but she couldn't see Diane saying good-bye to James in any meaningful way.

What she could see was Bobby. His eyes, such clear eyes, with such a wealth of love in them. The sun shining off the nutmeg color of his hair, hair that she reached up to touch, letting it run through her fingers because she knew it would all be gone the next time she saw him. He smiled at that. "It'll grow back."

And Connie kissed him. Put her mouth against his, and felt a swell of a love so pure, so sweet, so clear that it could never be sullied. She had not known then that there would never be another moment like that—or at least there had not been another up to now—when she'd feel such an uncomplicated thing for another person. She knew, too, that it would have changed if he'd come home to her, if they'd married as they'd planned.

Standing now, with her fingers in the gouge marks of his name, she remembered. Remembered breathing his breath, dreaming him in her, holding his body close.

And it seemed, for a moment, that it was not a memory. Hair brushed over her brow, hair that smelled of a shampoo—Breck—she hadn't thought of for thirty years, and a ghostly mouth pressed hers. And a soft, sweet sense of rightness, of completeness, rushed through her, all through her. Bobby himself.

She dared not move, for fear of losing the magic of the moment. She stood with her hand on the letters, his hair in her face, her heart filled with pure, sweet, uncomplicated love, and into the day came a sound.

A deep, rich, woman's voice, as clean and clear as it ever had been, singing a capella, "Hearts and bones and blood in a tangle . . ."

Connie smiled and fell into the sound, knowing, somewhere in her, that Bobby heard it, too. That James could hear his mother sing it for him, but mostly for Ellie, who'd somehow stumbled into their secrets and their sorrows and set them all to rights, simply by being, by needing to know the past and the truth and all the sorrows.

As Connie stood there, the sun broke through a tiny hole in the clouds and touched her face. Connie opened her eyes and smiled. A finger of God, her mother would say.

She laughed and moved toward the music, toward the one place in the world Mabel Beauvais might still sing, toward the hall where the people would be gathered, looking at the lives that had been lived, and were being lived. Now, even in their sorrow. Now, even in their joy.

At the door, a man she didn't know, a long tall drink of water who looked like Sam Elliot in the old days, swung aside, tipping his hat to her. "Well now, darlin'," he said, his eyes glittering. "Don't believe I've had the pleasure of your acquaintance."

He even talked like Sam Elliot. Connie inclined her head and held out her hand. "Connie Ewing," she said, and for the first time since she could remember, she gave him her smile. The real one.

For a real man.